D0946705

By Vella Munn from Tom Doherty Associates

Daughter of the Forest
Daughter of the Mountain
The River's Daughter
Seminole Song
Spirit of the Eagle

SEMINOLE
SONG

VELLA MUNN

SEMINOLE
SONG

A TOM DOHERTY ASSOCIATES BOOK
NEW YORK

CONNETQUOT PUBLIC LIBRARY
760 OCEAN AVENUE
BOHEMIA, NEW YORK 11716

This is a work of fiction. All the characters and events portrayed in this novel are either fictitious or are used fictitiously.

SEMINOLE SONG

Copyright © 1997 by Vella Munn

All rights reserved, including the right to reproduce this book, or portions thereof, in any form.

This book is printed on acid-free paper.

A Forge Book
Published by Tom Doherty Associates, Inc.
175 Fifth Avenue
New York, N.Y. 10010

Forge® is a registered trademark of Tom Doherty Associates, Inc.

Library of Congress Cataloging-in-Publication Data

Munn, Vella C .
    Seminole song / Vella Munn.—1st ed.
        p.   cm.
    "A Tom Doherty Associates book."
    ISBN 0-312-85896-5
        1.   Florida—History—1821–1865—Fiction.
2. Indians of North America—Florida—Fiction.
3. Fugitive slaves—Florida—Fiction. 4. Seminole
Indians—Fiction.   I. Title.
PS3563.U48S4   1997
813'.54—dc21   96-44497
                                                  CIP

First Edition: April 1997

Printed in the United States of America

0 9 8 7 6 5 4 3 2 1

To Dick, always.

And to Dale and Mary Ann, who must assume
responsibility for my love affair with the Everglades.
Long live the Mucky Duck and blackened redfish.

Acknowledgments

The writing of a book is a multifaceted adventure, part creative ramblings, part research and documentation. *Seminole Song* would have remained whirling about in my mind if not for what I gleaned from The Florida University System, the Seminole tribe of Florida, the Smithsonian, the Bureau of Indian Affairs, the Florida Historic Society, and the Florida State Archives in Tallahassee, all of which contributed to my understanding of that time and place in history.

My debt goes far beyond official sources. First and most essential, I am grateful to the spirit of the Seminoles who made and still make the Everglades their home. My understanding of the lives of slaves came, not from official history sources, but oral narratives. Linda Brent, thank you. The writings of zoologist Archie Carr did more than ground me in the Everglades ecosystem; he brought the land to life. Finally, thanks to the park ranger who took me deep into the Everglades and answered my endless questions. What an incredible day that was!

SEMINOLE SONG

1

Hate fierce as a hurricane whipped through the Seminole war chief. If he had been closer, he would have thrust his knife deep into the plantation owner and watched the man's lifeblood spill onto the ground. But Reddin Croon was too far away. Safe and powerful and cruel. Besides, as a war chief, a *tastanagee,* Panther had come to this enemy place to free his *honton,* his friend, not to murder.

But if the chance came—

On his belly, his nearly naked body vulnerable to the creatures that made the earth their home, Panther took in the newly erected master's house set several feet off the ground, the tiny one-room slave cabins, a horse pen, two barns. The plantation, hacked out of Pia-hokee—the Everglades—looked like an infected rattlesnake bite surrounded by healthy flesh. Panther's hatred of it burned almost as fiercely as what he felt for the white man.

Gaitor, big and strong, dark as night, had been run down and brought here by slave catchers. If it had been someone else, Panther might have left him to his fate, not because he didn't care but because his own life was at risk here and those who belonged to the Egret clan depended on his leadership for survival. But he couldn't turn his back on his friend. Gaitor had taught him the newcomers' language, shown him how to use the musket he'd taken from a dead soldier. Most of all, Gaitor had learned to walk in Seminole footsteps and howl like a black wolf to frighten the soldiers; he'd become a warrior.

Panther inched forward, stopping now with his chin resting on a knobby palmetto root, oblivious to winter's cold. Slaves, looking like baby alligators swarming over a floating log, labored in a nearby sugarcane field. A man on horseback rode among them, a whip clutched in his free hand. The air smelled of rot and swamp gases and hid from him the stench of the white land and flesh owner. Even as he measured the dangerous distance between himself and the wooden buildings, he again imagined his knife burying itself in Reddin Croon's belly. To be able to do that—

The sight of a stoop-shouldered Negro woman limping toward a shed caught his attention. She carried a pan from which water splashed with every slow and awkward step. When the plantation owner called to her, she stopped, head down. Croon yelled something, but from this distance, Panther couldn't make out the words, just the woman's reaction. Despite her loose blouse and billowing skirt, he could tell her body had tensed. Still, when Croon came closer, she didn't cringe. Instead, her head bobbing like a wind-blown leaf, she listened to what he was saying, said something in return. Finally, she turned her back on her master and started toward the shed again.

Croon, one hand wrapped tightly around a short switch, watched as she knelt and slid the pan in the small space between the bottom of the door and the ground. She tilted her head to the side as if listening to something coming from the shed. Her lips moved, moved again. When Croon yelled at her, she staggered to her feet and hobbled away.

A spider, nearly as large as his hand, crawled up and over Panther's thigh. He waited for it to disappear in the spongey undergrowth, then, snakelike, slid over the palmetto root. He listened to his spirit as it argued with him to wait until the safety of nightfall. But by then it might be too late for his friend.

In addition to the gray chill that pressed down around him,

there were enough shadows between him and the hut that he could reach it without fully exposing himself. That's why he'd worn nothing except a breechclout, so his body would fade into the surroundings. Slowly, grateful for the strength in him, he stood and darted behind yet another palmetto. His heart drummed furiously; he clamped his teeth together and willed it to quiet. If Gaitor was chained, he would have to find another way to free him, but if he'd only been thrown into the locked hut, Panther might be able to dig under the door with his knife until he'd made enough room that Gaitor could wriggle out.

And if there was no other way, he'd ask his friend if he wanted him to end things now—before Croon got to him.

The water-carrying woman was gone and Croon was walking toward the sugarcane field. Except for a sleeping dog, nothing living stood between him and Gaitor's prison-place. After closing half the distance between him and the dog, Panther sank to his knees. He pressed his lips tightly together and sucked in air, making the sharp, high-pitched squeaks of a baby alligator in distress. The dog's head shot up. Then, the loose flesh around his neck moving tidelike, he clambered to his feet and slunk toward Panther. Panther held his breath, his body motionless and taut as he continued the harsh sound. Matching the animal's pace, he slowly lifted the arm that held his knife and tightened his grip.

As he lunged for the dog's throat, he sent up a silent prayer to Breath Giver asking for forgiveness. The dog jerked violently backward, wrenching the knife out of his throat, but it was too late. As if the muscles had been stripped from his legs, the dog sank gracefully into a heap. He ducked his head; his tongue shot out as if trying to stem the blood. Then he spasmed and died.

Breath Giver, take this one to live among all animal spirits. Understand that I put the life of a man before that of a dog, that I could think of no other way. Panther spirit, guide me now.

After running his hand over the dog's side, Panther slipped around the animal and again studied the distance between him and the hut with its locked door. He wished he'd brought his leather bag of sacred medicine, his musket, powder horn, and bullet pouch, but those things would only slow him when he needed to move as silently as a water moccasin.

Shadows from the palmetto wall that surrounded the plantation reached out to caress the hut, seeming to protect it from harm, but if Croon decided to return to his captive or the water-bearing woman came back out again—

No! This was not warrior thought, not *tastanagee* thought!

"Gaitor." Panther's whisper wafted out from him with no more strength than that of a newborn bird. Leaves skittered and danced with the increasing wind, but nothing else moved. "Gaitor?"

"Panther?"

For a moment, Panther couldn't move. He'd been looking for his friend for two days and a long sleepless night and although he'd been certain he'd been tracking t   hose who'd captured the former slave, there'd been times when he wondered if his spirit was strong enough to bring them face-to-face again.

"You are well?"

"Nuthin's broke. What iffen they sees you? You gots to go! It ain't—"

"You speak too much, lowly clamdigger. Did they chain you?"

"My hands. To a post. But the chains, they weren't tight 'nough."

Panther understood. By compressing his fingers as tightly together as possible, Gaitor had managed to free himself. He might have torn his flesh, maybe even have broken bones in the effort, but a man who has once felt chains around his neck and then tastes freedom doesn't easily turn his back on that freedom. "The door?"

"I tried; it's solid. Someon' juss give me water, my first. I beens tryin' to dig out usin' the pan."

Panther grunted, then froze, his senses suddenly as alive as if he'd been touched by lightning. From where he crouched, he couldn't see any sign of danger, but he wouldn't have survived twenty winters if he hadn't taken to heart his spirit's instincts. He was panther; he lived panther. Trusting Gaitor not to break the silence, he breathed in a deep lungful of air and tested it for messages. Damp, heavy. Different somehow. The hut stood between him and the main house and blocked too much of the sugarcane field. If Croon—

"Leave. Run!"

Sharp pricks of warning slid down his spine. His muscles screamed with the need for action. *Leave! Run!* But he couldn't.

Calling on legs that had taken him through a chilled swamp, over hammocks, even across a small savanna since he'd last slept, he stood. Still nothing. He stepped back and to the side. He could see all of the house now. Despite its newness, it seemed to droop like sawgrass during the dry season, too big and gray and weary for its lush surroundings.

Someone was standing on the porch, a slight, female figure. Although she was so far away that he couldn't tell anything more than that about her, he felt her eyes lock with his. Then with a movement as graceful as a floating butterfly, she nodded in the direction of the cane field.

Acting on instinct, Panther bent and slid his knife under the door. "Use it!" he hissed.

"What—"

He didn't wait. Running with his first step, he bolted toward the trees. As he did, he glanced over his shoulder, not toward the warning woman but at the mass of sugarcane. There was no sign of the plantation owner. What had she— A flash of light at the edge of the field registered as a musket, but before his brain could acknowledge the awful truth, a roar like that of a bull alligator split the stormy day. He heard the sound; felt something slam into the side of his head; felt his legs crumple.

Heard Gaitor bellow and then nothing.

Panther woke with a weak sun touching his left shoulder and back. His belly felt as if he'd had too much of the black drink administered by shamans for purification, and he wondered if he was going to vomit. After taking several deep breaths, he managed to subdue the worst of his stomach's rolling, but the heavy air did nothing to quiet the drums beating inside his head. He tried to lift his hand to his temple; that was when he realized his arms had been lashed behind him.

He struggled to straighten his legs, but they'd been tied together and then pulled up and behind him so that his wrists and ankles were held tightly together. His mouth felt dry and swollen. Panic—no! Forcing his thoughts off himself, he arched up from the ground so he could use both his ears.

Insects buzzed. Somewhere an ax was being driven into wood, the *thunk-thunk* slamming into his throbbing skull. Pain told him he was alive. Lowering his head, he rested until he was able to open his eyes without feeling as if a spear had been driven into his forehead.

By turning slightly, he saw that purple-black clouds were building on the horizon. Already the wind was causing the dark green palmetto leaves to shimmy. Once the storm hit, he would be praying that a downpour didn't saturate the ground and drown him in mud.

The question of why he'd been tied like a pig ready for slaughter lasted only briefly; he knew the answer.

He'd been shot and knocked unconscious. The blood clotted in his scalp and down the side of his neck told him that. Someone had secured him and left him here because that person—it had to be Lieutenant Reddin Croon—wasn't done with him. Maybe he would be turned over to the bluecoats, who would torture him until he either died or told them where the small, scattered Seminole clans lived. And maybe Croon recognized him, would exact his own punishment.

A cry built in his throat, a wolf howl he'd used to terrify the soldier-boys who'd been chasing his people ever since warriors attacked the troops heading for Fort King and those already in it. But if he howled, his skull might explode.

Osceola, *Tastanagee Thloko*, Great Warrior of the Seminole, had raged like a wild beast when Indian agent Wiley Thompson seized him and placed him in chains; Osceola had avenged his humiliation by killing Thompson at Fort King. Panther's time for revenge would come, if he lived.

He'd been left where he'd fallen. He wanted to let his friend know he was alive, but several slaves were close enough that they might overhear, and even if he spoke to Gaitor in Seminole, one of them might understand and relay what he'd heard to his master.

The great storm cloud slid up into the sky and blocked out the sun. The air smelled wet and expectant, energy existing separate from and as powerful as the wind. Trees bent and fought like speared fish that don't yet know they've been killed. He heard the sound of running feet and guessed the slaves were trying to reach their cabins before the downpour began. Several ran past him, and when they stared down at him, he stared back.

It began to rain, heavy drops the size of the tip of his thumb slamming into his naked body, chilling him. He'd been tied with leather; once they were soaked, the bonds would stretch, but maybe not enough to allow him to free himself. When water ran off his back in tiny streams, he began testing the loops around his wrists, but the leather clung to his flesh like a constricting snake. The storm wouldn't last. Before nightfall, the clouds would return to their hiding place in the heavens, the sun would pull the moisture out of the earth, and the leather would dry and shrink.

The ground under him turned to slick mud. Maybe— The *hadjo,* crazy thought, nearly made him laugh; if he could flatten himself, he could slide under the door that kept Gaitor prisoner. His friend would cut him free. While the slaves and their owner waited out the storm, the two of them would run into the swamp and freedom.

Freedom. The taste, the smell, the need of it drove deep into him until he truly believed he had become *hadjo.* Would they keep him here like this until his arms and legs withered and became useless? He would die before he told any of the hated bluecoats where his people were, before letting Croon believe he feared the flesh-owner's power. But he wanted his death to be quick, a warrior seeking a warrior's end.

This helplessness was worse than dying.

He turned and opened his mouth, pulling water into his throat. His shoulders ached from the strain of being wrenched behind him, and there was a spreading numbness in his wrists. The rain continued to pound down around him, the sound all-consuming. He thought not of Gaitor and the sense of urgency that had brought him here, but of his clan, Osceola, the night that life had left his father's body. He wanted, needed to be back in the wilderness, needed to be a child again hunting and fishing at his father's side.

Thunder rolled, the sound alone enough to make the earth shudder. It was followed almost immediately by a great, branching tree of lightning that seared the purple clouds. He watched, fascinated despite himself, as it arched and re-arched through the sky. No matter that thunder and lightning were part of his life; he would always be in awe of Storm God's power. Another thunderclap surged after the first, potent and alive. He already felt as if he'd been thrown into the sea; now the downpour became even heavier as if urged on by thunder and lightning. Once again the sky lit up. Shafts of light pulsed and danced, momentarily turning the dark clouds gold.

With sound and brilliance and the need to live pushing him on, he strained against the sodden ropes. He felt the loops around his ankles give slightly, but although he rotated his feet in all directions, he couldn't free himself. After resting a moment, he did the same with his wrists. Ignoring the pain, he yanked and pulled, an animal driven half insane by helplessness. By defeat. He howled, the sound building and giving him strength until thunder abruptly cut it off. Osceola would understand; Osceola would howl with him.

"Panther?"

Gaitor. He opened his mouth, but rage and something else filled him, making it impossible for him to think beyond freeing himself.

"Panther? You live?"

Until Croon tires of me. Although his eyes remained open, he couldn't make himself focus on the rain-soaked world around him. Instead his mind's eye raced through the woods until he spotted his spirit lolling on a tree branch. Even though its dark body was at rest, the long, powerful claws and sharp fangs served as proof of the creature's power. Panther, his spirit, was free. While he—

Someone was coming. His nerves screaming the message, he once again pulled his shoulders off the ground and stared up into the rain. Croon wouldn't come out in this downpour; he'd be within his warm, dry new house, maybe drinking the white man's crazy-making drink, maybe yanking up his wife's skirt or the skirt of one of his female slaves.

Through the thick, gray cloud of rain slipped a small figure half bent against the storm. The woman's clothes clung to her frame as if she'd been sewn into them; her long, wet hair lay along her neck and over her shoulders like a black stream. In her hand she carried a knife.

"Panther?"

"Quiet!" he ordered Gaitor. The woman stopped a few inches away, looked back over her shoulder at the house, then stared down at him. Water ran off her. For no more than two heartbeats he thought of nothing except her dark, dark eyes, saw nothing except the courage in them. Her flesh was nearly the same color as his, but she wasn't Seminole. A slave?

She crouched. Her hand holding the knife stabbed outward; he waited for the pain that would signal his end, but it didn't come. Instead, his legs suddenly straightened, causing his thigh and calf muscles to shriek in pain. His arms, although still caught behind him, no longer felt as if they were being torn from their sockets. He tried to roll over to his side so he could see what she was doing, but she placed a small, strong, wet hand on the back of his neck, holding him there with her silent message. Trusting as he'd never trusted in his life, he waited while she first cut through the leather around his wrists and then freed his ankles.

He sprang to his knees. She remained hunched beside him, her big, deep eyes warning him not to get any closer. "Go!" she said in English. She pointed her knife toward the wall of trees. "Go, now!"

"I can't. My friend—"

From his prison, Gaitor uttered a protest, but Panther paid him no mind. His body might now be free, but the woman still held him with the power in her eyes. "He will kill you." She indicated the great house. Her voice was deep for a woman's, quavering and yet determined. "And if he sees what I've done, he will kill me too."

"Panther!" Gaitor shouted. "The knife; I's been diggin'. This mud's makin' it easy; just you gets outta here."

Already he could see that the space between earth and wood was greater than it had been earlier. Scrambling away from the woman, he stuck his hand through the enlarged hole. Gaitor grasped it.

"I don't want—"

"*He'll* spot ya fer sure! Run! I sees you back at the village."

Gaitor was right. He'd only jeopardize his *honton,* his friend, with his presence.

Willing his cramped muscles to hold him, he surged to his feet. His hand snaked out; he yanked the knife out of the woman's hand. She shrank away, eyes wide and frightened. Ignoring her, he sprinted toward the nearest tree. The palmetto seemed to reach out to embrace him, to cover him with darkness, and he breathed in the heady scent of freedom. Then, although the wilderness spirits called to him, he turned back toward the woman.

She hadn't moved. With the rain pelting down around her, she looked part of the earth. Still, her eyes were alive.

Don't ask, they said. *Don't ask why I freed you.*

2

"Come here."

Pretending she hadn't been aware that he'd entered her mistress's bedroom, Calida forced herself to look up at Reddin Croon. Her master had on an odd mix of clothing: a pure white ruffled shirt, too-tight pants that strained over his slight belly, mud-caked boots. He hadn't shaved today, but she could still see the tiny spider veins over his cheeks. What remained of his hair was slicked back over his too-big head and drew attention to his bulging eyes and fat nose. Everything about him was big. Huge.

"Did you hear me? I said, come here."

Willing her legs to obey, Calida put down her mistress's dress with the torn side seam and stood. She pointed at the dress. "Mistress Liana will be wanting this mended by tonight. Her father—"

"I know her father's coming. She's gone to pick him up. Gone." Croon's oversized hands clenched into fists and pulled the flesh tight over his thick knuckles. "He doesn't know what it's like, the damnable Seminoles—starting a plantation from nothing; he just doesn't . . . Why the hell I ever quit . . ."

When his words fell away, Calida sucked in a deep breath, but it did no good. Fear and loathing for the man who owned her attacked her until she thought she might shatter. "He won't be here until evening," he said at length. "Both of them." Jerking his head, he indicated the back of the hollowed-out, dark, fragile-looking house where he had his separate living quarters.

"Mistress—"

"She ain't around, my little pretty. No one; just you and me's in here. I sent the rest of the house servants outside. Maybe, if I'm lucky, the Seminoles'll attack the carriage with both of them in it. Come. Now."

No!

When Croon took a step toward her, she first cringed, then slid quickly around him and started down the long, narrow hall leading to her master's bedchamber. Her heart cried out with every footstep, but what could she do? She wasn't a Seminole savage; she couldn't run free and nearly naked into the wilderness.

Lieutenant Reddin Croon was following her. Even if she couldn't hear his heavy boots on the warped wooden floor, she would still sense his presence. His inescapable presence.

The door to his room was closed. She stared at it, already seeing the high, massive bed with the feather mattress flattened by his weight. There was other furniture in the room. Hadn't she cleaned and polished the two ornate oak dressers and the heavy night table on which he placed his empty whisky glasses? Hadn't she stared out the small window looking in vain for a heron or egret or rose-colored spoonbill, anything to keep her mind off what was being done to her body?

"Get in there."

No! Teeth clamped around her lower lip, she turned the knob and stepped inside the airless room. She felt darkness surround her, black and gray and brown shadows mocking her desperate need for light. He was right; it was only the two of them.

Behind her, she heard the door close, then his heavy hands were on her hips. "Been a long time, Calida," he said. "Too long."

Only three days.

"What did you think of him?"

Him? The savage? No. Master Croon didn't know she'd freed his Seminole prisoner; surely he didn't know that.

"Major General Jesup. What did you think of him?"

He didn't care about her opinion of the man who'd vowed to rid Florida of all Indians, the man who spoke easily and intimately with her master while they drank from Master Croon's precious liquor supply. "I barely saw him, Master," she said, her back still to him, her words clean and careful as Mistress Liana insisted. "He was only here overnight."

"He'll be back; he's damn glad I've settled in these parts. He's going to do it, mark my words. Accomplish what Major General Scott, Governor Call, even President Jackson haven't been able to. And I'm going to be right by his side advising him, reaping— Turn around."

If she'd gone to St. Augustine with her mistress and Liana Croon had decided to take in one of the concerts given at the courthouse, she would have been free to walk along the shore. She'd let the ocean waves lap around her feet, watch for stingrays playing near one of the sandy shelves, laugh at the antics of the quick-moving, stick-legged shorebirds, study the awkward and yet oddly graceful way pelicans dove for fish. She'd be alone, untouched by anything except the breeze.

Her master turned her around, guiding her with fingers that pinched her hipbones and made the flesh over them quiver in discomfort. His breath smelled of whisky and pork fat. His teeth were yellowed, one of them gray. How Mistress Liana with her rich ways stood being married to him—

"I've been thinking about you," he said. "Wondering when I'd get my hands on you again. Wondering whether this'll be the time I'd put my brat in your belly." He laughed and released her hips so he could grind a fist into her stomach. She winced but refused to retreat. Showing fear or revulsion, she'd learned, only excited him more. It was better to simply submit, to take her mind to the shore or even deep into the unending, terrifying wilderness.

"It won't change anything, you know," he went on. "Your having my seed in you. Black babies are easy to get rid of. Just sell them; *her* none the wiser. Long as you don't get fat and sloppy, I'll go on bothering you. You'd like that, wouldn't you?" He laughed at his joke, then before she could ready herself, he clamped his hand around the back of her neck and pulled her close. He smashed his hard lips against hers and forced them open with his probing tongue.

Warm water on her feet. Her dress caught up around her knees so she could wade out even farther. Looking for seashells. Collecting enough to bring back to her mother.

Her mother . . .

"You just going to stand there? You're no better than my wife. Dead from the neck down. Dead everywhere but her mouth, damn her. And Daddy's pocketbook; I can't ever forget that, can I?" He'd reared back in order to speak; now he jutted his face toward her again, still holding her in place. She closed her eyes thinking— thinking of how it tickled when the tiny shore fish nibbled at her toes and the sea breeze dried sweat on even the hottest day.

He ran his hands up the sides of her neck and into her hair, then closed his fingers around the strands, immobilizing her. No matter that twice now cramps had forced her to her knees; she would again take tansy and spirit camphor, even the roots and seeds of the cotton plant if she could get her hands on some. Destroying her unborn babies haunted her day and night, but to never be allowed to hold her child—to have it ripped from her—to spend her life fearing for its safety . . .

When she felt him grip her neckline, she put her hands against his chest and pushed. They were still so close that he was little more than a blur. "If you rip my clothes, Mistress Liana is going to know what you've done."

His mouth thinned down and his eyes narrowed dangerously. For a heartbeat she thought he was going to hit her. Instead, he swore and released her dress. "You think I give a damn?" he hissed. "A man's got to have some release."

What Mistress Liana thought or didn't think of her husband's needs, Calida couldn't say, just that she took great pride in having married a decorated military man and an intimate of President Jackson. She displayed Reddin Croon as if he were a fine stallion, while he made no secret of his determination to control her money.

Stallion.

"I could get a king's ransom for you." He ran a rough-tipped finger down her forehead, over her nose. He stopped with his finger pressing against her closed mouth as if daring her to bite him. "Don't know about Jesup. That man's military through and through; maybe he never thinks of anything else. But his officers—three of them asked what I'd take for a night with you."

If only she still had the knife she'd used to free the naked savage! She'd once seen a slave woman spit in her lover's face, remembered the look of shock and humiliation in the man's eyes. But Croon wasn't her lover; he owned her.

"Aren't you going to ask why I didn't oblige them?"

No! Just the thought— But if she said nothing, he would only hound her, tease and shame her. "You should have," she said, head held high and proud although she knew how much her defiance excited him. How dangerous it was. "You could have used the coins to pay off some of your gambling debts."

"Damn you, Calida. Throwing your airs around. You're asking to get yourself beaten until your back's in tatters."

"Then—then no one would pay for a night with me."

"True." Another of his non-smiles split his lips. He'd taken his hands off her while they were talking; now he went back to exploring her face as if he'd never done it before. "I didn't call for you while they were here 'cause I don't want any of those officers thinking your services come cheap. Light color like this." He gave her cheek a possessive pat. "Narrow nose, white lady's mouth. Hair nearly as straight as one of those savages. And you don't speak like a nigger; that's one thing my wife's done right, training you the way she has. Let them lust after you awhile; it ups the coins they'd be willing to part with."

He leaned down, grabbed her long skirt, and in a single motion pulled her dress up and over her head. She didn't fight him because she knew better than to offer any resistance. Already his pants bulged; his need for her would be over in a matter of seconds and then she could escape the airless room.

"You're a piece, Calida. A regular piece. Whoever your father was, he was no darkie. Probably not your grandfather either." He cupped his hand around her breast and squeezed. Desperate for escape, she closed her eyes. *Seashells under my feet, some crushed beyond recognition by the relentless surf. Some perfect and new, their color anywhere from purest white to dusty red.*

"Look at me."

No.

"Did you hear me? Look at me."

His hand still imprisoned her breast; his mouth hung slack, tongue half protruding. He was sweating. Dirty rivulets ran down from his temple to finally lose themselves in his shirt collar. His pig eyes had turned into dark shards capable of slicing off her flesh and exposing the bones and muscle and veins beneath. "You belong to me. Anything I want to do— Call me master."

"Master."

"Again."

"Master."

"You're damn right, Calida. Ought to take you to Orleans. Put you up against those fancy octoroons." When he released her breast, she struggled to keep her features immobile, knowing all too well the danger in letting him see any emotion. Couldn't he just get it over with? Let her put on her dress and go back to mending his wife's clothes?

"Undress me."

A small gasp escaped her before she could clamp it into submission. Although her master relished having her stand naked before him, except for dropping his pants, he'd always remained clothed. To have to look at all of him— "I've never—"

"I don't care what you've never done. If you're going to properly pleasure a man, you've got to be taught how it's done. That's it." Another of his non-smiles disturbed his war-aged features. "I've got to start educating you. Going to take a lot of time. A lot of time."

"Mistress Liana—"

"To hell with her! You heard me, undress me."

A necklace made of unblemished seashells carefully chosen and lovingly strung. Around her mother's neck they would serve as a constant reminder of love and beauty. Maybe two identical necklaces. Yes! One for each of them, a gift of love.

Her hands hadn't shaken when she sliced through the savage's bonds; they didn't shake now. Not looking at the man who owned her, she concentrated on her fingers. Although she wished she had her mother's bulk or that of most of the other slave women, she'd always taken pride in her slender but strong limbs, been grateful for her broad hands. They would fit around this man's throat, were capable of wrenching the life from him. At least they were in her dreams.

When she pulled it off him, Croon's shirt felt sticky with sweat; she couldn't stop herself from thinking about what he smelled and felt like, the hard and unthinking way he drove himself into her.

Seashells red with blood. With Master Croon's blood.

No matter how hot the day, his chest and belly never felt the sun; she saw that now. Although his face and hands and arms were burned nearly the color of leather, the rest of him reminded her of a hairless pig. No wonder Mistress Liana had her own sleeping quarters.

Croon slapped his belly, laughing at the ripe watermelon sound. "It didn't always look like this, not when I was in the military, I'll tell you. But that swill the cook puts on the table'd fatten a dead man."

She'd seen the picture of Croon in his military uniform taken when he rode alongside President Andrew Jackson. It hung prominently in what Mistress Liana called the drawing room so there was no escaping it. But whenever Calida looked at it, she saw not this panting, aroused creature but shiny buttons and a starched collar clamped tightly around a thick neck. Sometimes she caught her mistress staring at it. Whatever Mistress Liana thought of the man her husband had turned into since he'd left the military and become a plantation owner she kept to herself. Still, Calida had heard her crying at night.

Croon took her hands and held them up as if studying them for the first time. "You ought to be a blacksmith, they're that strong. You've got big feet too, big for as little as the rest of you is. You ever wonder about him?"

"About who?" she asked because he would only keep after her until she said something.

"The man who sired you. Ever wonder if your mama came to him the way you come to me?"

I don't come to you; you order me. "She never said. I don't ask." It was a lie.

"How come? Ain't you curious?"

"He was white."

"Sure he was white." Croon laughed and placed her hands on his shoulders. "And that's all you cared to hear, that's what you're saying, isn't it?"

"Yes."

"Mixing blood, that's what it is. If you spit out a baby even lighter than yourself, 'specially a girl, she'll fetch a fortune."

There won't be a baby; I can't . . . Trembling slightly now, she waited, wondering whether he'd punish her for her silence. But although his eyes took on a hungry look, he only wrapped his arms around her and pulled her against him. He began a grinding movement designed to push his still-clothed member between her legs. Fighting down revulsion, she spread her legs slightly. It had happened before; his need had been so overwhelming that he'd come before he could pull down his pants. He'd cursed and slapped her then—not hard enough to leave a mark. Then he'd ordered her to get dressed and leave him.

She could do that; oh yes, she could do that.

"I know what you're thinking," he hissed. "But it ain't going to happen that way. Not today." When he shoved her away, she stumbled but didn't lose her balance. She stood before him, naked, arms limp at her sides, thoughts of a warm beach slipping out of reach. For the first time since exposing him, she noticed a puckered scar on his right side between two ribs. Why couldn't the wound have killed him? When he unfastened his pants and shoved them down over his hips, she kept her eyes locked on his, refused to look elsewhere.

"I was watching the other night," he said. "Sinda and Jake. They were going at each other, so caught up in what they were doing that they didn't know anyone was there. Right under my window. All right, maybe not *right* under, but it wasn't hard for me to find them once I heard them ruttin' around. Sinda had her hand on Jake—right on him. They were moaning and carrying on like a stallion and a mare. That's what I want to hear out of you, Calida. Sounds like a mare being mounted."

Master Croon loved saying things to shock her; she should be used to them. Still, her stomach knotted, and she felt half sick. With his pants now puddled around his knees, he took her hand and slowly, relentlessly brought it closer and closer to his bulging manhood. "Control," he hissed. "You don't even know the meaning of it, do you? And you ain't ever going to. That's what I was going to teach that savage. Give him a lesson about who's in control he'd never forget—not that he was going to live long enough to give it much thought. But someone got to him first. Someone—who was it, Calida?"

He still hadn't made her touch him; that's what she should be thinking about, these precious last seconds.

"Who?" he insisted. "Was it you?"

"If I say yes, will you kill me?"

"You ain't worth much to me dead."

She breathed; tried to anyway.

"Or scarred up. Long as you've got your looks, you figure you aren't going to be beaten. How does that make you feel, knowing your looks are all that keeps you safe?"

"I can't change what I am."

"Damn right you can't. Just like me; I'll always be a soldier. And just like that Seminole; he'll always be a savage. All of them will. You know." He turned her hand so that the back of it was presented to his manhood. When she felt him press against her flesh, it was all she could do not to jerk away. "You didn't free him. Getting that close to a barbaric, you don't have it in you."

What was he going to do now? The question was still echoing inside her when the door behind him flew open and Liana Croon burst into the room. The look on her face—rage, hate, despair—seared itself into Calida's brain.

"You bastard!" Mistress Liana shrieked. "I knew! Damn it, I knew!"

"Keep your voice down. Your father—"

"My father isn't here! He was delayed. I came back—because I knew what I'd find."

Master Croon released Calida's hand and shoved her away. He reached for his pants but didn't yank them up over himself. "So he's not going to be a party to this little scene," he said almost conversationally. "Are you going to tell him?"

The rage went out of Liana's eyes, leaving only hatred and desperation. "You're nothing without him! All the money he's given you—"

"Because I'm the only man who'll marry his ugly daughter."

"That's not true! Reddin, that's not—"

Croon lurched toward his wife and struck her mouth. She shrank away, lip bleeding. Calida grabbed blindly for her dress but couldn't put her mind to the great task of dragging it over her head. She held it in front of her, gaping. Her master slowly, deliberately pulled his pants into place and fastened them. "You aren't going to say anything to your papa." He spoke through clenched teeth. "If you do, he'll insist you divorce me, and you'll have to go live with him. The humiliation—"

"It would be better than this. Than having you take up with a slave."

Calida felt violated. She should be used to it; still, being treated as if she didn't exist hurt.

"I'm hardly the first man to spend his needs on a darkie, my dear wife. Or maybe your papa kept you so ignorant you don't even know that."

"Stop it!" Mistress Liana ran the back of her hand over her mouth, stared at the blood. "I will *not* allow this!"

"How are you going to stop me?"

Mistress Liana rocked back on her heels. She blinked once, then glared through lowered lids. "*I'll* divorce you. Insist on getting everything, this miserable, so-called plantation, everything. My father will make sure you're driven out of here."

"You'll run this place? Don't make me laugh."

Uncertainty flickered across Mistress Liana's face. "I'll sell it. Take the proceeds and live wherever I want."

"No you won't."

Be careful, Calida wanted to scream. *He's deadly when he's like this.*

"Are you threatening me?" Liana asked.

"I'm telling you what's going to happen," Croon said in that deadly tone of his. "You're going to forget what you saw and when your father shows up, you're going to act the loving wife. You think your father's going to stand up to me for you? I'm a decorated war hero; you're nothing but a burden around his neck. Do you understand?"

"No. I won't—"

This time when he hit her, the sound vibrated throughout the room. Her head snapped back and she screamed. Then she came at her husband, her long nails reaching for his face. Master Croon ducked, but he wasn't fast enough. Liana's nails dug into the base of his throat and left five long, bleeding scratches in his flesh.

"Damn you!"

His fist, hardened by years of soldiering and the two years he'd spent wrestling a plantation out of the wilderness, slammed into the side of her neck. She fell backward, stopping only when her body hit the heavy dresser. She reached behind her in a desperate attempt to regain her balance, but he came at her again.

Calida stood, dress clamped between her fingers, seeing nothing except the one-sided battle before her. Mistress Liana, her eyes dazed, had sunk to her knees. She stared up at her husband, exposing her dead-white face to the little bit of light filtering in from outside. Her mouth opened and closed. She lifted a thin hand to her throat and touched the reddened flesh where he'd hit her. "You bastard!"

Croon kicked out. His boot landed in her belly, splattering her onto the floor. Moving as quick as a snake, he pounced over her, clamped his hands around her throat, squeezed, shook.

Calida screamed. She heard the sound, a mouse-squeak. Her mistress's head flopped back and forth as if it were a rag being shaken by a playful dog. Then, although horror and disbelief still assaulted her, Calida ran over to her master and began pounding his back. "Stop it! You're going to kill her!"

He only settled himself more squarely over his wife's limp body and continued the relentless shaking. "Stop it!" Calida shrieked. She fisted her hands more tightly, drew back, and hit him with all the strength in her. "You're killing her!"

Mistress Liana's body settled against the floor with a dull thunk. Her legs and arms danced briefly, then fell quiet. Barely aware of what she was doing, Calida picked up her dress and held it in front of her again. Her mistress's head was tilted at an impossible angle. Her mouth hung open and blood dribbled out.

Master Croon crouched beside his wife and held the back of his hand over her nose. He touched first the base of her throat and then his own where she'd scratched him.

"She's dead," he said.

Dead. Calida stumbled backward but couldn't think what to do after that. She watched, only half comprehending, when Master Croon stood and started toward her. "*You* killed her," he said.

"Me? No!"

Another step. "You hate the way she treats you; you've always hated the demeaning things she makes you do."

"No."

"Yes." The word felt like a blow. His eyes were wild, savage and determined. "Who's going to call me a liar—Liana? I'm the grieving widower. And you—" Another step. "You're only a slave. A slave who can't talk."

He was going to cut out her tongue! Another mouse-squeak escaped her, a helpless little sound that might be her last. She sensed him readying himself to lunge for her. The instinct that had brought her to the savage's side kicked in, and she turned and ran. Ran for her life.

3

Reddin Croon waited until dark before wrapping his wife's body in a blanket and carrying it out to the carriage she'd taken to St. Augustine. The moon would be out soon; he wanted to get away from the plantation with its worthless, wagging tongues before that happened. Still, it was all he could do to put his mind to the task he'd given himself.

This lifeless lump was his wife, a woman who'd come to him with her rich father's dowry and her desperate need for a husband worthy of her father's wealth. She was dead; the Seminoles had killed her. All he had to do was make sure his father-in-law Isiah Yongue believed that.

Leaving her crumpled in the bottom of the carriage, he went into the barn for the high-stepping mare Liana took such pride in. The mare nickered in irritation when he cinched a rope around her neck and dragged her from her stall. He quickly hitched her, then headed toward the slave cabins. As he passed the hut where he'd thrown the big runaway last week, rage replaced the numbness that had enveloped him all afternoon. The Seminole chief—Panther—had been a damned fool to come looking for the Negro. If the storm hadn't kicked up, Panther's scalp would be dangling from his front porch.

But he hadn't gotten back to the war chief in time and someone had freed him.

Calida.

Memories of the beautiful young slave replaced thoughts of what he would have done to both of his captives. He should have gone after Calida and hauled her back where she belonged, but he hadn't been able to move. While she bolted like a spooked deer, he'd stared first at her and then down at what was left of his wife. Calida with her doe eyes and sun-toasted skin was life and energy and spirit, while the woman who bore his name, who couldn't give him the son he needed—

Cursing, he wove his way around the worthless curs clustered around the slave cabins until he reached the one in which Joseph lived. He yanked open the door and stomped in. Joseph and his scrawny old wife were sitting on the floor, protected from the packed dirt by the rags they used as rugs. They were dipping wooden spoons into a shared pot that held some kind of gray soup.

"Get up," he ordered. "I need you."

"What? Massa—"

"I said"—he punctuated the order with a kick that caught Joseph's knee a glancing blow—"I've got a job for you to do. Now."

Holding his knee, the ancient carriage driver scrabbled to his feet. He kept his eyes on the ground, his bony body seemingly jointless. "Yes sir, massa," he muttered. "You wants I should put on mah shoes first?"

"You're not going to need them," he said tersely, then turned and walked out of the impossibly small cabin. Joseph knew better than to ask questions or stall; he'd be right behind him. Again Reddin's legs took him past where he'd left the Seminole trussed. Not only had the savage gotten loose, but the nigger had managed to dig himself out as well. As he glanced at the bits of cut leather, a smile—the first since rage overtook him earlier today—touched his lips. A man doesn't experience fifteen years of military duty without learning the meaning of control. Before this whole mess was over, he'd have what he wanted. What he needed.

He told Joseph only that he'd decided to start for St. Augustine tonight and Joseph was to drive the carriage. The slave gave him a disbelieving look but said nothing. Instead, he first reassured himself that the mare was properly harnessed, then climbed up onto his high seat. Reddin settled his bulk onto the coach's interior, careful not to let his feet touch his wife's body.

Once he looked behind him, watching as the emerging moon highlighted Croon Plantation—his land. It wasn't much, not nearly as grand as his father-in-law's, but more successful than the pathetic pieces of swamp closer to the coast, most of which had been destroyed by Seminoles a few months ago. Some of his neighbors were debating whether they dared remain or might have to desert their property until the Indian threat was over.

Reddin wasn't worried; he had President Jackson's ear and had already ingratiated himself with Major General Jesup. Hell, he even knew the territorial governor well enough to make a direct request for protection. Both the President and major general had promised him that troops would remain stationed nearby as deterrent against the savages.

Still, if he'd had time to kill Panther, the message would have gotten around; Osceola himself would understand that Reddin Croon wasn't a man to be crossed.

The carriage jogged and bumped along, but Reddin didn't try to fight the motion. Instead, he relaxed his muscles, pulled out a jug, and drank deeply. The whisky hit the back of his throat and he traced its progress into his belly. Already the fine edge of tension was being sanded away. He wanted to follow the drink with another, but if he did, he might make a mistake.

A thin trail that needed constant work had been hacked through the wilderness; except for that single way out, Croon Plantation was an island in the middle of nothing, cut off from so-called civilization.

Liana hated—had hated—that. No matter how many parties she threw or how often she went to St. Augustine, she still complained that he'd hauled her off to live with savages and slaves. She didn't care that his sugarcane fields were the richest in the territory because in his years of traveling he'd learned that land had to be treated right if it was going to produce. It mattered not at all to her that he'd already doubled the amount Isiah Yongue had given him for taking his homely daughter off his hands.

Well, she wouldn't be complaining any more.

He waited until the carriage had gone a mile before ordering Joseph to stop. The slave gave the reins a gentle, almost imperceptible tug, and the mare immediately dropped her head, obviously relieved that she was no longer being forced to put herself out. Reddin cursed the spoiled, worthless nag, then quickly calculated how much he'd get by offering her to St. Augustine's society ladies. If he told them how it grieved him to have his dead wife's beloved pet around, they would dig deep into their purses. Hell, maybe one of them would offer more than coins.

Not bothering to tell Joseph what he was doing, he climbed out of the carriage and walked around until he had an unobstructed look at the old man. The moon all but glinted off Joseph's white head; he'd pulled himself up as straight as he could, patiently waiting for his master to tell him what he wanted him to do next.

Reddin reached inside his coat and pulled a knife he'd once taken from a dead Seminole out of his waistband. It felt heavy, a sure weapon for a man who had the sense to stay sober. Joseph's brows furrowed when he saw what his master held, but before he could do more than start to lift his hand, Reddin hurtled the weapon at Joseph's chest. His bony fingers slapped at the knife now buried in him almost to the hilt. His eyes bulged and locked with Reddin's. As Reddin watched, the slave rose out of his seat, then pitched forward. His limp body landed on the mare's rump, causing her to jump. She pranced excitedly until Reddin grabbed the reins and yanked. Trembling, the mare watched him out of the corner of her eyes. Between her legs, Joseph lay utterly still.

When he was sure the mare wouldn't bolt, Reddin walked back to the carriage and climbed into it. He unwrapped his wife's body and forced her into a semblance of a sitting position. Then he slid away from her. Her neck was broken; a blind man would know that. Would her father look at her and believe both she and the slave had died at the hands of the Seminoles? No matter how many ways he tried to make the answer come out yes, he knew he was lying to himself. There was only one thing left to do.

Although touching her again repulsed him, he lifted Liana out of the carriage and placed her near the front wheels. Then he stooped, picked up a rock, and threw it at the mare's rump. She squealed, reared, then charged forward, dragging the carriage with her.

Reddin looked down. The wheels had passed over his wife's chest, smearing her bloodied dress with mud from this afternoon's rain. When Isiah Yongue arrived in St. Augustine, his son-in-law would be there, a grief-stricken widower who barely comprehended that his "beloved" wife had been killed by brutal Seminoles. After a short—very short—period of grief, he'd insist he would never know peace until the murdering savages were hunted down.

And as a former officer, he would be willing to lead any troops Jesup and the President—his friend—saw fit to assign to him.

When he tried to approach the mare, she shied away, and he had to lunge for the dangling reins. He thought, seriously, about taking a crop to the miserable nag. Instead, he ran his hand almost gently over the mare's sweating neck before unfastening her. Seminoles stole horses, damn it. That meant he couldn't get away with selling her, but there were other ways of making his story stick.

As he pushed his way into the wall of wet greenery, the moon seemed to be coming closer, silvered light outlining dense shadows. Teeth clenched, he listened to the night—the hissing, buzzing, growling night—and again congratulated himself on having stayed sober. The swamps that waited just beyond the road could all too easily trap someone who wasn't paying attention—who didn't understand the danger.

Calida was terrified of the world beyond the plantation. She'd be back soon, hungry and miserable. His.

Calida crouched behind a huge damp-barked tree. She'd started shivering even before it became night. Now, watching Master Croon walk away from the two bodies while leading the horse, she trembled so much that she could barely force her legs under her. She'd seen her master hurtle a knife into Joseph. Although she didn't understand why he'd done what he had afterward, the image of carriage wheels grinding Mistress Liana's body into the earth sickened her.

If Master Croon somehow knew she'd been watching him all day from behind brush and shadow, if he was even now sneaking up behind her— No. He'd gone in the opposite direction.

She whimpered and ordered herself not to look too closely around her. A minute passed, then five. If only it were daylight, maybe the wilderness wouldn't feel as if it was reaching out to strangle her. If she'd been allowed outside more, maybe she'd better understand the world beyond what had been painstakingly cleared. Maybe.

Still shaking, she stepped around the tree and half walked, half slunk toward the abandoned carriage. Mistress Liana was dead; she knew that. And the way Joseph lay left no doubt in her mind that Master Croon had killed him as well. What—

A scream sliced through the night sounds. Her flesh felt as if it had been touched by lightning and ice. Another scream began before the first finished echoing. It wasn't human, was nothing like any night-sound she'd ever heard. When she realized what it was, she clamped her arms around herself and leaned forward, gasping for enough air to quiet her stomach. Mistress Liana's horse, terrified. Somewhere in the swamp.

A third scream catapulted her into action. Mindless, she began running down the narrow road back toward the plantation, thinking—thinking what?

Her mother.

The mass of growth surrounding her sang its endless and eerie song, making her want to shriek at it to stop. The only time she left Croon House after dark was to go to her mother's cabin with the precious books she'd snuck out of Mistress Liana's library. Whenever she did, she walked quickly, concentrating on her goal and not the creatures that came out after the sun went down.

Tonight she was alone.

Ready to bolt into the wall of trees and bushes at the first sound of footsteps, she hurried toward the plantation as fast as her tender and stinging feet would allow.

Was she mad? Had what she'd seen and heard been a nightmare?

Sobbing, she struggled to shove the questions into submission. All that mattered was that her mistress was dead and her master— Her master what?

A sound like that of distant teeth snapping together made her whimper in fear. She strained to see, but the night kept its secrets. If an alligator or panther or other wild creature was out there— stalking her—she could only pray her end would come quickly.

Dying in a panther's jaws was better than letting Master Croon get his hands on her again.

The snapping sound was repeated. It was only with a great force of will that she kept from panicking. There wasn't anywhere to go, anyplace where she would be safe.

Only with her mother.

Knowing that was no longer true and hadn't been for years, she nevertheless comforted herself with thoughts of the soft and gentle woman who'd given her the only sense of belonging she'd ever had.

Faint candlelight flickered from inside the crudely built slave cabins. The light guided her first out of the awful darkness and then toward where her mother lived. She'd remained close enough to the plantation today that she'd have known if Master Croon had sent his foreman or slaves out to look for her. Maybe he figured she would return once she became hungry and tired enough, and maybe he was so grief-stricken over his wife's death that he couldn't think beyond that.

No. Whatever he felt about his wife, grief wasn't part of the emotion.

The thought that someone might grab her and hold her for Master Croon's return froze her in midstride. Then she reminded herself that if he had said anything about what had happened in his room, the other slaves would be talking about that tonight, not sitting quietly in their separate cabins. Not said anything? Why not? Didn't anyone know that Mistress Liana was dead?

Her mother was alone. Calida spotted her shadow as she passed between the open door and the candle she read by. Hand at her throat now, Calida slipped slowly closer. Her body hummed with fear of what the future might bring, but she *had* to see the only person she'd ever loved.

Pilar had stopped moving about and was now perched on a small wooden chair, her head bent forward. Her lips moved as she read and Calida heard or believed she heard her mother's mutterings as she went over Bible verses she could recite in her sleep. For longer than was safe, Calida stood with her arms wrapped tightly around her against the cold, her stomach pinched with hunger and nausea, and her heart and head filling with tears.

Pilar's hair was graying. Although she'd had Calida when she was little more than a child, the burdens she'd carried throughout her life had aged her too quickly. That and the accident that had crushed her right thigh and turned her into a cripple. Calida saw not the ragged dress and sagging breasts, but a woman with the determination to teach her only child how to read. A woman who'd shown that daughter that even though she couldn't escape the destiny determined by her light skin and man-pleasing body, she must hold her head high and keep her heart and mind separate from those who owned her.

"Mother?"

Pilar immediately dropped her Bible to the floor and kicked it under her long skirt, the movement as instinctive as Calida's had been when she ran from Master Croon. Her hand up to shield her eyes from the candlelight, Pilar stared out into the night. A slight if strained smile touched her lips. "Calida? What's you doin' here?"

Running.

"I've been watching you," Calida said softly. "Why do you open your Bible? You know the words by heart."

"Not all of 'em. Besides, it gives me comfort to see the words hasn't changed. Missy Liana has no need of you tonight?"

Although she was certain no one could overhear them, she slipped inside and took her mother's dry hands before saying anything. Then, holding her voice to a harsh whisper, she told her everything. Pilar started to tremble. She rubbed her daughter's arms as if she were a small, frightened child.

"Dead? Missy Liana and Joseph. You're sure?"

Unable to say the words again, she simply nodded. She gently pulled free and stepped over to the rough-finished pine table and picked up a small hard corn biscuit. "I can't stay here."

"Can't stay? Calida, no!"

"He'll want—he'll be after me all the time. Or maybe he'll take me into the quicksand like he did that poor horse. He— Just before I ran, he said I'd killed her. What— I don't know what to think."

Pilar's thick-knuckled fingers knotted. She stared, first out at the night and then into the flickering candlelight until Calida thought she might have taken her mind far from here. "I hates 'em," Pilar whispered. "I hates 'em as I's never hated in my life."

"No."

"Yes. Even more than I did the man who put you inside me."

Calida thought she might cry, but if she broke down, her mother would do the same, and how could she possibly leave her then? *Leave? Where?* "To have him pestering me all the time, the things he does—how did you abide it?"

"I hads no choice." Pilar ran her hand over Calida's face as if try-ing to commit it to memory. "But you—" Suddenly she gripped Cal-ida's arms with fierce strength. "I's been 'fraid for you for so long. From the moment your body turned to that of a woman. You're beau-tiful; I wanted you to be ugly."

"I wish I was." Her arms ached, but she couldn't bring herself to pull out of her mother's grasp.

"Where's you goin'? The runaway I give water to the other day— If the slave-catchers find you like they did him—" A spasm coursed through Pilar's body. "I'd rather have you dead than them brings you back."

Where are you going? She'd heard of white people who helped es-caped slaves go north—the Freedom Trail they called it, but this was untamed Florida, not Georgia or Alabama. Far from those who cared whether a black person lived or died at her master's hands. "The sav-age I freed." She started slowly. "If I can find him—if he remembers I saved his life . . ." *Find? But the Seminoles lived deep in the jungle and just the thought of them left her weak with fear.*

"The savage saw your face?"

"I think—yes. I know he did."

"He said nuthin'?"

"There was nothing to say, no time. He looked so wild; such rage was in his eyes— Oh Mama, maybe I'll give myself up to an alligator."

Pilar released her and sank back onto her chair. She stared at her bare feet for so long that Calida forgot her own desperate situation and worried that something was wrong with her mother.

"Follow the river, deep into the wilderness."

"What are you saying?"

"When I gave that poor captured darkie water, I asked where he been livin'. That's what he tol' me."

"Can you believe him?"

"I don't know." She groaned. "But there's nuthin' else."

Nothing else. Only, if she somehow survived the journey to wherever the Negro had been living and the Seminole was there as well, would he welcome her or slit her throat? Would she be no more to him than she was to Master Croon?

"The river," she whispered. "Come with me, please. Together—"

"No."

The word, although softly spoken, felt like a blow to Calida's heart. "I can't leave you. I don't want—"

"You has to! Do you think I wants you out there, alone? But for so long now I's wondered when your soul would cry for freedom. I knew it would happen; I seen the need burning in your eyes. Either you'll find the Seminoles—you won' be the first—or . . ."

"Come with me. Your eyes burn too."

"My leg, Calida. I'd only hold you back. You know that." She reached for a knife and a shawl and pressed them into Calida's hand. Then she gathered up the other corn biscuits and wrapped them in a scrap of cloth. She handed it to Calida, her mouth trembling. "I wants it to be more. If you wait, I'll go to the other cabins and ask—"

"No! I can't let anyone know I've been here." She looked at the burdens in her hands, then folded her arms around her mother and held her close. "I'll come back. As soon as I— I'll come back. And when I do, I'll take you with me."

"Don't talks 'bout tomorrow," Pilar said roughly. "And don't think of me. I'll be all right; you'll be all right. The Seminole . . ."

There wasn't anything left to say, was there? Calida thought as she continued to clutch her mother against her. She'd seen families torn apart, once shared Pilar's terror that Master Croon wouldn't buy both mother and daughter. When, with his stare so fierce that she'd felt stripped naked by it, he'd included her in his bid, she'd sent up a prayer of thanksgiving, even if it meant leaving Georgia and coming to someplace called the Florida Territory. It was only later that she understood why he'd wanted her.

She was leaving her mother; maybe she'd never see her again. With all her heart, she needed to tell her how much she loved her, beg her to flee with her. That leg! That twisted, prisoning leg! She felt as if she might explode with grief, and she couldn't leave her mother with that memory of her.

Instead, shattering inside, she kissed her mother on the forehead, spun away, and stumbled into the night.

Pilar waited until she could no longer see her daughter before making her way to the door. Her leg throbbed. She stood with one hand gripping the wood and her eyes already blurred with tears that might never end.

Be careful. Please. Please. May God look after you. Protect . . .

4

Screeching, a snakebird took flight from a nearby palmetto. Too sick and exausted to be startled, Calida stared at the long-necked black and white bird until it disappeared. Every muscle in her legs screamed at her to sink to the soggy, dank-smelling ground, but if she did, she might never rise again.

The river, at least this finger of it, was just beyond the tree the snakebird had been in. It seemed as if she'd been following it forever, although if she really thought about it, she knew she hadn't been out here for more than a week while it rained and rained and rained.

Out here.

The wilderness surrounded her, had swallowed her and might keep her trapped in its stinking, groaning, hissing belly forever. No matter how long she'd been walking, she couldn't get over her need to look up for a glimpse—any glimpse—of the sky. Most of the time, she couldn't see it for the mass of trees and brush that fought for light and space.

When she pressed her hand against the back of her hot neck, she felt countless mosquito bites. That first impossibly long and horrifying night, she'd come close to losing her mind because the insects wouldn't leave her alone, were trying to bite her to death, but as the hours and then the days passed, she no longer paid them any mind.

They, like the hordes of shadowy, screaming birds and animals, were everywhere.

Repulsed at the thought of drinking from the shallow, greenish, meandering river, she'd crouched openmouthed under leaves to catch the cascading raindrops. It should have been enough. While at the plantation, she hadn't needed more than two or three ladles of water a day, but back then her time had been filled with little more than tending to Mistress Liana. Now, always moving and always scared, her body craved endless moisture. Much of the time it ran sheetlike off her body, but the effort of getting it inside her—

Her eyes on the surrounding trees in case one of those horrible snakes was in them, she forced one bruised and lacerated foot after another. During the last storm, she'd taken off her torn, filthy dress and held it up to the deluge before scrubbing it between her hands. Although it chilled her, she'd put it back on wet because the single garment was all she had, and being naked made her feel even more vulnerable. The downpour hadn't ended until dark. By then it was too cold for the cotton to dry. She'd spent the night shivering and cursing herself for having lost her blanket in the underbrush several days before, but maybe it was her fever and not the cold that made her teeth chatter.

She was dying.

A hissing sound stopped her in midstep. She waited, not breathing, but it wasn't repeated, and after half a minute she forced herself to start walking again. Why didn't matter. Where mattered even less. All she knew was that she couldn't stop.

I love you, her mother had said. They'd been the last words she'd heard from Pilar, the last human voice. Since then there'd been nothing except hisses and whispers, eerie screams and coughs, endless and unfathomable sounds.

She was dying.

A tangle of roots just ahead clogged what her feverish brain perceived as some kind of trail. Because she had nowhere else to go, she clambered over it. The effort exausted her, and she fell to her knees. Moisture and rotting leaves seeped over her. Rocking slightly, she tried to lift her head, but her wet, dirty hair was so heavy and even if she could force her eyes to focus, she wouldn't see anything except this endless, living prison.

She would die in the wilderness, the horrible and terrifying wilderness.

After a meaningless length of time, she placed the back of her hand against her cheek. Her flesh felt so hot. The river. The stinking, churning, rain-swollen river. She was following it because . . . because her mother had told her to.

But why?

She should want the answer. She knew what she was running from; the memory of Mistress Liana's lifeless body, that poor trapped horse's scream. Those things had imbedded themselves into her brain. She'd told her mother good-bye because she didn't dare stay. And then she'd run into the fearsome jungle because she had nowhere else to go.

Go?

The hissing began again, closer, nearly as close as the wild sounds came at night. She wanted to get to her feet and run, but too many terror-filled nights and her growing fever had left her spent. She could only listen, stare into the living monster that was her world, and try to remember where she was going.

Follow the river. That's what her mother had said. It led—led somewhere.

A belly-deep roar split the air. Beyond screaming, she hauled herself to her feet. Five, or was it six, nights of this hell had taught her a great deal. She knew the sound of an alligator, what they looked like, their heavy slithering movements, the great jaws and uncountable teeth. This one was close; probably it was in the river—the river she was supposed to follow to . . .

Walking because if she stopped now she would never be able to start again, she kept her body and eyes moving. Except for the handful of corn biscuits, she hadn't eaten for the first three days for fear she'd poison herself, but finally hunger had forced her to try some berries and seeds. She watched the birds. If they ate something, so did she. So far she hadn't had any ill effects, but her weakening body told her she wasn't getting enough.

What did it matter? Fever consumed her; before long she would have to stop, and when she did she would die.

Alone.

To keep the thought from overwhelming her, she started counting her steps. Although she felt the weight of the clouds overhead, it hadn't rained yet today, which meant she hadn't had anything to drink. Her fevered body demanded water. Dragging one foot after another took so much effort, sapped her brain and left it incapable of anything except counting.

Walk. Just keep walking. Tonight you can . . . Tonight. Alone.

Panther stood motionless over a pond, his spear at the ready. Around him, the tops of the trees shook from the wind buffeting them. The air smelled of rain; the clouds were already dark purple. The others, seeking to avoid the approaching storm, were back in the village, but the clan's supply of fresh fish was almost gone. Besides, it was easier to fish than answer endless questions about how much longer the Egret clan and the runaway slaves who lived with them could stay in the small clearing created by a recent fire.

He wasn't a witch doctor. He didn't have the gift of sight. Still, he was the Egret clan's war chief, and in this time of war, everyone turned to him.

Tiny fish nibbled at his toes. He wanted to brush them away, but if he did, he would warn the two garfish swimming closer. In deference to winter, he'd put on leather leggings this morning but had stripped down to his loincloth before stepping into the pond. He loved standing here with the water flowing around him and the wind brushing along his back. This silence that wasn't really silence was important to him. Fishing or hunting alone, he could forget his responsibilities, his father's unavenged ghost, and the fear that the Egret clan could never outrun the army. He became a child again, concerned with nothing except filling his belly.

He became aware of a slight pull in his arm and realized he'd been holding his spear aloft longer than he usually did—longer than he needed to. One of the garfish was within easy reach. He drove the spear at the fish, aiming slightly ahead of it because the water distorted its location. The fish instantly curled its body upward as if trying to embrace the spear now protruding from its back. He yanked the spear and its prisoner from the water and gave thanks to Breath Giver for this gift of food. He pulled the fish free, flipped it onto the ground, and focused on the pond again, hoping the other garfish hadn't been frightened away.

That was when he heard the sound. Yes, Piahokee was never silent—its wild music only changed from day to night creatures— but this was something different. Something that didn't belong.

Stepping out of the water, he crouched low. He held his spear at the ready and judged the distance between where he stood and the closest gumbo-limbo tree. He could reach it in two steps, but that might be too long if a bluecoat had spotted him.

No, not a bluecoat. Two Seminole scouts kept a constant eye on the army camped near Raccoon Point. If any of the enemy had been sent into Piahokee, he would know.

Watching, listening, smelling, he pulled his surroundings into him until it told him what he needed to know. There was one, a stranger who walked without wisdom or direction or strength. In no hurry now, he faded into the shadows and waited. After a few moments, he heard erratic footsteps and quick, tortured breathing. Although many of the plantations were still inhabited by whites, none of them would be so foolish as to come out here alone. That left only one thing: a slave seeking safety.

For no longer than a heartbeat, he wanted to turn his back on the newcomer and fade into the wilderness. *Tastanagee* they called him. War chief. Head of the Egret clan. The weight of those responsibilities never left him, only increased with each passing day. The child he'd once been had delighted in watching turtles lay their eggs in the sand, had known where to search for alligator holes. Freedom had been something he took for granted; now it was precious and precarious.

The newcomer's breathing became louder. And because Gaitor and others had told him what it meant to be a slave, he couldn't walk away from someone who might need him. Still, he would wait until the stranger revealed himself before stepping out of the shadows.

It was a woman. Her long, black hair was plastered against the sides of her face making it impossible for him to see her features. Still, because her ruined dress left her legs and forearms bare, he knew she was young and so light-skinned that she might pass as a white who spent her life in the sun. She didn't have enough fat on her body, was barely strong enough to hold up her slight weight. Her legs were caked with mud; her arms had been scratched uncounted times. She had no weapon, no shoes.

A whimpering sound escaped her lips. She stopped and looked around. When her gaze passed over where he stood, he noted the bright splotches of color on her cheeks, her dulled eyes, the way her mouth hung open. She didn't see him, and he wondered if she was capable of focusing on anything, of reacting to anything.

When she sank to the ground as lightly as a discarded feather, he felt his hand tighten around his spear. She wasn't Seminole. He wasn't responsible for her. He wasn't!

Dying.

As the word pushed its relentless way into her thoughts, Calida tried to silence it; she'd fought it so many times, and yet it always returned to mock her. She shouldn't care anymore; death would be a relief. But something continued to burn and fight inside her, and she couldn't destroy that any more than she could the belief that she wouldn't live through the day. Forcing her eyes open again, she realized she was staring at the ground. A grub-filled branch was only a few inches away. She concentrated on the tiny white creatures, not with revulsion but with the simple understanding that they belonged here while she didn't.

She wanted to cry, to care. To no longer care.

A prickling of her nerve endings tore her from her study of the grubs, but she had to fight for the strength to look up. She stared at a pair of legs.

Naked. Dark and muscled. Not Master Croon.

The legs became narrow hips, a single piece of leather covering his manhood, lean and hard waist, a too-broad chest. He carried a spear. It was aimed at her.

Not breathing, she struggled to her feet and backed away from the man, the savage. She tried to study his eyes to know what he was thinking, but her mind felt as if it was shattering. It recorded his size and strength, the spear again, the jungle that surrounded him. His mouth was hard. His shoulders seemed to extend forever. Was there any end to him? Heat washed through her. She knew it was the fever and cursed its control over her.

Backing away, she again struggled to concentrate on his eyes, but all she knew was that they were black. His spear was pointed at her heart.

He was going to kill her.

Not dying anymore. Dead.

The last of her strength seeped from her legs. Still she willed herself to turn and run. She managed four, maybe five steps before he overtook her. His free arm snaked around her waist, and he lifted her off the ground, pulled her tight against him. She felt his cool skin, tried to scream, dug her ragged nails into his forearm. Growling, he flung her away from him. She tried to regain her balance, but there was nothing left of her.

Nothing except darkness.

Gaitor had just finished replacing a wind-torn chunk of bark from the roof of Panther's *chickee* when Panther stepped into the clearing. His friend carried an unconscious or dead woman over his shoulder, his burden barely heavy enough to unbalance his stance. Although others were already hurrying to Panther's side, Gaitor remained where he was, looking not at the woman but into Panther's eyes. The Seminole war chief returned his steady gaze and ignored old Pascofa who was trying to lift the woman's head.

Gaitor knew Panther had already taken note of what he'd been doing. Two days ago, Gaitor's hands had still been raw from the effort of digging his way out of the prison Reddin Croon had thrown him into. They were now healed enough that he no longer felt useless. To show his gratitude to Panther for having risked his own life coming after him, he'd been working on the *chickee*. He expected no gratitude, just as he knew Panther didn't want to hear the same words from him.

They were friends; that was enough.

"I never seen a fish like this one," he said when he joined those clustered around Panther. He indicated the woman. "She puts up much of a fight?"

"Not much." Panther shrugged to reposition her but made no

move to put her down or turn her over to someone. Maybe she was dead. "Has there been any word about the bluecoats?"

"No. But Osceola—"

"My chief?" Panther glanced around. "Where is he?"

"Not here," Pascofa said before Gaitor could speak. Suddenly everyone was talking at once. Thinking to let the others explain, Gaitor turned his attention to the woman, but Panther called his name. Again he met the war chief's gaze.

"Tell me," Panther ordered as if the nearly one hundred Seminole and Negro men, women, and children who made up the village didn't exist.

"Osceola sent a runner with a message," Gaitor explained. "He wants to talk to you, but he don't feel up to leavin' his village."

Panther didn't say anything, but then he didn't have to. The day Gaitor made his way back to the village, Panther had told him that Osceola the Great Warrior had again been taken by swamp sickness. Malaria, whites called it. Osceola lacked the strength to visit the far-flung clans that made up the Seminole nation.

"I tole the runner you'd come soon as ya could."

"Hm." Again Panther shrugged. When the woman started to slide off his shoulder, Gaitor leaned forward and took her slight weight in his own arms. She stirred and opened her eyes just enough for him to see that they were tinged with fever. She felt hot. Maybe she, like Osceola, had caught swamp sickness.

"Where you fine her?" he asked.

Panther's answer did little to satisfy Gaitor's curiosity, but he knew better than to push for more information. Once, he'd been told, Panther had been as talkative as any other, but the closer the army came, the more silent he became. Gaitor understood, maybe more than anyone else, that when a man's heart is heavy, there is little room for words.

The woman groaned and stirred again. Others crowded in around him eager for a close look at her. Her Negro blood had been thinned until she was the color of pineland brush. No one had to tell him why; some white man had fooled around with her mother, and maybe with her mother's mother. She was beautiful. At least she would be if she wasn't such a mess.

"She saved my life," Panther said.

"Saved? I don't under—the woman at Reddin Croon's plantation?"

Panther nodded but said nothing more. His eyes stayed on Calida. When Pascofa tapped his elbow, indicating he should carry his burden to the healer's *chickee,* Gaitor turned in that direction but kept his attention fixed on Panther who, like him, was taller than most of the others. "You know what Osceola wants, don't ya?" he asked. "He hates this runnin' en hidin'. He wants we should stand and fight."

"I want the same thing."

"But—"

"I am a *tastanagee,*" Panther interrupted. "It is not in my heart to hide like a deer." He looked around, his attention finally settling on a couple of Seminole boys so young that they couldn't run without falling. "I want them to know the world I did when I was their age. I want— I do not know when I will be back." Reaching out, Panther pushed hair away from the woman's face. His features didn't soften. He gave no sign of his emotions, and yet Gaitor understood. Panther, *tastanagee* of the Egret clan, owed his life to this maybe dying woman.

Just as Gaitor Man owed his to Panther.

The healer wanted to treat the woman in private. His magic, he said, would be strong only if nothing came between it and his patient. But Panther had asked Gaitor to watch over the woman, and he would do what his friend and chief wanted. Still, he knew enough to sit at the far end of the *chickee* so he wouldn't disturb the spirits and witches the healer would try to drive out of her. Because the *chickee* had no enclosed sides, others occasionally peeked in. When they did, the healer chased them off. He left Gaitor alone, however. There were, Gaitor admitted, benefits to being a head taller and much broader than most men.

The healer had ordered his wife to clean the patient. Calida stirred and moaned while water ran over her lacerations. Although she kept opening her eyes, Gaitor guessed she had no knowledge of her surroundings. It had taken his own strong legs more than three days to reach the village. This woman looked as if she'd been walking for much longer than that.

The healer took various herbs from several small baskets and dumped them into a larger one. Then he mixed them together with his sacred turkey feather and sprinkled water that he'd blessed over that. Next he put one tip of his hollow cane medicine tube in the mixture and blew on it. Only then did he take a handful and place it on the woman's chest. He chanted and called out to the evil spirits, exhorting them to leave her. His voice dropped to a whisper so no one could steal his magic words.

"Mama. Ma-ma."

Gaitor leaned forward, concentrating. She repeated herself, the single word both harsh and soft. Her surprisingly strong-looking fingers clenched and unclenched; her eyes fluttered several times but didn't stay open.

"Mama. Mama, please . . ."

Grunting in satisfaction, the healer placed more sacred herbs on her forehead. She tried to brush them away, but he grabbed her wrists and pinned them to the ground. A shudder worked its way through her body. She bucked and tried to escape.

"You will help me," the healer ordered Gaitor. "I can do nothing if she fights me."

Gaitor hurried over to the woman and did as he'd been ordered. Her eyes were wide open now but not focusing. Although her flesh still felt hot to the touch, her teeth chattered. Her chest heaved under what there was of her thin dress. When she sucked in her breath, her ribs stuck out.

"You lissens to me," Gaitor said. "If you wants to live, you gots to do as we tells ya."

"Mama?"

"I ain't yur mama, gal. I's a runaway, just like you."

At the word *runaway*, her eyes became bright and sharp. She stopped her struggling, blinked once. "Who—are you?"

"Ya don' know me. My massa called me Benjamin. Now I's Gaitor. I ain't never goin' back ta Benjamin."

"Gai . . . Where am I?"

He told her that she was in the village of the Seminole Egret clan but doubted she knew what he was talking about, or that she was capable of holding onto the explanation. Her recent struggle, plus the fact that she'd made it here alive, told him there was a hidden strength to her, but she barely looked sturdy enough for the lightest house chores. Of course if she'd been used as he figured she had, a strong back wasn't important.

"What ya doin' here, gal?" he asked. "Where ya come from? Panther, he says ya saved his life. Ya belon' to Massa Croon?"

"Croon?" She tried to sit up, fell back on the ground. "Where—?"

"He ain't here. No one is 'cept for the Seminole and fifteen, maybe sixteen runaways."

"Seminoles? This—I made it."

A sob caught in her throat at the end. She blinked at a tear, then closed her eyes. "Mama." She barely whispered the word. "Mama."

"Yur mama ain't here, gal."

"Not—I didn't want to leave her. I begged her to come. Told her I couldn't live without her, but . . ."

"But what?"

"He was going to kill me."

He wanted to ask who, but she might not be willing to say any more than she already had. He knew the fear, the horror of knowing someone held the power of life or death over him. He didn't talk about that helplessness and sensed she didn't want to either. "Tell me 'bout yur mama," he prompted. "She knows where you is, does she?"

"She told me—told me to follow the river. I didn't want . . ." Although tears dampened her lashes and ran off her cheeks, she didn't sob. "I didn't want to leave her."

He took her hand and squeezed it gently. The bones of her fingers shouldn't remind him of Lilly's, but they did.

Lilly, his wife.

Lilly, the mother of his son.

Lilly, who he hadn't seen for three years because his master had sold him away from his family and brought him to the godforsaken place called Florida.

Struggling against the memory of another time and place, of lost love, he released the girl's hand. He wanted to stalk away, but if she set to fighting again, she might harm herself, and he didn't want that. "You rest, you hear?" he ordered roughly. "You's safe here."

"Safe?"

"Panther'll make sure."

"Panther?" She opened her eyes again. Tears still swam in them. "Who . . . ?"

"You'll know soon 'nough. Iffen you lives."

5

Holding himself to a steady jog, Panther easily made his way through the wilderness. He'd left his chief a little after dawn, and if he didn't stop he would be back at his own village before nightfall. Osceola, weak but clearheaded, had wanted him to stay. There'd been five other war chiefs there, each willing to share his tobacco pouch.

But he wanted his people to know what he'd learned, especially Gaitor, who had to be told that the army had captured fifty-two escaped slaves near Withlacoochee Cove. His thoughts firmly on the Negro who'd become a brother to him since the long night the two had spent telling each other things no one else knew, he divided his attention between the uneven trail and the swampy land, which might conceal alligators or snakes.

Gaitor knew of Panther's hatred for all bluecoats, of his fear that his people would never again know peace and might one day be forced onto a reservation. In return, he knew that Gaitor still mourned the wife and child he hadn't seen for more than three winters.

Their tongues hadn't been loosened by *ueho'mee,* the white man's drink. When they found themselves the only ones still awake after a successful hunt, he had thought he'd only speak to Gaitor for a few minutes before retreating into the silence that had become part of his nature. That was before Gaitor told him he'd cast off his slave name, that living on white men's cattle, speared fish, and skinned snakes was better than what he'd had before he escaped his master.

Master.

After peering into the underbrush to assure himself that all he'd seen was a small deer, Panther let his thoughts go back to the word. Runaway slaves had been taking refuge with Seminoles since before he was born. He'd grown up hearing the Negroes talk about white men who owned other men's bodies, but he'd never understood what that meant. To be a Seminole was to be free; anything else was impossible. Unacceptable.

Gaitor knew that the color of a person's skin determined whether that person could live as he wanted or remained alive only as long as another willed it.

To have someone else have the power of life and death over him—

Was that why the woman had run? He understood a strong, healthy man like Gaitor fleeing into Piahokees, but the woman who'd cut him free didn't belong here. She'd been raised to live within her master's house. Her soft hands and legs had told him that. Although he hadn't seen her back, her exposed flesh showed no sign of having ever felt a whip. Why then had she risked her life by coming here?

And why had she freed him?

He shook his head in an attempt to remove her from his thoughts, but she remained there, a small, warm presence. She might be dead. If she was, he would never know more about her than he already did. But if she lived—

If she did, he would thank her for saving his life, tell her she would always have a place among the Seminoles. That was all.

It had rained much of the time he was on the trail, but it had stopped a little while ago, and the ground at the edge of the clearing had begun to dry. Panther took note of that in a single glance, then swept his eyes over the village. It was winter. They should have erected houses capable of withstanding torrential storms, but the twenty-some *chickees* were hastily erected structures without raised palmetto wood floors, attic storage area, or enclosed sides. Still, watching several children playing while their mothers either roasted ears of corn or pounded the dried kernels into meal gave him a sense of peace. At least they'd been here long enough to have raised their most vital crop along with sweet potatoes, beans, and squash. If they had to leave, they'd be dependent on what Piahokee provided because their cattle were gone, stolen by the army.

When the children recognized him, they stopped playing and studied him, awe and half-fear in the eyes of the youngest. He was used to that. Being war chief at a time when little except war mattered made him an object of wonder to those who didn't yet understand why the Egret clan had moved deep into Piahokee and why no man went about without a weapon, why the word *bluejacket* was spoken with hatred.

Nodding at the women, he moved through the village toward the healer's hut. He needed to call the clan members together, but until he'd learned whether the woman was alive, he couldn't put his mind to anything else.

The healer was nowhere to be seen. His heart twisted into a knot he didn't want to acknowledge. Then, recognizing Gaitor's powerful form hunched over something, he ducked his head to avoid the ferns that trailed down off the *chickee's* roof and entered. Gaitor looked up at him.

In the Negro's eyes, he found fierce determination and a pride that hadn't been there when, half dead from a whipping, Gaitor had been brought to the village by warriors who'd found him hiding in the swamp. Neither man talked about how Gaitor had begged him not to turn him over to his master. There was no need; the terrified creature he'd been that day had slowly disappeared, replaced now by a man.

"Yur backs early. I thought you'd be gone a lot longer."

Panther glanced over at the figure on the mat bed. The woman's scratches were already healing. Someone had cleaned her hair. Fever no longer painted her cheeks and neck with hot color. "She is better," he said.

"Faster 'en I thought she'd heal. Down deep she's a strong 'en."

Maybe that's why she'd freed him, because she'd sensed his

strength. The woman had opened her eyes and was regarding him warily, comprehension as to who he was dawning slowly. "I learned things you will not want to know," he told Gaitor. "General Jesup's troops have been on the move."

"Where?"

"Near Withlacoochee Cove."

Gaitor's features clouded. The cove was no more than a four-day journey from here. "What happened?"

"The bluecoat came across some escaped slaves. They tried to run, but he captured them."

"How many?"

The woman was following the conversation intently. Without understanding why, he wanted to protect her from hearing this. "Many. A few days later the general and his men found where Osceola was staying. My chief and the other warriors escaped."

"Found!" Gaitor spat the word. "Jesup forced the slaves to tell 'em, jus' as someone was forced to lead the army to the cove."

Panther had no doubt of that. He'd seen what was left of a Negro once after the army was done with him. The woman looked as if she'd been struck. If she was this easily horrified, she wouldn't long survive this life. And yet she'd made it here alive.

"What happen' to the slaves?" Gaitor asked.

"I do not know. My chief said no one has seen them since they were led away."

Gaitor stood and paced as far as he could in the small structure, turned, and glared. "They's back with their masters bein' shown as 'samples of what happens to those what tries to 'scape. Osceola ain't gonna to try to free 'em, is he?"

When he'd first come here, Panther had thought the big black man might be slow-witted, but that, he now knew, had been an act. "My chief and the others had to scatter when the troops found them. By the time the braves gathered again, it was too late. The slaves were gone." Leaving Gaitor, he stepped over to the woman and stared down at her. She returned his gaze, a mix of fear and something else swimming in her eyes. The something else, he decided, was determination.

"How did you know where to look for us?" he asked her. If there was any chance her master had the same information, he needed to know that—should have found out before leaving the other day. Only, she'd been out of her head then.

"I didn't."

Her English was precise, almost as careful as his. "You simply headed into Piahokee?" He didn't try to hide the disbelief in his voice. "Did you not care whether you lived or died?"

"Piahokee?"

"Whites call this place the Everglades. It is Piahokee to us."

"I cared; I didn't want to die. But I knew he might kill me if I stayed."

Killed? A woman like her brought a great deal on the auction block but not because of her ability to work. Was that what she'd fled, Reddin Croon's bed? He dropped to his knees and leaned over her, glad to see her shrink away from him. Frightened, she might be incapable of telling him anything except the truth.

"I do not believe you." Gaitor had drawn close and was standing behind him, anger seeping out of him. His friend's emotion told Panther a simple truth: the Negro wanted to protect the woman. "Piahokee destroys those who do not understand it. The Croon plantation is several days' walk from here, and yet you found it. Found me. How is that possible?"

The woman glanced at Gaitor, then met his gaze. "My mother," she whispered. "She said to follow the river. I did."

So simple. Could it be the truth, or was she here because Reddin Croon had sent her? "When I saw you, you were half dead. You had no shoes."

"I lost them." She waved vaguely. "The first day. It might have been quicksand; I don't know."

Her voice sounded tight, as if she was trying to keep her emotions buried where she wouldn't be touched by them. For a heartbeat, he wanted to leave her to rest and recover. But his clan's safety might be at stake. "Follow the river?" he challenged. "Even I could not find a small village if that was all I knew."

Her chin started to tremble, but she clamped her lower lip between her teeth and stopped herself. A strange fierceness took over and turned her eyes even darker. "It didn't matter. All that did was getting away from him. Staying where he couldn't find me."

"Hm. What is your name?"

She blinked at the sudden question. "Calida. And you?"

"Panther."

"Panther. It was you, at Master Croon's plantation, wasn't it?"

"Yes."

Her sigh seemed to engulf her entire body. "He would have killed you," she said. "If I hadn't set you free, you would be dead."

"Maybe."

"No maybe to it, Panther," Gaitor said. He held up his hands so Panther could see that the torn knuckles and blisters he'd received while digging out of prison hadn't completely healed. The message was clear: If either man had remained at the plantation, he wouldn't be alive.

"My mother"—Calida took a deep breath—"my mother told me to look for you. That you would help me. I didn't—there was nothing else I could do."

Panther felt a rope tighten around his neck. He couldn't deny a word of what she'd said; he owed his life to her. Only, if she remained here, her presence would jeopardize everyone else.

Isiah Yongue stood in the middle of his daughter's bedchamber as he took in every inch of the frilly but dark room. His stiff, sweat-stained collar jabbed at the fleshy sides of his neck, but the old man seemed oblivious to his discomfort. He'd been here for two endless weeks, ever since a distraught Reddin had met him in St. Augustine to inform him of his daughter's untimely death at the hands of murdering Seminoles. Reddin had made sure news of the "attack" had spread throughout the town. As he expected, the telling and retelling had given the story validity. Still, he lived in fear that his father-in-law, his former and very wealthy father-in-law, would learn the truth.

For the first few days, both men had been busy arranging for Liana's funeral. Several of Major General Jesup's officers had stopped by to gather all possible information about the attack. Wearing his badge of grief like a banner, Reddin was forced to admit that he and his slaves were of little help. His beloved wife, restless because her father's visit had been delayed, had ordered her carriage man to drive her to the nearest plantation so she could visit the mistress there. If only he hadn't let her go, she might still be alive. But, sensitive to her disappointment, he'd relented. After all, there'd been no sign of any Seminoles for weeks. He hadn't known what had happened to his wife until the next morning when his foreman burst in with the horrible news.

Folding his arms over his chest, Reddin half believed that things really had happened the way he'd said. Certainly he'd just been getting up when his foreman arrived; no one would dispute that. He'd ordered Joseph's ugly old wife to say she hadn't seen him the last night of the carriage driver's life. Unless she wanted to disappear the way the horse had, she would talk to no one, especially not Mistress Liana's father.

"This room sure isn't much," Isiah muttered. "Things sure as hell changed after she got married."

Because she married an army man who didn't know how to properly manage her considerable dowry. Reddin didn't need to hear the words to know what his father-in-law was thinking. Ignoring the dig, the lie, he walked over to the window and looked out at what he could see of his land. Damn it, he'd like to see anyone do better in the two years he'd had. Corn, beans, and pumpkins were the primary crops. Although they were doing well, he needed to clear more land. Only how could a man do that with a mere handful of slaves? With more and more of his neighbors being burned out by the Indians, he figured he had several choices. He could move out while he still had his hair or take over the unproductive farms and plantations.

Or he could rejoin the army.

"She won't be coming back," Reddin said, not caring whether he kept irritation out of his voice. "I don't know how you can stand being in here. Every time I do, I feel as if I'm going to explode." To give weight to his words, he moved toward the door.

"Did she ever love you?"

Damnation! They'd been dancing around this for days now. He'd hoped to get Isiah out of here and back to his own plantation without things exploding. "What does it matter? She's dead."

"And you wind up with everything."

"Do you think I want it this way?" Isiah hated weakness of any kind, and there was a delicate path to be walked between the so-called grieving husband and a spineless fool.

"The point is, Liana paid for this land with her life."

Liana had lost her life because she didn't understand a man's needs, not that he'd ever tell Isiah that. "Yes. She did." He tried to sound mournful. "If I could go back in time, don't you think I would? You didn't see her after—I did. There isn't a night I don't dream about that." Watching Isiah out of the corner of his eye, he was pleased to see that his words had had the desired effect.

"Where is she?"

"Who?" Isiah had a way of jumping from one topic to another that made it damn near impossible to keep up with him. When he first met the man, he'd thought him scatterbrained. Reddin now knew Isiah never stopped thinking; he just didn't always let folks know where his thinking had gone.

"My daughter's house servant."

"I told you, I don't know. My guess, the Seminoles got her."

"Either that or she ran off." Isiah walked over to the window and pointed, not at cultivated land but at the wilderness beyond. "Her mama couldn't say."

Isiah had talked to Pilar? He'd done his damnedest not to leave the old man alone for a minute, but it hadn't been possible. "Her mama couldn't say what?"

"Whether Calida left of her own free will."

"Not too likely. Calida hates being outside. There's nothing like a snake or gaitor to send her to shrieking."

"You know her that well?"

Careful. "Just what Liana told me." He pasted back on his mournful look. "We'd talk about it sometimes, laugh about how scared the girl was of anything that crawled. Rescuing her's just one more thing I've got to concern myself with." He pressed his hand against his head as if trying to ward off a headache.

"Not just you." Isiah swung around to face him. The window behind him turned his form into a dark silhouette, but although Reddin could no longer see the older man's eyes, he still sensed them boring into him. "I've been concerning myself with things too."

Careful. "Such as?"

"Such as what's going to happen around here if the Seminoles think they can get away with murdering white women. I know what it's like around here. The Seminoles take in escaped slaves. Even marry them sometimes. What if—" He ran his hand over his chin. Reddin imagined the stiff whiskers poking into his palm. "What if this Calida had taken up with a Seminole? What if she told them when my daughter was going to be out alone?"

"You're saying—you're saying Calida was part of it?"

"What I'm saying is, I don't know. Damn it, Reddin! Your wife's dead. So far all I've seen you do is put on a show for the funeral and go back to looking after your land."

I'm just biding my time until you leave, you old fool. Only, Isiah wasn't a fool. "I talked to General Jesup's men. I told them everything I know."

"Which isn't a damn lot."

"I wasn't there, Isiah. How many times do I have to say it?" Liana's room smelled like mildewed wood. If he could ever get Isiah to leave it, he'd never enter it again. "I don't know what happened."

"Don't you?"

"No!" The word exploded from him. "Spell it out, Isiah. Right now and right here. You've been hinting at something ever since you got here."

"What I'm saying is, if it was me, I'd be riding after the Seminoles avenging my wife's death."

"You think I don't want to? Look, if it was just me, if I didn't have this place to look after, bills to pay, slaves to keep an eye on, if I wasn't thinking every minute how I'm going to protect my land, I'd already be gone."

"I'll do it."

Isiah had spoken so softly that for a few seconds the words didn't register. But Isiah had folded his arms over his chest, a gesture he used only when something important was on his mind.

"What are you saying?" Reddin asked.

"That I'll take over managing this place while you look for my daughter's killers."

You're staring her killer in the face. Laughing to himself, he walked

back to where his father-in-law stood. "You've got your own plantation."

"Which doesn't need me around it all the time."

*Because you've been a landowner a lot longer than I have. Because
you're not in the wilderness and your slaves don't stop working the moment you turn your back on them. Go on, say it.* But he kept his thoughts
to himself, not because he was afraid of telling Isiah what he thought
but because he hated this place. He was a soldier. He'd resigned because a soldier was never going to get rich, while becoming Liana
Yongue's husband meant having wealth handed to him.

Only, Liana Yongue didn't need a husband anymore and the
plantation was his.

"You mean it? You'd take over here while I make sure those savages pay for what they did?"

"Not just the Indians. Calida too if she was in on it."

Calida.

6

The air smelled of pines and stagnant water, animal fat and cooking fish. At first those smells had only added to Calida's belief that she'd been forced into a nightmare world. But this collection of crude shelters surrounded by sawgrass and swamp had been her home for over two weeks. She still didn't understand it, but at least she no longer felt compelled to flee. Although his wildly painted face continued to unnerve her, she was grateful to the healer for extinguishing the fever she thought would consume her. Most of all she was grateful for the watery, pleasant-smelling mix of herbs and leaves that kept the mosquitoes away after she rubbed it on herself.

Ducking low so she wouldn't disturb the palm branches that hung down from the roof, she stepped out into the winter sunlight. The healer's wife had given her a brightly colored dress made from many different pieces of fabric to replace her ruined one. The garment was so loose around her neck that it was in danger of sliding off her shoulder. The skirt nearly dragged on the ground. It felt good to know her legs wouldn't give out under her. Still, this was the first time she'd ventured out on her own. Although the other Negroes seemed to be treated with respect, she didn't know if the same would happen to her.

Panther's presence was responsible. Panther, with his night eyes that watched her every move. Panther, who hadn't spoken to her since the day he returned from wherever he'd been. He was the village leader, that much she knew. He carried himself like a man comfortable with the mantle of responsibility and put her in mind of an overseer, except that he didn't carry a whip and no one addressed him with downcast eyes.

She didn't have to stare at the ground anymore. The realization had speeded her recovery and made it possible for her to get through the nights without her mother. She would have been able to explore, to savor this new feeling more fully if she hadn't always been aware of Panther.

She had saved his life. He hadn't asked why, and she'd been spared having to provide an explanation that had everything to do with knowing what it felt like to have her hands and heart bound.

She'd saved his life; he hadn't thanked her. Had barely spoken to her.

Looking around, she assured herself that Panther wasn't in sight. Many of the village's children had peered shyly at her while she was too weak to lift her head. Touched by their concern, she'd smiled at them with the result that they now greeted her as if they'd known her forever. Their parents were a little more reserved, but the big Negro who insisted on being called Gaitor had told her that being pursued by the army made them leery of everyone, even a half-dead runaway.

Following the aroma of cooking fish, she spotted a middle-aged Seminole woman hunched over a simmering metal pot. Sweat dripped off her forehead, and she wiped it away with the sleeve of her blouse. She looked up and gave Calida a tentative smile but didn't say anything. On still-tender feet, Calida wandered toward a younger woman with a coil of heavy, dark hair piled on her head. This one was pounding water-soaked corn kernels into a fine meal. Like Calida, she wore nothing on her feet, but hers looked so tough that she probably never felt discomfort. Mistress Liana had insisted her personal slave always wear shoes. Now, however, Calida had nothing. Maybe she'd never be anything except barefoot.

Casting off the kind of thinking that always brought a surge of terror, Calida stepped closer. The woman looked up and regarded her unsmilingly. If she'd known any Seminole, she would have tried to strike up a conversation. Only, this young woman didn't look Seminole, not entirely. Her features were a mix of Indian and Negro. One of her parents must have been a runaway. What did this near-child consider herself?

Panther spoke English. Where had he learned, and why?

The young woman said something to her. She shook her head and smiled. The woman repeated herself, then rose and extended her hand, which held a mound of damp corn mush. Grateful for what she hoped was a gesture of kindness, Calida placed it in her mouth. She expected it to be tasteless, but it was surprisingly sweet. She made a show of rubbing her stomach, which made the young woman laugh.

"I want to know so much," she said impulsively. "I feel—I don't know what I feel. No one talks to me. Just Gaitor, and he isn't around that much."

The woman tipped her head to one side, but she didn't speak, and Calida guessed she hadn't understood a word of what she'd said. But if one of her parents had been Negro, maybe she was pretending ignorance, holding back until she'd decided whether she could trust the newcomer.

The army men who visited Master Croon had kissed the back of Mistress Croon's hand. She did that to the girl, surprising herself as much as she must have surprised her. Releasing the girl's hand, she tapped her own chest. "Calida. My name's Calida."

After a moment, the girl pressed her hand over her small, high breasts. She said something Calida didn't understand. "What? I'm sorry. I don't—"

"Winter Rain."

Winter Rain. What a lovely name. Before she could tell her that, she realized Winter Rain had spoken without a trace of an accent. Why was the girl pretending they couldn't communicate?

If she stayed here, she would have to learn to speak Seminole.

If? Where else could she go?

Winter Rain dropped to her knees, picked up a long, narrow rock, and began grinding meal again. She glanced up at Calida, then as if dismissing her, hunched over her work. Feeling lonely, Calida continued her aimless wandering. Everyone, except for her it seemed, had something to do. As far as she could tell, all of the men had rifles. Just the same, two were skinning thin branches. Because she'd watched them earlier, she knew they were making arrows. Rifles? Arrows? Were they expecting trouble? A number of women and children were in the cornfield digging at the earth with long, pointed sticks. She wanted to make herself useful, but how could she ask to be put to work if no one understood her?

The sight of a tall, skinny Negro reminded her that she could talk to others like herself. She wasn't cut off after all. If the Seminoles had welcomed other runaways into their midst, certainly they'd do the same with her.

Why then did it feel as if most of the adult Seminoles avoided her? If they were acting on Panther's orders—

Questions without answers were giving her a headache. Firmly placing them in the back of her mind, she continued her walk around the village. She was careful not to get so close to any of the houses that people might think she was intruding. Still, she hoped she would be forgiven for staring at them. This was her world now.

But did she belong?

The reality of everything that had changed in her life hit her with the force of a blow. The Seminoles had set up their village in a small clearing that stood a little higher than the surrounding country. She didn't think the wilderness grew any closer here than it did at Master Croon's plantation, but it was hard to look at that awful unknown and not feel overwhelmed by it. She'd survived days and nights lost in that wet, creeping, crawling, stinking place—just barely. She should feel less intimidated now, but she didn't. Maybe, she admitted, it was because so much distance existed between where she was and her mother.

Thoughts of Pilar wrenched her stomach in yet another knot. She tried to distract herself by watching the antics of a couple of boys wrestling at the edge of the trees, but the diversion lasted only a few moments. Pilar been right. With her bad leg, she wouldn't have survived the journey here.

Would she ever see her mother again?

Hatred for Master Croon washed over her with such force that it replaced all other emotions. He was responsible for this! He had killed his wife—would kill her if he ever got his hands on her!

Arms wrapped tightly around her waist, she took a few deliberate steps closer to the giggling boys. Only then did she realize that one was Seminole while the other was Negro. "Enough! Ya makes 'nough noise ta brings gaiters!" a woman was chiding them.

At the woman's warning, the two boys broke apart. Their naked bodies were caked with mud. Laughing, the Seminole boy scampered away. Face downcast, the other shuffled toward the woman. A giggle escaped his lips. He clamped a dirty hand over his mouth, but it was too late.

The Negro woman carried a baby in her arms. It was nursing. In the silence following the boy's giggle, Calida heard the baby suckle loudly. As the sound died away, she fought to draw more air into her lungs. It didn't help. On legs that threatened to give out under her, she spun around so she no longer had to look at the mother with her innocent, trusting infant. Half-blinded by tears, she paid little attention to where she was heading. All that mattered was that she no longer see, no longer feel pain so intense it threatened to destroy her.

"Calida."

The voice came to her as if from a great distance, and for a moment she thought she could escape it. But then Panther called her name again, and she was forced to face him. His eyes never left hers as his long, powerful legs swallowed the ground separating them. Many of the Seminole men wore colorful dresses like the women, but she'd never seen Panther in anything except a loincloth. He intimidated her looking like that.

"You are well?" he asked.

"Yes. Finally." She prayed her tears had dried. "Panther, thank you. I would have died out there if it hadn't been for you."

"I owed you a debt. I have repaid it."

Was that all she was to him, a debt repaid? Telling herself that was how she wanted it, she gathered her courage for the rest of what she had to say. He hadn't been around much while she was recovering. The possibility that the army might find the village was a constant worry. Obviously, Panther spent most of his time concerning himself with that. "I, ah, I have to talk to you about something," she managed. "About what's going to happen to me now."

"I have been thinking about that too."

He had? Of course he had. The other women knew how to prepare food, while she didn't have the first idea how to gather it, let alone make it eatable. Forcing herself to go on meeting his eyes, she asked if she was welcome here. "I talked to Gaitor about that," she explained. "He wouldn't say much except that this is Indian land, and the Negroes who live with them do so because the Seminoles are willing to give shelter to runaways. That's what I am. A runaway." She thought the admission might make her shudder, but she remained calm. It was, after all, the truth.

"You are more than that, Calida."

Sensing this was why he'd sought her out today, she told him that she'd been a house slave and knew nothing about working the land, about anything that was necessary if one was going to survive in— what did he call it?—Piahokee. "But I can learn. If someone will show me, I can learn."

By way of answer, he grabbed her wrists and turned her palms upward. Feeling trapped when freedom now meant everything to her, she forced herself to wait him out. "Soft hands," he said. "Worthless hands."

Master Croon had been fascinated by her smooth skin. She'd hated her hands because of that, but until now she hadn't thought about how worthless they were. "I'll work. That's all I want, a chance to prove myself."

"Why do you not pull away? You hate my touch. Why do you not put an end to it?"

"I'm—was a slave, Panther. A slave. Do you know what that means?"

"Yes."

"Do you?" She indicated their lush surroundings. A breeze blew today. Erratic and yet insistent, it pushed the treetops first one way and then the other. "No matter what my master wanted from me, I had no right to say no. He owned me. My body was his to do—to do what he wanted with."

"And that is why you ran."

She already felt exhausted by the little she'd told him about her life with Master Croon. She could simply agree with what he'd said and be done with it, but he'd released her hands and she felt stronger now. She refused to admit that maybe his touching her was what had given her strength. "No. Not all of it."

"Tell me."

It was an order, and she'd been taught to never disobey an order. With him listening to every word, she told him about the day Master Croon killed his wife. "She brought a sizable dowry to their marriage. She told me that. I—"

"A dowry?"

"Money. She always said she had more money than him, that it was her family's wealth that made it possible for him to have his plantation."

"He killed her. Will her wealth now become his?"

"Yes. Unless—"

"Unless what?"

She'd been debating whether to tell anyone this for so long. At first her brain had felt too muddy to deal with the question. When she could finally think, she still couldn't make a decision because that meant telling people why Mistress Liana had become so angry. Her role in the argument. "Unless her father finds out the truth."

"The truth." A cold smile touched Panther's lips. "I will tell you the only truth that matters. Reddin Croon tells all who listen that Seminoles murdered his wife and carriage driver."

Seminoles? It all made sense now. That's why Master Croon had driven the carriage over his wife's body, why he'd thrown a knife at sweet Joseph. "Indians didn't have anything to do with it. *He* killed her. She died at his hands, her neck broken."

"You saw?"

Panther's tone captured her full attention. She stared up at him and tried to read his expression, but he'd shut his thoughts off from her. "Yes."

"Tell me, Calida. How much does he want you back?"

"I don't know."

"You must."

He'd spoken in a whisper, and yet there was an intensity about him that frightened her and held her in its grip. "I don't know," she repeated, then, taking a steadying breath, she told him about the fear she'd been fighting for too long. "I'm the only one who knows what really happened."

"You are a slave. Why would anyone listen to you?"

"Mistress Liana's father doesn't like Master Croon. Master Croon resents that Master Yongue has so much land while he would have nothing if it hadn't been for the dowry. Master Yongue never lets him forget it. If Master Yongue knew how his daughter died, he would have Master Croon thrown into prison. Maybe killed."

"This Yongue would believe you?"

She nodded.

"But if you were dead, the truth would die with you."

She'd been lost inside herself for the last several minutes. Panther's simple but not simple words forced her to focus on him. "Yes."

He nodded, the gesture short and economical. He kept studying her, and she wondered if he was waiting for her to dissolve into tears or beg him to protect her. She did neither. Being alone in Piahokee had done something to her, brought her closer to herself. Always before, she'd had her mother to talk to. Maybe Pilar couldn't protect her from what life handed out, but her mother's presence, and the presence of the other slaves, had made her feel not quite so alone. She'd spent most of a week in isolation until terror turned into acceptance.

"I know him," Panther said.

"Master Croon?" She couldn't help blinking at this sudden change in the conversation.

Panther nodded, reminding her of how graceful, how right his body was for the life he'd been born to.

"What do you mean, 'know'?" She hadn't asked him how he'd come to speak English. She wanted to, but other things kept on being more important.

"He was in the army then. I was with John Blount, waiting to be moved to a place called Texas."

John Blount was a Creek Indian. She'd heard Master Croon and General Jesup talk about him. "Texas? How did you get back here?"

"I never left my home," he said and then, eyes expressionless and by their lack of emotion revealing a great deal, he explained that Master Croon had been with the troops who'd been watching the Creek Indians while they waited to be moved. "They were still in their village because it was time for the corn harvest. They could not leave without food for the journey. The army was impatient; they wanted to be done with this. They had to wait for word from their government men and that too made them impatient."

"Why were you with them? The Creeks aren't your people, are they?"

"I am Indian. They are Indian."

There was more to it than that; there had to be. After another of those silences she wondered if she would ever get used to, he told her that Osceola had sent him to the Creek village to try to convince John Blount to remain here. "Even then, my chief and I did not trust the white soldiers. They said that all Indians who agreed to this reservation would be treated well and given enough land for their families, cattle, and crops." He ground his heel into the earth. "This is our land. We came from it and it is our mother. Our hearts do not know this place called Texas. Blount believed as I do, but his people were weary of fighting. They wanted a place of safety in which to raise their children."

"Did Master Croon discover what you were trying to do?"

"It does not matter."

"Not matter?"

"Lieutenant Croon and his men were greedy. All they thought of was themselves."

Panther called Croon a lieutenant, not master. Looking at him with the wilderness green and alive behind him and the wind making his hair look wild, she realized how different they were.

"Croon wanted the village's cattle. He stole them."

"No one tried to stop him?"

"Yes," Panther said, and in the simple word she realized he'd been one of those who resisted. "He wanted more than cattle. There were also Creek women."

Knowing what her master, her former master, was capable of, she couldn't suppress a shudder. "What happened?"

"The army men surprised some women and children while they tended cattle. They killed the cattle, beat the children, tried to take the women. Several other braves and I heard the children screaming."

She tried to imagine the scene. "How did you know it was Croon? It must have been chaos."

He frowned at the word *chaos,* then nodded. "He had ahold of a woman, was forcing her under him. I stopped him."

"How?"

He touched the knife at his side. Staring at it, she thought about the scar near Croon's ribs. She touched that spot on her own body. "You stabbed him there?"

"Yes."

"And— Do you think he recognized you?"

"That is why he did not simply kill me when I came to rescue my friend."

She knew what Master Croon was capable of; his punishment of runaways was horrible to watch—and every slave, her included, had been compelled to watch.

"I thank you," Panther said. "If you had not freed me, my death would have been slow."

His simple words shook her to her soul. "He isn't finished with me," she whispered. "He wants me silent so I can't say anything to Mistress Liana's father. He—he might cut out my tongue. Maybe he'll kill me. He also wants me because . . . because I have always pleased him."

No expression touched Panther's features. "Does he know you are here?"

"No. No," she insisted, although there was no way she could be sure of that. "My mother told me to follow the river, that that way I might find you. I didn't speak to anyone else, and she would die before she said anything."

He hadn't once turned his attention elsewhere. She was aware of movement around them, guessed that others were watching them, but Panther made the decisions for the village. He was the one she had to talk to, the one she had to be honest with. "Do you want me to leave?"

So motionless she couldn't tell whether he was breathing, he continued to stare down at her. He made her aware of her slight build, her slender legs in contrast to his long, powerful ones. His hands could and had brought down wild animals. They'd thrust a knife into Master Croon and maybe killed other white men. He was the war chief, a man of violence. "Yes."

Yes. She tried to make sense of the word.

"But it will not be. You saved my life, Calida. You will have shelter here."

"Even if my presence jeopardizes everyone's safety?"

"The army seeks us, Calida," he said. "We remain out of their grasp. Reddin Croon is only one man."

"He used to be in the army. Maybe he'll join again."

"He would leave his plantation?"

That made her laugh, almost. "He hates it. Having it brought him prestige, and he has succeeded where others failed, but he hates it."

Although Panther remained motionless, she knew he was thinking over what she'd said. Her future, her life even, lay in his hands, and she couldn't do a thing except wait. "Alone, you will die. I cannot turn my back on you."

She thought relief would flood through her, but it didn't. He was risking so much, for himself as well as the village, by allowing her to remain here. "Panther?" Her voice broke, and she tried again. "Mistress Liana taught me how to read and write. She was lonely much of the time. She wanted someone to talk to about books." Memories of the hours she'd spent at her mistress's side as a new world opened to her briefly clogged her throat, but she forced herself to continue. "Someday you may need my skill. Maybe I'm not useless after all."

"Maybe."

Winter Rain sat with her back to the sun. It had rained last night, and the heat felt good. She should go back to grinding corn. After all, she was a woman now and as such, expected to take care of her own food. Still, she didn't take her eyes off the pale-skinned Negro woman and Panther. What had she called herself, Calida? It didn't matter because Winter Rain had no intention of befriending her.

Calida didn't belong here. In the past it hadn't mattered to her how many Negroes took refuge in the village. They'd always been given a piece of land to cultivate. All the tribe had required of them was that they turn a portion of their crop over to the Seminoles.

But this woman had come alone, half dead, taking too much of Panther's time and attention when he should be thinking—

When Panther walked away from Calida, Winter Rain let out a long sigh. She studied him for as long as she could see him, taking in his long strides, the strength of his back, the proud way he held his head.

Someday, she prayed, she would be the one to brush and arrange his hair. If he had a wife to tend to it properly, he could wear it long and wrapped about his head in the traditional way instead of cutting it short.

If he had a wife—*her*—she would truly be Seminole. Everyone would forget that her father had once been a slave. Getting to her feet, she headed in the direction she'd seen Panther go. Spotting him, she started to call out his name, then stopped herself because he was speaking with some of the village elders.

She didn't want to love Panther. If someone else had taken her heart, she wouldn't lie awake nights scared he'd be killed before he understood how much she loved him. But he carried himself like a war chief. His voice was deep and low. He smiled at her. Talked to her. Made sure she always had a portion of meat.

With Panther's arms around her at night, she would no longer mourn her mother, who had been dead for five years. She wouldn't pray that her father would leave Osceola's village and come back to her.

Turning her back on Panther, she spotted Calida. The slave was watching Panther.

Winter Rain's belly muscles knotted, and her hand tightened around the grinding tool she still carried.

Calida didn't belong.

Wasn't wanted.

7

Calida straightened and absently wiped dirt from her knees. The day, although not hot, held no memory of winter. In the week since Panther had given her permission to remain in the village, she'd made friends with several of the Negroes, and no one had objected when she asked to be shown how to work the garden that raised so much of their food. Of the eleven coloreds, all but three were men. They accepted her more readily than did the Seminoles, but why should they put themselves out for someone who didn't speak their language and didn't know how to do the simplest things? The Negro women either already spoke Seminole or were learning. That, in part, was why she was working with them this afternoon.

Her hands stung. Looking at them, she spotted several new blisters. Everyone else, it seemed, had no trouble digging in the rich earth near the creek bed. Her mother's hands were rough, toughened by a lifetime spent working in her master's fields. She should have hands like her mother.

At the memory, anger and sorrow washed through her. She fought the hot emotions as she'd done so many times since leaving the plantation. If only she could make herself believe Pilar was all right, but she knew Master Croon too well for that. He would have tried to pressure her into telling him where her daughter was. If Master Croon had harmed—

No! Thinking about that always made her sick with helpless fear.

From what she understood, Gaitor had left two days ago to observe the army. She'd asked the Negro women where the army was, but their answers had been so vague that she couldn't make sense of them. Panther would know, only she didn't know how to approach him. He seemed so distant. Was it because he resented his debt to her? Hated the burden she represented?

Forcing her thoughts off the fact that she couldn't change him any more than she could change what she'd done, she realized she was staring at Gaitor. When had he returned? He was so far from her that he wouldn't have heard if she called out to him. Gaitor had worked alongside the healer until her fever broke. He'd talked to her, even held her when nightmares threatened to tear her apart. He was her friend. At least she wanted him to be her friend.

He wasn't alone. Belatedly she realized that several Seminole men were with him and that they were heading straight for Panther's house—*chickee*. Leaving the garden, she joined the others who'd been drawn to where Panther lived. She saw Panther step out into the sunlight, saw Gaitor extend his hand, watched as they shook hands and then clasped each other's shoulders.

Sliding closer, she tried to hear what they were saying. Unfortunately she didn't understand more than three or four words of what was being said. After no more than a minute, Panther held up his hand and pointed toward his *chickee*. Obviously he wanted to talk to Gaitor in private. She looked around hoping to find someone who could interpret for her, but none of the Negro women had left their work. Winter Rain stood nearby, not that it made any difference since the young mixed breed still had given no indication she understood English. When Calida started toward her and Winter Rain turned her back on her, she felt as if she'd been slapped.

Knowing she had no choice but to wait until the men were done talking, she went back to work. Her blisters continued to sting, but she refused to give up. Before long, she'd develop calluses and be able to match the speed and efficiency of the others. It felt so good to be well, to be growing stronger with each day. Maybe, if life among the Seminoles toughened her enough, no white man would want her.

It was afternoon by the time she spotted Gaitor again. She looked around for Panther but caught no glimpse of him. Walking on legs made stiff by hours of crawling around, she intercepted Gaitor. She didn't want to press him into telling her more than the rest of the village knew, but Panther had seemed concerned by what the Negro had told him. If it had anything to do with her—

"Not you. Least ways not right now," Gaitor said in reply to her question. "But there's trouble brewin'."

"What kind of trouble?"

"The army. They's still on the move."

"And you're worried about that. You and Panther and the rest of the men. Why?"

" 'Cause they's chasin' Indians."

"Chasing?"

"The Turtle clan. Maybe they'll catch 'em. Maybe they won't. That's what I cain't say," Gaitor said and then explained that the Turtle clan was in no immediate danger of being overtaken, but that they'd been on the move since last fall, and as a consequence their food supply was low and many of the members were weak and weary. Panther and the other leaders feared the clan would give up if the army kept after them much longer.

"What would happen then?" she asked. "They—the army men won't harm them, will they? I mean, if they surrender—"

"I cain't say what they'll do, Calida. They's like dogs what's been kicked too many times. You never knows when they mights bite."

She'd been a fool to ask the question. Hadn't Panther already told her about the time Master Croon and the men under him had attacked helpless women and children? "What are you going to do?"

"Maybe nuthin', damnation. 'En maybe we'll stop them."

It was the first time she'd heard Gaitor sound so angry. Chilled by his tone, she glanced toward Panther's *chickee*. She could just see his silhouette in the deep shade. "How? You can't—"

"Listen to me, Calida. I spent ma whole life thinkin' I was little more 'en an animal. I was like a dog, slinkin' with my tail 'tweens my legs 'til I hated maself. 'Til I couldn' takes it no more and ran.

Panther taught me what it is to be a man. He and I's goin' back in the mornin'."

"How many are there?"

"The army? More 'en a hundred men. 'Bout that many horses. They's got lots of supplies, much more 'en the Turtle clan does, that's fer sure."

"A hundred? You can't—"

"Without horses, they's just a bunch of damn fool men wanderin' 'round. That's what Panther wants to study on, whether there's a way to separate them from their horses. Don't you worry yourself none 'bout this, Calida. You's safe here. That's what matters, you's safe."

She'd like to believe that, to think of nothing except planting corn, but if the army could find the Turtle clan, Panther's tribe might be next. How could they possibly consider stealing horses? Surely they knew the army would retaliate. "When are you leaving?"

"In the morning, first light."

Night shrouded the village. Except for occasional campfires and the few stars she could spot through the trees, Calida felt trapped in blackness. Up until the sun set, she'd watched Panther and Gaitor as they prepared for a long time away from the village. They hadn't said much about what they were doing, but even the children seemed aware that something important was taking place. The sight of their muskets and spears and bows and arrows had made her shudder. Master Croon was so proud of his musket collection. Although she'd never handled them, never so much as touched one, she knew what they were capable of. Didn't Panther understand that a spear or knife stood no chance against a musket?

Master Croon.

She'd managed to keep him from her thoughts all day, but now that she was wrapped in darkness, he seemed to be everywhere. He'd once been a lieutenant, had commanded large numbers of men. He'd always wanted to do that again.

Stirring herself, she left the mat of leaves and branches that had become her open-air bed and approached Panther's *chickee*. Now that she was well, she could no longer stay with the healer and didn't feel close enough to anyone to ask for shelter. Maybe Gaitor, but he'd been gone most of the time. Besides, she was determined not to cling to anyone, to make her peace with the wilderness with its ceaseless sounds and sometimes overwhelming smells. Croon had trapped her within his walls; she loved their absence.

Panther sat alone, hunched over something he was working on. He didn't seem to need light; maybe his sure hands told him everything he needed to know. She wanted to simply walk up to him and ask her questions, but speaking to Panther took more concentration, more courage than she wanted to admit.

Light from a nearby fire flitted across his features. Sometimes they were all but lost in shadow; a moment later they danced with red lights. He looked so alive, so intense, so unapproachable. And yet she had no choice.

"Panther," she whispered. He stared in her direction. Although she knew she had to step closer, she felt safer surrounded by night—the night that such a short time ago had terrified her.

"Calida?"

The sound of him speaking her name made the decision for her, and she took the necessary steps. "I know what you're going to do," she said. "Gaitor told me."

"Sit down."

When Master Croon said that, there'd never been any question of whether she'd obey, but she didn't have a master out here. Still, she dropped to her knees and studied what she could see of Panther's face. He was like his namesake, dark and mysterious, maybe deadly. "I want to go with you."

"No."

Not why would she want to do such an insane thing but simply no. "You don't understand. If Master Croon—"

"No."

"Panther, I can't hide forever. I have to know what he's doing, whether he's out there."

"Women do not go to war."

War. She stared at his shadowed hands, seeing in them a competence, a sureness that took her breath away.

"Gaitor and I go to watch and learn, to talk of plans. Later, maybe, we will return with warriors. Gaitor did not see Croon with the other army men, Calida. He was not there."

"He told you that?"

"I asked."

Of course he would.

"There is another thing," Panther continued. "A thing you must know. One of my scouts went to Croon's plantation. He did not see him there either."

Had the night gotten darker? Barely aware of what she was doing, she scooted closer to Panther and fixed her attention on him. "Maybe—maybe he was gone that day."

"No. The scout talked to one of the slaves. Croon's father-in-law now lives in the house and runs the plantation."

A minute ago she'd asked Panther if she could accompany him so she could see for herself whether Master Croon had taken up arms. Still, she'd half convinced herself that he wouldn't leave what he'd worked hard for. She no longer had any doubts.

"Where is he?" she asked, not because she expected Panther to have an answer, but because the question wouldn't remain inside her. "He—he's friends with General Jesup. The general will let him do whatever he wants."

"General Jesup." Panther lay down the spear he'd been working on. His hands rested on his knees, the tips biting into his flesh. "Those who commanded the army before him were fools. They knew nothing of Piahokee, its secrets, its dangers. But General Jesup is a fighting man. War is in his heart."

"Are you afraid of him?"

Panther didn't answer. Silence spread out between them. She felt the weight of it and deeply regretted having asked her question. Panther was a war chief. From childhood, he'd been preparing himself to lead in battle. If he felt fear, he wouldn't admit it to her. "I'm sorry," she whispered. "It's just that—Panther, I think I've been afraid my entire life."

His fingers relaxed their tight grip, and she imagined them reaching out for her. Instead of shaking her hand as he and Gaitor had done, he would draw her to him and offer his strength as shelter. Safe within his arms, she would forget what it was to be afraid.

But he hadn't moved.

*   *   *

Panther and Gaitor left the village before dawn. Panther led the way because his eyesight was keener. Both men carried weapons as proof that they were ready to do battle. Still, their first concern was to try to find a way to stop or slow the army from surrounding exhausted Seminoles and runaways.

They stopped talking before the sun was high in the sky. Piaho-kee was their home, but the enemy had invaded it. Silence increased their chance of safety. With each passing hour, the air heated. Finally they stopped at a small creek to satisfy their thirst. Calida had wanted to come with them; she would only slow them down.

Was that why he'd told her no, or had there been another reason—one that had everything to do with not wanting her to risk her life?

A war chief doesn't allow other thoughts to take his mind, his eyes, from his goal. Angrily reminding himself of that, Panther scrambled up a moss-hung cypress and studied his surroundings. Much of the land ahead of them was open with only waist-deep grass to delay their progress.

Smiling to himself, Panther watched Gaitor slip around a young cypress. A man that big shouldn't be able to move as silently as a hunting cat, but Gaitor knew where to place his feet, how to blend in with his surroundings. That, plus his courage and honesty, was why he now called him a warrior. Why they smoked together.

"You was with Calida last night," Gaitor said, speaking softly and for the first time in hours. "Did you tells her 'bout what Croon's up to?"

"She knows he left the plantation." He didn't need to tell his friend that Calida believed Croon wasn't done with her. They'd already talked about that and come to the same conclusion.

"You was gone when she was sick. I thought she was gonna die. There weren't nuthin' left o' her; the fever had burned it all outta her."

"The healer—"

"It wasn't him what kept her alive."

"What do you mean? What did you do?"

"Not me neither. It was inside her. Her heart, it refused ta stop beatin'."

"Refused . . ."

"She ain't gonna let him git ahold of her again. She'll die 'fore she lets that happen."

Just as he would.

"She didn't talk none about it, what happen' to her back there with him. But I know it must have been somethin' awful."

No more awful than what Gaitor had endured. "No," he admitted. "She doesn't talk about that time."

"She's still scared. That ain't gonna go 'way anytime soon."

"How can it?" Panther asked with honesty he reserved for only a few, maybe Gaitor most of all. "All talk is about the army. She feels the unease, the fear. She wanted to come with us."

Gaitor stopped in midstep, the gesture causing Panther to do the same. "No! She's been through 'nough."

Gaitor's tone took his thoughts from what he'd been going to say. Intensity gleamed in his friend's eyes, that and something else. "I wants her safe. I wants things to be easy fur her now she's free of him."

Safe? Was that true for anyone? The weight of his responsibilities pressed on his shoulders. Added to that was his reaction to what Gaitor had just said. Calida had saved him from a long, horrible death. His debt to her . . . "She isn't your burden."

"Maybe. Maybe not. Thing is, I wants her to be." Gaitor glanced around and then started walking again. "She don't have no place to stay. Not so much as a roof over her head. I wants to give her that."

A roof over her head. Yes, she should at least have that. "Are you thinking to build her one? It might not be safe to stay where we are much longer."

"I know. There ain't nuthin' we can take for granted no more, is there? Still—what does I say to her? How does I tells her how I feel?"

Feelings weren't things a war chief dared acknowledge in times of war. Hadn't he learned that from his father and uncles, from the old *tastanagee*? One made decisions, led in battle. Thinking about the possibility of being killed or watching other clan members die stripped a *tastanagee* of his courage. Still, his heart felt joy and pain. He laughed when children laughed, sensed himself becoming calm and quiet at the sight of a spectacular sunset.

"I's 'fraid to say anythin'," Gaitor went on. "I knows she's grateful fur whats I did, but maybe that's all she feels fur me."

Gaitor had been torn from his wife's side. His arms hadn't held his son for nearly three years. Panther wanted Calida to care for the big, brave, lonely man.

Didn't he?

Smoke lay heavy in the air when Panther and Gaitor reached Hatcheelustee Creek two days after leaving their village. Dropping to his knees, Panther began slithering through the swampy land. Gaitor followed close behind. Despite the boggy ground and insects, he didn't regret wearing nothing except his loincloth. Clothing slowed a man and increased the chance of being heard, as did all but the most essential of weapons. He carried a knife at his waist; a bow and arrows were strapped to his back. He'd left behind his musket.

Catching a sound that wasn't part of the wilderness, he stopped and cocked his head first one way and then the other. Voices. A glance at Gaitor reassured him that his friend had had the same thought.

He began crawling again. When Gaitor first came to the Egret clan, he'd said it was demeaning for a man to slink through Piahokee like a snake, but he no longer did. An enemy with his eyes on what was around him seldom looked down at the ground.

The closer they came to the creek, the more the stench of burning wood and fat increased. The army was preparing meat to eat. He wondered if it was one of the Turtle clan's few remaining cattle; the army didn't have many men who knew how to hunt a creature capable of running. Anger, and fear he couldn't deny, raced through him. He was glad Calida hadn't come with them; he didn't have to think about her, worry about her.

Gaitor touched his ankle but didn't speak. Instead, the Negro rose to a crouch, every line of his body tense. Panther did the same; he heard hard laughter, an occasional whinny, hooves thudding on soft ground. And crying.

He increased his concentration. Faint whimpering reached him, reminded him of the feel of shards of rain driven by an angry wind.

"Children crying," he mouthed. "And women."

Had the army found the Turtle clan? A moment ago he'd been sweating; now he turned cold. Gaitor watched him, silently asking what they should do, but Panther didn't have enough answers.

Gesturing, he began crawling again. No one, not even Gaitor, would ever know this about the Egret clan's *tastanagee,* but at moments like this he felt sick. If the army had killed Seminoles and Negroes, he would spend the rest of his life asking if he couldn't have somehow prevented the slaughter. Others would tell him he was responsible only for his clan, that not even the great Osceola could protect everyone.

But women and children were crying.

Their sounds became even clearer, a murmur that reminded him of a limpkin's eerie call. Forcing himself, he eased aside the thick, heavy moss that surrounded him and peered at Hatcheelustee Creek. Fed by recent rains, the creek had escaped its banks and now flowed over the ground. Trees and brush growing nearby were surrounded by water. The army had camped on a high chunk of ground on the far side of the creek. He took note of the carelessly built campfire. Soldiers lounged around it. The horses had been tethered nearby and were being watched by several musket-carrying men. In the past the army had been careless about their horses, but no longer. More soldiers sat in small groups making it difficult for him to determine the enemy's strength. Enough. Too much.

Silent, Gaitor slid beside him. Tension danced between them, but Panther refused to acknowledge it. He had come here to learn what he could about the army, not react to that presence, because worry cheated him of his ability to think and plan. Still, when Gaitor pointed, he couldn't stop his belly from knotting again.

Three Seminole women, each of them holding a small child or baby, were huddled together. The women's eyes never left the armed and shabbily dressed soldiers who kept staring at them.

"The soldiers," Panther whispered. "Study them. Did you see fewer than this?"

"I think—yes."

"You are sure?"

"They's like ants, Panther. They swarm so a body can't count 'em. But—I's sure of it now. There was less before."

That meant others of the enemy had joined those who'd been hunting the Turtle clan. "They are full of themselves," he all but mouthed. "Careless because they think they have done a great thing by capturing three women."

"The army don' want to leave this place."

Panther couldn't argue with that. The Turtle clan had been moving toward Piahokee's heart. Fed by torrential rains, the plants and trees grew so close together that it was nearly impossible for a man to find a path. Endless fingers of water oozed their dark way through the underbrush. Alligators, snakes, panthers, and deer lived in the great mass, but it wasn't a place for a large number of men and horses. He could pray to the gods that, except for these few women, the rest had escaped, for now.

"What we gonna do?" Gaitor asked.

He thought, taking time with the decision. The soft cries of despair were often lost among the army's greater sound. If he didn't look at the small, defeated group, he could tell himself that he couldn't do more than return to his village with the news that the army wasn't interested in the Egret clan, at least not now. But he couldn't keep his eyes off the women and children.

He commanded nearly fifty warriors. This troop numbered over a hundred and might grow. Only a *tastanagee* who didn't care whether he saw tomorrow would order his braves to attack. Was there enough fight left in the Turtle clan that they would be willing to join their strength with the Egret clan? Could he and Gaitor find the fleeing clan? How many army men might be chasing them at this moment?

The sound of pounding hooves muffled by water sliced through his thoughts. More soldiers were approaching, the newcomers plowing through the water with no regard to their mounts' footing. Watching, he saw they were like the ocean wave, one after another bursting out of the wilderness until they equaled in number those who were already there. He breathed openmouthed, his fingers clamped so tightly around his knife that his knuckles felt as if they might break, but he couldn't make himself relax. He tried to study the captured women, but so many riders milled around them that he could no longer see them. Gaitor hadn't moved; tension flowed between them, hot and shared.

"The army's strength grows." Gaitor spoke so calmly that if Panther didn't know his friend, he might believe it didn't matter to him.

Ants. The army was like ants, never-ending. He wouldn't go back for his warriors after all. Two clans' warriors couldn't defeat this many of the enemy, and he wouldn't sacrifice their lives; the three women knew this.

Still, he couldn't make himself leave. He knew a little about how the army was run. Those with the fanciest uniforms, those who always rode instead of walking, were the leaders. The leaders were like the heads of a snake. Wherever they went, the others followed.

But if a snake lost its head—

Leaving Gaitor, he eased himself to the creek's edge. His body dripped water. As long as he made himself a part of the land, the foolish army men wouldn't know they were being watched. Maybe they didn't care; maybe their arrogance was that great. If he and Gaitor dared wait until dark, maybe they could drive a spear into the leader's heart.

A dark-dressed man who sat tall in the saddle and looked arrogantly around as if this was his plantation and not Seminole land caught his eye. Several of the lounging soldiers had scrambled to their feet and were watching him, but he paid them no attention. Instead, he moved his horse first to where the small clearing became Piahokee and then kicked the animal into Hatcheelustee Creek. Water lapped near the nervous horse's belly. The man increased the distance between himself and the others. Behind him, the troops laughed and called out to each other. Some approached the women. Panther didn't care about the ant-soldiers, only this one man. If he was a general—no, not a general.

Ignoring Gaitor's hissed warning, he heeded his screaming need and scrambled to his feet. He stood motionless, waited. Breathed and hated. After a moment, the man stopped looking around him and settled his gaze on him.

Reddin Croon.

"Panther!" Gaitor cried. "Damnation! What you doin'?"

What? "I want him to know I have found him."

Gaitor grabbed his wrist and tried to pull him back into the brush with him. "Damnation! We gots to get outta here, 'afores—"

Reddin Croon wasn't pointing him out to the others. If Panther had been a foolish man, he might have told himself that Calida's master—former master—hadn't recognized him. He knew different, knew and both relished and hated the moment.

"I want him to fear me. To think I am a spirit."

Heels grinding into his horse's flank, Reddin Croon started toward where he and Gaitor stood. Panther held his knife high so his enemy could see. Then as the man who'd once owned Calida, the man who carried the scar he had placed there, reached for his rifle, Panther spun and faded into the jungle.

8

It was the middle of the night. The sounds of gentle and not too gentle snores came from the silhouetted *chickees*. Winter Rain stood outside the small, lopsided shelter she'd built when Panther told them this was where the Egret clan would spend the winter. She couldn't say for sure what had wakened her; maybe the truth was she didn't want to admit that fear for Panther had made sleep impossible.

He'd been gone too long, he and Gaitor. She knew many of the women felt uneasy without their leaders, but that wasn't what caused her to strain to make sense of the night. Panther was a brave man, one who had risked his own life to rescue the big Negro who'd become like his brother. He wasn't foolish; he wouldn't allow an enemy's bullet to find him. And his Panther spirit protected him.

But was that enough?

Weighed down by fear, she made her way toward the storage building at the village's center. No one would mind if she used a little dried tobacco, and smoking might relax her enough that she could sleep. Not acknowledging what she was doing, she allowed her journey to take her near Calida. The foolish woman still hadn't built herself a shelter. Maybe she didn't know how to do that simple thing.

True, Calida had to first come into possession of a knife, and knives were in short supply.

Calida should ask Gaitor to help her. For reasons Winter Rain didn't understand, the strong, imposing Negro liked the scrawny runaway and felt protective toward her. But Gaitor hadn't had time to do anything except what Panther needed.

Panther. Safe. Please.

A sharp, low moan caught her attention. When it was repeated, she realized it came from Calida, who was nothing more than a small mound under a young pine. Curious, she slipped closer. Calida was having a dream, a night message from the spirits. She watched her legs and arms jerk, relax, then jerk again. She'd brought her knife with her so she could separate a little tobacco from what was in the large storage basket. If she slipped the knife into Calida's back, Panther would no longer have to concern himself with the foolish creature. He would be free to hear Winter Rain's love-whispers.

But to kill—

Calida gasped and sat upright. Winter Rain nearly faded into the shadows, but her curiosity held her in place. Calida first raked her fingers through her hair, then pulled her body into a tight ball. Only then did she look around. "Who—who's out there?"

"Winter Rain."

"What are you doing here?"

"Listening to the night."

For several moments, Calida said nothing. Finally, sighing, she stood and looked at her. As the silent scrutiny continued, Winter Rain remembered she deliberately hadn't spoken to Calida before. More than that, she'd pretended not to understand her. "A woman should not sleep in the open," she said sternly. "Even the most lazy can build a shelter."

"Maybe I don't want to sleep inside."

That made no sense. Telling herself she didn't care what Calida did, or why, she made a move as if to leave. But Panther looked at Calida in ways she didn't want. She had to learn more about the woman if she was going to fight her power over the man she loved. "You had a bad spirit dream," she explained without sympathy. "I heard you cry out."

"I know. No matter how hard I try, I—you wouldn't talk to me before. I thought, well, I'm not sure what I thought. Why is it different tonight?"

A bold question. Too bold. "Bad spirit dreams sometimes bring bad medicine to a village. I seek to know if you carry danger inside you."

"Danger?" Calida sighed. "I don't know. Maybe."

This wasn't right. Calida didn't belong here. The newcomer shouldn't be allowed to keep secrets. "Bad spirit dreams come to those whose souls are uneasy."

"Uneasy? I can't forget." Calida wrapped her arms around her waist and rocked back and forth several times. "During the day, I tell myself it doesn't matter anymore. That I've gotten away from him. But my mother—at night I can't hold back my fears for her. Why did I leave her? There must have been a way I could have brought her with me. Somehow."

"Quiet. You will wake the others. Where is your mother?"

Calida told her. When Winter Rain prompted, Calida explained what the plantation looked like, how the slaves lived. Sensing that the runaway was still holding something back, Winter Rain continued to press. Calida's hands weren't used to hard work. What did she do at the plantation? It seemed unbelievable that a white woman needed help with her clothing, dressing and getting ready for bed, taking a bath, but she'd never looked into the eyes of a white woman so maybe they were as helpless as Calida had said. If they were, Piahokee would kill her.

"This took all your time?" she asked when Calida fell silent. "Does a white woman have that many clothes?"

"Some do, but Mistress Liana didn't, not many new ones anyway. She said it didn't matter because she never saw anyone."

"This Mistress Liana. She was kind to you?"

When Calida nodded, Winter Rain stared at her in disbelief. "Then why did you run away? Your back bears no whip marks."

"I wouldn't have any value if I had scars."

But there were other kinds of scars, wounds that touched the heart. Her mother's death had taught Winter Rain that. It didn't matter that she didn't want to be thinking this; the sense that she was getting close to why Calida had fled continued to grow. Maybe if she understood, she'd understand what existed between Panther and Calida. Clenching her teeth, she forced herself to squeeze the runaway's hand. "I do not understand what it is to be a slave," she said. "My father was one, but it was before I was born. He never talked about that time."

"Is your father here?"

"He is with Osceola. He wants to fight the army. It is all he talks about. He would rather be dead than a slave again."

"So would I." Calida looked down at her trapped hand but didn't pull away. "You must miss him," she said softly. "Sometimes I think I can't bear being apart from my mother. Can't bear worrying about her."

"My mother is dead." Winter Rain spoke harshly, as she always did when she talked about her mother, because it was the only way she could keep from crying. "Smallpox. Three winters ago."

"I'm sorry. So very sorry."

What do you know of sorrow? Your mother lives. Angry, she released Calida. "Escaped slaves brought the disease with them. If they had left us alone, my mother would be alive."

"I'm sorry," Calida repeated and went back to hugging herself. "You were so young when she died, still a girl."

Yes, she had been. And her father's grief had been so great that he hadn't been able to think of anything else. She'd had to cry alone.

"I never knew my father," Calida was saying. "He was white."

"Was he your mother's master?"

"Yes. Whatever he wanted, he took. She couldn't fight him. If she'd tried, he would have killed her. When . . ."

"When what?"

"Nothing. Nothing. I don't want to talk about it."

But she was going to, Winter Rain thought. Otherwise how would she know Calida's strengths and weaknesses, why Panther looked at her the way he did? "You fear so for your mother. Why did you not bring her here with you?"

"I wanted to. Lord knows I've regretted every minute since then. But . . ."

"You were in too much of a hurry? I saw you when Panther brought you here. You had no weapon, not even shoes."

"I ran. When Master Croon killed my mistress, I knew I had to. My mother is crippled. She can barely walk." Her voice sounded flat, but emotion hummed beneath the surface.

"Did your master raise a weapon against you?"

"I didn't give him a chance. Winter Rain, I know what he's capable of. His violence. I looked into his eyes and saw something far worse than I'd ever seen before."

What had she seen before? Watching Calida, sensing the emotion that boiled inside her, Winter Rain had her answer. Croon had had his own use for her. Calida had run, not just because she feared for her life, but because death in Piahokee was better than what she'd endured.

Calida had turned her back on Winter Rain and was staring into the distance, where night was just beginning to give way to morning. For this moment at least, it was impossible for her to hate someone who wanted nothing more from life than freedom.

"I—I didn't know what to do," Calida whispered. "I was so scared. I begged my mother to come with me, but her leg—She said I would have to find Panther on my own. That he was my only chance."

Panther her only chance. The compassion she'd felt for Calida faded like a dewdrop under the summer sun. Panther was hers; he had to be hers.

She had nothing else.

Morning had become midday before Calida saw what she'd spent the day looking for. Panther and Gaitor stepped out of the wilderness. The sight of them—him—filled her first with relief and then a new kind of fear because she didn't want to care this much.

Careful not to ask herself why she needed to be closer to him, she joined those gathering around them. Because they spoke in Seminole, she caught only snatches of what they were saying. She knew they'd come across a large number of army men and that the braves and Negroes had left without doing battle with them. She didn't know what had happened to the members of the Turtle clan, just that what Panther said caused many of the villagers to mutter angrily and fearfully among themselves.

After what seemed forever, the group began breaking up. Only then did Gaitor approach her. She tried not to notice what Panther was doing, but her eyes had a mind of their own. Winter Rain was standing in front of the *tastanagee*, talking and gesturing urgently. Her entire being was focused on him. Her body seemed to dance toward his, then pull away.

"There's somethin' you gots to know," Gaitor said.

"I don't understand anything," she admitted. "You must be tired. I made some hominy. It's a little thin, but if you're hungry—"

An almost childlike smile lit Gaitor's heavy features. Taking his hand, she led him to the food preparation area she'd set up near her bed. Because she had only one bowl, a gift from one of the Negro women, she handed it to Gaitor and told him to drink as much as he wanted. He didn't stop until he'd swallowed at least half of the soupy concoction.

"What do I have to know?" she prompted once Gaitor had sat down. She refused to look around; Panther was the *tastanagee*. He was welcome everywhere. And he had no need of her.

"*He* was there."

He. Master Croon. Feeling sick, she fought off the impulse to tell Gaitor he was lying. "What was he doing? You didn't talk to him, did you?"

"Talk?" Gaitor spat the word. "He'd see us dead afore he spoke with a Seminole. Or one he considers a slave."

"Did he see you?"

"Yes."

"Yes?" she repeated. Maybe if she went on talking, facing the fear that came with the simple word would be easier. "Please tell me. Everything."

He did, his eyes never leaving hers. They'd been far enough away from Reddin Croon that Gaitor couldn't say what his military rank was, but there was no doubt that he was in uniform.

"I thought he might leave," she whispered half to herself. "I prayed he had. When Panther told me he was no longer at his plantation, I tried to make myself believe he'd left Florida."

"He's got hisself a fine horse. The way he stared at us, it's plain as day he's feelin' sure o' hisself."

"He recognized you? My god—"

"Me and Panther. That ain't all, Calida."

She wanted to get up and walk away, run, but she didn't have anywhere to go.

"On the way back, we come across a brave from another clan. Hawk Flying had been at Fort Dade, a prisoner. They let him go 'cause they wants him to spread the news."

What news? she wanted to demand but forced herself to wait Gaitor out. The explanation, which she guessed the rest of the village already knew, was that the army leaders were sending word through Hawk Flying and others that they wanted to meet with the leaders of the various Seminole clans. As proof of their desire for a successful meeting, they'd promised not to draw arms against the Seminoles until after the gathering.

Master Croon had told her something about Fort Dade, but she hadn't paid that much attention because it hadn't been part of her existence back then. Now . . . "What does Panther say? He can't go there. He can't! If Ma—if Croon is there, he'll kill him. I know he will."

Gaitor stared at her with new intensity. Ignoring him, she scrambled to her feet. Panther was some distance away talking with several older men. Not waiting for Gaitor, she hurried to Panther's side. Only then did she notice that Winter Rain was already there, glaring at her. Not wanting anyone except Panther to hear what she had to say, she had no choice but to stand there, silent and self-conscious, while the others studied her for a long minute before dismissing her. Finally, Panther separated himself from them and strode toward her. Winter Rain started to join him, but he waved her off.

"I'm sorry," Calida blurted. "I didn't mean to interrupt but— Gaitor just told me about Fort Dade. You're not going there, are you? It's a trap; it's got to be a trap."

"You are a *tastanagee*? You know how the enemy thinks?"

Was he deliberately trying to demean her? "*He'll* be there. What-ever he tries to do, the others won't stop him. Your life— He hates you. You know he does."

"Many Seminoles and whites hate each other."

How could he be so calm? "What do they want?" she asked. "Do they think every Seminole is going to surrender?"

"It is their wish. With us gone, they will claim Piahokee as their own."

He looked tired today. She would have noticed that earlier if she hadn't been so relieved to see him. He must have been on the move the whole time he was gone, but she didn't think that was what had put the shadows under his eyes. What happened to his clan, to the entire Seminole tribe, was a responsibility he'd borne since becom-ing a man. He was also responsible for her safety now. "I don't trust them, any of them. I know what Reddin Croon is like. He's army. That's all he's ever really cared about. What if they're all like him?"

"What would you have me do?" Panther asked.

"Stay here. Stay safe."

"Safe? There is no place the army cannot find if they look long enough."

It seemed impossible that any outsider would ever find the vil-lage, but she'd be a fool if she didn't admit that some Seminoles might turn in their own people in exchange for promises of safety. It seemed so overwhelming. All she wanted out of life was to learn how to live in harmony with Piahokee and to bring her mother here. Maybe one other thing. Children. And the right man to be a father to those chil-dren.

"Please don't go. If Croon's there, he'll kill you."

"To try and to succeed are not always the same."

"Panther, no! You said you saw at least two hundred troops. There'll be even more at Fort Dade. What if it's a trap? What if they're planning to kill all the Seminole leaders?"

He already knew that was a possibility. He'd discussed it with Gaitor on the way back, tried to imagine himself tied and helpless again, or worse. But he couldn't remain behind if the other chiefs wanted peace talks. Didn't Calida understand that?

Looking down at her, he found his answer. Her eyes, her too-soft mouth spoke of fear for him. Fear? His people knew him to be strong. Expected it of him. None had ever asked if he was afraid of war. Of dying.

Calida did.

Calida, who Gaitor loved.

Calida, whose presence might jeopardize the clan's safety if Croon learned she was here.

"I will tell you everything Hawk Flying said." He spoke around swirling emotions. "I thought about remaining silent, but I believe it is something you must know."

"Know what?"

"Seminoles raided Reddin Croon's planation. They freed Gaitor and me. They killed his wife and carriage driver. He has gone to war against them to avenge those deaths."

"That's a lie! That's not—"

"I know that. So do you," he said, his voice calm in contrast to hers. "But there are more ears to listen to him."

"The ears of other army officers. That's what you're saying, isn't it?"

"Not just the army. Hawk Flying said Croon insists he has the ear of the President."

Her hand spread over her throat; she took a long, dragging breath and briefly closed her eyes. "I forgot."

"What did you forget?"

"He knows President Jackson. They used to fight together. And he considers Major General Jesup a friend."

From what he understood, Jesup would be at Fort Dade. He couldn't imagine the President would lend his weight to this meeting, but if Reddin Croon was able to convince him to come—

President Jackson, Old Mad Jackson as the Seminoles called him, was Enemy. Several years ago he had signed a piece of paper that said all Indians in the eastern part of the country were to be removed from their land and forced to live in places called Kansas and Oklahoma. The Shawnees, Kickapoos, and Peorias were already in Kansas. Choctaws, Cherokees, and Chickasaws had been sent to Oklahoma. Only a few Choctawa, a handful of Creeks, and the Seminoles hidden in Piahokee remained on their ancestors' land. Croon would bring great honor to himself if he was seen as responsible for forcing the Seminoles to surrender. He would make sure that many troops were on hand to stop anyone from escaping Fort Dade. Croon was like a great alligator, dangerous and deadly.

"I am only one *tastanagee*. I cannot stop others from speaking to the army men."

She grabbed his arm, her grip so strong it hurt. "Why are they doing it?" she insisted. "Don't they want to be free?"

"It is hard to think of freedom when one is always running and hiding. When children go to sleep hungry. When newborns must be killed to keep them from crying."

Agony etched itself on her features. He wanted to ease away the emotion but couldn't. He wasn't used to talking to a woman this way. Seminole women concerned themselves with feeding, clothing, and caring for their children. They left fighting up to their men. But Calida understood, maybe even more than he did, about the danger that lay ahead for him, Osceola, and the others. She'd lessened her grip on him but hadn't let go. It wasn't a Seminole woman's way to touch or argue with a man she wasn't married to, but Calida wasn't Seminole. He didn't know her thoughts.

He was learning about her fears.

That and something that lay nearly hidden deep in her big, dark eyes.

"Reddin Croon, General Jesup, and President Jackson don't care anything about hungry children," she said. She sounded resigned, yet she continued to grip him. "All that matters to them is that they succeed. Whatever it takes, they'll do it."

"I know."

"Do you?" She glanced down at his wrist and frowned. He guessed she hadn't been aware that she'd grabbed him. He couldn't say the same, might never be unaware of her. "Panther, if you step inside Fort Dade, you might never leave it."

"It is not your concern."

"Not my concern? Panther, you're all— I care what happens to you. I care!"

* * *

Calida paced from her sleeping area to the jungle and then back again. It was dark, and Piahokee now belonged to creatures that hid from the sun. She should be settling down for the night, but she couldn't shut off her thoughts enough for that. In her mind's eye, she could still see the red marks she'd inflicted on Panther's wrist. Never in her life had she harmed another human being, and yet she'd done that to the man who'd carried her out of Piahokee when she was dying. She should fall to her knees before him and thank him for what he'd done.

But Reddin Croon had once forced her to her knees, and she couldn't do that again.

Although there was nothing to see, she continued to stare at the wilderness while her thoughts tumbled inside her. She had a decision to make, realities to face, but they kept slipping behind images of Panther.

Dreams of freedom, no matter how short-lived, had kept her going after she fled the plantation. Once her fever began to subside and she realized where she was, a sense of peace unlike anything she'd believed possible had settled over her. She was no longer a slave. That should be all that mattered. She should want to sing with joy, revel in the realization that she could hold her head high, but she'd never done that before in her life. How—

Learning the meaning of freedom had only a little to do with what she felt tonight. She was afraid, not just that Croon would get his hands on her again, but that Panther would sacrifice his life at Fort Dade.

Panther. Not anyone else.

What was she thinking? Everyone, even Osceola, was in danger.

But tonight only Panther mattered.

Groaning, she pressed her hands against the sides of her head. She'd only loved one person in her life, her mother, had never wanted to love another.

What was she thinking? She didn't love Panther! The man was a savage. He lived to fight and kill if necessary while all she'd ever wanted was peace.

Forcing Panther, briefly, from her mind, she made herself concentrate on what she'd learned about Croon. He had rejoined the army. Without his wife to keep him at the plantation, she shouldn't be surprised that he'd returned to his previous way of life. Croon had told everyone that the Seminoles had killed his wife. Certainly his wealthy, powerful, stern father-in-law didn't know the truth. Except for her, no one did.

Her.

Croon wasn't done with her.

The man hadn't put on a uniform because he wanted to avenge his wife's death. He was determined to find her, and this was how he was going to do it. He would find her. Someone, maybe a captured Seminole or runaway, maybe even Panther if they tortured him enough, would give her away.

No. Panther would die before he betrayed those he was responsible for.

Still, his life was in jeopardy because of her. He and the men, women, and children who'd given her shelter.

She couldn't stay here. If she did, eventually Croon would find her. Exact a horrible revenge on her—and maybe on Panther as well.

Her head throbbed, and she couldn't think straight. When she first fled the plantation, Piahokee had felt as if it was closing in on her. It felt like that again, not because she was still afraid of what dwelled in Piahokee's depths but because Reddin Croon might be coming closer. Determined to kill her. Or worse.

9

"You cain't be serious."

"I am, Gaitor. I have no choice."

"You's never gonna make it."

Didn't he think she'd already thought about the dangers? "I survived getting here. Please. You must know how to reach the Freedom Trail. Just tell me how to get to it."

Gaitor folded his massive arms across his dark chest. He looked so imposing, but she forced herself not to shrink from his scrutiny. She'd spent the whole night agonizing over her decision and was now exhausted but still determined. "I'm afraid for my mother," she admitted. "I have to get her away from there. If I don't . . . What if he's already done something to her? The things—" She couldn't go on thinking like this. If she did, she would make herself sick. "I keep telling myself he's with the army because he knows he can't find me on my own. But how did he come to that conclusion? If he tried to force—"

"Stop it, Calida."

She was grateful for the order. Looking around, she saw that the villagers were already up and moving about. There was a tension in the air that she had no doubt came from concerns about the upcoming meeting at Fort Dade. She'd tried to talk Panther out of going, begged him, but he wouldn't listen to her. All she could do was try to help her mother, to get them both as far as possible from Croon's vengeance. She'd carry Pilar the entire way if that's what it took.

"Gaitor, you know what it's like to be a piece of property."

"Yes."

"Aren't you afraid? Don't you want to get as far from that as you can?"

"My place is here."

Maybe it was. Despite herself, she envied him. "Mine isn't. It's with my mother. If you'd had family, you—"

"I did. A wife. A baby."

He tried to keep his voice emotionless, but she heard the truth behind those simple words. Impulsively she tried to hug him, but there was so much to him that she couldn't get her arms around his waist. He shuddered, and she stepped back thinking he didn't want to lose his composure around her. "Where are they?"

"I don' know. I was sold. They wasn't."

She'd known that Gaitor had been more dead than alive when he staggered into the Egret village, but unlike her, his wounds hadn't been inflicted by the unforgiving wilderness. His master had beaten him within an inch of his life, leaving him with nothing except the desperate determination to escape. Now she knew that that wasn't the whole story. He'd also been separated from his family.

If only there was something she could do, some way of reuniting him with his wife and child. But she couldn't. "Then you know what it's like for me. How I can't stop thinking about my mother. Worrying that I might have jeopardized her life. Wanting to take care of her."

"Yes. I knows."

She didn't tell him about her fear that her presence jeopardized the tribe's safety, most of all Panther's. He understood how she felt about her mother, and that was enough. When she again asked him to tell her how to find the Freedom Trail, he dropped to his knees and drew a map on the ground. With a start, she realized that the town he'd indicated was St. Augustine. There were people there, white people, willing to take her north. All she had to do was get herself and her mother to St. Augustine. Somehow.

"I'll takes you."

"You what?"

"Not now but later. After Fort Dade."

After Fort Dade was too late. She'd overheard enough to realize it might take weeks to reach the far-flung Seminole villages and that the leaders would have to meet and discuss and decide many things before they were willing to stand face-to-face with the army.

"You hears me, Calida. Don' you think to go by yurself. You'll never make it."

Gaitor was wrong. She'd managed to find the Egret village, hadn't she? As long as she followed the river, she could make her way back to Croon's plantation. She'd make mashed corn patties to eat along the way. She wouldn't have to rely on a few nuts and berries, not now that she knew which tubers and roots were eatable. Not only that, Gaitor had given her a knife, and a Seminole woman had presented her with a piece of leather and shown her how to make moccasins.

When she asked, Winter Rain agreed to give her a pig bladder for holding water. Winter Rain had also given her a stout oak stick to use to chase off any alligators who came too close. Calida had studied Winter Rain to see if she'd been joking. She hadn't been. Then Winter Rain had asked if Calida planned on leaving before nightfall. No, she wanted to wait until early the next morning so she could cover as much ground as possible before it got dark. Winter Rain had shrugged. When Calida begged Winter Rain to say nothing of her plans to either Panther or Gaitor, the younger woman had readily agreed.

As the afternoon inched along, Calida became aware of increased activity. Afraid that Panther was planning on leaving again, she found a spot to sit in sight of his *chickee*. Unfortunately, there were so many warriors about that for a long time she didn't catch so much as a glimpse of him. Several of the men were strangers engaged in serious conversation with the men of the Egret clan, Gaitor and other Negroes included. Finally, Panther emerged accompanied by a short, fat, proud-looking Seminole. Panther bent over the other man, listening carefully to what he was saying.

"Micanopy," she heard someone mutter. The name sounded familiar, but it was a minute before she remembered she'd heard Croon talk about him. Micanopy, Croon had said, had fired the shot that signaled the war between the United States and the Seminoles. Because she understood very little of what those around her were saying about Micanopy and Panther, she searched her memory. The incident had taken place near Fort King. A large number of infantrymen had been attacked by Seminoles who'd lain in wait for them, and no soldier had survived what Croon called the Dade Massacre, named after the major who'd been leading the troops.

Looking at Micanopy, she tried to imagine the man ordering the killing of so many others. He reminded her of a lazy, easygoing old dog content to sleep away his remaining days. Still, something must have burned inside him, must still burn to bring him here to Panther.

In sharp contrast to Micanopy, Panther looked like a man ready for war. He wasn't armed this afternoon, but the lack of weapons made little difference in his appearance. He carried himself as if he might have to do battle at any moment. His eyes were never still, always testing his surroundings. He often held his head cocked slightly to the right, and she guessed he was determined to hear everything. He used his height to look not just at those who surrounded him, but in the distance as well. She'd heard tales of his hunting prowess and now knew he succeeded because he hunted with his whole body and all his senses. If he could find the smallest deer hidden in the deepest shadows, was he capable of knowing her thoughts?

Shaking herself free of the question, Calida again tried to concentrate on what Micanopy was saying. He kept pounding his fat chest with his fist and often held a musket aloft. She wondered if he'd taken the weapon from some soldier he'd killed. When Panther spoke, he didn't boast, but the others held onto his every word. Both he and Micanopy were addressing the entire village now. Unfortunately, they spoke too rapidly for her to understand what they were saying. Looking around, she spotted Winter Rain. Hurrying over to her, she begged her to translate. The half-Seminole, half-Negro did so without once looking at her.

"Micanopy says there is no truth to the army leaders' promise of food and clothing for those who lay down their arms. He cannot smoke with the army men because he has killed so many of their brothers." Winter Rain fell silent, listening. Calida wanted to prompt her for more information but was afraid she might miss something important. Finally, Micanopy stepped back, ran his hands over his belly, and looked up at Panther.

His eyes taking in everything, Panther took the place of prominence. To her shock, he briefly locked his gaze with her. As long as they remained like that, she couldn't remember why she had to leave the village. Leave him.

When he began, his voice was low and deep, the voice of a man concentrating so much on what he needs to say that he is unable to ask himself whether others can hear. Winter Rain leaned forward. Her frown grew. She nodded.

"What?" Calida asked.

"Silence."

Upset by Winter Rain's sharp reply, Calida glanced over at her, but Winter Rain didn't take her eyes off Panther, and after a moment, Calida brought her reluctant gaze back to the war chief. He spoke without gestures. His body reminded her of a tree untouched by the wind. If she didn't know better, she might think he was talking about something of no more consequence than whether it was time to build a new canoe. But emotion coated his words, emotion that reached out to her and told her about a man who cared, who felt.

"What is he saying?" Her question was more insistent this time.

"He speaks of his hatred for whites."

She'd already guessed that. "Why does he—"

"Quiet!"

"What happened? Why does he hate them so much?"

"It is not for me to say."

Panther's speech had been much shorter than Micanopy's. For maybe thirty seconds after he'd finished, no one spoke. Then slowly, quietly, people began talking among themselves. Panther had already disappeared inside his *chickee* followed by Micanopy and the others who'd come with the older man. Gaitor remained outside a little longer while he spoke to the healer. Although he nodded to indicate he'd seen her, Gaitor didn't come over to where Calida now sat alone. She was relieved. Sick at heart but relieved.

Tomorrow morning she would walk out of the Egret village. She'd never see Gaitor or Winter Rain again. Never again see Panther. Fighting the pain that went with the thought, she turned her mind to her determination to get her mother away from Croon, but when she did, her fear that it was too late for Pilar grew.

Fighting too-familiar fear, she began walking. Two Negro women asked her to eat with them. A little Seminole girl tripped on an exposed root and fell, banging her chin on the ground. Calida picked her up and cradled her until her mother came to take her. She was still watching mother and daughter when she sensed that she was being watched. Without thinking what she was doing, she turned toward Panther's *chickee*.

His guests were seated in a circle under the brush roof, smoking and talking. She expected him to join them, waited for him to ease himself to the ground, but he continued to stand and study her. Finally, although she knew the danger in what she was doing, she started toward him. He met her halfway, his hunter's legs carrying his body effortlessly. She felt small and fragile next to him.

"I don't know what you were saying," she admitted when he remained silent. "Not all of it. Please, will you tell me?"

"I spoke of the past."

The past? That didn't make sense, or maybe it did. "I asked Winter Rain to translate, but . . ."

"She has heard my words before. They have little meaning for her."

She should tell him Winter Rain had hung on to his every word, but if she did, they might talk about that instead of what he'd said earlier. "Have you made a decision about Fort Dade?" she asked. "I know Micanopy doesn't dare show his face around the army. Are you going to stay with him?"

"I did not talk of decisions, Calida."

Because those things were for him and the other leaders to discuss in private? She wished she understood more about how such things were done among the Seminole; she wished she knew more about taking control of what happened in one's life. "What, then?" she prompted.

"What I feel inside."

He'd touched his chest much the way Micanopy had earlier but without Micanopy's boastfulness. She thought about his heart beating beneath that dark skin and powerful muscles. "What do you feel?"

"Hatred."

The word sounded clean and final. He hadn't had to give his response a second's thought. "Why?"

"Because of what the army did to my father," he said. His attention flicked off her. Out of the corner of her eye, she spotted the little girl who'd fallen. Her chin looked red, but she was laughing. Calida ached to hold her, to rock her, to never let her go.

"What did they do to your father?"

"Army men whipped him until life left his body."

She no longer cared about the little girl, her own mother, the decision she'd made about tomorrow. Only Panther mattered. "Oh, Panther. I didn't know."

"He was not yet dead when I found him. He did not die alone."

But he died in your arms and you're left with that memory. "Why? What did he do that—"

"It was five summers ago." His eyes glowed dark and hot. "There had been no rain for many moons. The sun sucked water from ponds and creeks, from the ground where our people had planted their corn and squash."

She remembered last summer's heat, Croon's concern that his crops would fail. From the window, she'd seen tobacco and other plants drooping, watched slaves carry water to them from the drying river. Even Mistress Liana, who had known little about how things grew, had shared her husband's concern. It had been one of the few things husband and wife had talked about. "What did your father do?"

"Not just my father. The entire clan. We left our village and went closer to the sea because it had rained there. That land had once been ours but was no longer."

Because whites had taken it from them. "Was he the only one?" she asked. "Did anyone else lose their life?"

"Not from a whip, but yes, from drought."

She didn't want to hear about that. Still, she knew she had no choice. "Many?"

"Old people. Babies and children."

"You found him?" she made herself ask. "Where were you?"

"Hunting. When I should have been by his side."

"Panther, I . . ."

"There were only women and children. My father had gone with them to trade for food. The whites called him to them, held out their hands in friendship. Then they grabbed him and beat him until there was nothing left of him."

No!

"They forced the women to watch."

It wasn't just his eyes. His entire body burned with an anger that came from his soul. Croon had hated the savages, as he called them, but his hatred existed because so many Seminoles managed to evade him. They refused to surrender, struck like poisonous snakes and then disappeared. But Croon hadn't lost anyone he loved to the enemy. Panther had. "Was Croon one of them?"

"I do not know. The women were too terrified to remember the faces of my father's killers."

But it could have been Reddin Croon. "That's why you'll never agree to take your clan to a reservation, isn't it? Because of what they did to your father."

"Because I know not to trust them."

She saw the truth in the hard way he held himself, the lack of emotion in his voice. Not trusting was only part of what he felt. The rest was hatred.

She wanted to touch him, but she didn't dare. "Panther, don't think about the way your father looked the last time you saw him. If you do, it'll haunt you."

He stiffened at the word *haunt,* and she guessed she'd spoken a truth he thought he'd kept to himself. "Was he a good father?"

"Yes."

Good. "And you loved him."

"Yes."

"Then think about that. Remember the way he was while you were growing up, hunting together, smoking together. Laughing."

He'd been looking off into the distance, and although she wanted it to last longer, he barely glanced down at her before fixing his gaze on the wilderness again. It was growing darker. Night creatures like bats and owls, like the panther he'd been named for, would soon be out. When the morning sun sent them back into cover, she'd leave, but it wasn't morning yet. "I love my mother, Panther. I know what you feel toward your father."

"Your mother lives."

Maybe. "Our parents will always live in our hearts," she managed. "Look for him there. Keep him inside you. If you feed your hatred for the whites, it'll take over everything, even your memory of your father."

He turned as if to leave. Not thinking, she grabbed his arm. He could easily have shaken her off, but he didn't. "The hatred I feel for the enemy needs no feeding, Calida," he said. "It will live forever. There is no way I can change that. I believe the same emotions beat inside you."

It was as if she'd opened herself up to him and he could now examine her every emotion. Her every thought. Without effort, he'd dug through the protective layers to the truth. "He believed he owned everything about me," she whispered because she had no choice. "That not even my soul was my own."

"He was wrong."

Wanting to believe Panther, she nodded. But Croon's power and arrogance had reached her even here in what should have been a place of safety. She couldn't turn her back on the man and what he was capable of, not as long as her mother lived, not as long as danger existed for the Egret clan. And maybe most of all, for Panther.

Emotion clogged her throat. She wouldn't tell Panther that she was leaving. She didn't dare.

"Come with me," Panther said.

Blinking, she forced herself back to the present. She was still holding onto his arm. Feeling self-conscious, she released it. He rubbed his hand absently over where she'd gripped him, and she imagined him feeling her heat. "Come? Where?"

"To Fort Dade."

She couldn't have heard him right. Surely— "No!"

"I have given you shelter, Calida. My people have accepted you. You have a debt to repay."

At the word *debt,* she struggled against an urge to strike him. She felt trapped, but more than that, she felt angry. "I don't belong there. There's nothing I can do. Unless—" Cold, she backed away from him. He watched her every move, and she knew she could never outrun him. "Are you going to turn me over to them?"

"No."

"No? Then why—"

"You can read."

She needed time to make sense of all this, but Panther stood too close. When he did that, he robbed her of a little of herself. She thought of the sound of his voice, not the meaning of his words, the way sunlight lost itself in his dark eyes, not the emotions glittering in them.

"I'm a woman, Panther. Women don't belong at peace talks."

"Peace talks! I am not so stupid to believe that."

"If you think it's going to be a trap, why are you going there?"

"Not a trap. Something else."

He wasn't telling her nearly enough, but the sun had fallen behind the trees and she was talking to a shadow. He'd become size and outline, deep rumbling voice, dark shining hair. The wilderness sang for him, maybe for both of them. Believing that, she couldn't keep her mind on this place called Fort Dade. "Calida, the Seminoles are one person and yet they are not. It is not our way to live together, to share the same leaders, to think and act with one mind."

She already knew that. The Egret clan didn't depend on their neighbors for survival, and except for watching the army's pursuit of the Turtle clan, they had little contact with the other villages. At Fort Dade, all those separate clans and villages would come together and their leaders would try to achieve some kind of unity, but maybe that wasn't possible.

"The army will present its demands. They will say what we can and cannot do. What will and will not happen to us. Those things will be written on talking leaves and we will be expected to sign our marks to them. I will not place my hand on something I do not understand."

But even if she read the documents he called talking leaves, could they trust the army to keep its word? What if those pages contained things Panther and the other leaders found unacceptable? "Panther, Reddin Croon has a piece of paper that says he owns me, but I'm not with him. Just because something is written down doesn't make it so."

"I know that."

"Then why are you having anything to do with them?"

"Because the Egret clan cannot spend its life running and hiding."

He was right. They'd been uprooted from their traditional village, hadn't they? Forced to live in temporary shelters, they hadn't had time to reestablish the huge gardens capable of feeding everyone. They'd lost many of their cattle to the army and settlers. And once the army had finished chasing the Turtle clan, they might turn their strength against Panther and his people.

Still, she didn't understand what he was saying.

"This is not an easy thing for me to do, Calida. I feel as if I have two minds. One says that I must listen to the army, must do as they say and leave my ancestors' land or I will not live to see another winter. Another voice screams at me to take my people and travel so deep into Piahokee that no one will ever find us."

And he wanted her with him, reading for him and the others, because knowing what the army said would help him make his decision. In the distance a baby cried. The sound wasn't repeated. Gaitor had told her that Seminole women sometimes pinched their babies' noses shut so they couldn't cry and give away where they were hiding. She'd heard two Negro women talking about the dead newborn the Turtle clan had left behind. It had, they'd said, been killed by its desperate parents because it wouldn't stop crying and the army was getting closer. If the Egret clan decided to flee, would they have to do the same to their infants in order to remain hidden?

"Will you help us, Calida?"

Would she walk into an enemy fort? No! She wanted to scream. No!

"What she say?"

Panther didn't look up when Gaitor ducked his head and slipped into his *chickee*. He wanted to be alone tonight, but that wasn't possible. If anyone broke his concentration, his thoughts, he was glad it was Gaitor. "She will go with us."

Silent, Gaitor sat across from him. Panther handed Gaitor his pipe and he filled it with dried tobacco leaves. For several minutes they smoked in silence, the glow from their pipes the only light. "I's glad and yet not glad," Gaitor finally said.

"She will tell me the truth about what the army men have written down."

"The truth? Ha!"

If Gaitor was the *tastanagee,* the Egret clan would already have bundled up their belongings and headed south deep into that wild land of panthers and bears, snakes and uncounted alligators. "I have thought on this for a long time," Panther admitted. "So long that my head beats like a drum."

"Micanopy and Osceola, they want things to end. You knows that."

He did. That was what made his decision all the more difficult.

"They calls themselves warriors. Micanopy boasted so today. He beats on his chest and talks about what a great warrior he is, but, ha! I knows better," Gaitor said.

"He is old and tired. His heart is weary of fighting. And my chief is sick."

"What 'bout you? You tired?"

When he first came here, Gaitor had kept his thoughts to himself. For awhile, Panther had wondered if his mind, his will had been beaten out of him, but as time went on, Gaitor became more of a man. His friend. The one person he kept nothing from—except how he felt about Calida. But then how could he, when he didn't have the answer himself?

"Yes, I am tired. Not my body, but my heart is weary." He pulled smoke deep into his lungs, but the tobacco he saved for times when he needed to relax wasn't doing its job tonight. "I have been thinking. Asking my spirit for guidance. If Osceola and Micanopy agree to go to Oklahoma, I will do as my chief says."

He waited for Gaitor to say something. Instead, the big Negro turned his attention to the stars. Was he asking himself what they looked like in Oklahoma? He hadn't asked Gaitor if he would stay with the clan if it left Florida. The decision was his, but his friend, like the other Negroes here, belonged with Seminoles. In Oklahoma, maybe, he would no longer be considered a runaway. His soul would feel free. Maybe.

"You needs someone who can reads, all right," Gaitor said. "Someone who ain't gonna lie to you. But Panther, what if Reddin Croon's there? How you gonna save her from him?"

10

Sweat trickled down Reddin Croon's back. He ran his finger under his starched collar, but the moment he released it, the fabric bit into his neck again. Despite the discomfort, the last thing he'd do was allow himself to be seen out of uniform.

The Seminoles would be here today. Finally. At least some of their chiefs would. Word was out that Micanopy was having second thoughts and had sent others in his place. As for Osceola, he was too sick, or so he said. General Jesup was concerned that without Osceola or Micanopy, the others wouldn't make a decision about whether to agree to the document commonly known as "The Capitulation of the Seminole Nation."

Looking around the crudely built Fort Dade, Reddin forced himself not to think about how many damned useless days he'd spent while first one thing and then the other cropped up to delay the peace talks. Chief Jumper was already here along with Holatoochee, both of them smoking all the tobacco they could get their greedy hands on. Chief Yaholoochee had been spotted less than a mile away. Yesterday a runner had brought word that Panther had agreed to join the others.

Panther.

Sweating, Reddin walked to the stable where his saddled horse waited. The Seminoles put great stock in horses. Wasn't that why they'd "stolen" Liana's? They'd sit up and take notice when they saw him astride the big red stallion. Only, he didn't give a damn what the rest of the Seminoles and their nigger "brothers" thought, just Panther.

If Calida had made it, she might be with him.

The soldier responsible for his horse backed away respectfully and saluted, but Reddin barely glanced at him. It'd been three months since he'd seen Calida, three long, hard months. Yeah, he'd had his way with a couple of his slaves, but they'd been quickies because his damnable father-in-law would have disapproved. Might have cut off his allowance.

Allowance! The word grated on him like a festering wound, but he wasn't about to turn the plantation—his plantation—over to Isiah lock, stock, and barrel. The money Isiah reluctantly let loose of had made it possible for him to purchase a real horse instead of the burned-out nags that belonged to the army. And although it sure as hell wasn't the same thing, money did some to make up for the loss of female companionship.

He'd tried to get Calida's mammy to tell him where her daughter had taken off to. If he'd had more time and privacy, he would have worked the truth out of the cripple, but Isiah was always around. He knew better than to arouse Isiah's suspicions, not with Isiah holding the purse strings. If he wasn't careful, Pilar might tell Isiah things that would make him suspect it wasn't the Seminoles who'd killed his precious and ugly daughter. And he was careful. Horny but careful.

Calida wasn't like those stinkin' field hands he'd been forced to turn to, not by a long shot. She was soft, quiet, intelligent, although that didn't particularly matter to him. Her high-yellow color appealed to him. He still remembered her silky skin, the way she felt under him.

If she was alive, he was willing to bet a month's pay it was because she'd hooked up with Panther. It had to be that. As far as he knew, Panther's clan was the only one anywhere near the plantation. She sure as hell hadn't been seen around St. Augustine or the forts. He knew because he'd asked.

Cursing impatiently, he urged his horse to the center of the fort. Logs had been set in a circle for the principals to sit on. Yaholoochee, who would represent Micanopy, had just arrived, but Reddin didn't care. Nothing mattered except catching sight of Panther and wringing the truth about Calida from him.

Don't make a single aggressive move. He couldn't remember how many times General Jesup had hammered that at the troops. He was sick of it. Just looking at the chiefs with their loud, moth-eaten blankets wrapped around their shoulders like some kind of armor made him want to run a sword into their bellies. A couple of privates respectfully approached Yaholoochee and indicated he was to sit near the other chiefs. As soon as he was seated, General Jesup stepped out of his quarters and, smiling like a damned idiot, ordered fresh tobacco for everyone. Reddin remained on horseback, sweating, ignoring Jesup's pointed glares. The Seminoles were savages, little more than animals. He by god wasn't going to sit down with them.

General Jesup had been smoking, saying nothing, for maybe a half hour while Reddin's horse moved restlessly under him when a red-faced and out-of-breath guard brought word that Panther was within shouting distance. Teeth clenched, Reddin positioned himself so that he could spot the warrior the moment he stepped inside the fort.

Panther wasn't alone. He'd brought a half dozen warriors with him, including, damn it, the big nigger who'd escaped from him the same day Panther had. When the nigger spotted him, he stopped in his tracks. Panther glanced over at the nigger, then, sober, did the same. Reddin stared back. He wanted to see fear, respect, something in the chief's eyes, but there was none of that. Instead, Panther's whole demeanor said he would kill him if he possibly could. Thinking about the knife scar in his side, he was forced to admit that he'd nearly accomplished it once.

"I do not want this man here." Panther indicated him. "He put ropes on me and my *honton,* my friend. I will not sit and talk peace with him."

"He's simply here as an observer," General Jesup explained, obviously surprised that Panther spoke English as well as he did. "All he'll do is report back to the President."

"He wants me dead."

"He isn't armed," Jesup pointed out. "None of us is."

If Panther believed that, he was a fool. The chief's glare said better than any words that he wasn't. "I tell you this, General. If Reddin Croon kills me, there will never be peace between Seminole and white."

"There isn't going to be any killing here, Panther. We haven't attacked any of your people since I called for this meeting, have we? What more proof do you need?"

By way of answer, Panther spoke quietly with the nigger, then nodded at the other chiefs and took his place across from General Jesup. Reddin had to hand it to Jesup. Despite what his detractors—and there were many—said about the man, he knew how to negotiate. A twenty-year-old doesn't join the army with the rank of second lieutenant unless he's impressed folks. Jesup began by telling the assembled chiefs that he was as weary of fighting as he knew they were. The campaign against the Seminoles was expensive. Those back in the capital were putting pressure on him to end the aggression. He agreed, completely.

What the Seminoles had to understand was that it wasn't possible for them to remain where they were. Ranchers, farmers, and plantation owners considered the land too valuable for that. But the Seminoles were being given something equally good in exchange for allowing themselves to be resettled. In Oklahoma they would be left alone to live as they wished. Although Jesup had never been there, he had it on good authority that the land was fertile, there was no sickly season during the summer, and the winters were mild. It didn't rain the way it did here. There were no alligators or panthers, no swarms of mosquitoes or poisonous snakes. No deadly hurricanes.

None of the so-called guests said a word.

Looking decidedly uncomfortable, Jesup ordered his aide to bring him the document that, he said, would demonstrate without a doubt to the Seminoles that the army meant to keep their word. Panther and the nigger exchanged veiled glances.

Clearing his throat, General Jesup began reading. Because he'd gone over the damned document so many times, Reddin paid little attention. Panther *had* been at Hatcheelustee Creek; he had no doubt of that. He'd seen the brave standing there arrogant as could be, as if daring him to fire. He hadn't—not because he didn't want the chief's blood spreading over the ground, but because he didn't trust his musket to reach that far. Panther must have known just how close he dared get and taunted him with his presence. Well, it was a different story this time. Panther was inside fort walls. There was no way he could escape.

Only, General Jesup would find a way to get him thrown out of the army if he killed Panther, no matter how much the savage deserved it. Chewing on his hatred, Reddin kept his gaze locked on the tall, powerfully built brave. Several times Panther looked over at him, his eyes unreadable. What did it matter? The point was, Panther was aware of him. Leery of him.

Good. Let him understand that the next time Reddin Croon got his hands on Panther, there wouldn't be any doubt of the outcome. Only, he wouldn't kill him, at least not right off, not until the savage paid for his arrogance.

Suddenly, Panther held up his hand, stopping General Jesup in mid-sentence. "I have heard enough. I hear you say many things about what is in the talking leaves, but your words and the truth may not be the same."

"What are you getting at, Panther?" the general asked.

"You want us to make our mark, which says we promise to abide by everything that is written there. You want us to trust like cattle who believe they are being led to water but may be slaughtered. I say we are not cattle."

What are you going to do, you ignorant savage? Hold things up while you learn to read? Although he could swear Panther and the nigger hadn't so much as looked at each other, the nigger got to his feet and strode unceremoniously out of the fort. Impatient, Reddin silently railed at his general to insist they get back to peace talks, but when Panther folded his arms across his chest, Jesup sat there like an obedient dog.

The better part of an hour passed. By then Reddin's horse had fallen asleep. He could jerk on the reins except that awake the stallion was more trouble than it was worth. The damnable heat rained down on him until he felt light-headed. Whisky, he kept telling himself. As soon as this charade was over, he'd have himself all the whisky he could get his hands on. He was so intent on not sliding out of the saddle that at first he paid no attention to the fact that the nigger had returned. Then he saw who was with him.

Calida. Alive. Walking close to the big black as if coming here was the last thing in the world she wanted to do. Head held too high for a respectful slave. Studying each soldier's face in turn. Finally settling on him.

He swore he saw a shiver run down her slender frame. Still, there was no look of surprise in her eyes, and he guessed the nigger had already told her what to expect. Even before she reached Panther's side, he understood her role. Liana, damn her, had defied the law forbidding any white to teach a slave to read or write. Even when he'd threatened to tell her father what she was doing, she'd countered by saying that if he insisted on keeping her in that godforsaken wilderness, she was determined to have someone to talk to about books.

Watching him and not the general, Panther explained that he wanted Calida to read the entire document before anything else was said. The way she stood close to Panther, the way the savage gazed down at her, Reddin knew. Calida *had* been the one to free him! If they were messing with each other, he'd kill both of them.

What did he mean, *if?* The savage was a fool if he hadn't taken her.

General Jesup turned the document over to Calida with not so much as a never-you-mind. That was the problem with a man who'd never known anything except the army. He didn't understand there wasn't a nigger in the world who was his equal.

Calida bent her head over the elaborate scroll. Several times she pursed her lips, and once she shook her head. All the time Panther didn't move from her side. Although black as night, she had the straightest hair of any colored he'd ever seen. It flowed over her neck and shoulders in a way that nearly drove him to distraction. She wore some kind of leather shoes and one of those multicolored abominations Seminole women wore. Her arms and legs weren't quite as skinny as he remembered them being, but there wasn't any fat to her.

Finally he realized what made the difference: She'd developed muscles.

At length she straightened and glanced up at Panther. He stared back but said nothing. She held the document a few inches farther from her face and read aloud. "The Seminoles and their allies, who come in and emigrate west, shall be secure in their lives and property. Their negroes, their bona fide property, shall accompany them to the West."

Damn her, out of that whole thing, she'd found what could cause the most trouble. Sounding infinitely patient, Jesup explained that the army was absolutely sincere in assuring the Seminoles that anyone who came in from the wilderness would be assured of safety. "We haven't worked out the logistics of getting you to Oklahoma. You'll be riding of course, but it might take awhile to get enough wagons here for the job."

"No."

"No?" Jesup repeated what Panther had just said.

"I care not whether it is wagons or iron horses. What is this bona fide property?"

"What belongs to you. I don't know how it could be any clearer."

Calida laughed, a faint whisper of sound, but there was no laughter in her eyes. When she spoke, Panther bent over her to catch the low words. They talked like that for several minutes while fury built in Reddin until he wasn't sure he could hold it inside. She was *his*, damn it! He'd bought her. Owned her. Her body belonged to *him*.

"I want to hear this from your lips," Panther said to Jesup. "Are the Negroes who live with us our bona fide property?"

Twice, Reddin had stalked out of the general's tent over this insanity about slaves belonging to the Seminoles and not their white masters, but in the end he'd given in because he knew as well as Jesup did that if the clause didn't stay, the Seminoles would never agree to leave Florida. "Let them keep their damn niggers," he'd said just last night. "They're probably ruined for any decent work anyway." That was before he'd known Calida was with the Seminoles. Still, there was more than one way of getting her back.

Jesup didn't once look at him while he explained that he was committed to upholding every word of the document, most particularly this clause. A relationship of long standing existed between Seminole and Negro, and he wasn't about to complicate peace talks by trying to return the slaves to their previous owners. He had the word of the United States government behind that, he wound up—when Reddin knew he couldn't truthfully make any such statement.

"If I give a Negro shelter then that Negro is my bona fide property? Are those your words, and the words of your president?" Panther pressed.

General Jesup nodded. Panther called the rest of the assembled Seminoles along with Calida and the big nigger to his side. They spoke quietly, intently. When they were done, Panther took the capitulation agreement from Calida. He held out his hand and an officer gave him a pen. No one spoke as he affixed his mark to it. The other chiefs followed suit. Reddin swore he could hear General Jesup sigh in relief.

"Just a minute here!" Reddin bellowed. Kicking the stallion awake, he pushed his way forward until the horse's nose was less than three feet from Panther and Calida. She started to shrink away, but Panther grabbed her arm.

"This here's *my* property." He jabbed a finger at Calida. "I want her back."

"Lieutenant Croon," Jesup warned. "That will be enough."

"No, it ain't. She's mine. I've got the bill of sale for her right in my belongings. How about it, Calida? You gonna stand there and deny you took care of my wife, my dead wife? That she's the one who taught you how to read?"

Tension lapped around him like waves from a stormy sea. Still, Panther willed himself not to give into the impulse to squeeze the life out of Reddin. The man was dangerous; he had to remain calm.

"I thought she was dead," Reddin continued. "She disappeared the same time the Seminoles murdered my wife. I figured they'd gotten her as well. Now I know she went running to them. I want her back. Now."

"This is not the time or place for this, Lieutenant Croon." The general sounded as if he was within a whisper of losing control. "We have just successfully negotiated a treaty with the Seminoles. That's what matters, not your claim on the girl."

"The hell!" Croon looked around, obviously trying to solicit support from the troops. "I know what that agreement says, General. I was involved in drafting it, remember. But she doesn't belong to the Seminoles. Never did and never will. And I can prove it."

No one seconded what Croon had just said. For a moment Panther didn't understand why the soldiers weren't standing behind one of their own. But most of these men were young and weary recruits who wanted nothing more than an end to this war. They were in the army because they had nothing else, no land, no slaves. What happened to Croon's property wasn't their concern.

But she wasn't his property. She was free.

Panther stepped forward and took the horse's reins. Reddin tried to jerk free, but he held on. "Listen to me." He spoke not to the slave owner, but to the army leader. "I have put my mark to this peace paper because I believed the words of a general. If she is taken from the Egret clan, all Seminole will know the army cannot be trusted."

Croon cursed and insisted that no one, not even the President of the United States, had the right to deprive a landowner of his rightful property. The soldiers shuffled uneasily. The other chiefs put down their pipes and made a show of getting ready to leave. Through all this, Calida was the only one who didn't move. Panther didn't look at her, didn't dare, because if she sensed his fear for her, she might try to run. He would not have her pursued by Croon and those he could order to obey him. He would not have her disappear into the wilderness.

"I grow impatient. She is *my* bona fide property. She is useful to me because she can read," Panther said.

"Because my wife taught her, damn it!"

Panther ignored Croon. "I will need her in Oklahoma. Without her, I will not go, and if the Egret clan stays, so will others."

Gaitor muttered something under his breath, but Panther didn't take his attention from the general. Still, he worried that his friend might do something foolish in an effort to protect Calida. "What do you say, General?" he demanded. "Will there be peace, or war because *my* bona fide property has been taken from me?"

* * *

Property. She was his property. Mired in her thoughts, Calida barely noticed what she was doing until Jumper explained that if she followed the path of the setting sun, she would have no trouble finding her way home. She thanked the chief for letting her accompany him and his followers this far, then struck out on her own. With every step she took, the need to make a decision grew.

Panther and Gaitor had stayed behind. Without giving General Jesup time to confer with his officers, Panther had told everyone that he intended to take news of the outcome of the peace talks to Osceola. As for Calida, she was to wait for him back at the Egret village. Croon was not to follow her. That was why Gaitor had remained at the fort, to make sure Croon didn't leave.

It had happened so fast. Before she fully understood what was going on, Panther had grabbed her arm and ordered her to follow Jumper. There'd been nothing in his touch or voice to let her know what he was thinking. The fire in his eyes—

It didn't matter. He considered her his property.

The wilderness squawked and hissed around her. When a brush to her right moved, she knew it wasn't caused by the wind. Trees grew so close here that the sun touched the ground only a few hours a day and it remained swampy. Not long ago just the thought of being out here alone would have panicked her, but no more. Not only had the Seminoles and Negroes shown her that Piahokee provided everything necessary to sustain life, but she'd survived on her own before. She could do it again.

She wouldn't think about the role Panther had played in her survival. She wouldn't!

Croon knew she was alive. He'd tried to get her back and had failed. Still, she was sure he wouldn't rest until she was back in his bed. If he was a fool, he might come after her on his own, but Reddin Croon was no fool. He had other ways.

Ways that might revolve around her mother.

She had to spend the night at the edge of a hammock and didn't reach the Egret village until late in the afternoon. By then, all she cared about was getting something to drink and eat. The villagers, eager for news about what had happened at Fort Dade, crowded around her. She told them everything she could, all the while looking longingly at a water basket. She was explaining, for at least the third time, that Panther wouldn't be back until he'd met with Osceola when someone gave her a tin cup filled with water. She grabbed it and drank deeply, only then acknowledging the kindness. Winter Rain, who'd listened to her every word, handed her a corn cake. "Do you believe the bluecoats' word?" she asked. "Will Panther be safe?"

The gentle way she spoke Panther's name caught Calida's attention. Winter Rain returned her stare with one that was just as steady, just as intense. Still, her mouth trembled. *She loves him. Winter Rain loves Panther.* "I pray he is," she whispered.

"I have listened to what you said. And I am afraid there will be no peace."

Winter Rain was a child, a girl who knew nothing about the world beyond this isolated village. Only, no matter how much Calida tried to make herself believe that, she couldn't. Winter Rain might be small and slender, but she was old enough to have fallen in love. And wise enough to understand a great deal. "The bluecoats want an end to this fighting."

"Do they?" Winter Rain challenged. "The leaders are proud and arrogant men. *My* people have defied them for years. They will not allow any Seminole to escape their grasp. Just as your master will not allow you to remain apart from him."

She'd spent the night with that thought churning inside her. How dare Winter Rain make her face it again. "The treaty—"

"Ha! The bluecoats have broken treaties before. So have the Seminoles. Gaitor told me about your master's fine land. Reddin Croon is a powerful man, one who can command others to do as he wishes."

"What are you saying?"

Winter Rain stood as tall as she could. Although she was still several inches shorter than Calida, Calida had no idea how to dismiss her presence—even if she wanted to.

"That you should not have come here. That your master will bring many bluecoats here with him, and the blood of our children will flow unless you leave, now."

11

Calida crouched at the edge of the wilderness and stared through dense foliage at Reddin Croon's plantation. She forced herself to take note of the expanded fields where tiny plants pushed their way to the surface. At this distance she couldn't tell what the plants were, but it didn't matter. She'd come here to get her mother and take her north. That was all she dared think about.

After too many long minutes of silent watching and listening, she slid to her right until she could clearly see the house where she'd once had to live. She'd burned the cast-off cotton dress Mistress Liana had given her and was now clad in one of her two loose, colorful dresses. This one had long sleeves, which covered her arms and protected them from insects. She'd fashioned the skirt so that it ended at her knees, since one any longer would tangle in the heavy brush. Although she could have made the journey without shoes, she wore leather moccasins because she could run faster in them. She carried a small bundle on her back that contained dried fish and berries and new clothes and shoes for her mother. She also had her knife because that way she could more easily harvest eatable plants. The knife, if she so needed it, would also serve as a weapon.

Could she kill?

A porch had been added to the front of the house. The horse corrals had been reinforced so that one side no longer sagged. Other than that, nothing had changed. One thing—Mistress Liana was dead and Reddin Croon was somewhere with the army.

Continuing her slow circle of the plantation, she spotted several slaves working just outside the lean-to where harvested vegetables were stored until they could be taken to St. Augustine. Some of the slaves were repairing a wagon. If Isiah Yongue was a wealthy man, wouldn't he have bought a new wagon? But maybe he didn't believe in spending money unless it was absolutely necessary. Maybe that was why he had so much wealth.

The ways of white men didn't matter. She was here to rescue her mother, to find the Freedom Trail Gaitor had told her about and stop thinking about Panther.

If anything, the slave quarters looked even more dilapidated than they had the last time she'd seen them. Parts of two roofs were missing, probably from a storm. She didn't need anyone to tell her that Isiah Yongue didn't care about his slaves' comfort. Anger coiled into a knot inside her. A few months ago it would never have occurred to her to be angry at a white man, because she'd been too afraid of them for that. But she'd tasted freedom, knew what it was to make her own shelter and search for her own food. She wasn't some animal living only for her master's pleasure, and neither were the other Negroes.

Only, how could she give them the freedom she'd found? She couldn't, she admitted. She could only rescue her mother.

Pilar lived alone in a cabin near the edge of the clearing. In the past, Calida had wished her mother lived in the middle of the slave quarters because that way she wouldn't hear so many of the terrifying sounds that came from that dark and frightening place, but Piahokee no longer frightened her.

Piahokee. Panther had given her that word.

Fighting free of thoughts of him, she willed herself to wait. This morning she'd rubbed crushed ghost-orchids over her arms and legs and neck to kill her scent and make her more a part of Piahokee in case Isiah Yongue had brought hunting dogs with him, but she knew better than to draw attention to herself in any way. Patiently, she waited.

An hour later, she left her shelter and slipped, using the shadows, to her mother's shack. In that time she'd learned that all the field hands were at work and the Negro woman in charge of the children had taken them to the road leading to the plantation. All but those too young to do anything except toddle carried cutting tools. Obviously, they'd been instructed to attack the vines and brush that constantly threatened to cover the muddy ruts.

She hadn't seen her mother.

Fear had an acid taste, which clogged her mouth and throat. There'd been no movement from her mother's cabin. If Pilar was dead—

Breathing deeply through her mouth and nose, Calida crept closer until she could look in the small opening that passed for a window. It was so dark inside that she wondered if daylight ever reached that tiny space. She turned her head first one way and then the other as she strained to catch any sound. She heard or imagined she heard breathing. No one spoke. No one walked about. Moving carefully, she rounded the corner and closed her hand over the frayed rope that served as a door handle. Her fingers tightened, but for several seconds she couldn't make herself pull. Her hard heartbeat reminded her of a bullfrog's courting sound. She needed to hear her mother's voice, to assure herself that she was all right and that no one was with her. She didn't want to be alone in this. She needed Panther. Panther, who feared nothing.

Finally, because she had no choice, she tugged on the rope until she'd produced a narrow opening and slipped inside. The cabin felt cool in contrast to the hot, humid day. Still, heavy, damp air had found its way through the rough walls. She waited for her eyes to accustom themselves to the gloom, breathed deeply again, and tried to find her mother in the smells that reached her. There was something, a presence. A quiet and gentle presence.

"Calida?"

Relief spread so quickly through her legs that she nearly collapsed. The harsh whisper came from the far corner of the room, where Pilar had made herself a bed from cast-off blankets and sacking. "Ma-ma? How are you?"

"Fine. Fine."

She wasn't fine, but then they both knew that. Hurrying over to the small mound, she dropped to her knees and pulled the too-frail figure to her breast. Her mother wasn't supposed to feel like an old woman. "What is it? Please, what's wrong with you?"

"You's alive. Praise the lord. You's alive."

Her mother hadn't known whether her daughter had survived the journey into the wilderness. Was that what had sickened her? Feeling so guilty that she wanted to scream from it, Calida sobbed into her mother's thin shoulder while Pilar's frail body shook with tears of her own. She had no idea how long they clung to each other, how long it took to put the past few months behind them. Finally though, her back protesting from the effort of holding her mother, she gently laid her back on her bed. To her relief, Pilar sat up. "You's here. I nevers— I tols myself I was never gonna see you again and that it din matter as long as you was alive. But my heart wouldn't listen."

My heart wouldn't listen. "Mama, what's wrong with you?"

"I'm gettin' old, child."

"No you aren't! You're young. You—"

"What are you doin' here? Did he grab—"

"No. No one knows I'm here."

"Then why?"

Didn't her mother know love had brought her here? She'd tell her everything in a minute, but first she had to hear her mother's voice, to pretend that it was strong again. Wondering who was the mother and who was the child now, she ordered Pilar to tell her what was wrong with her. Swamp sickness, Pilar said, shrugging. "The midwife's been here. She says it ain't nuttin' but this damnable swampland's gettin' to me. There ain't nuttin' she can do fur me."

"Mama?" With an effort, she kept her voice low and calm. "I was more dead than alive when I reached the Seminole village. I didn't care whether I lived or died, I was that far gone. No, it's all right," she assured her mother when Pilar placed a trembling hand on her cheek. "I'm all right. Stronger than I've ever been. I'm not afraid of Piahokee anymore."

"Piahokee?"

"Everglades. The Seminoles have healers, men and women who know which plants and herbs cure sicknesses." She clasped her mother's hand, careful not to hold it too tightly. If she took her back to Panther's village, Croon might find her there and exact his revenge—not just on her, but on the entire clan. But if she didn't do this, would her mother die? "They can help you."

"No, child."

"You don't know that. You haven't seen what they're capable of."

"That's not what I's talkin' bout, girl. Tell me, what'd you comes here for?"

"To see you. To make you free."

Fear contorted Pilar's gentle features. "I tols you not to ever come back. That the only way you gonna live is by stayin' wid the Indians."

"I couldn't do that. Mama, I love you."

"Ah, girl. If I was dead, you'd be truly free."

If you were dead, I'd have no one. "Don't talk like that, please. I'm not sure how long it'd take. Probably three days." *Or longer if you're too weak.* "But I know the way to one of the villages. They'll take care of you. Make you well."

Tears pooled in Pilar's eyes. Again she pressed her dry, too-hot hand against Calida's cheek. "I cain't, Calida. Don' you see that? I cain't."

The village felt different, as if something was missing from it. Determined to learn what that was, Panther strode into the clearing. He was immediately surrounded by clan members eager for information. Taking advantage of his height, he looked around for Gaitor but couldn't find him. There was no sign of Calida either. Because he knew how important his information was for the tribe, he forced himself to give them a thorough explanation of what had happened since he left Fort Dade. It had taken him the better part of two days to reach Osceola's village. Several lesser chiefs had been with the

Seminole leader, all of them eager to hear what had happened during the treaty talks and to watch Osceola's reaction. At first Osceola had maintained that the Seminoles would honor their agreement to leave their ancestors' land, but in private, he'd told Panther that he still didn't trust the bluecoats' word. It would, therefore, take the Seminoles a long time to get ready to leave—time that would allow them to watch and learn.

Panther told his tribe nothing about that private conversation, but then he didn't need to because only a fool would believe the enemy now spoke with an honest tongue. Maybe the Egret clan would indeed leave the village for unknown land to the west, but if they did, it wouldn't be for a while.

Once he'd satisfied the others' curiosity, he asked about Gaitor. No one had seen him. For all they knew, the Negro was still at Fort Dade. "I will go there tomorrow," Panther announced. "I must see with my own eyes that he is well and safe."

Two of the younger braves offered to accompany him, and although he could travel more swiftly alone, he told them to be ready to leave at daylight. If Gaitor had been imprisoned, he would need help.

Only when he announced that he was hungry and tired was he left alone. He wanted to ask about Calida, but if anyone knew where she was, they would have told him. Their silence meant only one thing. The brave and beautiful runaway was no longer among the Egret clan. Feeling old, he stepped inside his *chickee*. His bed called to his weary body, but he knew sleep would evade him. Someone had placed fresh water and food on one of his two shelves. He picked up a corn cake and popped it into his mouth, thinking not about who had done this for him, but that Calida had learned to slowly work moisture into dry cornmeal until it stuck together and could be carried wherever a person went.

A prickling along his spine caused him to turn around. For a moment, he told himself that the figure standing in the sun was Calida. She'd waited until he was alone, come to him alone. Then Winter Rain told him she had placed the food and water there while he was talking to the others. She hoped her gift pleased him.

"Thank you."

"It is so good to see you, Panther. I feared for your life."

Feared? Not sure how to respond, he turned his attention to the food. After drinking his fill, he took another bite. Winter Rain hadn't moved. He'd occasionally seen Calida and Winter Rain together. Calida might have confided in Winter Rain in the way women sometimes did. "When did she leave?" he asked.

"Calida?" Winter Rain shrugged. "Three, maybe four days ago. When I got up one morning, she was gone."

"You do not know where she went?"

"The runaway does not tell me what is in her mind, Panther. She took of our kindness. The healer gave her back her life, and in turn she left. I do not concern myself with one who does not belong. I would think you would do the same."

He wished he could. At the moment he wished he had never seen her. But he had, and he couldn't stop the questions ricocheting inside him. He tried to go back in his thoughts to that day at Fort Dade, but so much had happened since then that it was difficult. She'd been afraid, and he didn't blame her. After all, Reddin Croon had been there. Was that it? She'd been so afraid that she'd been incapable of thinking of anything except hiding from the man?

"She said nothing to you? You are certain of that?"

"Panther, she is not worthy of you. I—"

A shout of greeting cut through whatever Winter Rain had been going to say. The sound swung them both around, and to his great relief, Panther saw that Gaitor had just entered the clearing. He hurried to his friend's side and clamped his hand on his shoulder in greeting. Drying sweat clung to Gaitor's dark body, and he breathed rapidly. "Tell me," Panther insisted. "What have you seen?"

"Slave owners!" Gaitor spat. "Their smell fills the air 'til I thinks I be sick."

"Slave owners? What are they—"

"Gives me a minute." Gaitor leaned forward, planted his broad hands on his knees. "I's gettin' too old ta be runnin' like that. General Jesup, he done changed his mind. Them white men, they been railin' at him till there was nuthin' fur him to do but 'gree with em."

"Agree about what?" Panther asked although he already knew.

"Runaways." Gaitor swept his eyes over the Negroes crowded

around them. "Jesup, he says iffen a man can proves a slave b'longs ta him, then he's 'titled ta him. It don' matter none how long a darkie's been with the Seminoles, he's got ta go back."

A man cursed. A woman sobbed and clutched her child to her breast. Even the Seminoles who for the most part let the Negroes go their own way muttered that they'd known the army leaders couldn't be trusted. Despite his rage at having been deceived, Panther agreed. However, at the moment all that mattered was that Calida wasn't here. Reddin Croon couldn't get his hands on her.

Unless—

"Did General Jesup say whether he would help the slave owners get back their property?" he asked.

"They wanted him to, but he said that ain't no business o' the army. I thinks, I thinks he wants to wash his hands of the whole mess, but he cain't. What he says is, when the Seminoles come to turns themselves in to be taken to the reservation, that's when white folks can claim what's theirs."

"And if the Seminoles reject the peace plan?"

"Then there's gonna be more fightin'. You knows that, Panther. Jesup says he wants to talk to all the chiefs again."

"Does he think we are dogs waiting to do as he commands?"

That made Gaitor laugh. "I don' ask him. Let him finds that out on his own."

Panther agreed. However, he was only one chief. No matter how tired he was, no matter how much he wanted to find Calida, he knew what was expected of him. The other clan leaders would be joining Osceola as soon as they heard that the bluecoats had gone back on their word. He had no choice but to return to his chief. He told Gaitor that. Then, not caring who else heard, he told him that although Reddin Croon might try to find the Egret clan's village, it wouldn't do him any good because Calida wasn't here.

Concern replaced the exhaustion that had been in Gaitor's eyes. "Where is she? She got back, din' she?"

Panther reassured him of that. However, she'd left again. Where she'd gone, no one knew. Gaitor's only reaction was to let his arms sag at his side. "The Freedom Trail," he muttered. "That's where she went. I hopes . . ."

"You hope what?"

Before Gaitor could answer, Winter Rain stepped forward and touched Panther's forearm. "I remember." Looking up at Panther, she spoke earnestly. "I was so relieved to see you that I forgot. But I remember now. She was pulling her things together, looking frightened, muttering that she had to go north."

"You didn't try to stop her?" Gaitor insisted.

"No! She wouldn't listen to me. She kept saying"—Winter Rain pressed the heel of her hand against her forehead—"she kept saying she had to get where her master couldn't find her."

"Her master." Gaitor made the words sound like a curse. "Panther, he done left 'fore I did. Said he had to git home, that there was things he had to do at his place. Iffen he's found her—"

"No!" Winter Rain interrupted. "She would not go back there. She is terrified of him. All she talked about was getting away. Panther?" She squeezed his forearm. "She is gone. When Reddin Croon learns she is no longer among us, we will be safe. He will have no reason to come after us. It is better this way. Much better."

He had to go to Osceola's village. As war leader, he knew his responsibilities, but his mind had filled with images of Calida stumbling through Piahokee as she tried to find her way to freedom.

Freedom? Would she ever find it or—

A baby sobbed, capturing his thoughts. Glancing in that direction, he spotted Morning Doe exposing her breast so her baby could suckle. He felt the others' eyes on him, waiting for him, but all he could think about was the Seminole mother and her infant, the unbreakable bond between them.

Calida wouldn't leave Piahokee without trying to take her mother with her.

The sound of pounding hooves spun Calida around. Her first instinct was to run to her mother's cabin, but she forced herself to remain hidden. As the sound came closer, she ordered herself to relax and accept. She'd been waiting for this moment for days now and shouldn't be surprised. Still, knowing Reddin Croon was so close that he could bring her down with his musket made thinking difficult. On hands and knees, she slipped as close to the clearing as she dared.

A beetle scurried away, but she didn't concern herself with whether there was another. Croon and several men wearing bits and pieces of uniforms were riding down the road leading to the plantation. Although it was only midmorning, sweat slicked their faces and the horses' bodies.

Instinct screamed at her to run, but she'd spent the last four nights ministering to her mother and wouldn't turn her back on love and responsibility. During the days she'd remained hidden nearby, hoping against hope that her mother would feel well enough to go with her. Although Pilar's fever had subsided, she still couldn't keep down much of what Calida tried to get her to eat and was content to spend most of her time in bed.

The squeak of leather coupled with the horses' loud breathing convinced her that they wouldn't hear any faint sound she might make. Taking advantage of that, she circled the plantation until she was as close as she dared get to the main house. By then Croon and the other men had dismounted, and Croon was yelling at the slaves to tend to the animals. When she looked over at the cabins, she saw her mother at the doorway, one hand tight around her throat, the other gripping the door so she could stand. *Go,* Pilar had insisted just last night. *For sweet Jesus's sake, save yourself.* Calida hadn't, because one more day, one more herb gathered in Piahokee might have given her mother enough strength and they'd run together.

"What are you doing?" Isiah Yongue bellowed as he emerged from the house. He was barechested, his pants unbuttoned. Calida had no doubt that he'd been with the young house servant he'd brought with him. "You can't just ride in here and—"

"The hell I can't. This is my place, in case you've forgotten," Croon yelled back. The air between the two men seemed heavy and dark.

"Whose place?" Yongue taunted. "In case *you've* forgotten, my daughter's dowry is what paid for it. I've been making sure it doesn't—"

Croon silenced him with a curse. Calida couldn't tear her eyes from her master. She hadn't noticed this at Fort Dade, but he seemed less loose and sloppy, more like a military man than he had in the past. His belly no longer hung down over his pants. She'd always been afraid of him, and despite herself, that feeling increased today.

"If you will shut up for a minute," Croon was saying, "I've got something to tell you. This so-called treaty General Jesup tried to shove down everyone's throat is blowing up in our faces."

"What are you talking about?"

Calida was afraid the two men would go inside where she couldn't hear, but although that was obviously what the older man wanted, Croon made an insistent gesture to the watching slaves. Obeying, they slipped closer. He waited until all except for the distant fieldhands were within earshot before speaking. From where she crouched, Calida ignored the insects buzzing around her and prayed Croon wouldn't notice her mother's agitation. If only Pilar would stop looking around her, if only she would drop her hand from her throat.

Not that she blamed her mother, because at any minute someone might spot Calida.

"I'm talking about that insane document Jesup got the Seminoles to sign," Croon said, his voice carrying. "Not that it matters, because he's changed his mind. Finally."

Once again Isiah insisted he get to the point. Croon laughed, then leaned close to his father-in-law, speaking so low that she couldn't hear. Frustration ate at her, because whatever they were saying had everything to do with the war with the Seminoles, with Panther.

Panther. She'd fought his memory during the day, but at night while she lay beside her mother, her mind had filled with images of him.

"The Seminole leaders, do they know?" Isiah asked.

"If they don't, they will soon enough."

Risking everything, Calida inched closer. If everyone's attention hadn't been riveted on the two men, someone probably would have spotted her.

"What's going to happen then?" Isiah insisted. "If the Seminoles refuse to give up their slaves—"

"Some of 'em will; some of 'em don't give a damn."

Isiah nodded. "In other words, this is going to divide the Seminole nation. That's what you're saying, isn't it?"

Croon shrugged. Calida guessed he was doing that to frustrate his father-in-law, but it didn't matter. All that did was that what she'd feared would come true had. Because of pressure from slave owners, the runaways wouldn't be allowed to go to Oklahoma with the Seminoles. Croon was right. Some of the clan leaders would put their people first and not care what happened to the Negroes. But Panther—

Panther would never turn the Negroes over to their former masters. As a consequence, the Egret clan, those who stayed with Panther at least, would become fugitives.

It didn't matter. She had to save her mother. That was the only thing she dared think about.

Forcing herself to concentrate, she looked over at her mother's cabin. Pilar, her eyes wide with fright, stared at her.

Don't. Please! If Croon sees you—

12

Calida felt a branch give under her foot. Thanks to the spongy ground, it made no noise, but she might not be so lucky the next time. Inch by careful inch, she backed away from where everyone had assembled. Croon had ridden in with ten soldiers, but they grew in number in her mind until she felt as if she was looking at an entire army. They would hunt her down like dogs hunted wild animals. If she was lucky, they'd tear her apart, and if she wasn't, Croon would pull them off her, and she'd be forced back into the house, where—

There'd been a dog with Croon and the soldiers, but she'd paid it little mind. Where her former master had gotten it didn't matter; she couldn't let herself think about what use he might put it to.

Panther.

Shaking herself free of the name, the memory, she forced herself to take slow and careful note of her surroundings. She could no longer see the open and cultivated land that surrounded Reddin Croon's house, but she could still hear the murmur of voices. Croon and his father-in-law were continuing their argument. The soldiers had joined in, each of them announcing their reaction to the change in policy. She shouldn't have panicked. At the moment, no one cared about or even gave her a thought.

No one except for her mother.

She couldn't leave. Once, because she'd had no choice, she'd fled this awful place, but she wouldn't do that again because her mother was all she had.

Angry at herself for letting love and fear cloud her need to make decisions, she slipped even farther into the dense brush. Unless a great deal had changed about her former master, he would spend the rest of the day attending to his physical comforts. Once he'd cleaned up and had something to eat, he would start to drink. No. There was a new female house servant, the one Isiah Yongue had brought with him. It didn't matter who the girl belonged to, Croon would demand to use her, and Isiah might not care. In fact, he might decide that his son-in-law would be in a better frame of mind for thinking once certain needs had been tended to. As for the rest of the soldiers, they would probably content themselves with the women fieldhands.

Furious at the thought of how little say the slaves had in this, she clenched her fists until some of her anger subsided. Pilar would know freedom! If it took the last breath in her, she would make sure her mother discovered how sweet freedom could taste.

The Freedom Trail. North.

Not back to the Seminole village, because their presence would only jeopardize the men, women, and children who'd given her shelter when she would have died without them.

Not back to Panther because—

Images of his strength and courage lapped around her and threatened to distract her from what had to be done. She would wait until night, until she was certain that Croon and the other whites had passed out from drinking or lust or both. Then she'd slip into her mother's cabin and insist she leave with her—carry her on her back if that's what it took.

Filled with resolve, she headed toward the far side of the quicksand area where she'd made a shelter of sorts for herself. Bit by bit over the past few days she'd accumulated food, clothing, even another knife to sustain her mother and herself during the long journey north. She'd spend the rest of the day getting those things together.

Tonight—

A sharp, distant braying sound splintered her thoughts. As she listened, the howling became louder and more frantic. Heat washed through her but was immediately chased away by a chill that reached clear to the middle of her bones.

Wondering if the dog had picked up her scent, she forced herself to concentrate. The beast could simply be after a deer or rabbit. That hope died when she heard hoofbeats and Croon's sharp voice urging the dog on.

Then Croon called out her name.

He hadn't seen her, but maybe the hound—What did it matter? Run! She had to run!

Piahokee stretched out beyond her, a vast wilderness capable of hiding entire Seminole villages. But the dog was getting closer and Piahokee couldn't shelter her unless she headed into the quicksand, and the quicksand did to the dog what it had done to Mistress Liana's horse.

Fear surged through her even as she jumped to her feet and began running. She'd spent enough time around the quicksand in the past few days that she'd begun to learn where it was safe to step and what was bottomless and deadly. Did she know enough?

Forcing herself not to panic, she kept her pace at a fast trot so she could concentrate on where she was going. Croon had talked long and often about how keen a good hound dog's scent was. They were fast. There was no way she could outrun this one. Her only chance—

Only chance . . .

Mud gripped her right foot. She pulled free and plunged ahead. The dog. She had to stay in this slime until it trapped the dog. Less than a minute later, it happened again. Planting her weight on her left leg, she concentrated on yanking her trapped foot out of the warm ooze, but there was no safe place to stand, nothing solid. The panic she'd denied herself reasserted itself. Once, a thousand years ago it now seemed, someone had told her that if she didn't yank but slowly, calmly worked against the mud, she wouldn't become trapped, but how did one remain calm?

Looking down, she saw that both feet were now covered halfway up her calves. She wanted to shriek in terror, but there was no one—only the dog, and with it, Reddin Croon.

Mama, I'm sorry! I tried. Oh sweet Jesus, I tried.

No! She wouldn't give up like some speared fish! Working with her anger, she tried to stretch out on her belly. If she spread out her weight, it would slow her sinking. The stench of things rotting filled her nostrils, but she ignored it. Her mother needed her. She wasn't ready to die.

She wasn't!

By wrenching her body around, she managed to lower herself to her knees. She tried to stretch out, but the quicksand refused to let go of her feet. When she placed her elbows on the ground, warm, wet fingers of ooze instantly gripped them.

Don't panic! Oh god, don't panic!

"Calida."

Deep, calm, urgent and reassuring. She absorbed all that and more in the single word. Panther was half shadow, half reality. Later, if there was a later, she'd ask him how he'd found her, but for now, nothing mattered except staring at the thick stick he'd extended toward her. The braying echoed against the trees and slammed into her ears. Propelled by the sound, she wrapped her fingers around the stick and willed herself not to kick at the imprisoning slime. Panther's pull was relentless, and it was all she could do not to lose her grip. When slop sucked at her thighs, instead of allowing herself to think about how much more of her had become trapped, she looked up at Panther. Fixed her entire attention on him.

"Do not fight! Hold on. Just hold on."

She did because he'd told her to and she would do anything for him. Her skirt's hem felt weighted, but Panther, standing on a finger of dry land, continued to pull her toward him. It seemed to take forever. The awful howling grew, held—held. Turned into a frightened yowl.

"He is caught," Panther whispered. "Hold on, Calida. Hold on."

She couldn't feel her feet. Knowing what had to be done, she stretched out on the stinking mud. She felt bathed in it. And then her right knee touched solid ground. Teeth clamped against the scream that needed to break free, she waited while Panther released the stick, reached out, clamped his hands around her wrists, and pulled.

She was free! Dripping filthy water and ooze but free!

Blind to any other emotion, she scrambled to her feet and clung to him. His arms were around her, gripping so tight that it should hurt—would have hurt if she'd been capable of thinking about such things.

"You're safe, Calida. Thank you, Panther spirit. Safe!"

This was a clan *tastanagee?* He sounded as frightened as she felt. She wanted to look into his eyes to see if they mirrored what she'd heard in his voice, but she'd pressed her cheek against his chest. His warmth flowed into her; she couldn't get enough of it.

He'd saved her life. Come to her like some protecting angel and saved her life.

"Calida. Calida. I thought—thought . . . We have to leave. Now."

Of course. Why had she allowed precious seconds to pass before realizing that? The dog hadn't stopped howling—screaming, really. She heard the distant bellow that was Croon's angry voice and guessed he was trying to free his animal. If he was careless—please let him be careless—the quicksand would capture him as well.

"How—" Panther pushed her away from him, and for a moment the loss felt so intense that she couldn't think. "How did you find me?" she finally remembered to ask.

"I have been watching you."

"Watching? I don't—"

"Later. Now we run."

When, finally, Panther believed they'd put enough distance between themselves and the plantation, he stopped beside a creek so Calida could wash off the sticky mud that had come close to killing her. After scrubbing her arms and legs until her skin was chapped and red, she stood at the edge while she wrung water out of her skirt. The effort exposed her upper thighs and showed the muscles in her arms. He couldn't take his eyes off her, couldn't kill the image of her plunging into Piahokee when she realized the dog was after her and then her desperate and yet controlled struggle to free herself.

If she'd gotten any farther into the quicksand, or if he hadn't been so close, she would be dead.

She turned toward him, eyes big and dark and without the fear that had ruled her when he came across her after she'd fled her master. This was his land, the world he'd always known, but she was no longer a stranger in it.

"You shouldn't be here," she said, her voice soft. "I heard Croon talking about—there won't be a peaceful surrender."

"No. There will not be."

"Then—" She shook out her skirt. He watched the still wet fabric as it traced the outline of her legs. "What are you doing here?"

He couldn't tell her everything, not when he didn't understand himself. "I knew you would not leave without your mother."

"And you came looking for me?" She didn't seem to know what to do with her hands. For a moment she let them dangle at her sides, then she pressed one against her waist while the other played with her dripping hair. "Panther, why?"

Why? "Maybe so I would know whether you were leading Croon back to us."

She tensed at that, and her eyes became like a building storm. But although he hated seeing her reaction, that had been part of his reason. He wouldn't lie to her. "I wouldn't," she insisted after too long a silence. "He'd have to kill me before I betrayed your people."

"You do not know that. A man like Reddin Croon has ways of turning silence into words." He watched to see if she would shrink from what he'd just said. She didn't.

"I know me. I would never . . . Thank you." She took a step toward him, then stopped. Only then did he notice the slight tremor around her mouth. "You saved my life."

He didn't want to think about that. Glad for the distance between them, he made a show of studying her legs. "You can travel?" he asked. "You are not hurt?"

"No. I'm fine. Tired but— Travel? What are you talking about?"

"We must return to the village."

She didn't immediately say anything. Instead, she concentrated on him just as intensely as he'd done her. When she was through, it seemed to him that she was less sure of herself, as if she'd found something in him that made her uneasy. That should not be. She was brave, the bravest woman he had ever known. "I can't."

"Calida, the Freedom Trail is not safe for you. Croon will let many people know how much he wants you back. They will be watching for you."

His argument seemed to have no impact on her. He wanted to tell her that many escaped slaves never made it to freedom and because Croon had both money and connections, it would be more precarious for her than for most. But watching her with her wet hair splayed over her slender shoulders, he couldn't. "The Egret clan is no longer at the village," he said. "I have ordered them to move deeper into the wilderness."

"So they'll be safe?"

"I pray they will be safe."

She nodded, the gesture seeming to encompass her entire body. She had nothing, just the clothes she wore. When he reached the plantation this morning, he'd spotted her small pile of belongings and guessed she was collecting those things for the long journey north. She'd been there for several days, not leaving, risking everything by staying. He understood why. She was determined to take her mother with her.

"You cannot return to her. *He* won't let you."

"No. No." Wrapping her arms around her waist, she bent over as if trying to protect herself from further hurt. "I have to—she can't . . ."

"Listen to me, Calida." He wanted to touch her and take away a little of her pain, but she looked so distant and fragile. "He knows why you were there. They will find your belongings. He will never let your mother out of his sight."

"No. No. Panther, if he hurts—"

Taking her in his arms, he held her stiff body. He'd carried her when she was more dead than alive and should be used to the feel of her, but this was different, unsettling and yet what he wanted, what he needed. "You cannot help her. If you try, he will kill you."

"I don't care!"

I do. "You would lay down your life? I think not, Calida. Would that save your mother?"

"N-no."

"Would she find peace?"

"Stop it. I don't want to hear—"

Although she pushed against him, he refused to release her, and after a moment the fight went out of her. She looked up at him, so close that her features were a blur. Still, her tense and trembling body told him everything he needed to know. Much as she hated to admit it, she knew he was right. "Later, when he has gone, you can return for her," he told her. "But now, all you can do is stay alive."

"I tried," she whispered, and he wondered if she'd heard what he'd just said. "I begged her to come with me. But she's sick. Swamp sickness. I—I gave her what I could—herbs and plants I took from Piahokee. She's so weak."

He nearly pointed out that her mother could be dying, but she must have already considered that possibility. She wasn't crying. If she did, maybe when the tears were over she would feel better, but she was becoming like a warrior, holding her emotions inside. Trapped within her, they might make her strong, or they might feed and fester until they destroyed her.

"I make you a promise, Calida. Somehow I will let your mother know you are all right."

It had been dark for a long time. Calida lay beside him, sleeping. She'd said almost nothing all the time they were walking, and he guessed she hadn't been able to chase her mother from her mind. It was possible that Croon would torture Pilar in an attempt to get her to tell him what she knew about where Calida had gone. Calida had to have been thinking the same thing, sick at heart, and scared and helpless.

At least the long hours of walking had worn her out enough that she'd been able to fall asleep. Fear would return as soon as she woke, but for now, she looked like an innocent child.

No, not a child, Panther admitted. They'd stopped on a small hammock made up of strangler fig and pigeon plum trees. They grew far enough apart that the full moon reached the ground and caressed her features. He didn't want thoughts of her to fill his mind this way. Hadn't he told her he'd come after her so she wouldn't jeopardize the clan's safety? Now that they were together and heading back to his people, he should be thinking about the future.

Not how the moon made her skin look like still, smooth water.

Angry at something he refused to put a name to, he propped himself up on his elbow and continued to regard her. Gaitor loved her. Gaitor had wanted to be the one to try to find her. Why hadn't he let him then?

The answer was out there somewhere, or perhaps the truth lay within him.

The night was alive. The sounds that had been part of him since birth echoed around him and he briefly lost himself in them. As a child, there'd been nothing to fear except alligators and big cats, and witches and ghosts. He'd learned which plants to avoid and which fed his body. The shamans had told him stories of Seminole beginnings, and from those stories he'd learned how to walk a path that pleased the spirits. He'd filled his medicine bag with panther hair and sacred stones and thus had no reason to fear witches or ghosts.

But life was no longer that simple, because the army pursued them.

The whisper of a groan pulled him from his thoughts. Calida had stirred, the movement easing her skirt farther up her leg. Even before going on his quest for his protector spirit, he'd been aware of a girl's laughter, long arms and legs, a feminine smile. Those girls had been members of his clan, and although their growing up fascinated him, he remembered when they too were children. There was no mystery to them.

Calida was mystery.

She groaned again, the sound soft and yet filled with anguish. He leaned closer but held back from disturbing her. Dreams were messages from the spirits. It was not right to step between a person and those messages. Nightmares were different, but he didn't yet know what was causing her restlessness.

"No. N-no."

"Calida," he whispered. "Can you hear me?"

"Go—leave me. No!"

He called her name again, his voice still low. As before, she paid him no attention. "No," she hissed, more strongly this time. Her eyes were half open now but unfocused. Certain that the spirits hadn't been trying to reach her, he started to touch her, then stopped because sometimes there was honesty in nightmares.

"You can't. Can't. I will . . ."

"Will what?"

"Kill."

He opened his mouth to ask her what she meant, but before he could, her eyes shot open, and she stared at him in slowly dawning comprehension. He watched as tension seeped out of her body. He now regretted that he hadn't taken her in his arms and offered her comfort, but it was too late. She was once again in control of her thoughts, determined and strong.

"You called out," he explained. "A nightmare."

"I don't . . ." she began, and he thought she was going to tell him that she didn't remember it. Instead, she slowly sat up, pulled her legs tight against her body, and clamped her arms around her knees. She stared out at the night. He wanted to turn her toward him so he would know the truth in her eyes, but maybe she needed to keep that from him.

"I'm never free," she whispered. "No matter how much I try to deny what I did, it always comes back to me at night."

"We are unarmed in sleep, Calida. We cannot protect ourselves from what happens then."

"No." She rested her chin on her knees. "We can't."

She reminded him of a little girl torn from her mother's side. He expected her to tell him she couldn't go on with him after all, that she had to return to her mother. He didn't know what he would do then, whether he would force her and thus risk her hatred.

"Gaitor waits for you," he said, when that was the last thing he wanted to tell her. "He sent a message."

"A message?" she asked without looking at him.

"That he wants to build you a shelter. That it pains him to see you sleeping outside."

"He's a good man. Good and gentle."

He wanted to spring to his feet and plunge into the jungle because that way he wouldn't have to listen to her. But if he left, she would have to spend the night alone. "There will be no Oklahoma for the Egret clan," he said instead. "You understand that?"

"Because of people like Gaitor and me?"

"That is part of it. Calida, I never wanted to put my mark on the peace paper. I belong here, not—"

She shook her head, causing her hair to fly about. "I'm not worthy. Whatever you decide, don't do it because of me."

She was crying. He heard the emotion in her voice, and when he looked at her again, he thought he saw a glimmer of tears on her cheek. He brushed at the warm moisture. "Your mother would not want you to throw away your life for her. She wants you free. It is the way of a mother to put her children first."

"Don't." She began rocking, the gesture hard as if she wanted to hurt herself. He grabbed her wrists and pulled them off her knees, then yanked her around until she was facing him. The moon told him a great deal. In her dark eyes he found anguish and self-hatred, a woman lost and hurting.

"What is it?" When she didn't try to pull away, he placed her hands flat against his chest so she could take comfort from his warmth. She kept staring at him, not blinking, lips parted and vulnerable. "Calida, there can be truth in the night. Tell me."

"Tell you?" She stared at his chest, then focused on him again. She was still crying, silent tears pooling in her eyes before spilling over. "Tell you? Panther, I . . ."

He wanted to shake her, to threaten not to release her until she told him everything. Instead, he clung to silence because whatever was in her had to come willingly from her lips.

"I—I didn't put *my* children first. I—oh god, I . . ."

"Your children?"

"My babies. Master Croon put them in me and I killed them." Her head snapped back and then fell forward. She looked utterly exhausted. He wanted her to lift her head so he could better judge what was going on inside her, but she didn't.

"Tell me."

"Tell? I wouldn't let them live. Oh god, I wouldn't let them live!"

Acting on instinct, he wrapped his arm around her shoulder and drew her close. Instead of fighting him, she sagged against him. Her tearstained cheek heated his throat. He felt her hair on his chin, and when he lowered his head he was able to run his lips over the soft strands.

"Tell me, Calida." His people called him *tastanagee,* but tonight he felt weak. He hurt for her and could give her nothing except his body. Maybe she could take comfort from it, and maybe nothing would stop her agony. "Tell me about your babies."

"You will hate me. I hate myself."

"Calida. You saved my life when you could have left me for Reddin Croon. I know of your love for your mother. What you did, you must have done because you had no other choice." He'd never talked to a woman about such things and could only pray his words helped. "Did he know?"

"No. He . . ."

"What? Calida, do not stop now."

"He—he would have sold them. Torn them from my arms the moment they were born. I could not—for them to never know me—for them to be alone and frightened . . ."

He felt his grip on her tighten but couldn't make himself relax. He was no longer aware of the moon, the night sounds, even his clan's precarious future. There was only Calida's pain and their shared darkness.

"He—he wouldn't have wanted his wife to know they were his. That's why . . ."

"Why what, Calida?" He hated doing this to her, but her agony was like an infection inside her. Maybe she would be whole only once she'd exposed the wound to the air, to him.

"Why—oh god—why he would never let me keep them."

I will kill him. With my own hands, I will kill him.

13

Gaitor straightened, his senses instantly on the alert. When he spotted his war chief and Calida walk into the small opening where the clan now huddled, he forced himself to relax. Someday, if he lived long enough, he would stop reacting like a runaway.

Someday.

Several of the children called out a greeting. One little boy toddled over to Panther and clamped his arms around his legs to prevent himself from falling. Panther lifted the boy and rested him against his hip, rubbing his nose playfully against the smaller one. The boy giggled. Panther laughed.

Gaitor couldn't take his eyes off Calida. He took careful note of the way she watched Panther, her fisted hands, her painful attempt at a smile. Panther glanced at her, returned his attention to the boy, looked at her again. Then after saying something Gaitor couldn't hear, Panther handed the boy to Calida. She looked as if taking the wiggling burden was the last thing she wanted to do, but when Panther continued to insist, she held out her arms. The boy studied her gravely but didn't draw away.

Panther had found her, brought her back to where she belonged. There was no joy in either of their faces, and yet they stood close to

each other, communicating in a way Gaitor couldn't understand. He
didn't try to join those gathering around Panther and Calida. Sooner
or later his chief would look around and spot him. Until then, he
would watch and learn.

Questions were being thrown at Panther one after another until,
if it were him, he would have insisted on silence. Instead, Panther
patiently answered each and every one while Calida stood nearby,
her head cocked to one side as she tried to make sense of the Seminole language. Although her arms must be feeling his weight by now,
she still held the little boy. The child no longer leaned away from
her. Instead, he placed his hands on her shoulder to help balance
himself. She looked over at the boy and smiled. Gaitor felt his body
stiffen. Calida had never smiled like that at him.

Why had she willingly returned?

What had happened between her and Panther during their days
and nights together?

When, if ever, would she look around for him?

The final question, the one that in the end was the most important, gnawed at him until he wanted to stomp it into the ground.
When his wife had been torn from his arms, he'd vowed to never
love again because that was the only way he could survive. Then he'd
allowed Calida to get close to him, dropped his barriers.

How could he erect them again?

At length, Panther's eyes locked with his, but the war chief made
no move to come closer, and because he needed time with his
thoughts, Gaitor remained where he was. Finally, Calida handed the
child over to its mother. Although the two women smiled at each
other, he didn't think either of them spoke. He wondered if there
was a language between women that revolved around children and
needed no words.

Eager to be distracted, he looked behind him and discovered that
he wasn't the only one who hadn't joined those crowded around the
war chief. Winter Rain stood at the edge of the wilderness. Behind
her grew a large, smooth-barked gumbo-limbo tree, which cast its
shadow over her. Her eyes were fixed on Panther.

While the rest of the clan had been making its way through the
jungle toward the small clearing, Winter Rain had gone to visit her

father at Osceola's village. She must have just returned. Eager for news of Osceola, he started toward her. He stopped when he realized she still wasn't aware of his presence, although he'd made no attempt at stealth.

She continued to study not the gathered clanspeople but the man who stood in its center. Something about Panther held her attention, something—

"Winter Rain," he called out. After a moment, she tore her eyes off Panther and faced him, reluctantly it seemed. "You's back."

"Yes."

"How is he?"

"He?"

"Osceola," he prompted. "He any worse?"

"Worse? I do not know."

Surely she knew how vital news of the Seminole leader was. "Ya saw him, didn' ya? He have any message for Panther?"

"Panther?" She stared at the *tastanagee* again, mouth tight. "He brought *her* back. Why? She wanted to leave. Why did he not let her go?"

"I don' know. Winter Rain, this is 'portant. What did Osceola say?"

"Osceola? I barely saw him. He stays in his *chickee*. The healer is with him all the time trying to cool his fever. He—he does not look strong enough to walk."

Panther needed to know that.

"My father—my father says that Osceola will become strong again."

"I prays yur father is right."

Winter Rain blinked and then frowned. "You are not sure?"

"I seen swamp fever afore. It comes en goes. Every time it attacks, it leaves a body weaker."

Sighing, she ran her hand through her dark, curly hair. "I spent much time with my father. I have never seen him look so defeated."

"Defeated?" Winter Rain's father had always put him in mind of a shark. It was as if once he'd tasted freedom, he'd made the decision to die rather than lose it again.

"It has already begun to happen," Winter Rain whispered. "My father says that some clans have turned their Negroes over to the army so they will be allowed to go to the reservation."

Although he'd known that would happen, the reality of it rocked him. "What about someone like me, Gaitor?" she asked unexpectedly. "My mother was Seminole, but I look like my father. If the army sees me, will they say I must become a slave?"

He didn't know. In truth, the question had never occurred to him. "What's your papa gonna do? He ain't gonna surrender, is he?"

"No. He chooses death over that."

"So does I."

She stared up at him, her gaze intense. "It's *her* fault. She read the talking leaves and told us the army would allow Negroes to stay with Seminoles. She lied. She—"

"Calida did not lie."

"How do you know? She—"

"I was there, Winter Rain. You wasn't. I knows what happened."

Winter Rain wasn't ready to agree with him. He understood that in the way she held her body, the firm tilt to her chin. "I *have* to talk to him," she said. "My father says he must know what is happening."

Gaitor allowed his attention to be drawn back to Panther and Calida. They continued to stand side by side. Although only Panther was speaking, Calida was obviously part of everything being said. They'd been alone together for two, maybe three nights. In that time—

From the way Panther had kept glancing over at where Gaitor stood, Calida guessed he was waiting for his friend to join the discussion about what the Egret clan was going to do, but Gaitor had remained where he was, just as Winter Rain had done. Only now, hours after they'd returned to the village, were Gaitor and Winter Rain approaching.

"I missed you, my friend," Panther said by way of greeting.

"And I missed you." Gaitor nodded gravely, then stepped back in a gesture designed to leave Winter Rain standing in front of Panther. Calida felt worn out, not just physically but emotionally as well. She deeply regretted having told Panther what she had, and yet maybe she wouldn't have survived if she'd tried to keep the pain wrapped inside her. He'd held her through the night and made it possible for her to finally fall asleep. In the morning, he'd talked about how snails, frogs, turtles, and even alligators dug deep into drying mud during a drought in order to survive. He'd said nothing about unborn babies. She should be grateful and yet—

"I bring a message from my father," Winter Rain said after a prompting from Gaitor.

A moment ago Calida had wanted to leave the others so she could clean up after the long walk, so, away from Panther, she could clear her thoughts. However, before Winter Rain had said more than a half dozen words, that no longer mattered. Three clans had already agreed to the army's new terms. They'd either turned over their Negroes or were making plans to take them to one of the forts. Once that was done, they would begin the long journey to Oklahoma and peace—or at least what they hoped would be peace. Other clans were expected to do the same.

"My father says he will never again allow chains around his wrists," Winter Rain finished. "He would rather be dead. I—maybe I should run with him."

"With him? Why?" Panther asked.

"Because—" Winter Rain's eyes were too large. "Because maybe the army men will look at me and say that I am Negro, not Seminole."

Panther muttered something Calida couldn't hear. He studied not Winter Rain but Gaitor. She needed no explanation to understand the silent message taking place between the two men.

Panther would never turn Gaitor or the other clan Negroes over to the army. The fact that he'd risked his life by coming after her was proof of that. Reddin Croon had always reacted to any sign of rebellion with swift punishment; Reddin Croon and the army were the same.

"Does ya know what ya's doin'?" Gaitor insisted. "This ain't just 'tween you en me. We's talkin' 'bout the whole clan."

"I know."

"Does ya?"

"Yes." Panther sounded weary and determined at the same time.

"I choose freedom. And I promise freedom for all who walk in my footsteps."

Freedom. That, she tried to remind herself, was why she'd come here with Panther. She couldn't help her mother, couldn't reach her without putting both their lives in jeopardy. But was that the only reason? Her mother had given her life. Shouldn't she be willing to surrender that life if it meant giving her mother freedom?

Despite everything Calida had to do, the rest of the day passed slowly. Because Panther was concerned that the army might find this spot, in the morning the clan would be moving even further into Pi-ahokee. As it grew dark, Panther gathered everyone around him and relayed what Winter Rain had told him. Those who wanted to surrender were free to do so. He would even accompany them to within sight of Fort Dade to make sure they got there safely. Those who decided to remain with him needed to prepare themselves for what might be unending flight. No one had said they wanted to go to Fort Dade. Men, women, children, even the clan's oldest members had pledged their allegiance to Panther.

It was, Calida knew, because they believed in him and trusted him to keep them out of the army's hands.

She wished it was that simple for her.

Restless, wishing there was someone she could talk to, she wandered through the hodgepodge of brush shelters that had been thrown up over the last few days and would be abandoned tomorrow. There were few conversations tonight. Those who spoke did so in soft whispers. Even the babies seemed to understand that crying would further burden people who had enough to think about.

Panther and Gaitor as well as some of the other able-bodied men were nowhere in sight. Because Panther hadn't told her what he was going to do, she could only guess that they were studying their surroundings, maybe checking to see if tomorrow's journey would truly be safe.

Winter Rain sat near a large, flat rock on which lay a number of roots and tubers. She was pounding them with a grinding stone. Watching her, Calida recalled the girl's fear that the army would see only her Negro blood. Winter Rain had never felt the bite of a slave chain. She was slender and healthy with a gentle way of carrying her-self that would catch a man's eye. Despite her cooking skills, she wouldn't spend much of her time in her master's kitchen.

Sick at the thought of what Winter Rain might be forced to en-dure at her master's hands, Calida stepped closer. Still, when Win-ter Rain acknowledged her presence, she couldn't bring herself to speak about what was on her mind. Instead, without waiting for an invitation, she sat down near the girl. "What is your father going to do?" she asked. "If Osceola is too sick to fight—"

"My father would rather die than surrender."

Like Panther. "Will he come here? Join the Egret clan?"

"I do not know. Osceola gave him land to farm when he escaped his master. He owes a great deal to him."

But he'd married a woman from the Egret clan and had a daugh-ter by her. Much as Calida wanted Winter Rain to tell her more about what had happened after her mother's death, she didn't feel she knew the younger woman well enough. She watched her in silence for a few minutes, impressed by Winter Rain's economy of move-ment.

"My father wants me to join him," Winter Rain said. "He has al-ways wanted me by his side."

"Are you going to?"

Still looking down, she shrugged. Silence settled over them again, which gave Calida time to think, to remember. Winter Rain's eyes hadn't once left Panther while she told him about what she'd learned from her father. She'd noticed the girl watching Panther before, sensed a disquiet, an eagerness in her manner whenever she was around him. Now, with no sense of shock, she realized Winter Rain loved Panther.

"My place is here," Winter Rain whispered. "I belong with my mother's clan. It is not for me to say what my father should do."

"If Panther wasn't the *tastanagee,* would you feel the same way?"

Her question brought Winter Rain's head up. She seemed torn between anger and determination, reminding Calida of a doe risk-ing her own life to protect her fawn. Only, Panther was no fawn.

"Everyone says that Osceola is the great Seminole leader, but that is only because he has long spoken to the army men, because he has always raised his voice to say what is on his mind. Is he a skilled hunter? No. Does he have the courage to take his clan where it has never gone before? No. Those things are what Panther does."

And you love him for that.

Unable to think of anything that might keep the conversation going, Calida tried to concentrate on the steady rhythm of Winter Rain's work. Yes, she was little more than a child, but she had skills she might never have, and she belonged heart and soul with the Egret clan. She was worthy of Panther; she hadn't ended two innocent, helpless lives.

The air reeked of Indians. No matter where Reddin Croon looked, he could see the half-naked, stinking savages. General Jesup, lucky for him, was inside Fort Mellon's excuse for officers quarters. It might be hot and sticky in there, but at least the general didn't have to look at Seminoles. Didn't have to smell them.

Thoughts of how much he wanted to run a bayonet through every one of the three hundred Seminoles who'd come here filled Reddin's mind as he made his way through the seated and standing groups. Osceola was camped near the officers' cabin along with other such noteworthy leaders as Arpeika, Coa Hadjo, Emathla, Tuskinia, and Coacoochee. General Jesup was so damn proud of what had been accomplished; it didn't matter to him that Panther and his clan continued to defy the army's orders to surrender.

General Jesup was a fool.

Only by clenching his teeth until his jaw ached was he able to squelch his impulse to kick at the scrawny brave staring up at him from where he'd plopped himself in the all but boiling mud. These so-called human beings were worse than animals. At least the creatures who made their home in the god-awful Everglades knew enough to run from armed men. The Seminoles, however—hell, they acted like the army was here to wait on them. They didn't know the meaning of the word *defeated*. It probably never entered their simple minds that the soldiers could wipe them out in a matter of minutes.

Muttering under his breath, Reddin carefully made his way around the mass of humanity until he reached the separate stockade that held the slaves that hadn't already been reclaimed by their masters. It made him laugh; it really did. The niggers had honestly thought they'd be safe living with the Seminoles. Well, they'd found out different, hadn't they?

All except for Calida.

He'd done it before more times than he cared to admit, but once again, he peered in through the poles that made up the stockade looking for some sign of her. She would stand out. Damn it, he knew that, so why was he—

The line of a long neck distracted him. True, the nigger gal was on the scrawny side, but she was better than nothing, a damn sight better than a Seminole whore. Three well-armed soldiers guarded the dejected group of slaves. It wouldn't take more than a quick flaunting of his rank to get the soldiers to turn their backs. He wouldn't take her out in the open because he didn't need any waggling tongues. Still, it had been too damn long since he'd mounted a woman. Since he'd had Calida.

The taste of her name inside him distracted him from the skinny black woman. It *had* been her at his plantation. Damn it, he had no doubt that it was she who'd gotten his new hound in such a state when he'd given it one of her dresses. She'd escaped by making her way through the quicksand while the stupid dog had just about gotten himself killed. Fortunately he'd managed to get the mongrel out in time, but the swamp had swallowed Calida's scent.

Maybe it had swallowed her.

The unwanted thought that Calida might really be dead this time rammed its way into him. He hated being consumed by her. Damn it, she was nothing but a slave. His slave. He could have a hundred just like her.

He didn't want a hundred; he wanted her. He owned her.

Grumbling to himself, he banged his fist on the stockade door and waited impatiently for the guard to open it. He recognized the man but for the life of him couldn't remember his name, not that it mattered. "I've got me an itch." He pointed at the female slave. "I want her to scratch it."

"I don't know, Lieutenant. Her master might show anytime. If—"

"You let me worry about that, understand! This isn't gonna take long. Just bring her over here."

The man still looked uncertain. "Look," Reddin compromised. "What if you get your turn at her once I'm done?"

"You think so?"

"Why not? You keep an eye out for me so I can have a little privacy. I'll do the same for you."

That did the trick. Grinning, the soldier plunged into the midst of the dark bodies. He emerged less than a minute later holding onto the woman's arm. Reddin didn't bother looking at her face. By the way she was breathing, quick and uneven, he figured she knew what was coming.

As a lieutenant he'd been issued a tent to stay in. The damn thing trapped the unbearable heat and humidity, but even if it didn't, he wouldn't use it for what he had in mind because Calida's mother was in there, and there wasn't enough room. At the soldier's suggestion, he dragged the silent woman to the far corner of the stockade. The soldier trailed along behind him, talking nonstop.

"Do you really think they're all going to go to Oklahoma?" he asked. "I mean, after all this time we've spent chasing after them, it seems so simple. I just don't trust the Seminoles, don't trust them at all."

"If you don't, you're smarter than just about every other white man here."

"You mean it? You think they're going to pull something?"

It depended on what was meant by "pull." Troops had more or less stumbled onto where Panther's clan had been staying, but the Seminoles had already left. He'd offered his dog to try to sniff out the Indians, but that hadn't been successful. What that meant was that the Egret clan was savvy enough to know how to hide their tracks. Panther didn't want to have anything to do with this damnable treaty and right now there wasn't a damn thing the army could do about that. He didn't trust the rest of the Seminoles not to start thinking like Panther.

If they did, Fort Mellon could clear out in a matter of minutes. There wouldn't be anything left except that miserable bunch of niggers, this now-whimpering woman being one of them.

Niggers and Calida's mother.

Smiling, he shoved the slave against the stockade wall and dropped his pants. The soldier spun around so he couldn't see but didn't step out of earshot. If Calida was alive, sooner or later she'd learn where her mother was. She'd come after Pilar once before; that's why she'd been at the plantation.

If she was alive, she'd be back.

And then—

14

Micanopy sat across from Panther, a look of great patience on his fat face. With him and Gaitor were Jumper, Cloud, and Alligator, all respected Seminole chiefs. Panther kept his attention on Micanopy, who, although more than a head shorter than him, outweighed him. Micanopy was slow moving and slow talking, but the great Cowcatcher of the Alachua band had been one of Micanopy's ancestors, and Micanopy wore his bloodline proudly. Someday, Panther guessed, Jumper, who had married one of Micanopy's sisters, would push Micanopy aside, but that day hadn't yet arrived.

"The numbers grow daily," Micanopy was saying. "Already the fort is full, and yet still more Seminoles come."

"Is that what the general is waiting for?" Panther asked, careful to keep his question casual. "For the walls to burst?"

Micanopy snorted and patted his belly. Then his expression turned serious. "No. They wait for you."

"Are those the general's words?"

"I speak not for the general," Micanopy insisted. "My words are my own. I walk my own way."

Beside him, Gaitor hissed under his breath. "What is your reason for telling me this?" Panther asked. "I have made my decision.

You know that. I will not step inside the white man's fort. I do not trust him. I do not believe what he says."

"You anger him."

"It is a little anger," he countered. "I am only one *tastanagee*. General Jesup has much more to concern himself with."

"Not the general."

Panther didn't have to look at Gaitor to know they were thinking the same thing. Reddin Croon had been wearing the uniform of an army man for several months and was at Fort Mellon. "Anger is not a good thing," he said slowly. "Sometimes it robs a man of his senses and he becomes foolish."

"And sometimes it turns him into a sharp-toothed alligator."

That was true; he would be wise to never forget that. Although Panther needed to understand as much as possible about what was happening at the fort, even more important was hearing everything the other chiefs could tell him about Calida's former master. Was Croon acting under General Jesup's orders? he wanted to know. Or was he on his own, free to come and go as he wished? Jumper and Cloud provided the answers. Croon and the general sometimes argued, and although it angered the general to have another question his decisions, he didn't seem to know how to silence Croon.

"I do not know what he is doing there," Cloud said. "He has taken a number of army men for himself. It is said that he pays them well, that they no longer listen to their commanding officers. But they have nothing to do. They simply wait."

"And Croon? Does he wait too?"

"He has much to fill his time. He takes slave women to his bed; no one stops him."

"That is all?"

Cloud shrugged. "We do not concern ourselves with a lieutenant. Osceola is still sick. We are all tired. We want peace and a new place to live."

Feeling old, Panther looked around. Because he'd wanted privacy for this conversation, he'd asked Gaitor and the chiefs to join him on a small hammock out of sight of where his clan was now staying. He believed the spot he'd chosen for his people was safe, but it hadn't rained in weeks. Already the surrounding swamps were dry-

ing up, fish were dying, and the ground was too parched for planting. The sun had always burned this land; he knew that. But this year
the clan wasn't ready. They would have to move soon if they were
to have enough food. He hated telling the children and old people
they couldn't stay here and rest, but he would as soon as he knew
what Micanopy and the others had come to him about.

Micanopy leaned forward. He was no longer smiling. "General
Jesup grows more angry with each day. He is tired of waiting for
Osceola to say when we will leave Florida."

"Osceola is too sick to speak?" Panther didn't believe that. He suspected Osceola was deliberately testing the army's patience.

"He is still chief. But my turn will come. Soon."

Hearing Micanopy say that worried him. Although Micanopy
strutted like a snowy egret in full plumage, he was no leader. "What
would you do differently?" he asked. "To decide to leave the land of
one's ancestors is not an easy thing. We do not know if our spirits
can follow us to another place. The army wants us to turn our backs
on people who have become like us."

"The Negroes are runaways," Jumper insisted. "We gave them
shelter, but we will not risk our lives for them."

Anger surged through Panther, but he was careful not to let it
show. "They have become our allies. A man does not turn his back
on a friend."

"Friend!" Jumper spat. He didn't look at Gaitor. "I must think of
all Seminoles. If we are to live, we must listen to the white man's
words. Walk another way."

Panther didn't agree, but he might be in the minority. The men
who were sharing tobacco with him were free to come and go around
Fort Mellon because they'd agreed to give up the Negroes who lived
with them. He, on the other hand, would be thrown into the stockade if the army got their hands on him. Gaitor hadn't wanted this
meeting. He'd argued that Micanopy and the other chiefs were no
longer worthy of being called men because they'd gone back on their
word. Only Panther could hold his head high.

But was there pride in being a fugitive?

"You say you must walk another way," he challenged Micanopy.
"Is that why you are here? To tell me what that way is?"

Panther sensed a change in Micanopy and Jumper, an end to easy conversation. "We are a patient people, Panther," Jumper said. "We are not quick to fight. We want only to plant and hunt, to fish and trade. Being at war is not something that comes easily. But there's a time for the end to patience. In that, we and the army are the same."

"Are you?"

"Yes." Jumper stood. A moment later so did Cloud and Alligator. Only Micanopy remained seated. "You walk alone, Panther," he said. "Your clan is the only one that refuses to join with the others at Fort Mellon."

That wasn't true. However, the others still hiding consisted of isolated families. "I walk one way. You walk another," Panther said unnecessarily.

"No longer." Jumper stepped closer. Panther was saddened but not surprised to see him draw his knife. "General Jesup wants you; he demands to see you." Jumper spoke through lips drawn tight over his stained teeth. "Until that has happened, he will not say when we will leave Florida."

Flanked now by Jumper and Alligator, Panther willed himself not to move, to accept that men who'd once been his friends might have become his enemies. Although he had no doubt that he could kill one of them before he himself died, he wasn't ready for death.

If he was dead, the Egret clan would be without a leader. Gaitor would have lost his brother.

Dead, he would never again see Calida.

Panther and Gaitor had been gone for two days. No one knew where they were, just that they hadn't been seen since their meeting with other Seminole chiefs. Repeatedly, Calida told herself that his absence was none of her concern. But with the air around her feeling hot and heavy, it was impossible not to ask herself what had taken him from his people. She'd always believed that freedom would be a wonderful thing. To be able to go where and when she wanted—

It wasn't like that for the Seminoles. Scouts constantly searched the land around them to make sure it was safe. Children weren't allowed to roam beyond the clearing's boundaries and everyone's belongings were bundled for easy carrying should flight be necessary.

They no longer had a village; this thin soil would never grow crops. The men spent much of their time hunting, while women and children scavenged like animals. All everyone seemed to talk about was whether the army would find them and what would happen if they did.

She worried about that too, but fear for her own safety was unimportant next to her concern for her mother and Panther. Pilar was sick. She desperately wanted to return to the plantation for her mother, would have if Panther hadn't ordered her to stay here. If she hadn't been forced to admit that her mother couldn't make the long walk. Pilar wanted her daughter safe and that might be the only thing she could give her.

But to abandon her mother . . .

Leaving the shrinking creek where she'd been washing up, she started back toward where the clan was staying. It was so hot that it hurt to breathe. As always, she kept her eyes and ears alert for any sight or sound of Panther—and for the army. Pushing her way past heavy brush that stuck to her sticky flesh, she spotted an Indian she hadn't seen before. He was flanked by two Egret clan guards, but he wasn't acting like someone who'd been taken prisoner. Curious, she slid closer, but the newcomer was speaking so rapidly in Seminole that she understood little of what he was saying except that the conversation had something to do with Fort Mellon.

After a few minutes, the newcomer signaled that he wanted something to eat. The gathering started to break up then, small groups of Seminoles speaking quietly among themselves, occasionally glancing at her. When she approached Winter Rain, Winter Rain turned away as if to leave. "Don't, please," Calida begged. "That brave said something that upset everyone. What is it? Is Panther—has something happened to him?"

"Panther? Is he all you think about?"

"No. Of course not. But no one knows where he and Gaitor are. He isn't—"

"This is not about Panther. Micco is a Creek Indian. He wears two faces."

"Two faces?"

Winter Rain grunted as if Calida should have already understood.

"Because he has become a friend of the army men, he is free to walk among them. He was at Fort Mellon but does not want to be there anymore because there is evil in the place."

Calida needed more of an explanation but didn't want to anger Winter Rain by asking another question she'd probably consider stupid. After a minute, however, the younger woman continued. "Micco says that the hatred and distrust between Seminoles and the army grow daily. One says that the other must do something. Then the other says that that thing cannot be done until something else is."

Not sure what Winter Rain was talking about, Calida nevertheless nodded. "Did Micco say whether anyone has left for the reservation?"

"None. General Jesup says that will not happen until all Seminoles are ready, until the Egret clan joins the others. Osceola tells him that no one can speak and act for us, but the general does not want to hear that. Perhaps he is afraid that the government men will be angry with him if a single Seminole remains here."

An uneasy thought struck Calida. As far as she knew, both Panther and Gaitor had left without telling anyone where they were going. If they'd agreed to meet secretly with the army— No! Panther would never turn his clan or the Negroes over to the enemy. But what other explanation was there? "Micco looked at me several times," Calida said. "So did others. What did he say?"

"I told you."

No she hadn't, not everything. "Reddin Croon is at the fort, isn't he? That's what Micco was talking about, something Croon's been saying or doing?"

"Croon is not alone."

"What do you mean?"

"He has someone with him. A woman."

Of course he did. If at all possible, Reddin Croon wouldn't be without a woman at his disposal. "What does that have—"

"Her name is Pilar."

Calida stared stupidly at Winter Rain. "My mother?"

"Yes."

Suddenly, frighteningly, Calida understood. "I came for her once," she whispered. "He knows I'll try again."

"Are you stupid, a deer walking into a trap?"

That didn't matter. Pilar should have been left at the plantation, where she could rest and hopefully get better. Instead, she'd been forced to accompany Croon, maybe walking the whole way. "Did Micco say how she was? I have to—"

"You do not do anything!"

"You don't understand!" Calida shook her head until it throbbed. "She's sick, but he doesn't care. As long as he thinks he can use her, he'll make her, force her— My mother . . ." She didn't want to appear weak, but a horrible image of Pilar barely clinging to life threatened to overwhelm her. "If I'd never defied him—"

"It is too late for such talk. Micco says that Fort Mellon is full to the bursting with armed soldiers. You will never be able to reach her. Forget—"

"Forget!" It was all Calida could do not to shake Winter Rain. "I will never forget my mother. Never!"

Winter Rain returned her glare, seeming not to care or understand what had her so upset. "It does not matter what you do. No one can free her."

"Panther—"

"No!"

"Yes," Calida countered, although why she was arguing with Winter Rain she couldn't say. "He's the only one. He knows—he knows how to move silently, how to keep himself hidden."

"Reddin Croon captured him once; have you forgotten?"

She wouldn't let herself think about that, not with Panther her only hope. "It won't happen again. I know it won't." If only Panther were here. He had no right leaving the way he had, not when she needed him. "I'll ask him to—I'll go with him. Together we'll free her."

"Why?"

"Why? If—if she's forced to stay there, she might die."

"That is not what I am saying. Why would the Egret *tastanagee* risk his freedom, his life even, for your mother?"

Calida wanted to throw an answer at Winter Rain, to throw arguments at her one after another until Winter Rain stopped asking her stupid questions, but she couldn't speak. Panther had left without telling her where he was going or when he would return. Why should he? She wasn't one of his people. She was a woman who had denied life to the babies inside her.

"I'll go alone," she whispered. "I have no choice."

"Micco says she is sick. Maybe she is already dead. You risk your life for a dying woman?"

Fighting the impact of Winter Rain's words, Calida closed her eyes so she could better imagine not what her mother might look like now, but what she'd once been, the way she'd held her daughter, shared secrets with her, loved her. "She's the only person I've ever loved. I can't—I can't leave her like that."

"You already have. Twice."

Winter Rain's hard honesty pulled her out of herself. She had no idea what the other woman was thinking, but it didn't matter. "The first time I ran because she begged me to. Because I knew what he'd do with me if I stayed. I came back; I had to see her. I had to. But"—self-loathing made her sick to her stomach—"but I ran again. I was afraid, and I ran. He wants me; he's using her to get to me. I can't let her be hurt anymore. I won't." She felt exhausted.

"You would risk your life for a woman who has come to the end of hers?"

Don't say that! "She's all I have. All I've ever had." Why was she standing here arguing with Winter Rain when any more wasted time might mean her mother's death? Calida had some idea of where Fort Mellon was. Maybe she could get the Creek Indian to tell her more. At least she'd hear from his lips how her mother was faring. She could leave here today, and if the fort wasn't any farther away than she thought it was, she should reach it in no more than two days.

Two days? Did her mother have that much time?

She started toward where Micco was waiting to be fed but stopped when Winter Rain grabbed her arm. "I do not understand. Reddin Croon will kill you."

Kill? Maybe, if she was lucky.

"You risk your life? It means so little to you?"

"My mother gave me life. I have— I love her."

"More than you love your own life?"

That didn't matter. Didn't Winter Rain understand? "I love her," she repeated. "She's the only human being I've ever loved."

Winter Rain didn't release her. Neither did she demand more of an explanation. "You do not know how to find the fort."

"I'll ask. Micco—"

"No, not Micco. I will take you."

"You? Why?"

Winter Rain's hand fell away, but although Calida was free, she couldn't think about moving. "I can't let you take the risk," she insisted when Winter Rain didn't answer her question.

"Your mother, is she beautiful?"

"Yes," she said, although that was no longer true. "Her hands—she has such gentle hands."

"My mother's hands were gentle too," Winter Rain whispered.

She'd been wrong. Because heat sucked her strength, it had taken nearly until the third night to reach Fort Mellon. Without Winter Rain leading the way, Calida had no doubt that she would have gotten hopelessly lost trying to find the army stronghold located on the shore of Lake Monroe. They'd said little to each other, both during the long days of walking and at night when they fell asleep as soon as they'd had something to eat. Still, because Winter Rain had told her about her dead mother's gentle hands, Calida believed she understood why the other woman had agreed to guide her. Someday, she silently vowed, she would find a way to repay Winter Rain and thank her for making the journey less lonely. And she would do everything within her power to make sure Winter Rain didn't take any more of a risk than she already had.

It was dark. As the sun was setting, they'd climbed a tree and watched soldiers drive the horses inside for the night. With the memory of the fort's thick, high walls haunting her, she tried to concentrate on how to reach her mother. It couldn't happen tonight because she didn't know enough about the fort's interior, but maybe by tomorrow night . . . "Winter Rain?"

"What?"

"When it gets light, I want you to leave."

"What will you do?"

"I don't know yet. I—somehow I have to get inside."

"You? No."

She wanted to tell Winter Rain she was wrong, but what difference would lying make? There were hundreds of Seminoles staying inside the fort along with whatever slaves were still there, but the slaves probably weren't allowed to move about. And with her light skin, she would stand out.

"I am only another Indian woman," Winter Rain said unexpectedly. "No one will look at me."

"They'll see your Negro blood. You've done so much," she finished. "I can't have you risk—"

The sudden sound of pounding feet stopped her. She sprang up and peered into the dark, trying to make sense of what she'd heard. The distant thudding became closer, louder. She grabbed Winter Rain, thinking to shelter her behind her. Her hand brushed against something hard and sharp. Winter Rain had drawn her knife. Doing the same, she backed both of them until their buttocks came in contact with a large tree.

"What—" Winter Rain gasped.

"Quiet!"

She heard a woman's excited voice followed almost immediately by a child's cry. It now seemed as if a hundred people were running toward her, but that made no sense.

Sense or not, it was happening.

Again and again like a human wave, people passed on either side of them. Some of the runners must have realized there were others besides them out there, but they were only interested in putting distance between themselves and the fort and didn't so much as slow their pace.

Someone laughed. A moment later someone else did the same. Concentrating, Calida made out individual bodies. When she saw an older man lumbering her way, she planted herself in front of him. He stopped and might have fallen if she hadn't grabbed him. Calling on the Seminole she'd learned, she quickly identified herself as a runaway slave and asked him what was happening.

"They lie!" the man bellowed. "The bluecoats cannot be trusted."

"Is everyone running away?"

"Everyone!" He laughed. "The army men are stupid. *Hadjo.*

Crazy! They think Osceola is sick and a fool, but he is not. He has seen through their lies. We are not cattle. We will not be taken from our land." He struggled in her grip. She needed to let him go, but first she had to know what the army men were doing.

"I do not care," he insisted. "They are the cattle, stupid creatures waiting for knives to pierce their hearts."

"Are they following you?"

"It does not matter. Osceola and the other chiefs say we are to leave. We leave." He started to struggle again, and this time she released him. She looked around for Winter Rain, but there were so many shadowy figures that she couldn't tell one from the other.

A musket blast shattered the night air and sent unseen birds to squawking. "Calida!" Winter Rain gasped. "What—"

"The army!" They were coming after the Seminoles. That meant they were leaving the fort and wouldn't so much as look at her if she snuck into it. Not bothering to tell Winter Rain what she intended to do, she began weaving her way through brush and bodies toward where she believed her mother to be.

"Calida? No!"

"I have to find her! I have—"

Winter Rain grabbed her flying hair, forcing her to stop. "You can't!" she gasped. "They will kill you!"

Although it brought tears to her eyes, Calida managed to yank her hair out of Winter Rain's grasp. She couldn't think about anything except her mother; if Winter Rain didn't already understand that, she never would. Silent, she again started running. Just as silent, Winter Rain kept pace.

The heavy fort doors hung open. Light from a half dozen burning torches made it possible for her to see that. A stream of Seminoles continued to pour out of the opening, and although soldiers occasionally discharged their weapons, she didn't see any Indians fall. Twice someone ran into her; once she was knocked to her knees. Still, she managed to make her way into the fort. Even more torches burned in here. Everything was confusion, Seminoles and army men struggling, yelling, horses milling about. The stench of long-unwashed bodies assaulted her. The air felt old and trapped, so hot she could barely breathe. Trapped? No, she didn't dare think about that.

She made out several small structures that reminded her of the shelters at the plantation used to protect crops from rain. That might be where some of the army men stayed, not that it mattered. A number of slapdash *chickees* had been erected in the center, and near them were circles for sitting made of rocks and logs.

Her attention was drawn to something that resembled an animal corral. Its wooden gate was closed, but there was enough space between the logs that she spotted a dark face peering out from a crack. This must be where the runaways were forced to stay. She started toward it but stopped because Reddin Croon would want to keep her mother close to him.

The shelters? No. There wasn't anyone in them. But the handful of tents might be places for officers to stay. She began to shake at the thought of encountering Croon, but her determination was stronger than her fear. Her mother? In there? Not breathing, she placed one foot in front of the other.

Before she could take another step, someone called her name.

15

Spinning around, Calida found herself face-to-face with Gaitor. "Git out!" he ordered. "Git out whiles you can!"

"My mother—"

"There's no helpin' anyone 'cept yurself, girl. Everyone's leavin'."

Everyone who could. Driven by the desperate need to find her mother, Calida tried to step around Gaitor, but he stopped her. She felt the weight of his hand around her wrist and willed herself not to fight him. The air smelled of sulfur and sweat, of too many people in too little space for too long. It had smelled like this on that awful day when she and her mother stood on an auction block while strange white men pressed around them. She'd been a child then but not so young that she didn't understand what it meant to be helpless.

She'd never be like that again!

"I *have* to find her!" she insisted. "I know she's here. *He* brought her here."

"It don' matter." Gaitor pulled her with him until they stood near the wall, out of the way of the confusion. Flickering flames painted his face in bloody colors until she barely recognized him. "Nuthin does 'cept stayin' alive."

"What are you doing here?"

"He is with me."

Yet another musket shot cut through the screams and curses, but the sound wasn't loud enough to prevent her from recognizing who had just spoken. As with Gaitor, firelight bucked and danced over Panther's features. A child might shrink in fear from the ever-changing images. She wanted to draw away from Panther, not because she was afraid of him, but because—because why?

"Is this your doing?" she demanded as she indicated the confusion swirling around them. The solders were gathering into a number of tightly bunched groups. It didn't look to her as if they had any interest in stopping the mass exodus, just staying alive. "Is this why you left us? So you could— Panther, have you seen my mother?"

"That is what brought you here?"

"Yes!" She had to yell to be heard. "Where is she? Please, where is she?"

"Calida, there is no time. If you are seen—"

She couldn't remember when Gaitor had released her and Panther had taken hold of her. Energy pulsed through him. He felt alive with a sense of urgency; his emotion imprinted itself on her. Feeling all but consumed by it, she quickly told him what she'd learned from the Creek Indian. "Winter Rain led me here. She didn't want to, I know she didn't. But she did."

"Winter Rain?" Gaitor insisted. "She should not—where is she?"

She pointed toward the gaping hole that was the fort's entrance. "I don't think she came inside. I told her to stay where it was safe." Had she?

Something passed between Gaitor and Panther, but with fear driving her, she couldn't concentrate on making sense of it. Gaitor whispered something in Seminole; Panther responded, and then Gaitor was gone.

"What—"

"Calida, listen to me," Panther interrupted. "It was not my wish to come here. I wanted nothing to do with the white men, but I could not defy Micanopy. I did as a *tastanagee* must. And I spoke to Osceola, again and again until his thoughts were changed. The army men did not know I was here because I stayed far beyond the fort walls."

Even so, Panther had risked his life. Maybe later she would care what he and Osceola had said to each other, but right now she couldn't think of anything except Panther's presence—not even her mother. "What are you doing in here? You shouldn't be—"

"Not all knew to leave."

And he'd taken it upon himself to bring that message to everyone. The risk had been even greater for Gaitor because the Negro would stand out, while Panther might be able to lose himself in groups of Seminoles. But that, like her mother, didn't matter.

Panther was an eagle, a great bird of prey. Fierce courage and pride glittered in his flame-colored eyes. His body gave out a powerful message of determination. He would never surrender, never allow himself to be placed behind bars. She wanted to climb onto the fort's highest place and demand the soldiers leave him alone. Panther had been born free. He should be allowed to die free, when his time for death came naturally.

Panther.

Alive.

"Calida?" He pressed closer. She hated not being able to see him any more and yet she loved the feel of his hot and all but naked body against her. "I can do no more here. It is time to leave. Time for both of us to leave."

She could do that for him. She'd had enough of sweat-smell and yelling and white men's weapons. Incapable of thinking beyond that, she started to stumble after him. It seemed as if she'd been inside the fort forever, and yet she knew it had only been a few minutes. So much had happened, so many emotions.

The fort reminded her of a seething anthill. Some of the Seminoles were already deep in the wilderness while others ran back and forth as if they had no idea what to do. She wanted to yell that freedom lay beyond the yawning door, but the Indians had willingly come here. Only they could decide whether to stay or leave.

It was simpler for her and Panther.

At least for her.

Her. No, not just her.

"I can't!" she wailed. "Not without my mother."

"Calida, no!"

"You don't understand. You'll never understand." A child nearby began crying. Its sobs tore through her. "She's all I have. I can't—"

Panther's grip tightened. Thinking to tell him he was hurting her, she swiveled toward him. He wasn't looking at her. Instead, his attention was fixed on the opposite side of the fort.

She couldn't see—couldn't fight her way through the milling Seminoles and soldiers. It was insanity: Indians running first one direction and then the other, soldiers pointing muskets but not firing. Firing into the air. Taking forever to reload. Sweat ran off her. Her body smelled of fear.

If it hadn't been for Panther's strength—

Not Panther. Reddin Croon.

She tried to tell herself it couldn't be him. There were so many people. Men, women, children, terrified babies, all in motion. The man standing just outside the tent could be anyone. She didn't understand what the buttons and ribbons on his uniform meant and didn't care, didn't want to be looking at him.

To have found the man who had her mother.

Panther lashed her to him, his arms acting as tethers. She fought not him, but the horrible sense of confinement. There might have been a moon; she couldn't remember whether she'd seen it earlier. But something, probably the flaming brands caught to the fort walls, pushed back the night, and after a few more seconds she no longer had any doubt.

She'd found Reddin Croon.

And he wasn't alone.

Croon was dragging her mother behind him. Pilar's fingers were clamped around the rope that circled her neck, but she wasn't fighting him. Rather, she seemed to care about nothing except keeping pace with her master so she wouldn't be strangled.

An animal. He was treating her as if she was an animal.

"No! No!"

"Calida, don't!" Panther warned. She tried to wrench free, but his strength far outstripped hers. Hatred soured in her belly and mouth. Still fighting, she watched as Croon took in the scene around him. Most of the other soldiers wore next to nothing, which made her think they'd already been asleep when the Seminoles started to leave.

Croon, however, was dressed in full uniform. She wondered if he'd deliberately stayed inside his tent until he could present himself as an officer.

He hauled her mother behind him as if she were nothing more than a cur.

"No!"

"Calida! You can't—"

Hating Panther's warning almost as much as she hated Croon, she kicked and twisted in the *tastanagee's* grip. He only held her more firmly and then—

And then Croon saw them.

She saw his lips moving, felt his fury and triumph slam into her. The baby was still crying. Its mother tried to calm it. She didn't care. There were only Croon's hard little eyes and Panther holding her against him. Giving her his strength, keeping her from her mother's side.

Croon started to smile. She knew he was doing it deliberately, but it didn't matter. Nothing did except watching his hand tighten on the rope around Pilar's neck, seeing him jerk on it. Watching her mother fall.

"No! No!"

Her mother forced herself back to her feet. She marveled at Pilar's strength. Relief surged through her at the sight of it.

Still smiling, Croon lifted his musket. The long, dark barrel wavered and then steadied. It was aimed, not at her, but at Panther.

Panther.

Screaming, she threw herself in front of the warrior, but he must have known what she was going to do because he shoved her aside and started toward the slave owner. She quickly regained her balance and charged after Panther. Not Panther dead. No! Not Panther dead!

The musket became larger and larger in her mind until she couldn't see anything else. Flame-light glinted off the awful barrel. It didn't move; nothing did except for Croon's fingers, and his fingers were capable of bringing the weapon to life. Of spewing death at Panther.

Panther, whose body had absorbed night and fire.

"No!" Even before the scream was out of her mouth, she saw her mother hurtle herself at Croon. Pilar hit Croon at the instant the musket bellowed. Not breathing, Calida waited for Panther to fall, but he remained upright.

Strong.

She reached for Panther but had no idea what she was going to do when and if she touched him. She wanted to clutch him to her and assure herself that he hadn't been shot, but her eyes had locked onto her mother, and she couldn't pull free.

Croon had staggered a little when Pilar hit him, but he quickly recovered. Spinning, he faced Pilar. Calida screamed again, the inhuman shriek a warning to her mother to run.

The warning came too late.

As she watched helplessly, Croon swung the musket around and slammed it into the side of her mother's head. Pilar fell as if she was nothing more than ripe fruit hitting the ground. Despite the night, Calida saw blood spill over kinky graying hair.

"No!" She wrenched free of Panther, or maybe he released her. She didn't know which, and it didn't matter. There was only one thought: killing Reddin Croon for what he'd done.

Backing rapidly, Croon managed to keep equal distance between them. No matter which way she stepped, someone blocked her path. Although she desperately wanted to shove at the confining bodies, she held back because some of the women carried babies. Someone was beside her, someone big and strong, roaring like a jungle cat.

Suddenly Panther launched himself. At the same instant, Croon grabbed a girl and shoved her into Panther's arms. The girl, off balance, clung to Panther, slowed him. Croon ran. The bodies and darkness swallowed him. Freeing himself, Panther took off after him, but Calida couldn't concentrate on that.

Her mother lay crumpled and motionless on the ground. Dropping to her knees beside her, Calida gently lifted her mother's head and cradled it in her lap. Someone brushed against Pilar, jostling her. Calida slipped closer to her mother and used her own body as a shield.

"Mama. Mama, I'm here. Mama, please, can you hear me?"

Pilar moaned and muttered something that made no sense. Leaning down, Calida peered into the precious face. Pilar's eyes were half open but not focusing. With her free hand, Calida tried to brush the hair off her mother's forehead. Blood soaked her palm and fingers. "Mama. Oh Mama."

She no longer heard rifles being fired. Whether the soldiers had been ordered not to or hadn't reloaded didn't matter. Her mother's body was limp, quiet. Feeling gently, Calida discovered that Pilar was bleeding at the side of her head. More torches were being lit. The fort's interior now looked as if it had been touched by a blood-red sunrise. The stench of white bodies, of sulfur again assaulted her.

She would not let her mother die in this place.

Straining as she'd never done before, Calida managed to wrap her arms around her mother and then staggered to her feet. It would be easier if she placed her over her shoulder, but this way she could be surer no one ran into them. At first she couldn't see the fort opening. When she finally spotted it, it seemed so far away. Still, she began walking, staggering really.

She'd covered less than half the distance when she could no longer ignore the screaming pain in her upper arms. Telling herself she would only rest for a few seconds, she sank to her knees. As before, she cradled her mother's head against her. This time she didn't look at her. If Pilar was dead, she didn't want to know, not yet.

A careful survey told her there were now many more soldiers than Seminoles inside the fort. A large number of the soldiers were bunched around the solid enclosure that she guessed held recaptured slaves. Her heart ached for those poor souls. If she didn't leave, she would be forced to join them, or worse.

Although the thought of taking up her burden again brought tears to her eyes, she crouched over her mother, grasped her shoulders, and struggled to bring her to a sitting position. Sweat popped out on her temple and stung her eyes, but she couldn't release her mother long enough to wipe it away.

Strength. Somehow.

Someone touched her arm. Fear exploded inside her. Looking up, she made out Panther's red-tinged form. As quickly as it had come, her fear died, replaced by an emotion she didn't understand. "Let me," he said softly. "You can't carry her."

Let me. Crying from gratitude, she slid aside so he could cradle her mother in his warrior's arms. What had nearly undone her seemed so easy for him. She needed to ask him if he'd found Croon and killed him, but that would have to wait until her mother was safe. When Panther began trotting toward the fort opening, she kept pace. Pilar's head fell back limply.

Several soldiers stood just outside the fort, but they weren't try-ing to stop anyone. Instead, they simply stared as she and Panther slipped past them. Still, she half expected to feel a ball in her back. When it didn't come, she looked up at Panther.

"They do not know what to do," he said. "Today the fort was full of peace talk. Now everything has changed."

The why and how of that was important—maybe as important as learning whether Panther had killed Reddin Croon—but neither of those things mattered as much as what they were doing.

Darkness swallowed them. Without flaming torches to hold back the night, she quickly became blind. When her eyes adjusted to the dark, she was able to make out trees and bushes, shadows and shapes. She became aware of jungle smells, rotting vegetation, fra-grant flowers, moss and earth. Those scents were wonderful.

She wanted Panther to put her mother down so she could tend to her but trusted him to know how far they had to go in order to be safe. Now that it was just them and the night, she heard her own breathing, and Panther's. She strained for any sound coming from her mother but couldn't hear anything. The air was damp, which kept her sweat from evaporating. It must be the same for Panther, worse because he was carrying a heavy burden. If her mother was dead . . .

Dawn touched the tops of trees by the time Panther set Pilar down. The older woman had stirred from time to time, and he had felt her slow, uneven breathing so knew she was still alive. But if Croon had only hit her a glancing blow, she should have regained conscious-ness by now.

Calida, who'd said nothing during the long journey, immediately dropped beside her mother. Much as he wanted to know how Pilar was, Panther understood that Calida's need was greater. He watched as she ran her fingers gently over her mother's cheeks and forehead.

The rest of Calida's body was so still, as if she couldn't put her mind to it. Her voice came out a singsong whisper, a woman softly begging her mother not to die. He thought of when he'd done the same thing with his father and knew what she was feeling.

"Calida? She needs water and something to eat. I will—"

"N-no."

It took him several seconds to realize that Pilar had spoken. Calida sobbed and bent closer. Over and over again she whispered her mother's name, told her she loved her. Pilar's eyes were half-opened, but he couldn't tell whether she could see anything. His father hadn't once opened his eyes, hadn't known that his son had been there to ease his dying.

"What do you want?" he asked. "Whatever you need, I will get it for you."

"No. It doesn't—" Pilar lifted her arm and reached out weakly. Immediately Calida grasped her hand and held it to her breast.

"You need water, Mama. He'll get— Panther, please."

Much as he wanted to obey Calida's request, he was afraid to leave the two women alone. Army men might have followed the escaping Seminoles, but that wasn't what kept him here. He didn't want Calida to be alone if Pilar died, didn't want her to cry alone as he'd done.

"Panther?" Pilar whispered. "You's Panther, ain't you?"

"Yes."

She sighed. Despite the shadows still clinging to the ground, he watched her struggle to fully open her eyes. "Takes care of her, please. She's never had no one 'cept me, and now—"

"Mama!"

"Don't, Calida. Please don't."

Calida cried softly. The sound put him in mind of a newborn wildcat's mewing. He wanted to hold her, to tell her it was going to be all right, but he couldn't and they both knew that. When he rested his hand on her shoulder, she shivered. The day was already hot; she couldn't be cold.

"Did you find him?" Calida asked. "Croon. Is he dead?"

"No."

"No?" She didn't seem to know what to do with the word. "Where—"

"I do not know where he is, Calida." He hated having to tell her that, hated that his knife hadn't found Reddin Croon's throat. "The night swallowed him. I am sorry."

She briefly covered his hand with hers when he said that, then she went back to caressing her mother's face while he fought the sense of helpless rage tumbling through him. He'd wanted to kill Croon, not for himself, not for Pilar even, but for Calida. If Croon was dead, she might be able to bathe in freedom. To forget she'd once been a slave.

Calida wanted to know what it had been like for her mother during the time she was at Fort Mellon. He started to warn her not to tax her mother's strength, but maybe it didn't matter. Pilar was having trouble breathing, and she'd stopped trying to keep her eyes open. Her body lay as limp as a lily torn from a pond and discarded. Still, she talked.

Reddin Croon had brought her to the fort when the Seminoles first began to gather in it. He'd paraded her about every day and made sure everyone knew she was Calida's mother. He was most careful to tell the scouts and runners.

"He wanted Calida to know where she could find you," he said when Pilar paused for a breath. "You were his bait."

"Yes," Pilar said.

"Mama, you knew what he was doing?"

"Yes."

Calida sobbed deep in her throat and turned haunted eyes on him. He didn't know what to say, could only wait for Calida to tell him what was happening inside her. "Why didn't you run, Mama? Did he keep you tied all the time?"

"No."

"Thank heavens. Thank heavens." She seemed to be trying to comfort herself. "Then—then you were free to move about?"

"Sometimes."

"The Seminoles were free to come and go, weren't they?"

"Yes." Pilar took a ragged breath that ended in a strangled cough. "The army men, they didn' wants to anger the Seminoles."

"The gate was left open?"

"Y-es."

"Do not say it, Calida," he warned. Still, he knew Calida needed to ask her mother certain things and this morning might be all the women had.

"Why didn't you leave, Mama? If sometimes he left you alone and the gate was open, why didn't you run away?"

Pilar's chest rose and fell. It was still for so long that he wanted to press his ear against her breast to see if he could hear her heart. Then her mouth trembled and he remembered to breathe, himself. His hand still rested on Calida's shoulder. He felt her tremble.

"He broughts me there, Calida. He tols me to stay in the tent."

"But you could have left. You—" Calida's voice caught. "Oh Mama, why didn't you run?"

He felt Pilar's effort as she slowly opened her eyes. They focused, briefly, on her daughter's face. "I couldn't."

"I know you were sick and your leg—I understand that. But Mama, freedom . . ."

Freedom wasn't the only thing Calida was thinking about. If her mother had run, Calida wouldn't have been drawn to the fort, wouldn't have risked her life. Pilar knew that. But for reasons Panther didn't understand, Pilar had remained with Reddin Croon.

"Mama, I'm making it out here," Calida said. Her voice was filled with love, not recrimination. "I'm not afraid. Not afraid of Piahokee anyway."

"P-iahokee?"

"What the Seminoles call the Everglades, Mama. Remember?" She'd been massaging Pilar's wrist and fingers. Now she drew her mother's hand up to her face and gently kissed the palm. "You knew he wanted me to come to him. He was using you."

"Y-es. Calida?" Pilar coughed again, the sound deep and dry. "I was so scared for you. So scared that nuthin' else mattered."

You could have done more than live with fear. You could have found your own freedom. "You're free now, Mama," Calida whispered. She glanced over at Panther. He felt assaulted by the anguish in her eyes.

"Rest, Pilar." Although Calida had already done it several times, Panther brushed the hair away from Pilar's forehead. "Just rest for a while."

"No. No. Where—" Pilar arched her back up off the ground and looked around, although he wasn't sure she saw anything. "Where is we?"

He could tell her that not far from here was a dense grouping of passionflower vines that was home for large, beautiful gold and black butterflies, but that might not matter to her. Surely all she cared about was how far they were from the fort. "Safe," he said finally. "Reddin Croon cannot find you here."

"Safe?"

"Yes, Mama," Calida mouthed. "Safe. You can get well here. He won't ever bother you again. The healer. I'll talk to the healer. He'll come here—Panther can find him and he'll come here—he'll use his herbs and prayers. You'll be fine. Just you see. You'll be fine."

Panther wanted to silence Calida, to comfort her so she wouldn't need to go on lying, but he couldn't take his eyes off Pilar. The older woman's limp body seemed to take on new life. The muscles returned to her shoulders and arms. She looked around her, and the faintest of smiles touched her lips. He was glad it was dawn and that she could see the untold shades of green, dark bark, the tiny frogs and brightly painted snails that clung to many of the trees. He wished it would rain this afternoon so she could watch lightning slash unending paths across a purple sky and feel the energy.

"Calida?" Smiling, Pilar pulled her hand free and pressed it against her daughter's cheek. "You's free, honey. You's free."

"So are you, Mama." Tears spilled from Calida's eyes and dampened Pilar's fingers. "So are you."

He thought Pilar was going to speak. He waited, waited. Instead, slowly, gracefully, the older woman's chest settled down into itself and her fingers slid off her daughter's face.

16

She couldn't cry. As unexpectedly as they'd begun, Calida's tears dried. Still, she felt their pressure inside her, wished she could set them free because crying would end the awful pain. Maybe.

Although she knew it no longer made any difference to her mother, she continued to smooth Pilar's eyes and nose, her chin, her slender throat. She couldn't bring herself to touch her head where Reddin Croon had wounded her, but the rest of her mother—the rest of her was still perfect.

"It is all right, Calida," Panther whispered. "She is at peace now."

She didn't want to hear those words, and yet they helped. With every passing second the day became brighter. She wanted her mother to see that. They should have been able to walk through Pi-ahokee together. She'd show her mother where alligators dug their holes, and because the time would be for them alone, because there was no need to run or hide, they'd wait until baby alligators made an appearance. With Panther's help, they'd slip through the dense vegetation to where mother deer hid their young. They'd watch beautiful gold and black butterflies, brightly painted tree snails, newborn anhingas in their nests high in moss-draped cypress, grace-ful white or red herons. Together they'd learn that there was nothing to fear in the wilderness they'd once been terrified of. Panther would teach them its secrets. Together . . .

There was no together. Her mother was dead.

"We cannot stay."

Calida hated him for saying that. A moment ago she'd been overwhelmed by gratitude because he'd made it possible for her mother to die free. She wasn't ready to leave this place, wasn't ready to face the world again. Didn't he understand?

"Calida. We must leave."

"No."

Instead of arguing her down, Panther drew Calida away from her mother's body. At first he held her shoulders, watched, waited. When she didn't try to pull free, he began massaging the back of her neck. She felt his thumbs against her spine, the pressure gentle and sure. She didn't believe herself strong enough to stand, and yet her body felt as tight as a sun-hardened vine. She didn't know herself, needed to tap the depth of her emotions so she would understand, was afraid to begin. Panther was making it possible for her to stay with her mother's memory, to breathe without pain slicing through her. There was peace in his hands, peace and understanding.

"She was who she was, Calida." His breath puffed along her hair. "She was born a slave and lived a slave."

No. Don't say that.

"But she did not die alone. Think always of that."

The tears were there, building and boiling, receding sometimes. Just out of reach when she needed them. They would come. She knew that. But for these few minutes before Panther told her to stand, she let him be strong for her. Listened to him and believed.

The jungle was waking up. She heard birds and insects, sensed grass and trees bending under the sun's weight. Piahokee stirred around and inside her. Brought her back to life. With Panther's hands still on her, she leaned down and settled her mother's lids over her eyes. She took Pilar's hands and squeezed them before folding them over her chest. Now her mother looked as if she was sleeping, not dead.

"I won't ask you to take her back with us," she whispered. "It's too far."

He grunted by way of answer, and she sensed he was waiting to see what she would say next. "I want her to be free even in death. Here—I think she would be happy here."

"This is not her place. She was afraid of Piahokee," Panther said.

"But we were together. When she breathed her last, we were together. It will be all right."

"If it is right for you, Calida, that is what is important. We cannot stay. You know that."

"Yes." She kept her eyes on him. "I do."

After a brief period of silence, Panther stood and walked a little way away from Calida. He cupped his hands over his mouth and made a deep coughing sound like that of a bull alligator. A few seconds later, something in the distance returned his call. "Gaitor," Panther explained. "He will come."

Gaitor wasn't alone. When he emerged from the trees, Winter Rain was with him. Calida should have been concerned for the younger woman's safety. Why hadn't she once thought of her? Thinking there must be something she could say, she forced herself to stand and walked over to her. Winter Rain looked down at Pilar and without saying a word gathered Calida into her arms. That was when the tears came again.

"I can't believe this! I goddamn cannot believe this! All of them. Every last one of those savages."

Reddin shifted his weight, but there was no comfortable place to sit on the log that served as a miserable excuse for a chair. As it was getting light, General Jesup had sent word that he wanted to talk to his officers. Because the general's quarters were barely large enough for his bed and belongings, they'd been forced to gather at one end of the all but empty fort. Several officers were missing, maybe because they were out looking for Seminoles, or maybe because they wanted to avoid their commander's wrath.

"They should have never been allowed to talk among themselves the way they did. If I'd been given the freedom to control them the way I wanted to, none of this would have happened. President Jackson understands the Seminoles. Why he listened to those bumbling fools in Washington—"

Although it was impossible to close his ears to General Jesup's ranting, Reddin didn't try to concentrate on the words. He'd known this was going to happen. Damn it, any soldier who thought savages would allow themselves simply to be led away from land they considered theirs was a fool. Time and time again he'd told Jesup it was a mistake to treat the Seminoles, particularly rebellious chiefs like Osceola, like honored guests. Unless the Indians understood who was in control and felt that control, they would constitute a threat.

How and why the decision had been made for the Seminoles to desert the fort didn't matter. Jesup could spend the next five days laying blame, but it didn't change the fact that the so-called treaty had been broken before it had been given a chance.

It took all Reddin's self-control to remain where he was while Jesup continued his tirade, but he knew better than to risk angering his commanding officer further. Finally, with hesitant suggestions from other officers, Jesup agreed to send out well-armed troops to try to round up what Seminoles they could. As for Jesup, he had a letter to write.

"There's only one thing I can tell the President and adjutant general," Jesup muttered. "That the campaign for Indian migration has utterly failed. All this time, all the plans we made, they've been for nothing."

"Maybe not, sir," Reddin ventured. Calida had been here last night. So had that miserable so-called chief. He had no doubt that keeping Pilar with him was what had brought Calida here. As for Panther—

They would have to wait. "This experiment has taught us a vital lesson," he told the general. "We now know without a doubt that it's impossible to deal logically and honorably with savages. They've had ample opportunity to study the army's strength, and yet they continue to defy us. Any rational and thinking human being, anyone with any intelligence at all, would understand that to defy the army is folly."

General Jesup grumbled something Reddin didn't hear. The other officers, some of whom hadn't so much as opened their mouths before, muttered agreement to what he'd just said. He nearly laughed. How like them to wait for someone else to make a volatile statement.

They'd pipe up when it when it wasn't them putting their reputations on the line.

"They aren't human, General. They're no better than niggers. Animals."

He thought General Jesup might disagree. He didn't blame him. After all, *he* certainly wouldn't want to have to admit that animals had bested him. "Maybe," Jesup muttered.

"There's no maybe to it, sir. We could go after them and try to get them to agree to another treaty, but what would be the point? We can't trust those savages' words."

"No. Only a fool would do that." Jesup gestured at his aide, who'd been standing nearby. "Our mission is now clear, gentlemen. We have a new and irrevocable official policy. One that I firmly believe will not be circumvented by politicians. It was their decision to send the Seminoles to reservations, not the army's. They've failed miserably."

A minute ago Jesup had said he was the one who'd failed. Reddin wasn't about to point that out to him. Neither, he knew, was anyone else.

"In my official role as head of the Seminole campaign, it is my considered opinion that only a policy of extermination will render Florida safe."

Extermination. Although several officers exchanged uneasy glances, Reddin didn't share their reaction. The Seminoles were nothing more than animals. When a dog turns on its master, that dog is killed. When a panther or alligator threatens a man's slaves, that man orders the creature shot.

The Seminoles were, finally, getting what they deserved.

He stood at respectful attention as General Jesup dictated the message he wanted delivered to Washington. It might take as long as three weeks before the army received any communication back, but Reddin had no doubt that President Jackson, who'd spent his military career battling Seminoles, would concur that extermination was the only way to ensure Florida's safety. In the meantime—

Reddin frowned at the memory of practically having to grovel at his father-in-law's feet in order to get Isiah to let loose of enough money to allow him to purchase his own troop. If the Seminoles hadn't unwittingly helped his cause by stealing a few cattle, he might still be talking himself blue. However, Isiah hated losing anything he'd paid for as much as he hated unhanding a single coin.

The soldiers at Fort Mellon would have precious little to do until they'd gotten their new marching orders. However, not all of them would be content to sit around doing nothing. Many would like nothing better than to take off after the Seminoles, especially if they were paid handsomely.

Pleading the necessity of looking after his belongings, Reddin bid the general good-bye. However, instead of going to his tent, he stared down at the spot where Pilar had fallen. He'd hit her, hit her good, but damnation, she'd stopped him from killing that savage!

A shudder ran down his back at the memory of what Panther had looked like as he charged him. If it hadn't been night and the fort hadn't been full of people, he had no doubt Panther would have overtaken him.

Panther and Calida had been together. That meant he'd been right all along. She was living with the Egret clan, was part of the damnable rebel bunch that had refused to be part of treaty negotiations.

Not caring who saw him, he ground his boot into the earth. He could no longer use Pilar to get to Calida, but maybe it didn't matter. He would soon have the men he needed for a protracted expedition into the damnable Everglades. Once they knew they would be going after Panther himself, he'd probably have his choice of soldiers—at least the ones who could by rights call themselves soldiers.

His mouth fairly watered at the thought of running Panther into the ground. Maybe they'd make him a general then. A general—did he want that? With the need to put his plan into action driving him, he couldn't put his mind to what he'd do when and if the promotion was presented to him. One thing he did know: His relationship with Isiah Yongue would change. Never again would he have to defer to the old bastard.

And he'd have Calida back.

Calida couldn't remember ever having been this tired. She hadn't done that much today, just walk and then walk some more, but exertion took so much more effort these days. It was the sickly season of summer, and although she'd managed to avoid the fever that had once again taken hold of Osceola as well as several members of the Egret clan, she felt half-sick most of the time.

Nightfall brought little relief. It helped to no longer have to search for shade, but even in the middle of the night, the air still burned. Breathing took so much effort that she could barely stir herself enough to swat at mosquitoes.

Not caring where she landed, she dropped to the ground and leaned against a rotting tree trunk. She heard others talking in low tones. A baby began to cry. The sound was immediately cut off, and she imagined the infant's mother pinching its nose to keep it quiet. That was the worst part. Hard as the constant travel was on her, at least she only had herself to consider.

When something stung the side of her neck, she swatted at it with a heavy hand. She should get up and help the other women prepare the evening meal, but if she waited a few minutes, maybe she'd regain a little of her strength. And if she didn't . . .

Someone whispered her name. Fighting free of her lethargy, Calida recognized Winter Rain coming toward her. Grunting, Winter Rain dropped beside her. "Have you seen them today?" she asked.

By "them" she knew Winter Rain meant Panther and Gaitor. She shook her head. The two had left yesterday morning; they hadn't returned last night. It wasn't the first time.

Winter Rain pressed a hand to her forehead. "They never rest. They are like hunted animals who care for nothing except staying alive."

Panther hunted? No. He was determined to keep the Egret clan hidden from the army, that was all. "They have a great deal to think about and do."

"I know. I have never done the things I now do every day, never thought we would spend all our time hiding. Running." Winter Rain leaned forward and rested her chin on her bent knees. "When I was born, the Egret clan had so much land. We raised corn and other crops. Unless there was a drought, we had more than we needed. I loved to watch our cattle, especially the calves. I wanted to be a boy so I could protect the calves from wild animals. That was our life then, waiting for new plants to climb out of the earth. Now there is no time to plant or care for cattle. We have no home." Sighing, she looked around. "It is as I said about Panther. The Egret clan has become hunted animals."

Earlier, Winter Rain included Gaitor in what she said; now, probably because she was too tired to guard herself against the truth, all she talked about was Panther. Calida had watched and listened enough that she knew Winter Rain's feelings for Panther ran deep. Why shouldn't they? Panther and Winter Rain had known each other since Winter Rain was born, and their lives had run along the same course. Pulling herself away from painful thoughts of how little she had to offer Panther, she asked Winter Rain if the other women had begun to prepare dinner. Not yet but soon, she was told. There wasn't much corn left. Once it was gone, they would have to depend totally on what they could find in the wilderness. "We will have to move even slower then," Winter Rain said. "It will take much time every day to find food."

If she hadn't been so tired, Calida wouldn't have minded. She enjoyed going out with the other women while they searched for plants and berries and roots. It was a simple thing to be doing and helping feed the clan's children gave her a sense of satisfaction that had been missing from her life since her days were spent making clothes for Mistress Liana.

That too was a thought she didn't want. She'd begun to get to her feet when she heard soft, solid footsteps approaching. In the dying light, Panther's body slowly revealed itself, proud and strong. She sensed more than saw Gaitor, not that it mattered, because she couldn't take her eyes off the *tastanagee*.

While many of the men now looked beaten down by the constant travel, Panther had became more hardened. More powerful. More remote. His deep and dark eyes spoke of his concern for his people. If he didn't look as if he could endlessly walk and hunt and search for the army, if his body didn't say it was capable of protecting them from harm, she might have felt despair. She didn't, because strength rode with Panther and she believed the message.

Winter Rain sucked in an unsteady breath. "You are all right?" she asked. "You saw nothing?"

Silent, the two men lowered themselves to their knees near the women. Gaitor held out his hand, and Calida squeezed it. He did that a lot these days. She always felt comforted by his touch, but she didn't think about him when he was gone, and she didn't feel toward him as she sensed he felt toward her.

"He has many men with him."

Calida didn't dare go on looking at Panther. Even with it nearly dark, she knew she couldn't hide her emotions from him, and Panther had enough to worry about without concerning himself with her. Maybe he didn't care; they'd said so little to each other for weeks now that the closeness they'd once shared had become mist in her mind. "Where is he?" she made herself ask.

"North of us. Little more than a day away."

Sweet Jesus. Weak from the effort of keeping everything locked inside, she could only wait for Panther to speak. Instead, taking her hand again, Gaitor told her that Reddin Croon's small army was camped near Grasshopper Slough. From what he and Panther had determined, the soldiers had been there for two days but were preparing to leave again. Panther and Gaitor had managed to get close enough to learn that Croon was acting on information he'd gotten from a newly captured slave from the Bear clan. Reddin was convinced the Egret clan was heading even farther south into Piahokee. Fortunately, that was all he knew.

"We're safe then?" Winter Rain asked while all Calida could think about was that Panther had risked his life getting that close to Croon. "They don't—"

"They have a dog with them. A hound."

The dog that had tracked her when she fled Croon's plantation. Remembering its relentless pursuit of her, she couldn't suppress a shudder. Panther was watching her, saying nothing, learning too much. She wanted the night to swallow her. She also felt braver because of his presence. "Did Croon try to make the slave lead him to us?"

"Yes," Gaitor said. When she opened her mouth to ask more, he shook his head, warning her not to press.

"What is his army like?" she asked. For weeks now they'd known that the soldiers Croon had selected were trying to overtake them, but that news had come from other Seminoles. Now Panther and Gaitor had actually seen them.

"Strong."

She pulled free from Gaitor and turned so her attention was focused on Panther. He wasn't close enough to touch, which should have made her feel safe from his impact, but it didn't. "How strong?"

She thought Gaitor might answer. Instead, Panther leaned forward and stared at her, his features immobile and unreadable. "He has nearly fifty men with him. They are healthy and well armed. They hate traveling in the heat. They hate him, but there is no talk of leaving him. They are well paid."

"Croon won't stop, not until he has me back."

"Not just you, Calida."

That was true. Reddin Croon hated the entire Egret clan. He probably held the clan responsible for everything that had happened at the fort. Maybe he hated Panther most of all.

"The rest of the army is content to stay where they are. They will wait until summer has lost its strength and then they will join Lieutenant Croon, and the troop's strength will swell like storm clouds," Panther said. "It will never end."

She'd never heard him say that before, and it frightened her. He didn't sound defeated, simply resigned. Still, how could anyone imagine a lifetime spent running? "What are we going to do?" Winter Rain asked.

Panther and Gaitor exchanged glances. "It's somethin' the whole tribe's got to know 'bout," Gaitor said. "They will soon. Arpeika's on his way here."

Arpeika was the elderly shaman who wanted to take over leadership of the Seminoles because he said Osceola was too sick, and Micanopy, who'd once distrusted the army as much as anyone, now wanted to work out a new peace agreement. Arpeika would never let that happen, and with the force of his medicine and spiritual power behind him, he met no argument.

"You have talked to him?" she asked. "What does he say?"

"Wait," Panther cautioned, "until I tell everyone."

"No!" The force behind her voice surprised her, but she didn't try to control it. "Panther, Croon wouldn't be after the Egret clan if

I wasn't here. You and I both know that." When he didn't move or speak, she went on. "If I leave—"

"No." Although quiet, Panther's voice carried more strength than hers. "We need you. You are strong and healthy."

Need. She wanted to be needed.

"And even if he had you, he would keep after us."

"He wouldn't iffen he was dead."

"What are you saying?" Winter Rain demanded of Gaitor.

"That the Egret clan will never know peace as long as Reddin Croon lives," Panther said.

Panther made it sound so simple, when it wasn't like that at all. She imagined him crouching in the dark just beyond the light cast by the fire from Croon's camp. His senses would be alert to everything that happened around him, but his eyes would never leave Croon. In his mind, he would be plunging a knife into Croon's chest. Relief surged through her at the thought of Croon's death, but it was short-lived. Panther might not escape before the others caught him. His own blood would seep into the ground next to Croon's.

"What are we going to do?" Winter Rain asked. "Otter can hardly walk. I can't stand to look at his foot. And Little Pond is so big with child. Panther, we can't keep on like this. We have to rest."

Something unseen and unspoken passed between Panther and Gaitor. "I know," Panther said. "I will leave in the morning."

"Not alone, you won'ts. This ain't nuthin' yur gonna do on yur own," Gaitor insisted.

"What are you talking about?" Calida asked. "You're not going back to where he is, are you?"

Panther didn't answer. Given how little they'd spoken to each other since her mother's death, she should be used to his silence, but she hated it. "You can't. Panther, your people depend on you."

"I will return when I am finished."

"You aren't immortal. Your knife against his musket, against all those weapons! He'll kill you, and even if he doesn't, someone else will."

"You have that little faith in me?"

Why did he ask that? "I know what the army's like." She struggled to keep her voice under control. "What Reddin Croon is like.

When I was with him, he told me things, things I wish I'd never heard. He was with those who found the bodies of the troops that were killed on their way to Fort King. He was part of the battle of Withlacoochee. Panther, he was one of those who survived the ambush."

"And he hates."

"He hates. He'll have surrounded himself with men who feel the same way."

"I am not a frightened bird, Calida. I will not fly from my enemies."

She knew that; she'd sensed his courage from that first day. But courage wasn't enough; it had to be tempered with wisdom. Standing, she placed herself in front of him. She'd hoped he'd remain sitting so she might continue to feel strong, but he slipped silently and gracefully to his feet. He looked down at her, waiting, maybe unreachable. "You are *tastanagee*," she said. "I understand that. But a war chief who risks his life is a fool."

"You think me a fool?"

How could she possibly answer when she could barely think? "Panther, you're so much like the big cat you were named after. You're brave; you know no fear." She didn't know whether that was true, but at the moment it didn't matter. "But a panther acts on instinct. He kills because he needs to in order to stay alive. When he's attacked, all he thinks about is killing because that's all he knows. He doesn't look at his enemy and understand there may be more of them than him. He doesn't think about what will happen to his cubs if he's dead. Panther, you're a man. That makes you different from a panther. You have to put your people ahead of your need for revenge."

"I must rid my people of their enemies."

If only he could; if only there weren't so many of them. Night had closed down around them. She was no longer aware of Gaitor and Winter Rain. "If Croon kills you, who will take your place? Arpeika? He's filled with hatred. It's a sickness inside him that stands between him and wisdom. That hasn't happened to you." *I pray it hasn't.* "I can't believe you'd put your wish for revenge before everything else."

"She is right, Panther," Winter Rain said, startling her. "Gaitor walks by your side, but many of the Egret clan would not accept him as their leader if you were dead. Will we become part of those who follow Arpeika? If we do, I believe we are doomed."

Calida sent Winter Rain a silent message of gratitude. Thinking to reinforce what the other woman had said, she grabbed blindly for Panther's hands. Instead, her fingers brushed his flanks. Startled, she nearly drew away but forced herself not to. He was alive. Warm and healthy. Whatever it took to keep him safe, and near her, that's what she would do.

"Panther, please." Her fingers closed around his hands. She hated the panic in her voice. "Killing Reddin Croon won't change anything. The army will keep on coming. We'll go where they can't find us. Lead us. We'll follow you."

"You do not want him dead?"

I want you alive. The words echoed inside her, frightening her as maybe she'd never been frightened in her life. Losing her mother had nearly killed her. She still couldn't fall asleep without thinking about her, and sometimes the pain was more than she could bear.

Calida didn't want to care this much about Panther. She wouldn't care!

"I want to follow the *tastanagee* known as Panther. I don't want to be ruled by a hate-filled old shaman."

17

Isiah Yongue probably wouldn't recognize him. Smiling for the first time in months, Reddin finished shaving and put his sweat-stained shirt back on. He'd lost so much weight that it now hung on him. Patting his flat belly, he admitted there were some benefits to having spent an entire damn summer trying to survive the Everglades. He'd lost every bit of fat, and his legs were now hard as tree trunks, although the rest of him felt weak. He was also heartily sick of being mosquito bit and trying to remind himself of why he'd started on this damnable disaster, to say nothing of listening to his men complain.

After struggling with his boots, he combed his dirty, too-long hair. Feeling every inch the lieutenant, as much of one as was needed in this hellhole, he started toward General Jesup's tent. He barely glanced at his troop, which to a miserable man was laid out on the ground. Summer had done them in, damn it. Nearly done him in as well, not that he'd ever admit it. He'd chosen the strongest men he could find, but they'd been no match for the heat and drought. He'd tried to inspire them by reminding them that the Seminoles were in even worse shape because they had old people and children with them and couldn't rely on food reinforcements from both the army and the few plantations they'd come near. But in the last few weeks, they'd stopped listening to him. It had only gotten worse when his hound sickened and died, damn him.

It didn't matter. It was September. Summer's back had been broken. Besides—he licked his dry lips—he had a new plan.

General Jesup was sitting outside his tent. When Reddin showed up here last night, much to the relief of his men, who only wanted to rest and complain and see if there was any whisky they could buy, Jesup had bid him welcome but not much beyond that. It didn't matter. Before this meeting was over, General Jesup would be admitting that Lieutenant Croon had a solution for at least one of the problems bedeviling him.

The general, who was smoking on his pipe, looked up but didn't stand. Reddin saluted and received a halfhearted salute in return. "I haven't seen you for what, three months," Jesup observed. "I'd hoped your campaign would be more successful than mine has been."

"So did I. So did I." Jesup handed him a pinch of tobacco. Although he thought it a miserly amount, Reddin gratefully accepted the gift, not speaking until he'd filled and lit his pipe. "At least none of my men is sick; I'm grateful for that. I've also managed to keep a lot of Seminoles on the run."

"You've done that all right. And you didn't come away from it empty-handed."

Pleased that the conversation had already turned in this direction, Reddin glanced at the small group of Negroes huddled under his men's watchful eye—not that he feared the slaves would try to run, not after what they'd been through. The bastards were beyond caring about anything. "I understand you've had some success with runaways turning themselves over to you too," Reddin observed.

"A few. Not as many as you have."

"That's because my men and I have been able to stay closer to the savages." Careful not to antagonize Jesup who, he'd heard, had a short fuse these days, he offered that it was easier for exhausted and demoralized Negroes to surrender to a small group of soldiers than the large troop Jesup commanded. "Take a look at that bunch. They're played out. They'd rather go back to their masters than spend any more time with the savages."

"Hm. They're in the minority, and we both know that."

And none of the slaves had been from the Egret clan. That's what kept eating away at him. Still, he was determined to take victory from any source he could. "It'd be more if policy was changed," he said, carefully watching the general's reaction.

To his relief, Jesup didn't argue. Smoking, speaking slowly, Jesup acknowledged his frustration with governmental decisions. At the time the Seminoles had been signing the treaty, all Negroes with them had been considered the Indians' property. Under pressure from slave owners, that had changed, a decision that was directly responsible for the disaster that had taken place at Fort Mellon.

Now, in an attempt to facilitate an end to the cat-and-mouse game being played by the army and Seminoles, President Jackson had ordered the army to offer freedom to any runaways who gave themselves up. Unfortunately, many residents of Florida considered them war plunder and when possible seized them for the reward money being offered by their masters, or those who claimed to have been their masters. As a consequence, only Negroes more dead than alive left the relative safety afforded by the rebellious Seminoles. That kept the Seminoles strong, too damn strong.

"I know you've kept the President apprised of how things are going," Reddin said. "Has he given any indication he's willing to once again reassess the situation?"

"He'll do whatever it takes to end the hostilities. He's got enough on his mind without this so-called war. It's an embarrassment to him to have to still be fighting Seminoles after all these years."

That was the answer Reddin hoped he'd get. "What if the Negroes were put under the army's protection?"

Jesup pulled the pipe out of his mouth and stared at it. "Our protection? We don't need to be looking after them."

"Just for a little while until we can ship them off to the reservation."

"Spell it out to me, Lieutenant. What are you talking about?"

Patiently, carefully, Reddin outlined a plan that had been born out of frustration, embarrassment, endless and futile searching, mosquito bites, and boots worn down to nothing. And a need to win that was almost more important than life itself. In essence, what he'd come up with would call for a return to the original agreement with the Seminoles that had made them agree to be sent to the reservation. But why should the army wait until they had all Seminoles under their control before getting the Negroes out of their hair? They'd offer sanctuary to the runaways, promise they wouldn't be returned to their masters. All they had to do was turn themselves in. "It'll break the Seminoles' back. A lot of their strength, their damnable stubbornness, comes because they've got niggers among them and those niggers don't want to surrender because they know they'll be sent back to their masters. But if they think they're going to Oklahoma, well, if it was me, I'd jump at the chance."

General Jesup stared at him for a long time, but Reddin didn't mind. This was, after all, a switch in army policy and as such a decision that couldn't be easily arrived at. He didn't care what happened to the niggers hiding out in the Everglades. If truth be known, he hoped they'd rot in there and be eaten by alligators. But the more niggers he came in contact with, the greater the chance he'd meet one who knew exactly where the Egret clan was. Where that devil Panther was hiding out with his nigger companion.

Where to find Calida.

Gaitor waited until the evening meal was over before approaching his chief. He wasn't surprised to see that the clan's Negroes had gathered together and were talking quietly among themselves. If he wasn't so close to Panther, that's where he'd be.

Panther had told him he was going to try to track down the alligator who'd made the signs they'd come across earlier in the day. That meant his chief had gone to what remained of Gray Creek. As Gaitor made his way around the Seminole families grouped throughout the small clearing, he took careful note of their condition. Little Pond had had her baby, but the infant had been sickly from the beginning. Calida, who seemed as healthy as she'd ever been, often cared for the little one while the mother searched for the food she needed to suckle it. He wondered if either the mother or Calida knew the baby was going to die.

None of the other children looked as if they were at the end of their strength. He would have felt better if old Hill Climber hadn't died yesterday and his toothless wife the week before. The Egret clan was tired. Tired and hungry.

The smell of fresh blood told him Panther's hunt had been successful. He slipped around the chest-high ferns that grew to the creek's edge and peered into the dying light until he spotted Panther squatting on the opposite side. He was using his knife to cut open a dead alligator's belly. The creature was small, little more than the length of a half-grown child. Panther gave him a rueful smile. "When I saw the tracks, my mind made them larger than they were. I do not need help bringing this one back."

"That ain't why I's here, Panther."

"You were quiet today. You had much on your mind?"

Panther didn't have to ask that; surely he knew he'd been thinking about what a Creek Indian had told the clan yesterday. "I's wonderin' iffen we can believe the army this time."

"I cannot answer that for you, *honton*."

Honton. Friend. Was Panther deliberately reminding him of everything they'd been to each other? "Sara wants ta leave."

Panther nodded. Sara, whose master had been going to sell her, had fled in panic a little more than a year ago. Fortunately, she'd come across another escapee who'd planned his flight carefully and knew how to reach the Seminoles. The other Negro had no complaints. Nothing he experienced living with the Seminoles was worse than what he'd left behind. Sara, however, remembered only that she'd once had a cabin to live in, more than the clothes on her back, enough food to feed her belly. She hated snakes and insects, hated eating alligator and turtle meat.

"I cannot stop her," Panther said. "I will not stand before anyone who wants to take the army's offer."

Although he'd guessed Panther would say that, he wished his friend would ask him to stay, thus relieving him of this decision. "You knows why I's here," Gaitor began. "I cain't go back. My master, he'll kill me."

"Yes."

"I never thought there'd be anythin' 'cept livin with Indians fur me. But Oklahoma—it could be safe there."

"It could be."

"Not just for me," Gaitor hurried on. Panther had finished gutting the alligator. He would want to take it back to the clan so they could cook it. "I's thinkin' 'bout everyone here. Maybe 'bout Calida most o' all."

Panther dipped his bloody knife in the creek and washed it with a fern he'd pulled from the bank. "She could breathe free and safe in Oklahoma," he said. "I have given that much thought."

"I'd take care o' her. Make sure she never wants fur nuthin'."

"Yes. You could."

Things had changed between Gaitor and Panther. Although neither of them had said anything about it, he'd seen something in Panther's eyes the day Calida's mother died that he'd never been able to forget. Yes, Panther had felt Calida's grief and had wanted to avenge Pilar's death just as he'd been driven by the need for revenge after his father's brutal killing, but it was more than that. It had been in the way Panther studied Calida that day, the way he still looked at her when he thought no one was watching. Panther and Calida hardly ever spoke to each other and when they did, it was only about what they absolutely had to.

Calida had told him she believed Panther hated her, had hinted she'd done or said something to make Panther feel that way, but Gaitor didn't believe that.

He knew his friend, his brother, too well.

"There's sumthin' else I been thinkin' 'bout," he went on. "You git the runaways out o' here en them slave owners, they ain't gonna care what happens no more. The army won't have their backing no more."

"That is true."

What is it, Panther? Whatever you's thinkin', say it. "I needs to learn more 'bout this so-called offer," he conceded. "I ain't gonna make no decision lessen I knows whether the army's gonna keep their word." He stopped watching what Panther was doing to the knife and studied his face. "I ain't gonna jeopardize Calida."

Panther stood. Water streamed off his naked legs. Crossing the creek with the alligator slung over his shoulder, he laid his hand on Gaitor's shoulder. His eyes, already dark as night, became even blacker. "I will miss you, my brother. You will never leave my heart.

But maybe the army can be believed this time and you will truly face freedom. I want that for you."

Freedom. Panther had grown up believing he knew the meaning of the word. Freedom had a smell, a taste. It lived in an afternoon's downpour, in a purple sky shot through with lightning, in the simple pleasure of fishing or watching butterflies collect on a tree. Being chased by the army hadn't blunted his appreciation of the things that had always been part of his world. He'd wanted to tell Gaitor that Gaitor could still stand proud and safe once he was in Oklahoma, but how could he when he couldn't even imagine what the place looked like?

After placing the alligator before the clan's oldest woman, he went in search of Calida. He found her, as he thought he would, with Little Pond. Little Pond had been carrying her newborn all day. Now she was making herself a meager meal from a turtle and a few roots while Calida sat off by herself rocking, always rocking, the unmoving baby.

Leaning down, he ran his finger over the little one's forehead. Its flesh felt dry and limp, the same way Pilar's had.

"There's no hope for it," Calida whispered. She kissed the tiny nose. "It barely has the strength to suckle, and it can't keep anything down."

The baby hadn't been named; Panther didn't know whether Little Pond's uncle intended to give it one at death. He wanted to take it so Calida wouldn't have to continue to cradle what might not see the morning sun, but there was no look of horror in her eyes, only quiet acceptance.

"I am sorry," he whispered. Suddenly more tired than he'd been in days, he sat beside her. She wore her skirt just long enough to cover her thighs, so she could move about easily. He'd never seen her legs look so taut, so prepared for the life that had been forced upon them. She was thinner than she'd been when she first came to live among the Seminoles, but her eyes remained bright. "I do not want this for any of my people."

"Am I one of your people, Panther?"

He didn't know how to answer her. In the past, Negroes either lived with Seminoles or they didn't, depending on what they wanted. Now everyone shared the work, the worry, the food-gathering. "You heard about the army's offer?" he asked. "Do you believe what the Creek said?"

"Whether I believe or not doesn't matter. Even if the army does as they say they will, I'll never make it to Oklahoma."

"Because of Lieutenant Croon."

She gave him a rueful smile and went on rocking the baby. The little one looked so peaceful that for a minute he nearly believed what his eyes were telling him. Calida lost her warrior's edge when she was around children. She became a woman, a mother. The woman she'd once been had submitted to her master because she'd had no choice, but that had changed. If Croon ever got his hands on her again, he would have to kill her.

"If the Negroes are gone, you would have less to worry about," she said. "Fewer mouths to feed. Maybe—maybe you think there won't be any reason for the army to chase you if slave owners are no longer pressuring the army to return their property to them."

He'd thought about that; he wouldn't tell her otherwise. "We have killed. General Jesup and President Jackson will never forgive or forget that. Neither will those who wish to take over our land."

"No. No, they won't." She folded her slender frame over the tiny one in her arms. "He's going to be safe soon. Safe and free."

She was free but not safe. Knowing he couldn't give her what she most wanted in life became a knife twisting inside him. "Gaitor may leave."

"Gaitor? But he's your brother."

"He is a man who hears promises of a different life. It is something he must think about. I will never stand in his way."

She sighed. The sound hung between them for a moment before drifting off in the breeze. "Listen to the night," she whispered. "Look at the stars. Endless stars. Beautiful. When it's like this, and I can smell food cooking, and I know I don't have to walk any more today, I'm happy."

She looked content. He wanted to tell her that, but words that came without thought when he was talking to anyone else evaporated like the little water left in Gray Creek whenever he was around her.

"What do you want, Panther?"

"Want?"

"Ever since the Creek told us about the army's offer, everyone has been talking about what they should do, what they want to do. At least the Negroes. But what about you? What do you dream about?"

"Yesterday. The world of my childhood."

"Not what it might be like living in Oklahoma, no longer at war?"

"Whites murdered my father, Calida. They turned my clan into frightened rabbits running for their lives. That is what I dream about. The only truth I know."

Calida wanted nothing more than to forget what Panther had said, but the words refused to leave her mind, her heart. They'd been together day and night since he brought her back to the clan and yet they barely spoke. She sometimes imagined that he was looking at her, but when she studied him to see if that was true, he was always doing something else. Always busy. It was the way she wanted it, she told herself. In a moment of unbearable pain, she'd exposed her deepest emotions, agony that sometimes ate at her soul. She shouldn't have.

That was why she never spoke to him unless she absolutely had to, because whenever she caught her image reflected in his eyes, she remembered the night when he held her and she told him about killing the babies Reddin Croon had put inside her.

She had to stop thinking about herself! Tonight was for Panther, Panther who knew nothing except the burden of keeping his clan safe—and sleeping alone.

Feeling both brave and frightened, she went to where he'd bedded down at the edge of the clearing. The stars reminded her of flickering, darting fireflies, but there was no moon. Still, her body knew where to find him. In her mind she saw him stretched out on a soft mat of leaves and ferns. He wouldn't be asleep yet; maybe he never slept anymore. Master Croon had insisted she keep herself clean for him. She'd never imagined she'd want to groom herself and come willingly to a man, but tonight she did. She didn't ask herself why, didn't dare face the answer.

Or maybe she already knew.

"Panther?"

"Calida."

His voice belonged to this place. It knew how to find wind tunnels not taken up by wilderness sounds so that it came to her clear and honest. Wanting to run, needing to stay even more, she first stood over him and then dropped to her knees in front of him. "I— I can't forget what you said earlier today. I've been thinking . . ." She should have thought out what she was going to say—maybe she had—but the words had faded the instant she saw his solid outline. "Have you talked to Gaitor again? What is he going to do?"

"He does not know."

Say more than that. Make this easier for me. "I wish I could give you yesterday."

"Yesterday?"

"I asked you what you wanted and you said you wished for yesterday. Your childhood again."

He sighed. She so seldom heard that sound from him. Hurting for him, she nearly extended her hands to him, stopping only because she was afraid of her reaction should she feel his body's heat. "Life was so different when I was a child," she told him. "My mother and I lived on a huge plantation in Mississippi. There were more slaves than I could count. The master and mistress had fine carriages and horses. My mother was a house slave then. It was her job to clean the kitchen. I had no chores. I could do whatever I wanted." She couldn't say why she was talking about this, maybe so he would understand more about her—if that was what he wanted. "The master's dogs were always having puppies. I loved playing with them. While my mother worked, I was looked after by another slave, a huge old woman with arms that swallowed me when she hugged me. For a long time I didn't know what was happening to my mother while she was in that fine house. I remember—I didn't understand why she so seldom smiled or laughed. I thought there could be nothing more wonderful than spending my days in there." Her throat constricted unexpectedly, and she had to work at being able to speak again. "I was so innocent then. So happy. Panther, I know about yesterday."

"It is behind us. We should not think about that time."

Was he right? "But what do we do if there's no promise in today? How do we keep from giving up?"

"That is what you want to do, give up?"

"No. No. But Panther, I have nothing to go back to. Croon will never allow me to go to Oklahoma. This"—she swept her hands in a slow circle to indicate their surroundings—"this is all I have." *And you.*

He didn't speak.

"Do you want me to leave?" she asked when she could stand his silence no longer.

"No."

"Then—what?"

"I do not know, Calida. I am thinking about what you just said. It makes my heart heavy."

His heart? She'd sought him out because she felt weighed down with the reality of his life. "I don't understand. What—"

"To have nothing except running and hiding is a sorrowful thing."

Hot tears stung her eyes. She should have told him how much she enjoyed the alligator meat, how the stars looked close enough to touch. Those things should come easily from her; that way she wouldn't have to examine the emotions she'd been so careful to keep hidden.

"Do not tell me that you do not think my way, Calida. I do not want lies between us."

No lies between us. But if she told him the truth, he would know she fell asleep thinking about him and that he often followed her into her dreams, commanded them. She would have to tell him she couldn't look at him without being put in mind of a dark and powerful panther. That she needed his arms around her.

"It's all right." She could hardly speak. "Even if I never have a roof over my head again, it's better than what it was when I was with him."

"You have no regrets?"

Not about fleeing her master. "I will never go back; you know that. I'll kill myself before— Panther, I don't want to talk about that."

"What then?"

She wanted to snatch away her words and find safety in inconsequential things, but it was too late. Maybe it had been too late from the moment she started walking toward him.

"I'm part of why you're running," she told him. "If I wasn't with you, Croon wouldn't have spent the summer chasing us."

"You do not know that."

"I do! I know what he's like. Panther, I'm sorry. That's what I wanted to tell you tonight, that I'm sorry."

"That is all?"

No. I want to ask you to touch me, to hold me, to understand I'll never want more than that, but I'm so weary of being alone. I need you to tell me what's in your heart, what your thoughts are as you're falling asleep. Who you think of when you wake. "I owe you, Panther. I have only one way to pay on that debt."

He was once again using silence to force her to expose herself to him. She should tell him she was terrified of a man's body because of what Reddin Croon had done to her, and yet she couldn't look at him without wondering what it would be like to make love to him.

"If you want me," she whispered. "I will submit."

"Submit? Is that how it would be?"

Thank heavens he hadn't touched her. If he had, she might be incapable of speech. "What do you want me to say?"

"The truth, Calida. Is submission the truth?"

"I—yes."

Silence flowed around them, but this time, she believed, it wasn't because he was in control. Rather, he was trying to find the truth of his own emotions as well as hers. "You do not want to sleep with a man, do you?"

"I—no. I . . ."

"Go then."

"What?"

"Listen to me, Calida. Listen and believe. My man's body wants you. I will not lie about that. But unless you want the same, I will not touch you."

18

The five Negroes who'd decided to accept the army's offer had spent the day collecting their belongings. Now, weighed down with as much food as the rest of the clan could give them, they were ready for the long journey to St. Augustine. The four men and Sara had asked Gaitor repeatedly if he would go with them. He didn't blame them for asking. After all, he understood Piahokee as they probably never would. He could bring down game they'd never see, protect them.

What angered him was that they didn't understand why he'd turned them down. Wishing they'd leave so he wouldn't have to look at them anymore, he picked up his bow and arrow, thinking to spend the remaining daylight hours looking for game. The sky was dark and brooding. The wind had picked up. It was going to rain. After months of nothing but the life-stealing heat. It didn't matter. He needed to be alone.

He hadn't seen Panther all day, not since last night, in fact, when he'd spotted Calida walking toward the *tastanagee's* bed. A cramp seized the hand wrapped around his bow and forced him to admit how tightly he'd been holding the weapon. If Panther walked into view at this moment, he might bury an arrow in his brother's chest.

Shoving the thought into submission, he started toward the wilderness. He hadn't left the clearing before he heard Winter Rain call his name. Walking heavy-footed, she came toward him. He tried to remember whether she'd been around to watch the Negroes bundle up their belongings but couldn't recall. No wonder; his mind had been on Panther and Calida—of whether they'd spent the night together.

"You are not joining them?" Winter Rain indicated the Negroes. "You spoke to them earlier. I thought— Do you not want what the army offers?"

He could tell her he'd spent the night asking himself that very question, or trying to. Morning had given him only one piece of wisdom. Here, for the first time in his life, he felt like a man.

"Don' worry yurself none 'bout it. I's here. That's all that matters."

"I am glad."

She was so much smaller than him that he felt like a giant around her. He'd always thought of her as a child, until the night at Fort Mellon when he grabbed her and insisted she hide with him. The moment his arms closed around her, he'd found a woman's body under the too-big dress. He'd been frightened the soldiers would discover the same thing.

"There'd be fewer mouths to feed iffen I was gone."

"You fill your own belly, Gaitor. And more. What did the others say? Are they disappointed you are not going with them?"

"They don' understand. They's tired o' runnin' en hidin'. They wants to rest."

"And that does not matter to you?"

"Sometimes a man's got to do things so he can go on holdin' his head high. Bein' sent someplace like I was someone's pet dog ain't gonna do that."

"Panther needs you. The Egret clan needs you."

He indicated his weapons. "That makes me feel like a man, providin' for folks. I . . ."

Something pulled her attention from him. Looking in the same direction she was, he spotted Calida, alone, watching the Negroes as they shouldered their belongings, and without looking back, began walking away. "Why is she not with them?" Winter Rain asked.

Maybe because she would rather be with Panther.

"I know why," Winter Rain continued before he could speak if he was going to. "She went to him last night."

That mattered to Winter Rain? The answer came to him in bits and pieces. She was always quiet when Panther was gone. A smile often touched her small mouth when she saw him, and she sometimes gave Panther berries and roots she'd collected. With a wrench, he recalled having to hold her prisoner that night at Fort Mellon because she'd been desperate to learn if Panther was safe.

"We cain't stop 'em from what they do."

"If she left—"

"She won't 'cause she cain't."

"Can't?"

"Reddin Croon would never allow her to go to Oklahoma."

Winter Rain blinked, then nodded. "Then she is like the Seminoles, trapped in Piahokee."

Winter Rain wasn't Seminole, not all of her. But neither was she Negro. Her black-skinned father, who was still with Osceola, had vowed to die before surrendering to General Jesup's troops. He considered himself Seminole, fought and spoke and was willing to die like one. Gaitor knew nothing about Winter Rain's mother, just that she hadn't survived a sickly season when her daughter was a young girl.

Winter Rain had spent her entire life with the Egret clan, was as much a part of them as he was. "We's gonna leave in the mornin'. We cain't stay here 'cause the army might make those darkies say where they come from."

"It does not matter," Winter Rain said on a sigh. "I have walked and run and hid for so long that I do not know anything else."

A few minutes ago he hadn't wanted to do anything except bury himself in hunting because that way he might not have time to think about Panther and Calida together or about the decision he'd made to stay here. He didn't want Winter Rain's emotions on his shoulders, but they were there. "You's gonna be all right, gal. I promise yous that."

"Do you, Gaitor? Can you?"

Tears spilled from Winter Rain's eyes. He'd never seen her cry before and could think of only one thing to do. Dropping his bow and arrow, he took her into his arms.

From where she stood on the opposite side of the clearing, Calida watched the two embrace. Winter Rain looked so small next to Gaitor, but instead of pulling back and trying to protect herself, after a moment the girl wrapped her arms around Gaitor's solid waist and gazed up at him. Calida was too far away to sense what was passing between them. All she knew was that for a long, long time neither of them moved.

Barely aware of what she was doing, Calida ran a hand up and down her arm, finding goose bumps. The air was weighted with the threat of blessedly wanted rain; she wasn't cold. Still, she needed to feel something, anything. Human warmth.

Unable to watch any longer, she turned away from Gaitor and Winter Rain. Her gaze settled briefly on where she'd last seen the Negroes, but she didn't want to think about them either.

Little Pond's baby had died this morning. She'd been sitting beside the young mother, neither of them speaking, when the tiny chest collapsed for the last time. They'd waited, not breathing themselves, and when the infant remained still, they'd each bent over it, crying softly. She'd finally convinced Little Pond to hand her the dead baby so she could wrap it in a blanket and place the body in a tree in the Seminole fashion, the way Panther had done for Pilar. Then she'd held Little Pond while Little Pond prayed for her child's soul.

She'd needed to be strong then and had believed she'd been able to give Little Pond the strength and compassion she needed. But there hadn't been anyone to hold her either then or now.

Panther wasn't in the village today. He'd been gone by the time she got up this morning after a long and restless night. He wouldn't want to watch the Negroes leave; she understood that. It made it easier for her to know he wasn't studying her, remembering what had and hadn't passed between them last night.

Was he thinking about her right now? Was he remembering?

He didn't want her.

She didn't deserve him.

She'd been a fool to approach him last night.

Unworthy.

* * *

He'd seen miserable examples of flesh before, but this beat all. The niggers who'd been straggling into Fort Peyton over the past week were a sorry bunch barely worthy of a second glance. Why their owners had been so all-fired determined to get their hands on them remained a mystery to him. If one of them had been his, he would have shot him and put him out of his misery.

Still, Reddin continued to carefully scrutinize each scrawny, mosquito-bit black as he or she passed through the fort's gate, and if a soldier dared to say the slaves didn't look as bad as he said they did, he cut the man off. These ignorant boys didn't know how to judge flesh.

Calida wasn't among them. He'd hardly expected her to waltz in bold as she pleased, but even if she tried to disguise herself, sooner or later he'd spot her because he'd put himself in charge of getting everyone's name down. There wasn't a darkie around here who was going to be sent to Oklahoma without Reddin's first saying so.

Today's lot, four men and a woman, looked better than most. He didn't know how far they'd had to walk, or where they'd come from, but he was about to. After ordering them to line up so he could talk to them one at a time, he jotted down a physical description before asking the woman her name. Sara, she said, looking at him as bold as she pleased. She wasn't going to tell him the name of her former master. She didn't have to, she told him. She was free and going to Oklahoma. Stifling an urge to slap her until he'd gotten that uppity notion out of her head, he told her she'd be given two meals a day and a change of clothes. "The general's still working out the details of how you niggers are going to be moved, so don't go asking a bunch of stupid questions about when it's going to be, you hear me?"

"We was tole—"

"You weren't told anything because no one knows. Look, there wouldn't be any amnesty for you if it wasn't for me, so don't you be pushing me, you got it!"

Some of the arrogance went out of the woman's eyes. He guessed she wasn't as stupid as she'd first appeared. She wasn't bad looking— a little old—although maybe it was just the way she'd been living lately that made him think that. He'd have to work on her some, get her to thinking like a slave again, but that should be easy enough. Once she got it in her head that he was in charge and could make things as easy or hard on her as he wanted, she'd come around.

Pushing her aside, he studied the first man. After a minute, he wrote down his height, approximate age, and weight. The nigger was missing the middle finger on his left hand, which made any further physical description unnecessary. Unlike the woman, this man knew better than to look him in the eyes. Still, there was nothing subservient about him. "How long you been walking?" he asked almost conversationally.

"Seven days."

"Hm. Then you were a long way from here. No wonder it took so long for word of what's happening to reach you."

"Yes, massa."

Yes, master. Good.

"You're going to be taken good care of here," Reddin said, even though he didn't give a damn about that. "The President's given his word." He didn't bother to mention that Jackson's word was subject to change depending on how he reacted to pressure from slave owners. "Seven days, you say. Then you've been with a clan that wants to stay as far as it can from here."

"Yes, massa."

"And what clan is that?"

The woman, who'd been standing nearby, took a small step toward him. "Does we have to tell you that?"

"Of course you do. How else are we going to keep track of which clans have gotten word? You don't want other runaways not knowing what's happening, do you?"

The man he'd been talking to began shaking his head, but Reddin didn't take his eyes off the woman. He indicated the paper he'd been writing on. "As near as we can figure, more than half of the clans have been accounted for. That's good, real good. Now—" Pen poised expectantly, he waited.

"Egret," she said. "We was with the Egret clan."

Careful to keep his reaction to himself, he scribbled down the name as if it meant little to him. He told the woman—Sara—she was dismissed but that he wanted her to look him up as soon as she'd eaten. When she gave him a puzzled look, he told her he'd had a woman looking after his things, but she'd hurt her foot and was having trouble getting around. In exchange for a little bit of work, he'd make sure she got more than one dress to wear, shoes, first crack at the meals, maybe her own bed. He didn't say where that bed might be, and the look in her eyes told him she already knew. He didn't have to go at it this way. If he wanted, he could have forced things out of her, but if he did, he might have to answer to Jesup, and this was no one's business but his.

The word had came from Arpeika. Although the old shaman was too busy to personally bring news of what the army was doing, he'd made sure runners were sent to each clan. As a consequence, Panther knew that large numbers of soldiers were moving up the St. John's, Indian, Kissimmee, and Caloosahatchee Rivers.

He waited until the runner had left before allowing the news to sink in. Feeling weary, he leaned against a tree and studied what was left of the Egret clan. Five Negroes had left the first day. Although he'd hoped the rest would remain with him, a week later, three others had struck off. It had rained most of every day, which meant everyone had spent hours huddled under trees, their stomachs rumbling, while they waited for the downpour to end and animals to venture out again.

He'd barely spoken to Calida since the night she came to his bed, and she hadn't so much as looked at him. Because of the relentless heat and humidity, she often went about with her skirt rolled around her waist so that all except her upper thighs were exposed. Her thighs and calves had no extra flesh on them. The muscles stood out, evidence of how much time she spent on her feet. She never complained. Even when a meal consisted of nothing except boiled onions, she ate only as much as necessary to keep her body going, and she always made sure the children got enough.

He'd done it all wrong. He should have taken her that night. He'd wanted her; he wanted her to know that. But every time he searched for the right words, he wound up remembering that she'd almost fallen apart the night she'd confessed that she hated herself, and why. If he believed he could bring it up again without causing her too much pain, he'd make sure she understood he didn't blame her for what she'd done. He'd never been a slave; he'd never walked in her footsteps. But he knew what it felt like to lie helpless at the feet of the man who'd captured him. To no longer own his body, to be a woman deprived of holding her babies in her arms—

Forcing his thoughts on what he needed to do, Panther pushed away from the tree and strode over to Gaitor. He told him he intended to start for the St. John's before the day was over so he could see for himself the army's strength. He wanted Gaitor with him but said nothing because the offer should come from him.

"I wondereds when you was gonna git 'round to it," Gaitor said. "We's wastin' too much time as it is. We's gots to know iffen we's still safe."

"Wait," Panther admonished when Gaitor reached for his spear. "First we must tell everyone what we are doing. If we have to run, they need to be ready."

Sober, Gaitor nodded. A few minutes later, they'd gathered the clan around them. As briefly as possible, Panther explained what he'd learned about the massing army from the warrior sent by Arpeika and what he and Gaitor were planning to do. He expected to be asked numerous questions. Instead, the others only regarded him gravely. Obviously they knew he'd told them everything he could. They trusted his decision.

He filled a bladder with water, took a few strips of dried fish, and slung his bow and arrows on his back. Knowing Gaitor would soon catch up to him, he turned to leave.

Calida was standing a few feet away. In her hand she held a bag that she said was filled with dried plums and persimmons. "Be careful," she whispered as she extended it toward him. "Please be careful."

He stared at her offering. "You need this. You have so little."

"I have time to look for more. You won't. Don't let them see you, please. Whatever you do, don't let them see you."

He took her gift, not sorry that their fingers brushed and it might be a long time before his flesh forgot what hers felt like. "I will be back."

"Will you, Panther?"

"You think different?"

"I don't know. When I heard you talk about getting close to the army, I was so scared I could hardly stand. I'm sorry. I shouldn't tell you that. You need to think about what you'll be doing, not listen to a woman's foolish fears."

"You are not foolish, Calida."

"Aren't I?" It wasn't a smile really, more like a wistful sigh that had fought its way to the surface. "I want things I'll never have. If only I knew how to make the thoughts stay away." Straightening, she clamped her arms by her side. "May Panther Spirit walk with you today. May you see with his eyes, listen with his ears. Run with his speed. May his courage beat in your heart."

That was warrior talk. It pleased him that she'd learned the words and was handing them to him. He wished he could approach her with a woman's heart and words. That way, maybe, she would no longer carry sorrow inside her. She would forgive herself and go forward in life.

Life?

Did they have one, or would the army steal everything from them?

Neither Panther nor Gaitor said much all day. Communicating with gestures, they took turns leading the way first to and then up the St. John's River. A few months ago it had looked more like a stream than a river, but it had rained enough recently that the river now filled its banks. Duckweed, sawgrass, and pond-apple trees that had looked dead were coming back to life, and they saw fish each time they studied the river's depths. There'd been a downpour just before dark, and although Gaitor had felt half drowned by it, Panther had kept on walking, and Gaitor hadn't asked him to seek shelter.

Now it was the next afternoon. Listening intently, Panther tried to pull apart each sound to reassure himself that only things that belonged were here. A few feet away, Gaitor did the same. Panther was asking himself if they dared take time to fish when he heard a faint sound that chilled his blood. Crouching, he cocked his head first one way and then the other. The sound was repeated, leaving no doubt that he had indeed heard a horse whinny.

"Army," Gaitor mouthed. His eyes narrowed and his jaw clenched. Hatred flowed from him like sweat.

Army. Not bothering to nod, Panther sprinted away from the river. He didn't stop until he was certain shadows and thick brush hid him. Gaitor slid beside him, breathing deep and silent.

After determining that the sound came from upriver, Panther began walking again. He took care with every step, because silence could make the difference between life and death. He had no doubt that Gaitor would do the same, was driven by the firm grip on life.

The sounds became louder. Hoofs thudded into the ground like drumbeats. Birds squawked and then fell silent. Motioning for Gaitor to climb the closest cypress, Panther sprinted to another and scrambled up it. The mass of vegetation all around hid the approaching army until it was nearly underneath. Still, the sounds the men and horses made told him a great deal about pace and size. The enemy was moving slowly, as cautiously and silently as at least twenty horses could. Although he'd sometimes wondered what it was like to ride a horse, Panther wouldn't want to own one because their large bodies weren't made for speed in the thickly tangled, soft earth of Piahokee. Besides, horses were easily frightened.

Because of his position, he spotted the enemy before Gaitor did. He was right; no soldier walked. The horses were small and scrawny-looking things. Their pace, he now realized, was slow because the beasts were forced to carry so much. In addition to the riders, they were weighed down with muskets, sleeping blankets, food provisions. Two mules pulled a wagon. Straining to see all he could despite the heavy shade, Panther forced himself not to think about the threat these army men represented. As he was trying to determine who was in charge, he realized he'd been wrong; not everyone was on horseback. A woman, barefoot and tethered to one of the men by a rope around her neck, walked in their midst.

Features grim, Gaitor pointed at the woman. Motionless, Panther waited until she was no longer half hidden by the men. When he recognized Sara, his already tight belly knotted even more. A glimpse of her back made him physically ill. She'd been beaten. Her dress was shredded there, dried blood staining the once colorful fabric. Reddin Croon held the rope.

Although Panther would've like nothing better than to hurtle a knife at Croon's chest, he remained a silent observer until the soldiers had passed out of sight. Then he dropped to the ground.

"Amnesty!" Gaitor hissed. "They lie! The army has always lied!"

"It does not matter. This is what I think. Somehow Croon learned that Sara came from our clan. He is forcing her to lead them to us."

Gaitor showed no reaction; obviously he'd already come to the same conclusion. "We's run from 'em 'afore. We'll do it again."

True, but not if they didn't reach and warn the clan in time. A sense of urgency washed through him; still, for a moment, he couldn't make himself move, not with the image of Sara's back imbedded in his mind. His father's back had looked like that when he last saw him, when he'd had to carry his body home for burial.

"Panther?"

"I will kill him. With my own hands, I will see him dead."

"Not iffen you lets hatred git the best o' you. That'll blind you, and he'll be the one doin' the killin'."

19

As if they knew what he was going to say, as one, the remaining members of the Egret clan stopped what they were doing and turned toward him. Panther felt winded from his long run but knew it might be a long time before he dared rest.

"They have Sara," he gasped. "She brings them here."

A beat of silence ended with the first question. It was followed by more until Gaitor stepped forward and reminded everyone that the longer they stayed here, the less time they would have before the army arrived.

"We still run?" a warrior asked. "We do not stand and fight like Seminoles?"

"Do you think this is what I want?" Panther demanded. Weighed down by his position within the clan and the decision he'd been forced to make, he lifted his bow and arrows off his back and held them aloft. "What good are muskets if we no longer have powder? Our ancestors' weapons are no match for what the enemy brings with them. We must use wisdom, not just courage. We must let Piahokee hide us. Protect us."

"I am not a rabbit!" the warrior insisted. "I will not—" Before he could finish, his wife grabbed his arm. Her voice thin with fear, she reminded him that he had two children. She wanted them to have more than a memory of him.

That speech seemed to act as a catalyst for the entire clan. Silent, their faces pinched with concern, they hurried to their belongings and began pulling them together. Panther put his weapons back in place, then looked around for Gaitor. His friend was with Winter Rain, their conversation intense and private.

"It's him, isn't it? Lieutenant Croon."

He'd been aware that Calida was among those listening to him, but until this moment, he hadn't had time to think about her reaction. "Yes."

"Sweet Jesus. He's stalking me. As long as he's alive, he'll keep on stalking me."

"It is not only you."

"Sara—how is she?" Calida asked.

"He hasn't hurt her so much that she can't walk, but she has been whipped."

Mouth pale and eyes too big and deep, Calida stared at him for a long time. "She tried to protect us," she whispered. "But she couldn't stop him, couldn't fight him. In the end, he broke her."

She was thinking about what she'd endured around Croon. Panther wanted to clear her mind of those memories but couldn't. Not caring whether it was wise or not, he grabbed her arms and pulled her close. "Listen to me, Calida. You cannot allow your fear for Sara to overwhelm you. You must think about freedom, only freedom."

"If I turn myself over to him, he'll let the rest of you go. Release Sara."

"No! I am *tastanagee!* I say you will not do that."

"But—"

"No!" He was hurting her; he could see it in her eyes. But if he didn't continue to hold her, she might run toward the army. "Tell me something, Calida. If Croon had you again, would you willingly give yourself to him?"

"No. No." She shook her head until he was sure she'd made herself dizzy. "Never."

"And if you fought him, what would he do?"

"I don't care. I—I can't!"

"He would kill you."

She accepted that with the briefest of nods. "At least it would be over then."

"For you, but not for the Egret clan. Listen to me. Listen and believe. Reddin Croon is driven by hate and the need for revenge. For power. You and I have spoken of this before. You know it is true."

"Y-es."

"Then go with the others."

"The others? What about you?"

Gaitor and Winter Rain were walking toward them. It was time for Panther and Gaitor to make their plans. He had to send Calida away. "I'll do what I must."

"You're going to try to kill him, aren't you?"

As *tastanagee* he had no choice, and she knew that. And if she'd learned anything about him during all the time they'd been together, she'd understood this was the way he wanted it. "I can not leave Sara with him."

"Sara? Panther—" Calida began.

"You have not seen what he did to her." *You do not have my memories of what my father looked like.*

"It's too dangerous. Please—"

"Lieutenant Croon searches for many Seminoles. He will not be studying the shadows for a lone man."

"Not alone, Panther," Gaitor said. "This is gonna be the two o' us."

"I know, my friend. Go, Calida. Now."

"No." She wrenched out of his grip but remained where she was. Her eyes glittered and her nostrils flared. She reminded him of a frightened but determined doe protecting her young. "Give me a knife, a spear."

"You are a woman. You do not—"

"I don't care, Panther! Don't you understand? He's going to be here soon. He won't be thinking about an ambush. All he'll be thinking about is that he's chasing us, getting closer. He'll be arrogant, determined. Careless." Calida fixed her gaze on the knife strapped to his waist. "I know how to use it. I'll surrender to him; at least that's what he'll think I'm doing. I'm the only one who can get close enough to him, you know that. By the time he sees I have a knife, it'll be too late."

She was right. If she was anyone else, he might have been swayed by her argument. But this was Calida, the woman who'd saved his life, the woman who waited in his dreams. "A woman does not fight. Does not kill."

"She does if she's had to endure what I have."

Although she looked so slight that she shouldn't be able to withstand the faintest breeze, he saw beyond that to raw determination. She was ready to lay down her life if it meant ending Croon's threat to the Egret clan, to the entire Seminole people, and if Croon killed her, Panther would have to live the rest of his life without her.

"I am *tastanagee*. I say that you are a woman, useless in battle. It is for you to hide. I will have it no other way."

She stared at him as if he'd slapped her. Still, hand uplifted, she stepped toward him. Winter Rain grabbed her wrist. Gaitor hurried to her other side and spun her away from him. "Go!" Gaitor ordered. "He's right. You don' belong here. We don' want you."

Calida tried to pull free. She was still struggling with Gaitor when two braves approached. Gaitor shoved her at them. "Gets her outta here. Now."

As she was being pulled away, Calida glared over her shoulder at Panther. Despite the cost, he refused to drop his gaze from the hatred she threw at him.

"Panther?" Gaitor said after a length of time he couldn't judge. "Forget 'bout her. Think like what you is, *tastanagee*."

Was that possible?

She should have fought more, should have insisted that Panther let her remain with him. She was right. Damn it, she was right! If Croon saw her, if he believed he could put his hands on her, he would forget everything else.

Barely paying any attention to what she was doing, Calida allowed herself to be dragged farther and farther from Panther and Gaitor. She tried to remember how many weapons the two men had with them and whether they'd said anything of their plans, but she couldn't keep her thoughts on anything except the image of Panther standing proud and strong and silent.

He had been born with rare courage. He didn't know the meaning of fear when it seemed that she'd never known anything except that emotion. That was why she was here and not with him.

Winter Rain said something about the need to stay where the bushes grew the thickest and to move as quickly and quietly as possible. Nodding, Calida kept her attention fixed on where she was going, not behind her.

"You will not do a foolish thing, will you?" Winter Rain asked. "It is safe to let you walk by yourself?"

"Safe? Yes."

"I want to believe you. Calida, if you run back to Panther, you will risk his life. The army will soon reach our camp. He must think about that, only that. Not you."

"I know; I know. I should have told him to be careful. Should have said a prayer for him."

"All here ask that Breath Giver guide Panther's step. He does not need your white man's prayers."

About to tell Winter Rain that she would never consider herself white, Calida realized what the half-Seminole woman was talking about. She'd been raised on beliefs that came from her masters. She'd embraced those beliefs because she'd never had anything else, but the god she'd prayed to had never given her what she wanted most of all: freedom.

"I feel useless. Worthless." The moment the words were out of her mouth, she regretted them.

"I cannot see what is in your heart. I do not understand it just as you do not understand mine."

Winter Rain was right. Still, Calida was afraid to say anything for fear the girl would recognize her for the coward she was. She'd changed so much since that panic-filled day when Mistress Liana died. Piahokee felt more familiar to her than Reddin Croon's house ever had. If she could kneel at the edge of a creek without fear because an alligator might be there, why couldn't she turn around and confront the man who'd turned her into a fugitive?

Why couldn't she stand beside Panther? Match his courage?

* * *

Damn miserable hound.

After lifting his aching rear end out of the saddle long enough to restore circulation, Reddin once again faced facts. If the rock headed hound hadn't gulped down that poisonous lizard, the mutt would be with him instead of barfing until he died. That, among more damn things than he wanted to think about, was the difference between him and the men who'd agreed to take what was left of the money his father-in-law had reluctantly given him in exchange for going after the Egret clan. Because they'd never hunted with dogs, they didn't believe that having one along could make running down the Seminoles any quicker or easier.

They were wrong, damn it! And if he still had the miserable mutt, he'd show them.

Sara was walking too slowly. Just because it was going to be pitch black before much longer was no reason for her to slack off. He jerked on the rope so hard that he yanked her off her feet and had to rein in his horse while the Negress staggered upright. Fear flecked through with something else shone in her eyes. She had the look of a woman who understood who was master and who slave but also understood that her worth extended beyond what her body could provide. He didn't know how she felt about leading him to the Seminoles. Her lacerated back was proof that compliance hadn't come willingly, but even that hadn't brought her to her knees, not completely. He wondered if she knew a secret about him, one he didn't know himself. Maybe it was like that with all women and she just wasn't as good as hiding it as most women were.

As Calida had been.

Sara. That's what the nigger had said her name was, not that it mattered. She'd willingly let him bury himself in her and yet when he did, he suspected she'd taken herself off to someplace he couldn't reach.

Calida had been like that.

When he had her back again, it wouldn't be like that anymore. This time—this time he'd own all of her.

After an inordinately long period of time, Sara was ready to get going again. The men with him hadn't stopped moving, but then they'd been going so damn slow that he and Sara hadn't fallen behind. He'd wanted to get a horse for her so she wouldn't slow them down, but there hadn't been one to spare, at least not unless he was willing to pay handsomely for it. One of the men had suggested Reddin let Sara ride with him, but he'd be damned if he'd do that for a slave.

Although it was approaching night, it was still hot, and the air seared his lungs. The only living creatures that didn't seem to notice the baking heat made unbearably humid by the rain were the damnable bugs. The miserable horses . . .

Several minutes passed before Reddin pulled his thoughts back from wherever it was they'd gone. He was riding this half-dead nag because General Jesup refused to see that he was about to break the Seminoles' back. He had a way to find Panther, damn it. The whole rebel Egret clan. Osceola was nothing more than a dying and dried-up chief. Whether he remained in the swamp or was under army control didn't make any difference. Panther was the one who'd refused to have anything to do with a treaty. It was Panther who thumbed his nose at the United States Army and gave the rest of the Indians a new hero.

With Panther dead or in chains, the Seminoles would by god be singing a different song.

Reddin looked around to make sure no one was watching before allowing himself a cold smile. General Jesup was a fool. No matter what other people said and thought and wrote, Jesup wasn't any better than the bumblers who'd come before him. And when he, Lieutenant Reddin Croon, came back from this little adventure with Panther's head on the edge of a bayonet, he'd be the one placed in charge of the war against the Seminoles.

His back ached. Cursing under his breath, Reddin rose in the saddle again, not so much to look around as to ease out a few of the kinks. When his gaze happened on Sara, he tried to distract himself by imagining what he'd get her to do for him once it got dark. Unfortunately, his imagination didn't make up for reality. Sara was long in the tooth. Her breasts sagged and her rump felt like rising dough when he kneaded it. She might be able to scratch a few itches but not enough.

Only Calida could do that.

For the second time in less than a minute, he tried to stretch his spine. He was barely aware of the faint outline that was all he could see of Sara when he noticed that she'd stopped plodding along. Head high now, she stared intently in all directions as if trying to push back the night. He strained to hear but couldn't detect anything except hissing bugs and squeaking leather. He thought sure she would look back at him to see if he'd noticed the change in her, but obviously she was too distracted to remember where she was. Slowly, he reached for his musket. As he did, he glared at the men nearest him until they glanced his way. Something he took to be befuddlement twisted what he could make out of their stupid features, but at least they had the sense to follow their commander's movements.

When he yanked on the rope, Sara stopped and turned toward him. He smiled. Her mouth fell slack when he held up his rifle. "Panther!" she shrieked.

Galvanized by the name, Reddin stared into the wilderness. It seemed to be breathing, laughing at him. To have locked itself in black.

From where he crouched no more than twenty feet away, Panther sensed more than saw Croon's reaction. He could smell the man's fear, but it was more than that. Croon could hardly contain himself at the prospect of putting an end to the game they'd been playing for so long.

It was different for Panther. He'd been aware of little beyond Sara's wounded back, thought of little except the effort of carrying his father's body home for burial. Screaming like his namesake to frighten the horses, Panther catapulted himself at Sara. She shrank away but had barely moved before he reached her. He freed her with a hard slashing motion. "Run! Hide!" he ordered in Seminole. She obeyed by staggering toward where he'd been and where Gaitor waited.

Croon was lifting his musket to his shoulder. So were other soldiers, but only Croon mattered. Gaitor had made him promise that he wouldn't let revenge blind him to danger, but Croon was so close and his knife was so sharp. The man was stiff and clumsy. The musket seemed too heavy for him. He would have time. A powerful jump, a quick slash. That was all it would take to slice Croon open from crotch to knee. He would bleed to death before nightfall.

Calida would never have to fear him again.

Panther gathered his legs and ordered his muscles to obey his command. The knife felt solid. He watched as Croon's musket settled on him, saw the man's finger tighten on the hammer, but he still had time.

Then something with the force of a thunderbolt slammed into his side and nearly threw him to his knees. Despite his shock, he realized he'd been shot. Because he was still looking at Croon's musket, he knew the ball hadn't come from him. But if he stayed here beyond another heartbeat, Croon would finish what another soldier had begun.

On legs that were forgetting how to work, he plunged into the brush that had sheltered him a few minutes before. He heard men yelling, heard the squeal of frightened horses. His side felt on fire. Still gripping his knife, still running, Panther clamped his free hand over the wound and forced night fog from his mind.

He would run.

Until he died.

His breath wheezed every time he pushed it out. If he didn't silence it, they would find him before Night Spirit hid him. Consumed by the need for quiet, he barely noticed where he was going. He tripped over something and fell. Only by biting into his lower lip was he able to keep himself from crying out. His face burned as if he'd walked too close to the sun, and yet his arms and legs were cold. His heart beat furiously as if trying to escape his chest. Forcing himself to stand again, he shook his head to keep from passing out.

In a few minutes it would be too dark for anyone to find him. If he could last until then—

The horses were still whinnying. Because of the ringing in his ears, it was impossible for him to determine how far away they were. He'd been a fool. He'd forgotten his warrior's wisdom.

Because he'd looked at Reddin Croon and thought of what the man had done to Calida.

His mind flitted from one thought to another like a butterfly seeking a flower. Incapable of running any more, he kept up a staggering trot. He stepped into a spongy bog and then out of it. His feet scraped over tree roots. He bled.

Night caressed him. The air was as hot as it had ever been and sapped what strength he had left. Mouth open so he could pull more air into his lungs, Panther concentrated on sounds. A few minutes ago it seemed as if the army men were so close he could have reached out and touched them. Now the horses no longer screamed. A few still whinnied occasionally, their sounds faint.

He could—he could rest.

Earlier in the day, Gaitor and he had stopped beside a small pond. They'd agreed that if they were separated, they would look for each other there. Because he'd spent his entire life in Piahokee, Panther didn't need daylight to know what direction to go, but what had seemed a short, easy run earlier now was so hard.

He fell again. This time he couldn't say whether he'd tripped or his legs had simply given out. He lay on his good side and thought about nothing except how much it hurt to breathe. Several minutes later, he pulled himself out of the pain enough to check if he was still bleeding.

He was.

Working blindly, he felt around him for a leaf or fern to press against his side to stem the flow, but his hands only came in contact with bits and pieces of hot, rotting material.

Calida. Think about her. About seeing her again.

Strength welled up from some unknown place deep inside Panther, and he managed to stand again. He walked slowly now, carefully, like an old man who has lost the branch he uses to support his body. It didn't seem to be as hard to breathe as it had before, but maybe that was only because walking took all his concentration. He thought about the village of his childhood, of the night he and Gaitor went from strangers to brothers, of his prayers that his father's spirit would find peace. Mostly he thought of how Calida's eyes sometimes glittered like stars.

She'd wanted to come with him. If she had, she might now be dead. Or worse.

In a slow and dulled way, he realized he wasn't alone. He tried to pull in the scent of whatever it was, but all he could smell was his own blood. He stood on legs splayed wide to support him and cursed the tortured sound of his breathing. If he was dying, a panther would know. Would stalk him. But a panther was patient.

Croon?

No. Croon and his men didn't know how to be silent.

"Panther?"

"Gaitor."

Turning toward the voice, he took a child's step. His knees gave out, and he felt himself slumping into a tangle of arms and legs. He was trying to lift his head off the ground when Gaitor reached him.

"Damnation. What you do that damn fool thing fur?"

He wanted to tell Gaitor about giving Calida peace of mind, of the overwhelming need to be the one to kill Reddin Croon, but when he opened his mouth, nothing came out.

With hands that probed and poked but knew how to be gentle, Gaitor assessed his injury. Finally the Negro rocked back on his knees, a rough hand still on Panther's chest. "You cain't walk, can you?"

Panther could tell him that he'd try, that if Gaitor would give him just a bit of help, he'd make it to where the Egret clan was, but it would be a lie, and if Gaitor didn't know it now, he soon would. "You cannot carry me," Panther managed. "Where is Sara?"

"Here," the woman whispered from somewhere in the dark. "Panther, you saved my life. He would have killed me. I know he would have."

At least he'd done that; he should be glad. "Why are there no more troops than these?" he asked. He wasn't sure whether that was important.

"I dons know," Sara said. " 'cept that Massa Croon and that general man had a big argument when the massa tole him what he was gonna make me do. The general, he says the army gots to—to honor its 'greement with the Negroes."

He didn't need Sara to tell him what Reddin Croon thought of that; her back was proof. Gathering strength from bits and pieces of his body, Panther told Gaitor that he had to get himself and Sara back to the Egret clan as quickly as possible. If necessary, the clan members would separate and hide, anything to keep Croon and his men from finding them.

"What 'bouts you?" Gaitor cut in before he'd finished. "I ain't gonna leave you here."

"You have to." Panther forced himself to remain propped on his elbow. "I will rest and follow—" His mouth dried. He swallowed and swallowed again. "I will follow later."

"The hell—"

"Gaitor! We have no time for this." He should shut his eyes; all he could see was a blood-red haze. "I will only slow you. The clan must be told. Only you can—only you can do that."

Gaitor cursed under his breath but didn't argue. Panther was grateful for that because he lacked the strength for any more conversation. Still, he would miss his friend's touch, his presence. Fighting the pain drumming through him, he and Gaitor briefly discussed where the clan would gather should it be necessary for the members to separate. If he were strong, it would take a three-day journey to reach the clean, hot sand where sea met land. Now . . .

After washing Panther's wound with drinking water and pressing a moss bandage against it, Gaitor handed him what was left of the food and water and told him he would return as soon as he could. Then, silent, Gaitor slipped into the wilderness with Sara close behind. Panther concentrated on the fading sound of footsteps until he could no longer hear them. Gaitor hadn't called him a fool, but both men knew the truth. He had put his need for revenge before safety, and maybe his life would end tonight because of it. Only, it wasn't just revenge. Reddin Croon had had him bound like a captured animal, had turned him and his clan into fugitives, but the man hadn't taken his body for his pleasure as he'd done with Calida.

Calida.

What might have happened if he'd let her come with him?

His elbow began to ache. Moving as carefully as possible, he stretched out on the damp, heated ground. His side screamed; he sucked in air, fought the pain. He was shaking and yet his face still felt so hot. He would rest for awhile. Then . . .

His thoughts had gone somewhere where he couldn't find them when he spotted twin red spots of light in the distance and forced himself to concentrate. Understanding, he wrapped his hand around his spear and waited for the alligator.

20

Calida's legs burned. Her lungs ached and pulling air into them made her head pound. Still, the thought of stopping never entered her mind. Gaitor and an exhausted Sara had reached the Egret clan at daylight. In clipped tones, Gaitor had told everyone what had happened, and she'd forced herself to listen. Panther, shot by Reddin Croon!

Only Gaitor was to return for Panther because it wasn't safe for more than him to get closer to the army. The rest, Calida included, were to scatter and eventually join up again at Sea Point. Before he left, Gaitor had to consult the healer and dispatch runners to Osceola and other chiefs.

Panther might not have that much time. That was why she'd insisted Sara tell her how to find him.

Her hips moved rhythmically. By keeping her attention split between the ground beneath her and what lay ahead, she kept up a steady pace that might—please—allow her to reach Panther before he died.

I'm coming, Panther, I'm coming, she chanted to herself as sweat poured off her. She carried water but had drunk only sparingly because Panther might need it. Gaitor had assured her that he'd left

Panther with something to eat, and because she hadn't wanted to deprive the clan of what little food they had, she hadn't tried to take any with her.

She had a knife, prayed she'd be able to find the herbs she'd seen the healer use.

He *had* to be alive. Croon *couldn't* have killed him.

It was late afternoon now. She should be approaching the creek where they'd been forced to leave Panther. She cursed the necessity of having to move in a wide arc around the troops with their hated leader, but it couldn't be any other way. She'd heard them once, and although she couldn't say why, for a few minutes she had debated sneaking closer. In the end, fear for Panther had kept her on course.

She paused briefly to grab a couple of fresh persimmons. The sweet fruit quieted the worst of her hunger and brought needed moisture to her throat. She tucked the other one in her pocket for Panther because he *would* be alive when she reached him. He would.

The vegetation, which had already been so thick that she could barely find a trail through it, became even more clogged. It wasn't the first time she'd walked where it felt as if the plants might envelop her. Still, she felt trapped, unable to see more than a few feet in any direction. Because the glossy-leafed palms and rain-fed cypress put most of their energy into their tops, they created a curtain that nearly shut out the sun. The air down here felt old and trapped. She longed for the clearings Panther had always found for them to stay in. She missed the great stretches of pines in dryer areas.

When a large snowy egret rose into the air ahead of her, she watched the pure white bird with its soft, fluffy feathers disappear through a slit of an opening. Mistress Liana had had a hat made from egret feathers. She'd put it on once when no one was watching and imagined herself the grand lady. Now, although she could have a dozen plumes if she so desired, she preferred to see the birds alive. St. Augustine, which had once fascinated her, no longer held any appeal. She prayed she would never see it again.

She heard a cough, stopped. It wasn't a human sound. She knew the difference between what came from a man's throat and the noise an alligator made. After nearly a minute, the cough was repeated, to her left and ahead. A hunting alligator can be silent, but sometimes when they want to frighten their victim, they bellow like that. Panther had told her so.

Moving cautiously, she concentrated on each step. Because she hadn't seen the army for several hours, she thought about calling out to see if Panther answered, but Croon might have left some of his men behind to search for him. Her belly tightened at the thought that they might have found him—might have found his body. If they'd left him because he was useless to them, maybe that was what had attracted the alligator.

A grunt followed by an angry shout pulled her from her thoughts. Despite the sense of urgency eating away at her, she forced herself to move slowly and silently. Because women weren't allowed on hunting trips, she hadn't been able to watch the men as they stalked game, but it came easily to her. Crouching low, her knife held firm and ready, she followed where her senses led her. Several times she stopped to listen. Something heavy and slow was moving through the grasses just beyond where she could see. She knew the sound an alligator made as it dragged its awkward body over land. This was it.

She slipped around a palm, careful to remain in the generous shadows. Pushing aside a fern, she spotted the area Sara had told her about. Because it had been fed by rain for several weeks, the creek overflowed its banks and oozed through the vegetation on either side.

She saw the alligator first. The deadly monster-sized beast lay with its mouth half open and its tail just out of the water. It was staring at something.

Panther.

He lay on his side. His right hand was draped over a spear, but he didn't seem to be holding onto it. She strained to catch the rise and fall of his chest, but he was too far away for her to see. How long had he'd been locked in confrontation with the alligator? She'd heard his shout a few minutes ago, but he was motionless now.

The alligator's mouth opened a few more inches. Its tail moved lazily from side to side like a panther waiting for sleep to overcome it, but the massive creature wasn't falling asleep. It was waiting to eat.

"Panther." His name came out a harsh and yet barely audible hiss.

The *tastanagee* didn't move.

"Panther?"

The alligator must have heard. Either that, or it had grown tired of the waiting game. Slowly and ponderously, it lifted itself onto its too-small legs and began inching closer to Panther. When it had covered half the distance, while she was still trying to come to grips with the danger the creature represented, Panther lifted his head off the ground. His hand tightened around the spear, and she saw the muscles along his back grow hard and ready. He must have heard her, but maybe there was nothing left of him except the need to keep the alligator from attacking.

Pushing away from the tree, she started toward the combatants. Her knife would be no defense against thick scales. She would have to use Panther's spear. *I'm here, Panther. I'm here.* She kept her desperate message inside her because she didn't dare draw Panther's attention off his foe. A moment of weakness, of inattention, was all it might take to prompt an attack.

Inch by silent inch she eased closer. Despite what she'd told herself, it worried her that Panther hadn't sensed her presence. The alligator didn't seem to notice her either. If her legs were strong enough and her reactions quick enough, she should be able to reach the spear before the beast completed its deadly lunge. But if she had to wrestle the weapon out of Panther's hand—

"Panther. It's me."

He made no movement to indicate he'd heard, yet she sensed a change in him. It wasn't that he'd relaxed his guard in any way. Rather, it was if he was now sharing this moment, this reality with her. She didn't dare concentrate on him because if she did, she might miss something vital in the alligator's movements.

The beast seemed to be enjoying himself. If it was possible for alligators to be playful, this one was. He'd found what he considered easy prey. He could wait, draw out the act of killing.

She would die before she let that happen.

Beyond any emotion except determination, she continued toward Panther. Only now did the alligator acknowledge her presence by briefly turning its head in her direction and lashing its tail back and forth. She could sense it readying its ponderous body for a charge, but she moved first. Pushing off, she covered the ground still separating her from Panther in a single bound. She bent down and grabbed the spear, barely aware that Panther had offered no resistance. Screaming, she ran at the alligator. All she could see was the massive head with its jaws open wide. Beyond those deadly teeth was a soft and vulnerable throat. She aimed at that dark spot, tightened her hand around the spear, lunged forward, and plunged it deep into the animal's mouth. The great jaws snapped shut. She felt something hard rake across the back of her hand, but didn't take time to determine whether she'd been injured.

The alligator began thrashing in a frenzied circle. Horrified, she watched as blood seeped out from between its teeth. She'd never killed anything before. This creature was huge, much longer than Panther was tall, so wide across the back that her legs couldn't span it.

Recoiling from what she'd done, Calida nevertheless continued to stare in fascination. The beast lifted its head and then slammed it against the ground as if that could dislodge what barely protruded from its mouth. The jaws snapped open. Little feet clawing furiously, it turned in a short circle and half ran, half slithered into the creek. She watched it slowly disappear, shuddered when the water around it turned red.

Panther.

By ordering her every movement, she managed to walk the few steps back to him. Her body trembled as if thunder was rumbling through it, and for too long, she couldn't think what to do besides stare down at the *tastanagee.* Her *tastanagee.*

He'd managed to work himself into a sitting position, but his white lips told her how much the effort had cost. His hand slid to his side, and he pressed. His nostrils flared.

"Panther!" Thinking only of him now, she sank to her knees beside him. He made a queer little movement as if to increase the distance between them and then slumped forward gracefully, silently. She caught him and helped ease him back to the ground. He breathed quickly and shallowly with the faintest gasp at the end of each breath. His eyes were open and fixed on her, but she wasn't sure whether he saw her.

Before giving herself up completely to him, she looked back at the creek. She could just make out the scales along the alligator's back. The stained water around it bubbled and churned. She wondered if it was dying and how long that would take.

"You should not be here."

She didn't want Panther to exhaust himself by talking. At the same time, the need to hear his voice was a sharp pain. "You're all right," she said in a singsong tone she couldn't control. "You're going to be all right."

When he didn't acknowledge what she'd said, she began caressing his shoulder. Even so weak that he could barely keep his eyes open, he was strength, and she took in some of it for herself. "What about the soldiers?" she asked. "I didn't see or hear anyone. They didn't leave anyone here to look for you?"

"None would stay. I heard them arguing with him."

She wouldn't think about Reddin Croon. Only Panther mattered. "I—I didn't take time to collect any herbs." Unless he told her he didn't want it, she would continue to touch him. "I think—I think I can find what you need."

"It does not matter."

"Not matter?" Did he know he was dying? Oh please—

"You *must* go, Calida. You belong with the clan, safe where the army cannot find you."

The only place she wanted to be was here; didn't he know that? "I can't leave you; I won't."

"No! Calida—"

"Stop it, Panther!" Tension and fear made her voice sharper than she wanted it to be. "I defied your orders, yours and Gaitor's, because I was determined to find you. Do you think I'm going to leave now? Do you?" She jerked her head at where she'd last seen the alligator. "He isn't the only one, you know that. Another will come after you, and you don't have your spear anymore."

His lids slid over his beautiful black eyes. Alarmed, she crouched over him. To her relief, his chest moved steadily in and out and the vein at the side of his neck pulsed with life. If she didn't look at his side, she could believe he'd simply fallen asleep. When he woke, he'd tell her he was going hunting and then—

No. Not hunting. He'd hold out his arms and she'd go to him and they'd—

He didn't want her here. She didn't dare forget that.

Spurred on by the need to do something so she wouldn't have time for thinking, she gently removed the wrapping Gaitor had placed over his wound. The sight of the raw flesh nearly made her cry out in alarm. After a moment, she forced herself to touch the flesh around it. It was too hot.

"Panther? I've got to find some gumbo-limbo bark or medicine vine to pull the poison out of you. It won't take long; I promise."

He opened his eyes. She was afraid he'd repeat his order that she leave, and she'd be forced to argue with him, but he didn't. "Thank you," he whispered, "for saving my life."

She hadn't yet done what she'd come here to accomplish. Unless—no!—*until* she had, there was nothing to thank her for. Holding her emotions tight within her, she reached for the water bladder she wore slung over her shoulder and helped him drink. Although he didn't say anything, his raging eyes told her how much he hated this weakness. She still shook from the aftereffects of having killed the alligator but struggled to keep all reaction from him. Although she'd told him she had to leave him to search for the necessary herbs, she wasted precious time telling him what had happened after Gaitor and Sara reached the clan. He nodded; his eyes remained clear enough that she believed he understood everything she said.

"Why did you do it?" The question burst from her before she could stop herself. "Gaitor said Sara was free and that you should have run. Instead, you attacked Croon."

"I tried. I failed."

He'd saved Sara's life. Wasn't that enough? "Why, Panther?" she insisted. "There were army men all around. Surely you knew they'd try to stop you. You risked your life. Why?"

"I wanted him dead."

She already knew that. She nearly told him so, but before the words could burst from her, she forced herself to remain silent. Panther had a thousand reasons for hating Reddin Croon. He, and others like him, had turned the Egret clan into fugitives barely able to keep their children fed. That was enough of a reason, wasn't it?

Maybe not.

"I saw Sara's back. You looked at it and remembered what happened to your father, didn't you?"

"Yes."

"Is that why? You couldn't save your father, but you could avenge what had been done to her?"

"No."

She was exhausting him when he needed to conserve his strength for the long walk ahead of them. *No.* His response echoed inside her, made it impossible to let go of her need for the truth. "What are you saying?"

His blink was so slow that she was afraid he wouldn't open his eyes again, but when she could again look into the midnight depths, she saw that he was still fully conscious. "I wanted him dead so he could never touch you again."

It seemed to take forever to find what she needed. She knew it would have been easier if she'd been able to concentrate on her task, but her thoughts remained back with Panther. He hated being weak. Without his saying anything, she knew that bothered him more than the pain. Remembering how helpless she'd been as Reddin Croon's slave, she understood what he was having to deal with. She also knew that nothing she said or did would make it easier for him.

A *tastanagee* was supposed to be strong. He'd spent his entire life with strength flowing through his veins. And now he couldn't stand, had to rely on a woman's help to do something as simple as swallow. If there'd been a way she could have given him a drink without touching or looking at him, he might not have to dwell on it, but she couldn't change that any more than she could silence his last words to her.

He'd thrown wisdom and maybe his life aside because he'd wanted to end Croon's threat, had been consumed by vengeance.

Reddin Croon had owned her. She should be the one filled with rage.

Unless . . .

Terrified that Panther had died while she was gone, she slipped toward him but didn't speak until she saw him stretch out his leg.

Fighting back tears, she lowered herself to her knees beside him. When he opened his eyes, she showed him that she'd filled her skirt with peeling bark and soft vine. Needing to say something, she told him that she first had to crush the bark in water before she could apply it to his wound. He nodded, then watched through lowered lids while she worked. Feeling grit on her hands, she wished she had time to bathe. She started to run her fingers through her hair to see if it was tangled, then forced herself to stop. Panther was hurt; he needed to rejoin his clan. Surely he didn't care whether she had leaves and twigs in her hair.

They spent what was left of the day doing very little. At his prompting, she cut a straight branch and then sharpened one end so she would have another weapon. She broke off a limb to use as a crutch tomorrow. Although she wanted to move Panther farther from the creek, she didn't want to deplete what little strength remained in him. She got him to eat the persimmon and after a short search, found some tubers, which she scraped clean and fed to him. He insisted she take her share of the food, and because she'd gone all day without anything except a piece of fruit, she did as he said.

She couldn't count the number of times he fell asleep, and she told herself it was because he knew the wisdom of resting so he could grow strong again. She changed the wound dressing frequently, not because it needed it, but because she wanted to see if the bark and vines were having any effect. As it was getting dark, he told her that the wound no longer felt hot.

She slept beside him. Again and again she stirred herself to listen for alligators, panthers, or soldiers. Whenever she sat up, she felt his body tense and knew he was listening to the night with her. Twice she heard the scraping slither of alligators and yelled and pounded the crutch against the ground until they left. After the second time, Panther's arm was waiting for her when she lay back down. Not speaking, he drew her against his good side. She needed to rest if they were going to travel tomorrow, but Panther's touch and warmth stirred something deep inside her and kept her awake—so awake. Whatever that something was hummed and throbbed until she thought she might scream, until she wasn't sure she could keep her hands off him.

She tried to think of other things, but only the rhythm of his breathing and his flesh separated from her by a single layer of cloth mattered. The night sang and moved around them.

Panther was in awe of Calida's strength. Holding her last night, he'd been aware of how small she was, but her size was deceptive. He'd railed against his helplessness, not because he was a *tastanagee* with a clan to lead, but because he wanted to be strong for her.

Only, she didn't need that from him.

Using the thick branch she'd given him to lean against, he'd managed to walk without help most of the time. His side felt as if tiny, sharp teeth were chewing on him, but he took himself away from that by watching her walk.

Instead of going back the way Calida had come, they took off at an angle designed to take them toward where the Egret clan was fleeing. He'd hoped the vegetation would become less lush and they'd be able to travel faster, but the dense brush and trees seemed endless. Still, a part of him didn't mind.

They traveled at a slow pace all day. Except to talk about where Reddin Croon's troops might be and whether any of the former slaves were or would ever be on their way to Oklahoma, they said little. He searched his mind for words to break the long silences, but in truth, he needed all of his strength simply to keep moving. If someone asked him which of them was the leader in this journey, he wouldn't be able to say. They seemed to be working in unison, frequently judging his endurance and altering their pace as conditions warranted. As afternoon sagged into evening, he was forced to admit to himself that he was barely capable of walking, let alone deciding where his steps would take him. Although she said nothing, he had no doubt that Calida knew. It wasn't quite dark when she pointed toward a small hammock. They would, she told him, spend the night there. Slumping to the ground, he rested his head against a tree trunk and almost immediately fell asleep. He didn't wake until he smelled roasting fish.

Calida's face was expressionless as she explained that she'd first whittled a slim spear out of a branch and then waited beside a quiet pool of water until a large fish swam so close that she was able to spear it. She'd used the flint she carried in her pocket to start a small fire. "I have never seen a woman fish," he admitted. "I have never thought of it as something a woman would do."

"And I never thought I'd be living in Piahokee, Panther."

"If you could, would you walk away from it?"

"I don't know. I'm free. Whatever it takes, at least I'm free. I can't think beyond that."

The fish tasted delicious. He swore he could feel it seeping throughout his system and returning a measure of strength to his spent muscles. He nearly told her that, but never in his life had he admitted weakness to anyone. The sun had set by the time they finished eating. Calida redressed his wound, then told him she wanted to look for berries or roots to eat in the morning. If she could fish, he thought, he could help her with what he'd always believed was women's work. However, before he could make the decision to stand, sleep claimed him. He didn't wake until morning sun touched his eyelids. She lay beside him, hair tangling about her face, a long-fingered hand trailing over his side. If he'd killed Croon, she might spend the rest of her life looking as peaceful as she did at this moment—as lovely.

The second day was a repeat of the first. He'd hoped that a night's rest would restore him, but if anything, he was weaker than he'd been before. He tried to hide his condition from Calida, but from the way she studied him, he guessed she knew the truth. She talked more than she had before, her voice low and easy. She frequently fell silent as they listened for sounds that might warn of danger. In between those silences, she told him that she used to walk along the beach near St. Augustine and had collected a large number of the seemingly endless seashells. Once she'd seen a play with her mistress. Going to a play, she insisted with a delighted laugh, was like entering a new world.

He listened not so much to the words, but to the warmth in her voice. Because she asked, he told her a little about what it had been like to know from birth that he'd been chosen to lead his people in times of war, but he didn't want to talk about that. Piahokee surrounded them. They were trapped in it and yet he didn't want to be anywhere else and believed she felt the same way. The voices of a thousand birds, insects, and animals hummed around them. Despite the heat, they seldom saw the sun because the trees formed an almost unbroken ceiling. He wondered if she felt as small and insignificant as he did with dense vegetation clogging the world in all directions. He was *tastanagee*. He shouldn't feel this way, should deny the emotion. But it was the truth and he would only be lying to himself if he said different.

The sea was still several days' journey ahead, but they were nearing a treeless area where, before the strangers forced them from it, Seminoles had once planted corn and other crops. All members of the Egret clan would stop briefly at this sacred place on their way to their final destination. He believed they'd reached it in time to meet up with some if not all of the clan.

When they were within a fifteen-minute walk of the home of his ancestors, Panther stopped. He leaned against his staff until his heart no longer felt as if it wanted to escape his chest and listened again to the wilderness. He'd been right; in the distance he could hear the faint murmur of voices, Seminole voices. Calida stood only a few feet away listening to the same sounds. Her long, dark hair was tangled and a few small leaves clung to it. Her legs had been scratched in several places. She'd have to make herself a new dress. Her back was straight, her eyes clear.

"Calida."

A shiver so slight that he might have imagined it slid through her.

"I owe you my life," he said. "Twice now you have stood between me and death."

"You've done the same for me."

He didn't see it that way. He wanted to tell her how deep his debt to her ran, but he was a warrior who had already said all he could. Barely aware of what he was doing, he held out his hand, and she came toward him. She placed her hand in his, and he let his staff fall to the ground. She was a wild bird, frightened and yet incapable of moving. Trembling, lips slightly parted, small and brave, a warrior in her own right.

Maybe she wasn't afraid of him after all.

Maybe she felt something far different.

"Our time alone is almost over," he said.

"Yes."

He wanted to ask her if she was sorry that they were rejoining the others but couldn't think how to form the words. One of them had stepped closer to the other; maybe they were both responsible.

The birds and insects and animals fell silent; either that or he couldn't concentrate on them. He no longer felt the heat and was unaware of his wounded side. It had been just the two of them for so long that he couldn't remember anything or anyone else. And now—now that was ending.

But not yet.

Not until he wrapped his arms around her and pulled her against him.

Feeling strong and weak and full of raw wanting, he lowered his head toward her. She stood on her toes, gripped his shoulders, drew herself even closer to him.

Her lips were moist. Soft. Giving.

21

Calida looked out from the shadows at the small group of Seminoles. There were only twelve, including Winter Rain and Sara. She didn't see Gaitor, which bothered her. She prayed the others had gone on ahead or would soon join those who'd reached what had once been undisputed Seminole land.

Beside her, Panther too watched. She felt not the day's heat, but his. He'd held her and kissed her. No, that wasn't the truth. Her arms had enveloped him at the same time he'd reached for her. She'd welcomed, maybe even initiated what they'd done. She had no explanation for it, didn't want it. Hadn't she spent two days carefully keeping her physical if not emotional distance from the *tastanagee?*

She'd been weak. A moment of weakness, that's all it had been.

She knew that was a lie.

"We made it," she said with a heartfelt sigh. "And they are here, at least some are."

"I would be dead without you, Calida."

He had to stop saying that. Panther was like the wind, ceaseless and ageless. Reddin Croon's bullets were incapable of killing him. They had to be!

A small voice that said she was trying to make Panther into

something he couldn't possibly be demanded to be heard, but she shoved it aside. Panther was alive, and that was all that mattered. Because she didn't trust herself to look at him again, she stepped to one side and waited for him to lead the way. He wouldn't want his people to see him leaning on her any more than she did. The depth of his weakness would remain unspoken between the two of them, just as so much of what she felt and needed remained trapped inside her.

"Panther! Panther!"

Winter Rain ran toward them, her long hair a wild cloud around her small face. Calida was afraid Winter Rain would hurt Panther, but when the younger woman's gaze fell on the walking stick and then his bandage, she stopped. Crying a little, she stared up at him. Panther waited until the others had joined her before explaining. Calida wanted to hide from the scrutiny that came her way. Most of all she was aware of how Winter Rain's attention flicked from Panther to Calida, and then back to Panther again.

"You risked your life for him?" Winter Rain asked when Panther told them about the alligator. "You did that for him?"

A heavy sense of finality accompanied the question. Calida wanted to tell her that it hadn't been like that at all, that Winter Rain shouldn't believe a bond had been forged between her and Panther when she wasn't worthy of such a thing, but now wasn't the time or place.

"You—you did not see Gaitor?" Winter Rain asked.

"No," Panther whispered.

"He went looking for you," Sara cut in. "I begged him to stay, but—"

"When did he leave?"

Although her explanation was garbled, by the time Sara finished, Calida knew Gaitor had been consumed by concern for Panther. She didn't have to look at Panther to know he was worried about his friend; they both were. As skilled a tracker as Gaitor was, he should have found them. In fact, she was surprised Gaitor hadn't overtaken her.

Panther turned in a slow circle, his eyes fixed on his surroundings. He seemed to have forgotten where he was, that he was still wounded, that Calida stood beside him. Catching Winter Rain's concerned look, she struggled to keep her own fears for Gaitor under control.

"Someone has to go after him," Winter Rain insisted. "He—I did not want him to go. I pleaded with him, but he would not listen."

"The risk is too great." Panther's voice was low and intense. "No one will search for him."

"No one?" Winter Rain grabbed Panther's arm. "What if he is hurt? He—I should have gone with him. I should—but I was afraid."

"Panther speaks the truth," Calida said, although she hated every word she was forced to say. She sensed Panther's deep frustration at not being able to go in search of his friend. "The army is close; we need to put more distance between ourselves and them. Gaitor could be anywhere."

Winter Rain sobbed and went on staring up at Panther. "I know," she whispered. "I am sorry. I should not have said . . ."

Her voice trailed off, and in the silence that followed, Calida listened to the labored sound of Panther's breathing and hated his weakness as much as he did. Finally, Sara said she still had some of the herbs the healer had given her for her back and wanted Panther to use them. Calida thought he might argue that they needed immediately to be on the move again. When he didn't, she wasn't sure whether it was because he was too tired to go on or was hoping to give Gaitor more time to overtake them.

Heart twisting, Calida watched Panther walk away with Sara. He hadn't once looked at her since the clan members recognized them. He was grateful for what she'd done—their embrace had told her that—but maybe what he felt for her went no further. How could it? He knew she'd ended her own children's lives. She was unworthy of anything except contempt and hatred.

Not sure what to do, Calida tried to focus on her surroundings. Except for Winter Rain, the rest of the clan had followed Panther and Sara. "It is not good between you and Panther?" Winter Rain asked abruptly. "He does not want to be near you?"

Too physically and emotionally weary for anything except the truth, Calida told Winter Rain she had no idea what Panther was thinking. "He fears for Gaitor. There's no one who can go after him?"

"I wish. Oh, how I wish. If I could have gotten someone to go with me, I would not be here now." Winter Rain swallowed and her hand went to her throat. "But we are women and children and old people. There are no warriors with us, none except for Panther. You love him, do you not?"

Love. "I—I don't know."

"You do not know your heart?"

"I'm tired, Winter Rain. Too tired to think."

"I think not." After a glance in Panther's direction, Winter Rain spent the better part of a minute studying the wilderness while Calida waited and hurt. "If he is dead—" Winter Rain began. "I have never seen Gaitor like that. He was a wild animal, he wanted to go back for Panther that much. But he could not until he had provided for us. He said—he told me he hated being torn apart like that. When you left, it took all my strength to stop him from following you."

"Why did you?"

Calida felt Winter Rain sink into herself. "I—we had no meat. The braves had gone on ahead to see if the journey was safe."

"Was that the only reason? Because you wanted him to bring down some game?"

"No." Winter Rain stared at her without blinking. "No," she repeated.

"Maybe it was because you were afraid of what might happen if the army overtook you and neither Gaitor nor Panther was here."

"Yes." Winter Rain didn't sound convinced. "We would be helpless. When he had calmed down, that is what Gaitor said. That he could never again face himself if something happened to us. But he was even more afraid that his friend was dying. He—" She pressed her hand against her cheek. "He promised me that he would return."

Wondering if Gaitor's hardest decision had been to leave Winter Rain, Calida tried to remember whether she'd seen the two of them together more than usual. When she first came to the Egret clan, they had numbered over a hundred. Now there were less than twenty. True, many were finding their own way to the sea as Panther had ordered, but there was something fragile and vulnerable looking about those clustered around Panther.

They were her life. *He* was her life.

Only, she wasn't worthy.

Beyond words, she gripped Winter Rain's hand and hung on. She sensed the other woman's fear, but it was all so mixed in with what she was feeling that she couldn't sort any of it out. She'd helped Panther return to his people. He now belonged to them. And she?

Calida's heart belonged to Panther. Winter Rain had only to look at the former slave to know that beyond any doubt. It might have happened while the two of them were alone together, but maybe Calida had fallen in love long before and that was why she'd gone off alone in search of him.

Alone.

Despite her resolve not to, Winter Rain studied her surroundings time and time again until it was too dark to see. She'd been terrified at the thought of Panther alone and wounded out there; her fear should have eased now that the *tastanagee* was back.

But it hadn't. Night had swallowed Gaitor.

Too restless to join the others, Winter Rain paced from one end of the opening to another. She'd lived here briefly as a child and remembered following behind her mother as she harvested corn. If her mother was still alive, she could ask her how she'd felt when they left. If her father was nearby, she could ask him the same thing. Only, her mother was dead and her father was with Osceola. She'd stayed with the Egret clan because . . .

It didn't matter. Nothing did except reaching the sea so they could join up with the rest of the Seminoles.

No. That didn't matter either.

Nothing did except that she should have gone with Gaitor. She was young and strong. No one needed her here. Calida had had the courage to strike out on her own, or maybe the truth was, Calida had been so consumed by fear for Panther that nothing else had mattered.

Tonight, watching the stars flicker to life one after the other, Winter Rain prayed not for Panther's health, but for Gaitor's life. She couldn't think of anything except him, knew she couldn't sleep until he returned.

Why?

All he'd done was touch her cheek with a rough but gentle hand. And he'd smiled down at her, a smile he'd shared with no one else. *"I will be back,"* he had said. *"I will not let anything happen to you."* To her. Not to the others. To her.

Her neck began to cramp, and she was forced to stop her study of the sky. As her gaze fell on the knot of people around what remained of the small deer Gaitor had killed, she realized that all of them were turning in the same direction. A moment later, a tall, dark figure emerged from the night.

Shaking so much that she could barely keep her feet under her, she managed to half stagger and half run toward Gaitor. She reached him a heartbeat after he placed himself in front of Panther, who was lying on a grass mat.

"You return, my friend," Panther said simply.

"You are alive, my friend," Gaitor said just as simply. He dropped to his knees and held out his hand. Panther returned his grasp while tears flowed over Winter Rain's cheeks.

She didn't remember pushing past the others, but she must have because she was now only a few inches from Gaitor's massive shoulder. Not trusting herself to speak and afraid to let anyone see how grateful she was, she stood, wrapped deep in her thoughts, as Gaitor explained what he'd been doing since he left the others. The route he'd taken had brought him near Reddin Croon's troop. Although he'd been wild to reach Panther as quickly as possible, he also knew it was necessary to learn what the enemy was up to. Slipping as close as he dared, he'd overheard an argument between Croon and his men.

"He was fussin' 'en fussin' at them 'bout how they let Sara get away and didn' go after either you or me. Kept at it sumthin' fierce 'til one of 'em tole him he didn' have to take it no more. Next I knew, they was all leavin'.'"

"His men deserted?" Panther asked.

"Right 'fore my eyes. Croon, he been drinkin'. Kept on drinkin' long after they was gone. He said he was gonna kill anyone who walked out on him, but they grabbed his musket 'fore he could git his hands on it. They laughed at him there at the end. I thought—"

"He's alone?" Calida interrupted. "Alone and unarmed?"

"Not unarmed, gal. It took him awhile, but he finally hauled his weapon out o' the bushes where they throwed it. But he ain't gonna do much damage with it like he is."

Calida clenched her fists and looked out at the night. "Where is he?"

"I don' know, gal. Last I saw him, he was passed out, but that was a while ago."

Gaitor went on to explain that when he reached where he'd last seen Panther, he spotted signs telling him that two people had left together. Guessing that Calida had been the one to find his friend, he'd hurried after them, but he'd spent so much time watching Croon and the others that he'd never caught up to his chief. "You moved some there, Panther," he finished. "Made me think maybe you wasn' hurt near as bad as I thought."

Although the conversation now centered on whether the group should leave at first light or take a chance on waiting through the day so everyone could rest, Winter Rain heard little of that. She was aware of Calida's continued nervousness. Despite what both Gaitor and Panther had said about Reddin Croon having lost his teeth, Calida still feared the man.

Threat. Danger.

No matter how many times she tried to reassure herself that Gaitor had snuck away from the army men without their being aware of his presence, Winter Rain continued to feel sick at the thought of what he'd risked. Gaitor was everything she wasn't, so strong that he feared nothing, wise and courageous. He'd always been gentle around her. At first she'd been afraid of him because he was so big, because she sensed his deep and all but consuming anger at having been treated as less than human. But over the months, he'd become a Seminole warrior, a man proud of who he was. A man capable of leadership.

Remembering he'd had nothing to eat, Winter Rain shyly handed him some of the roots she'd dug earlier that day. He barely glanced at her at first but then fixed his attention on her. "Thank you," he said simply. It seemed that he was reluctant to turn from her. Finally someone asked him a question and he did. Remaining where she was, she studied the way Panther and Gaitor acted around each other. Despite his weakness, Panther obviously still saw himself as the clan's leader. Just the same, he and Gaitor discussed everything as equals. She'd always been aware of the bond between them, but it seemed even stronger than before. She wondered if it had been strengthened at the moment a bullet tore into Panther. His life had been at stake. Nothing else should have mattered. Still, Gaitor had put Sara's safety before Panther's, not because he didn't care what happened to his chief, but because the clan's survival had come first.

The toll on Gaitor had been incredible. It must have been just as hard for Panther, but Panther had had Calida—

Calida, who hadn't once taken her eyes off the *tastanagee* and had risked her own life by going into Piahokee after him.

Weary from the long day of walking and worrying, Winter Rain suddenly wanted nothing more than to stretch out and sleep. She wouldn't think, wouldn't remember the way Calida gazed up at Panther. Or that Panther had eyes only for Gaitor and Calida and none for her.

Her tears had dried. Admitting how little she mattered to Panther tonight, she waited for them to return. Instead, despite a small ache deep inside her, she felt no need to cry. Numb, Winter Rain slipped away from the group, but instead of heading toward the pile of leaves she'd collected for her bed, she wandered toward a massive cypress. Staring up at it, she thought about the first time she'd climbed a tree. Her father had helped her reach the lowest branches and then encouraged her as she slowly made her way higher. She'd been so brave then. Maybe not brave so much as determined to prove to her father that she was worthy of his praise. Her mother had come upon them, and although she'd scolded her husband for risking their daughter's neck, her voice had held laughter and love.

"Winter Rain?"

Another voice. From the present. Male. "Gaitor? What—"

"I saw you leave. You's all right?"

"I—I'm fine. I was just thinking—" Gathering her courage, Winter Rain faced him and wasn't surprised to see that he'd blocked out the night sky. "Thinking about something that happened a long time ago."

"I don' think 'bout the past. Tries not to anyhow."

He'd never told her that. The truth was, they'd seldom said anything to each other. "You must be exhausted. And hungry. I can get you—"

"Later. You's really all right? I saw you was cryin'."

"It does not matter," she said with conviction. "Gaitor? I am glad you are back. So glad."

He brushed his fingers lightly over her lower arm. A shiver raced up her spine and stopped her breath. It was too dark to see into his eyes, for him to look into hers and maybe guess how off balance she felt. "We cain't stay here," he said. "Just 'cause Croon's men left him don't mean there ain't more whites 'round."

"I know."

"I don' like it bein' like this fur you. Not havin' no folks 'en all, you should at least know where you's gonna sleep."

"It's all right, Gaitor. It's all right. At least I am free."

"We's all free. Tonight."

He said it so simply when it wasn't simple at all. Overcome by the need to give him something, she gripped his hand. Her fingers barely surrounded his, but she held on anyway. "When we reach the sea, the Seminoles will be strong again," she promised him. "Don't think about anything else."

"You believes that?"

"I cannot not believe," she told him honestly.

"Neither can I, 'cause that's all there is."

Was it? Something soft and alive had begun to grow inside her. She wasn't yet ready to examine it, but the time would come. In the meantime, she'd stand here in the dark beside Gaitor while his chest expanded and contracted and his hand continued to hold hers.

Out of the corner of her eye, she noticed that the clan members were scattering, leaving Panther to rest. Only Calida remained within the light of the dying cooking fire. Calida's hands were tight by her side, her fists clenched. The woman held herself hard and still as if she was battling something strong and wild inside her.

Then Gaitor thanked Winter Rain for giving him something to eat and she forgot about Calida.

Reddin's throat tasted of vomit. He gagged but didn't throw up because his stomach had already emptied itself. Cursing, he dragged

himself off the spongy, stinking ground and managed to haul himself into a sitting position.

He was alone.

The bastards he'd paid good money to were gone. They'd deserted him.

It was Calida's fault. Hers and that ignorant, dangerous savage,
the one he should have killed the other day.

Calida, damn her. Damn her!

When his head pounded, he forced himself to calm down, but
that didn't kill the stench of hatred that now filled him. The bastards
who'd left him to die had made a crucial mistake. They'd left his
horse behind.

Looking around, he was forced to admit he didn't have an idea
in hell where he was. In the morning, he'd be able to get his bear-
ings from studying the rising sun, but right now, swallowed by the
god-awful Everglades, he felt more alone than he had in his entire
life. Fear nibbled at his nerve endings and would have consumed
him if he hadn't still been half drunk. As it was, fear was like a
toothache that pulsed and receded but never left.

His plantation. Where the hell was it? North, but where the hell
was north? It didn't matter; he'd get that figured out with first light.
He'd go home; not because he'd given up, by god. Not that by a long
shot. But those bastards who'd deserted him had bled him dry of
money, and he couldn't go after Calida again until he had some coins
to dangle in front of the new troops he intended to recruit. It didn't
matter what Isiah Yongue said. That old hunk of alligator bait was
going to let go of more money. If he didn't—

Not soldiers. Slave-catchers.

Feeling suddenly sober, Reddin allowed a broad smile to split his
face. Why the hell hadn't the thought about that before? Slave-
catchers were perfect. They knew how niggers thought and were half
bloodhound anyway. Hell, for a few more coins, he could get his
hands on a real dog this time.

The dog would tear Panther apart. And then Calida . . .

"Don't you be sleeping too well tonight, girlie," he hissed. "I'm
comin' for you. And this time it's going to turn out different."

22

When he tried to move, Panther's muscles screamed in complaint. Relaxing, he eased back on the ground, but even though the pain in his side subsided, he knew he wouldn't be able to fall back asleep.

It was the middle of the night. The moon, nearly full, spread a cool white light over the ground but left the nearby trees sheltered in darkness. By turning his head, he made out most of the others stretched out on their makeshift beds. Not recognizing Gaitor's form, he remembered that his friend had left his side earlier to talk to Winter Rain and wondered if the two were still together.

Calida too had watched Gaitor and Winter Rain. He'd sensed her reaction in the tight and unnatural way she held her body. Alone. She'd looked so alone.

He'd wanted to end that for her, but he hadn't known what to say or do, and then it had gotten dark, and he'd been too tired to think.

Now it was the middle of the night and something had wakened him. Eyes shut so he could listen, he concentrated, but whatever that something had been now eluded him. He felt uneasy, but he'd been that way for so long now that the emotion seemed normal.

Nothing had changed by the time he opened his eyes again. The moon still called to him. Piahokee continued to keep its ageless secrets. His ancestors' spirits whispered and murmured and gave him a small measure of peace. The wilderness had always sheltered and sustained the Seminoles; he would be wise never to forget that. But in the past, there'd been no white men hungry for land, no soldiers.

So much had changed.

Not all of those changes involved the world around him. Some stemmed from inside.

By concentrating on every movement, he managed to first sit and then stand. His legs trembled, and his heart beat out of rhythm, but he would feel stronger in a few minutes. He had to, because tomorrow he would lead his people east.

It was impossible to determine which sleeping outline belonged to Calida. She wouldn't be nearby; hadn't she made it clear that she wanted nothing to do with him? She'd sought him out, saved his life, helped him return to the Egret clan. She'd stood near him earlier tonight, but she hadn't spoken to him. For most of the time they'd been together, she hadn't said a word or touched him.

He wanted to shake his head to see if that would clear it but wasn't sure he could continue to stand if he did. The sea seemed so far away. Just thinking about the journey ahead of them made him wish he was a child again. He would never tell anyone how he felt tonight, barely acknowledged the emotion to himself. But being shot had wounded him in ways he was still learning about. It was so hard to always be brave. To be chief. A woman—

No. That wasn't right. He'd been about to tell himself that it was a woman's nature to let a man go to war, but Seminole women were strong. They remained in the village because the children needed them, and without children the Seminoles would be no more.

Calida was Seminole, in her heart, where it mattered most.

Not sure what he had in mind, he took a few uneasy steps. His legs felt strong enough to hold him, and he walked even farther. A child whimpered once. An old man snorted, stopped, began snoring steadily. Beyond the grassy area, Piahokee made its own sounds. Thinking of little except wanting to hear more of the night, he left the sleepers. He might not be able to return to bed before what strength he had seeped out of him, but the laborious task of walking gave him scant energy to think about anything else.

He wasn't the only one awake after all. The moment he spotted the shadow, he reached automatically for the knife he always carried, but although he now held it in his hand, he felt no sense of alarm. There were no soldiers nearby. Gaitor had told him that and he believed him. That left only members of the Egret clan, or his ancestors' ghosts. Instead of calling out, Panther waited on legs that were too rapidly losing all feeling.

The shadow moved. He studied it, not because he didn't now know who was out here with him but because there were so many things he still didn't understand about Calida, and this was one way of discovering more. She had learned how to move in time with Piahokee, to accept it. At night when there was little breeze, the wilderness was a gentle, almost languid place. It was as if surviving the sun took so much out of it that it did nothing except rest once the burning heat gave up its daily attack. Calida wasn't resting. She was alert, testing her surroundings, testing him. And yet she did it at Piahokee's pace.

"You cannot sleep?" he asked softly. He didn't dare move. His head felt both heavy and empty.

"You shouldn't be out here, Panther."

"If I should not, then the same is true for you."

She didn't say anything, which left him wondering whether she agreed with him or not. If he could think how to put the words together, he would have asked her. He wanted to feel something of her seep into him, nothing more.

"Gaitor's wrong," she whispered as if she didn't want to hear the sound of her own voice. "Croon isn't defeated. I know he isn't."

"Is that what keeps you from sleep?"

"That and other things."

What other things? He was certain he'd asked the question, but she wasn't reacting in any way so maybe he hadn't.

"I keep thinking about the sea." She was still whispering. "I want to hear it. To study the birds that live there. To smell—I love its smell."

He didn't care about that, didn't care about anything except her voice and nearness and . . . "It will take several days to reach the great water."

"I know."

She didn't know what to do with her body, or with him. He wanted to make sense of what he'd just learned, but no matter how hard he tried, he couldn't stop mist from seeping into his mind. Without thinking he reached out, but his groping hands didn't find a tree. Instead, he felt Calida's shoulders and then her arms, a breast.

And then nothing.

Legs spread, Calida shoved her hands under Panther's armpits. She tried to stop his fall, but his weight was too great, and she slumped to the ground with him partly on top of her. As soon as she'd caught her breath, she wriggled out from underneath and pressed her ear to his chest. His heartbeat, although too fast, was strong. He shouldn't have tried to walk as far as he had. He knew he needed to rest.

Sitting so close that her hip pressed against his side, Calida lifted Panther's limp arm and pressed it to her breast. He would soon be well. His eyes might open in a matter of seconds, and when they did, she would draw back into herself, protect herself from him.

But for now—for this dark and quiet moment—she would lean over him and press her lips to his.

When she did, the first of her tears clouded her vision and dropped onto his flesh.

Dismounting, Reddin gave scant attention to his horse, who stood with its head nearly dragging on the ground, eyes glazed. He shouldn't have ridden the nag the way he had. After a lifetime spent around horseflesh, he knew better. But he'd be damned if he'd spend one more night out in that godforsaken jungle, especially when he had his own bed waiting for him.

The plantation didn't look all that different from the last time he'd been home, but then Isiah had already done just about everything he could to bring the land into production. He'd seen both soldiers and landowners on his way here, and every one of them had maintained that the Seminoles were so far from here, thanks to pressure from the army, that they no longer threatened anyone's safety. Reddin didn't believe that. The man who trusts a Seminole to stay in the swamp is a fool.

Not bothering to wipe his boots, he slammed his way into the house and stomped toward the kitchen. Opening the door, he startled the skinny but pretty Negress cutting up vegetables. Obviously, Isiah had brought his own cook with him. Studying her, Reddin admitted that his father-in-law had chosen well. Where, he asked without bothering to introduce himself, was Isiah Yongue?

"At the corral, massa," she told him. "He done bought hisself a new stallion. It come yesterday 'en he's been with it most o' the time since."

Did she resent that? If so, Isiah hadn't taught her her place. Taking the wooden spoon from her, Reddin ladled out a chunk of meat and briefly cooled it between thumb and forefinger before popping it in his mouth. "I'll be back. When I am, I want the biggest bowl of this you've got. And then when I'm done, maybe I'll let you give me a bath."

She blinked but gave no other indication of her reaction to his boldness. He wondered if she knew who really owned the house she lived in. It didn't matter; she would before too much longer.

Going back outside, Reddin noticed that a slave had taken charge of his horse and was in the process of giving it a drink. He had to hand it to his father-in-law: The old man knew how to run a plantation. The corral was around back. Stomach rumbling and another kind of hunger nagging at him even more, he decided he wasn't going to put up with much nonsense from Isiah, not after what he'd been through.

Isiah, as lean and fit looking as ever, sat on top of the corral fence. The stallion was at the opposite side and was flanked by two slaves, who each strained on ropes around the big roan's neck. Just outside the corral trembled a mare. Her tail stuck straight up in the air; her eyes were white and wild.

"You think he's going to set her with everyone watching?" Reddin announced without preliminary. As he expected, Isiah spun around. To his great amusement, the older man all but lost his balance.

"Damn you, you gave me a fright! What are you doing here?"

"Three reasons. One, I'm hungry. Two, I've got a hankering for a piece of your cook. Three—well, why don't we talk about that later. You got any whisky?"

Isiah nodded reluctantly and climbed down. When he indicated Reddin should follow him into the brand-new barn, Reddin guessed he didn't want anyone overhearing what they said to each other. It rankled him that they weren't heading for the house—his house. But Isiah was right. What they said to each other should remain private.

"I heard," Isiah said the moment they were inside. "Your men deserted you. They said—"

"I don't want to hear what they said. It's a damn bunch of lies. I need more money."

Even in the faint light, Reddin easily read Isiah's reaction. "If you think I'm going to throw away any more money on this damn fool vendetta of yours—"

"It's mine to throw and don't you forget it."

Isiah sighed. Reddin didn't need to be hit over the head to know the man didn't want to talk about this. In the silence that followed, Reddin turned his attention to his surroundings. He'd wanted to build a barn, but Liana had insisted the house first be brought up to her standards. He'd wanted a stallion. Unfortunately there hadn't been a proven one to be had for the kind of money he'd had to spend. He'd only been gone a few months and Isiah had accomplished both of those things, among others.

So who the hell's plantation was this anyway?

"She's quite a piece," he told Isiah. "That cook of yours—can she really cook, or are you just giving her something to do when you're not fooling with her?"

"You keep your hands off her."

"Me! Damnation, she's sleeping under my roof!"

Isiah held up his hand, but with both the stallion and mare squealing now, Reddin knew no one could hear a word they said. "So," he said when it looked as if he'd rendered Isiah speechless, "what else did you hear about me?"

"Not much. There's a lot more important news than what you're up to, believe it or not. The niggers General Jesup said were going to be sent to Oklahoma? Well, it hasn't happened, and it isn't going to as far as I can see. The bulk of them are being brought to St. Augustine. As for what's going to happen to them once they're all here, well—" He shrugged. "When and if the army and government and their owners ever get together on this, I guess we'll know."

The news about how the runaways were being treated didn't surprise Reddin. It must be reaction to the long hours in the saddle; suddenly he was too tired to care whether this so-called war went on forever or was wrapped up before nightfall. It didn't concern him, not in the slightest. Only Calida and the damnable Egret clan did.

Mostly getting Calida back.

That and reclaiming his plantation.

"I'm planning on going to St. Augustine myself as soon as I rest and have something to eat," he said. "From what I've heard, there's slave-catchers there, a lot of them."

"Slave-catchers?"

"Yeah. Those so-called soldiers who all but left me for dead don't know the first thing about fighting Indians. I don't know why Jesup or the President hasn't thought about this before, but if a body wants someone pulled out of the 'glades, they'd be smart to hire proven trackers."

Isiah tipped his head slightly to one side. Now that his eyes were accustomed to the darkness, Reddin had no difficulty reading the skepticism in the older man's eyes, not that it surprised or bothered him. "I won't be here long. Just until morning," he explained. "I'll take a fresh horse. And I'm going to need more money."

"No."

"I didn't come here to argue with you, Isiah. The last time you made me beg. It isn't going to happen again."

"I said no, Reddin."

"You want everyone saying you don't give a damn that the Seminoles killed your daughter?"

"I'd think you'd give a damn whether this place succeeds or fails. It takes money to run a plantation, damn it. Money that can't be wasted chasing after ghosts."

"Ghosts? You think they're ghosts?" Reddin was losing control and had to be careful, but Isiah was pushing him. "I've seen them. Hell, I shot one of them. A war chief."

"He's dead?"

"Yeah, he's dead," Reddin insisted although he had no way of knowing that. "*She* was living with him. Can you believe that? *She* was living with that bastard."

"Who?"

Didn't Isiah know anything? "Your daughter's personal slave, in case you've forgotten. Sleeping with that brave, bold as you please. I almost had them, damn it. I'd 'convinced' one of the runaways to take me to where the clan was hiding. Somehow Chief Panther found out about it and came after her. That's when I shot him." Laughter bubbled out of him before he could stop it. "I hope to hell she had to bury him."

"So this chief is dead. Reddin, the Seminoles are on the run. I will *not* waste any more money on this obsession of yours. There's no discussion to it."

Damn him. Damn, damn, damn. He nearly pointed out that the plantation was his and how he spent the money that came from it was his business, but he and Isiah had gone over this before to no avail. Little light reached this far into the barn. He was speaking to a shadow, the shadow of an old, stubborn, and worthless man. "You don't get it, do you?" Reddin challenged, although he couldn't say why he was bothering. "One of those savages killed your daughter. Is that what you're telling me? That it doesn't matter whether her killer gets away because she didn't mean that much to you?"

"I never—"

"It sure as hell sounds like it." He'd started shaking and couldn't put his mind to how to stop. "Fine. What you do or don't do is your business, but I'm telling you one thing right now, and you'd better not forget it. I'm not letting *her* get away with it. Runaways are either turning themselves in or being captured left and right and still *she's* out there defying me. Laughing in my face. She's not getting away with it. She's not!"

"Shut up."

Reddin was so surprised by his father-in-law's order that for several seconds he did exactly as he'd been told. Then: "Don't tell me what to do, old man. I'm not—"

"You killed her, didn't you?"

Reddin went cold and then hot. "What are you saying?"

"You killed my daughter." Isiah looked beyond him to the half-opened door. Reddin's eyes followed the same path as he assured himself that they were alone.

"You're crazy."

"No, I'm not. And you killed the carriage driver so there'd be no one to talk about what you'd done."

"That's—the Seminoles—"

"The Seminoles had nothing to do with it."

Although his body continued to ricochet between hot and cold, Reddin forced himself to fold his arms over his chest in a nonchalant gesture. "Go on. Tell me how you came up with this nonsense."

"Slaves talk, Reddin. You should know that."

Calida had been the only witness and she was gone. He felt a burning in his upper arm and realized he'd been gripping himself there. He forced himself to let up on the pressure. "Sure they talk, even when they've got nothing to say. Only a fool would listen to them."

"Not a fool; someone who wants to get at the truth. Joseph's wife was there the night you hauled him out on his last carriage ride, in case you've forgotten. She started thinking about that, then she talked to some of the other slaves and learned that no one had seen any sign of Indians. You should have done a better job of cleaning up after yourself, Reddin. The slave who washed Liana's bedding after her death remembered a stain on it that might have been blood. Why?" He leaned forward and seemed to shrink at the same time. "Why did you do it?"

He started to tell Isiah he didn't know what he was talking about, that the slaves had lied to him, when suddenly he no longer cared. Isiah Yongue was at least thirty-five years older than him, and although he was in good shape for a man his age, he didn't have his size or heft.

"I want you off my property, Reddin. Now."

"Your property? Wait a—"

"Either you get back on your horse, or I'll have you charged with murder."

"No one will listen to a bunch of slaves."

For an instant Isiah seemed to shrink again, but before Reddin could take advantage, he rocked forward. "Maybe. Maybe not. But I can promise you this: General Jesup is going to know everything, and the President, if that's what it takes to stop you. You'll be ruined. My daughter's dead, but at least you'll never wear a uniform again."

Reddin was lunging before he knew he'd been going to do it. The first blow landed on Isiah's throat and threw him against the nearest stall. Isiah's hands clutched at his throat. His eyes bulged, and he made a sick gurgling sound. Reddin hit him again. This blow struck the older man on the side of the head and sent him sprawling onto the floor. Before Isiah could move, Reddin started kicking him. His boots made a sound like rocks being thrown at a watermelon.

Outside, the stallion screamed again. The sound of hooves beating against the ground echoed in time with Reddin's heartbeat, and he went on kicking long after Isiah stopped moving. Then he forced himself to pick up the body and carry it to the far corner of the barn, where he hid it under a pile of cornstalks.

When Reddin went outside, the stallion was riding the mare. All eyes remained on the two animals as he headed toward the house and the bedroom where Isiah had slept and kept his valuables. His mind was on how much cash Isiah might have had on him when, just before his boots reached the stairs, he spun around and headed toward the kitchen. He reached out, grabbed the female slave around the neck, and began propelling her ahead of him.

23

Even the air smelled less free here. No matter how many times Calida told herself that the Egret clan should remain close to the rest of the Seminoles, with all her heart she wished they'd stayed anywhere else. They hadn't yet reached the sea before a runner brought word that Osceola wanted his people to move as close to St. Augustine as possible. After conferring with the runner and then Gaitor, Panther had told his followers that Osceola did not believe the Seminole people should be scattered after all. There'd been no Green Corn dance this year, and Osceola had vowed to the Great Spirit that that would never happen again. The wilderness around St. Augustine was ancestral land; the Seminoles would not allow themselves to be forced from it.

When Calida had argued along with others that they were safer deep in Piahokee, a somber-faced Panther had pointed out the irrefutable: Piahokee was not a kind mother. Even if they could stay in one place long enough to raise crops, the crops wouldn't be ready to harvest for a long time. The Seminoles weren't raccoons who scrounged for food. Osceola was tired of eating roots and berries. Whites had stolen his land from him. He would steal in return for desperately needed supplies, either by sneaking into St. Augustine itself or taking from the remaining plantations.

The idea of getting anywhere near the plantations had horrified Calida, but before she could speak, Panther had said something else. He was willing to move the Egret clan, not because he agreed with his chief, but because he wanted to try to change Osceola's mind.

"Osceola is worn down," he'd told her later that day. "His illness clouds his thoughts. His weakness makes him ask himself whether Great Spirit has deserted him. He wants to be near his parents' and grandparents' home. He wishes for all his people to join him there. And he believes that by staying close to the army, we will know everything we must about them. I say it does not matter what they do as long as we are far from them. Still—still my heart yearns for the land of my childhood. The land of Breath Giver."

Now, staying on a tree island surrounded by a plain covered with sawgrass, Calida had to admit there was some wisdom to what Osceola had decreed. Yes, they could reach St. Augustine in a little less than two days. Still, the town seemed so far away that she seldom thought about it. There was comfort in knowing other clans were nearby.

For hours at a time she felt safe.

This afternoon she was sitting in the shade after having stretched a deerhide Panther had given her on a wooden frame for tanning. Although he'd said it was her gift because she'd killed the alligator, she planned on making him new moccasins. If he was going to be meeting with Osceola and the other chiefs, she wanted him to go to them looking like a true *tastanagee*. Still, doing something this personal for him made her uneasy.

Made her think of him when it was easier not to.

A tiny white butterfly had been flitting around her bare feet. Now it landed on her big toe, tickling her. Stopping her work, she studied the fragile creature. So much of the land was defined by dark greens and deep shadows. The butterfly didn't seem to fit and yet maybe Breath Giver had placed it here so the Seminoles would know there was beauty in their lives.

Panther was walking toward her.

Unable to take her eyes off him, she watched the raw mesh of muscle and bone. So many of the Seminoles were thinner, more tired than they'd been when she first came to live with them, but hardship only seemed to make him stronger. Still, his eyes were deeper, darker these days, as if the weight of his responsibilities had drawn him into himself.

He had been born to this unkind land, was more a part of it than the butterfly even. He put her in mind not just of his namesake, but an alligator as well. She'd studied alligators for hours until she knew that beneath their bulky bodies and long stillness lay a creature made for survival. Panther had their hardness, their durability, their ability to accept.

Still, there was much more than that to him.

He'd decorated his body with intricate symbols made from various dyes for a meeting with Osceola and the other chiefs but had washed himself clean since returning.

He had shown her how to embrace the wilderness; she knew that now. By the simple act of living, he'd taught her how to survive. More than survive. When he returned from a successful hunt, she sensed his pride and took a little of that for herself. When he slipped into Piahokee so he could watch the army, she sensed his courage and determination and some of that seeped into her. He said she'd saved his life, but he'd given her one.

"You have been quiet too long," he said once he was standing over her. "I want to know your thoughts."

Not all of them; I can't. "They don't matter, Panther. You have so many to be concerned about. I'm just one."

"One." He held onto the word. "Tell me. You still do not want to be here, do you? It is because you fear Croon's presence."

Her emotions went so far beyond that that sometimes she couldn't think about Croon at all. Panther was a large part of her thoughts, maybe all of them when it shouldn't be that way. "I understand," she whispered. He looked so big. She wanted him to sit and yet was afraid to have him any closer. "About how hard it was for you to leave here. When you tell Osceola why we can't stay, does he listen, or is being where his ancestors are buried all he talks about?"

"He speaks of many things." Panther lowered himself to the

ground. Although he made only a whisper of sound as he did so, it was enough to disturb the butterfly. Calida watched it until she could no longer see it before forcing herself to look at Panther again.

Wild.

Wild as his name.

"You will do what you have to," she managed. "What is best for the Egret clan. Don't put me before them."

"I cannot think of you first, Calida. I do not dare."

But he wanted to. Why? she wanted to ask, but maybe she already knew. Something existed between them. Even when they barely saw each other for days, just the thought of him felt like the energy that precedes a storm. Sometimes, mostly at night, that energy rolled over her like a thunder-and-lightning-filled cloud. She'd told herself she was the only one who felt that way because it was somehow easier. If she thought he wanted her as much as she wanted him—

No!

"Summer is almost over," she said. Maybe no other conversation was safe. "It'll be easier once it isn't so hot."

"I do not care." He looked around him, then suddenly sprang to his feet and held out his hand. "Walk with me. I am tired of doing nothing."

He never did nothing. Still, his hand beckoned to her, and she didn't try to stop herself as she placed hers in it. He brought her effortlessly to her feet, held on a few seconds, then started toward the surrounding and sheltering trees. Shaking and scared and hungry in a way she barely understood, she followed him. She shouldn't do this! She couldn't walk away from him.

He took a thin trail that led to a creek where the men often fished. Calida tried to make herself think about how good it had made her feel yesterday to know that all the men of the Egret clan were back together, but she was looking at Panther's back. Feeling him.

He stopped beside a log whose top trailed in the water and created a tiny dam where fish could rest. Joining him at the edge of the bank, Calida stared down. There were three, maybe four fish here today. They weren't large enough to be worth spearing, but if a warrior was patient, a larger fish might come to feed on the smaller ones. That, she'd learned, was the way of the world. The stronger fed on the weak. And the army was so powerful.

"Winter Rain says she thinks Gaitor is going to ask her to marry him," she said in a rush. "He has been bringing her gifts."

"Is it what she wants?"

"Yes. I'm sure—yes. She smiles when she talks about him. He makes her feel safe; she told me that."

"I pray he will always keep her safe," Panther said.

They both knew how little control any of them had over their lives. She didn't want to talk about that. "She's been lonely for a long time. She didn't want anyone to know how hard it has been for her."

"She told you that?" Panther sat on the log. She joined him but kept far enough away that she couldn't feel his body heat.

"Two nights ago. Gaitor was gone. He hadn't said anything, but she was sure he wanted to see where the army was."

"Yes."

Panther was watching the pool. She wondered how he could concentrate on that when her thoughts were like leaves caught in a storm-wind. "She—she talked about when her mother died. Winter Rain was a small child, but not so young that she doesn't remember. It was hard for her, very hard."

"Her mother was sick for a long time."

Although Panther wasn't looking at her, Calida nodded. "Winter Rain wanted to do things for her but didn't know what. She—for a long time, she believed her mother would have lived if she'd brought her the right things to eat, given her more water." Panther. She would think about Panther and not—not . . .

"I did not know that," he said. "I was learning to be a war chief in those days."

Learning to be a war chief. What did that mean? She risked a glance at him and found that his profile was all angles, rocklike. "I didn't know there was such a place as Florida when Winter Rain lost her mother. I was a child myself. Innocent."

"And then Reddin Croon bought you and your mother."

"Yes."

"That time is behind you, Calida. Winter Rain survived her mother's death. You are surviving yours. And *he* cannot touch you here."

Couldn't he? In ways Panther didn't understand, in ways Calida could barely bring herself to acknowledge, Reddin Croon was still part of her existence. Dragging her gaze off Panther, she tried to concentrate on the fish until the water blurred.

"I—I want Winter Rain and Gaitor to be happy. To know peace."

"Peace. I cannot give them that."

He held himself responsible for their future? No wonder he had been so somber these days. "Don't make that your burden, Panther. You're *tastanagee*. You're not Breath Giver."

"Breath Giver's spirit should be stronger within me. If I had his wisdom, I would know what the Seminoles must do."

"No. No." She'd grabbed his hand without knowing it. Now that she held it, she couldn't let go. "Don't do this to yourself. Please. If the President can't put an end to this war—if Osceola can't either—it isn't your responsibility."

"Isn't it, Calida? My heart is filled with a great weight. There is only one way for that to change."

For a long time now she'd thought she understood what went on inside him, but she hadn't known the depths. Her head pounded, and tears pressed against the back of her eyes. Like him, her heart was heavy, only, for her, it had little to do with concerns for the living. The dead—those who had never known life . . .

"And maybe that burden will never lift," Calida finally thought to say.

"I know."

Panther sounded both tortured and resigned. Still, when, finally, he looked over at her, she saw only a hint of pain in his eyes. The rest of the message—

He was thinking of her. Aware of her.

Run!

"The first time I saw you, I was filled with anger and fear," he said. "I hated being helpless. You freed me. That was all that mattered, that I was free. But since that day, you have been part of my life."

He could talk about his fears. Why couldn't she do the same? "My mother died free because of you," Calida whispered. "I—thank you. My gratitude—"

"Only gratitude?"

No. Don't you know that? A storm raged inside her. She wanted to jump to her feet and run from it, from him, but distance wouldn't make any difference.

Not wanting him to touch her but needing it too much, she sat with her body as tight as a drawn bowstring.

"Only gratitude, Calida?" Panther asked.

"What do you want from me?"

"The truth."

The truth! Sweet Jesus! "Don't do this to me. Please."

"If not now, when?" He hadn't taken his eyes off her. They cut into her like a just-sharpened knife, and yet she wasn't bleeding. Instead—instead she felt more alive than she did even when a storm raged around her and thunder and lightning seemed like they were exploding inside her. She felt buffeted by him. Whipped and whirled and thrown about.

"I do not know how much time is left to us, Calida," he said. "To the Egret clan, or the Seminoles. Maybe all we have is today."

Today. "That—that's why Gaitor and Winter Rain are reaching for each other, isn't it? Because—"

"This moment is not about them. We are together, you and I."

The storm was getting darker, heavier, more deadly. More exciting. She should tell him she wanted to go back to the others where she could again—maybe—feel safe, but he was right. There might not be a tomorrow for them.

"What do you want me to say?" Calida asked.

"What is in your heart."

She couldn't do that, could never do that. And yet remaining silent might be even worse. "I'm not afraid of you."

He looked surprised by that. "You once were?"

"I don't know. I was so terrified of Reddin Croon that I didn't know there was any other way to feel. From the moment he became my master, he didn't allow me to be around any other man, not even another slave."

Panther didn't move or speak, and she felt compelled to continue, or maybe the truth was, she couldn't stop herself.

"My mother—she believed I needed to know the truth about how I came to be. There was no . . ." She'd almost said the word *love* but couldn't around Panther. "My father took my mother whenever he wanted her. However he wanted her. She never forgot that, and when she was no longer with him, she swore she'd never let another man touch her, not even another slave. She always told me—she told me that nothing mattered more than not belonging to a man. Being free in that way."

"You grew up believing her words?"

"Yes."

"Only, her words were a lie with you because your master owned your body."

She shouldn't have started talking about this, wanted nothing to do with honesty after all. But she'd come here with Panther because he was that important to her and maybe—maybe there'd be less pain if she released some things she thought she'd hold inside for the rest of her life. "I hated him. Hated and feared him. He made me feel trapped. I couldn't talk to my mother, to anyone." The storm brought to life by Panther's presence continued to rage around her, but coldness had seeped into her bones and made it impossible for her to feel his energy, his presence even. "I was like a wild animal with ropes around its neck. But an animal fights. I knew he'd kill me if I tried. There was nothing—nothing I could do."

"And when you saw what he had done to me, you knew how I felt."

She would think about him, only him. That way she would survive. How had she forgotten that? "Holding that knife in my hand made me feel strong for the first time in my life," she admitted. "Cutting you free—it was as if I'd defied him." She could smile at that, smile and sense again the power that had surged through her at that moment. "He couldn't have you! I'd denied him that."

Something slammed into her even before she'd finished speaking. Desperate to understand the emotion, she reached for Panther. His heat seared her fingertips, and she jerked back.

"Do not."

"Do not what?"

"Hide from me. From yourself."

She didn't want to. Suddenly, powerfully. Not understanding what was going on inside her, she straightened and kept her eyes steady on him.

"I did not want to feel this way," Panther said. "A *tastanagee* who buries himself in a woman is weak in battle."

Panther would never be weak. Didn't he— He wanted to bury himself inside her? She started shaking.

"Listen to me. Listen and think only of today. The past is dead. Buried."

I want to believe. Oh, how I want to believe.

He ran his knuckles over Calida's cheek and chin, down over her throat. "I am not Reddin Croon," he said.

"I—know."

"Your head does. But does your body?"

He hadn't asked about her heart. It didn't matter, because she wouldn't have been able to answer him anyway. "I'm afraid."

"Of me?"

"No," she told him, although being near him made her feel as if she was walking into a hurricane.

"Of what then?" Panther asked.

How could she answer him? How could she face herself? But she'd already told him so much; this shouldn't be impossible. "I—I know what it can be like between two people. Gaitor loved his wife. Winter Rain's parents loved each other. But . . ."

"But you are not them."

Reddin Croon called all Indians savages, and before she'd come to live with the Seminoles, she'd believed the same thing. She never would again. "I want—" She closed her eyes and spoke from behind the shadows she'd created. "I want what they had, but my body doesn't trust. I—I'm afraid to try."

"I do not believe you."

Instead of refuting what Panther had said, she struggled to remain safe and silent in darkness, but he was making it impossible. Turning his hand around, he tested her with his fingertips. When they dipped below her dress's loose neckline, she started trembling again. He could kill; she'd seen him wrench the life from animals the Seminoles needed. Those same hands could be gentle. So gentle.

Alive.

Calida felt feverish. She needed to be cooled by the violent wind that accompanies a storm. She wanted to walk into the middle of it.

Panther was the storm.

Unable to hide within herself after all, she opened her eyes a slit. He sat so close that he was little more than a hazy outline. This way she could make him a dream figure in her mind, could reach for shadow and mist, feel flesh and muscle and bone. Not think. Simply react.

When he touched her breast for the first time, she nearly slapped his hand away. Feeling her nails bite into her palms, she realized how hard she had to fight to kill her instinctive reaction.

Reddin Croon had done that to her. Made her hate being touched.

But he wasn't here today. Panther was.

Panther, who had carried her, more dead than alive, to his village and given her shelter. A place to be.

"Do not think of him."

"I won't. I promise; I won't."

Still, for long and agonizing minutes she couldn't completely thrust her former master from her mind. Other women reached for the men they—for men they trusted, but what came easily to them was one hard-fought battle after another for her. She wouldn't feel as if she was being torn apart if she ran from Panther; she'd stop shaking, put an end to the explosions taking place inside her if he didn't have his hands on her.

But she wanted them. Needed them. And because she did, she faced each battle and rode the waves.

He didn't speak, and she was grateful for the silence that allowed her to concentrate on what was happening inside her, to cling to each moment, each gentle or insistent touch, to battle against yesterday's memories.

She was winning. Panther was making that possible.

He'd removed her loose blouse without her knowing how he'd done it. Now he leaned toward her and blew his hot breath over her shoulders and breasts, touching and yet not touching. He slid off the log and brought her down with him. She was off balance and had to brace her hands against the ground behind her. Smiling, he again leaned into her, painting every inch of exposed flesh first with his breath and then with his mouth and tongue.

The storm's energy coiled in her belly. She couldn't think how to stop the sensation, or if she wanted it to end, and it grew. She had barely touched him, had no idea what a man wanted from a woman, knew he deserved more than what she was giving him.

Her back ached from the unnatural position, and she grabbed him around the neck with one hand to straighten herself. Her naked breasts pushed against his chest, pressed and tightened and expanded. He slid an arm around her waist and took over the monumental task of sitting upright for both of them. Before she could think to thank him, he covered her breast with his free hand. His manhood probed against his loincloth, and for a heartbeat she couldn't think of anything except how Reddin Croon used her to satisfy his need. Then, as if he knew what she was thinking, Panther slid his hand from her breast to her chin and tipped her head upward. Holding her gently, he touched her mouth with his.

"I will not hurt you," he whispered. "Believe me. I will not hurt you."

He gave her strength. Ignited her. The fire burning in her belly and breast consumed all fear and allowed her to walk out of the past. This man had given her shelter and a place to belong. He'd held her mother while she died. She could give him—give him her body.

Her mind.

Arms laced around his neck now, she drew him in through her pores. They seemed to share the same air, the same flesh even. Her heart beat like that of a captured bird, but she wouldn't think about that. Would concentrate on flames and thunder and lightning and him.

Gentle and yet insistent, he laid her out on the ground. He slipped her skirt down over her hips without asking permission, but then she'd given it by lifting her hips. He'd never seen her naked before, had he? Maybe at first when she'd been unconscious—

It didn't matter.

He did it all. Everything. Traced her body with his fingers. Held her eyes with his. Climbed into her thoughts until nothing remained except him. Stole Piahokee's heat and replaced it with his. Took her hand, first flattening it over his chest, then his waist, his belly. His eyes asked if she was ready for more. Terrified, she shook her head. Then, still terrified, she opened her mouth to say yes, but she couldn't speak. She should have already known that.

He couldn't either. His eyes told her the truth of what he was feeling.

She touched him then, not the male part of him because he was too new to her and she too new to wanting a man for that, but at least she needed no guidance, no help to run her fingers over his high cheekbone, the solid collarbone, his ribs.

He came to her inch by inch until she thought she would scream before they were no longer two separate people. He eased himself into her, kissing, touching at the same time so she couldn't tell where to focus. Before she knew it, they'd joined. Become the same. He wouldn't begin pounding at her! He wouldn't!

Not her warrior.

Still, she tensed and would have remained like that if he'd left her mouth alone, but he didn't. She lost herself in his kisses, his hot and fast breath, the size and strength of him protecting her from the world. Becoming her world.

The lightning he'd caused to shoot through her earlier had never died but had simply simmered while she gave her body over to him. No longer content with that, it flickered countless fingers of heat through her. Every time he pressed himself into her, the wavelike rushes he ignited added more energy to the storm until she no longer thought to try to control it, to protect herself.

Now she rode with him. Forgot who and what she was. Embraced the moment. Buried all sorrow.

For now.

Surrendered herself to him.

For now.

Reddin Croon sat across from General Joseph Hernandez. In the firelight, the Spanish American's nose seemed even larger, his mouth more sour than Reddin remembered it. He had had no use for the man since he'd failed to protect plantations around St. Augustine from attack nearly two years ago. If it had been up to him, he would have sent both Hernandez and the equally ugly Zachary Taylor to the remote frontier of the Mississippi Valley where Taylor had come from. However, both men were firmly entrenched at Fort Peyton on Moultrie Creek a day's ride southwest of St. Augustine. And because Hernandez had taken responsibility for the capture of the slave known as John Philip, Reddin had no choice but to meet with the man.

"He can be convinced," Reddin insisted. "There isn't a man alive who can't be persuaded to change his mind."

"I don't want him dead, Reddin."

He hadn't said anything about killing the captive, had he? He wanted him alive, at least until he'd told his captors everything he knew about the Seminoles' strength. From the moment he'd heard that one of the most militant slaves, a nigger who'd become one of Osceola's trusted warriors, had been brought in, he'd been forming a new plan, and he wasn't about to leave Hernandez until he'd put it into motion. "Neither do I," Reddin said. Glancing down at his hands, he thought about how easy it had been to kill Isiah. A miserable slave wouldn't be any harder. "Neither do I."

"It sure sounds like it."

"I said nothing of the sort. What I said was, if this nigger has been by Osceola's side all these months, he knows everything the chief does about where the rest of the Seminoles are."

"Why do you think I've been telling John Philip he can go to Oklahoma as soon as we're done with him? I don't want him so scared he can't talk."

Hernandez was a lily-livered nigger lover. Who cared whether John Philip's heart stopped from fear, just that it didn't happen until he'd led the army to the Egret clan and Calida and Panther. "He's a slave. He knows what a whip feels like."

"The government doesn't—" Hernandez began.

"Are they here? Damn it, are they?"

Hernandez tugged at the corners of his mouth and drew them down even more. The so-called fort was a joke. If the Seminoles decided to attack, it wouldn't last a day. The army didn't dare wait for that. They had to keep on the offensive.

"You've got how many men?" Hernandez asked.

"Here? Not a hundred right now, but I've got three companies of regulars and two made up of citizen soldiers under my command. I thought you knew that."

"I just wanted to be sure." Reddin managed to keep from smiling, but it took effort. "Once we combine that force with the two companies I'm willing to bring in from Palatka, we'll bring the Seminoles to their knees."

"Two companies? Do you have any idea what it'll cost to get and keep them here?" Hernandez asked.

"Yeah. I do know." Reddin made no attempt to disguise his intensity as he leaned forward. "I'm willing to do that, at my own expense, General. I have the resources. I'm committed to ending all resistance."

"I heard you were looking to hire some slave-catchers. What happened to that plan?"

That so-called plan had blown up in his face, not because it wasn't a good one, but because he hadn't been the first to think of it after all. While he'd been forced to waste precious time getting things in order at the plantation, every man who claimed he could bring back a runaway had gone to work for other slave owners. Most of them were as worthless as the soldiers who'd deserted him, but a few had met with success. None of them, as far as he knew, had gotten anywhere near the Egret clan or clapped eyes on a beautiful octoroon known as Calida.

However, as soon as Reddin could get his hands on John Philip, her luck would change.

24

Turtle Follower had broken her leg. If they'd still been on the move, Panther would have had had no choice except to leave her behind, but because he still hadn't convinced Osceola to leave the area, the healer had splinted the leg of the young mother of two. Barely able to get around, she depended on Calida to care for her children.

Panther crouched at the base of a palm and watched. Although the children were pretending to wrestle alligators and took turns playing that role to the delight of several younger children, he paid them little attention.

Calida was a woman of great patience. If she ever grew weary of the children's energy, she kept it to herself. This afternoon she sat near the makeshift wrestling ring as she applauded first one and then the other. She occasionally admonished them to be gentle and never once allowed them to make enough noise that their voices carried, but she understood that children couldn't spend all their time being quiet and still.

She loved her young charges. Listening to her faint laughter, Panther had no doubt of that. In the not quite two moons since their bodies had finally joined, he'd discovered how precious children were to her. No one had had to ask her to take care of Turtle Follower's children; she did so willingly, joyfully.

After easing himself to his feet, Panther walked closer. As Calida always did, she sensed his presence this time as well. Her eyes said nothing of how she felt about seeing him after a two-day absence, but then he'd come to expect that from her. She never kept her body from him. She seemed to need him at night as much as he craved her. But she remained silent; they both sought silence. She knew he feared that the time of the Seminoles was coming to an end, something he'd told no one else, not even Gaitor. What, other than Reddin Croon, did she fear? He wanted nothing more out of life than to spend his days and nights free. What did she want? She hadn't told him.

"How is he?" Calida asked.

Knowing she was asking about Osceola, whom he'd just left, Panther explained that the chief's fever had broken, but he was too weak to walk, or to make decisions. "His words have not changed. He speaks only of being near his ancestors."

She barely nodded. He wondered if she might leave the children and go into the wilderness with him, but she didn't move. In the past when he returned, her eyes had betrayed her anxiety and hunger, but today her emotions remained deeply buried, hidden from him.

"Turtle Follower is no worse?" he asked.

"She hates the way her splint itches, but the swelling is gone."

"Do you want to spend the night with her? She needs your help even then?"

"No." Calida's fingers clenched. She didn't look at him. "No, she doesn't."

"You will join me then?"

Mouth trembling slightly, she nodded. Before Panther could say anything else, one of the children let out a sharp squeal. Calida jumped to her feet, ran over to him, and pulled the little boy against her. With one hand clamped over his mouth, she hugged him. Red marks from a bite on the back of his hand explained his outcry. It wasn't the way of a Seminole woman to coddle her children, especially a son, and Calida knew that. Still, she held the boy for a long time, rocking, whispering low in her throat. When she at last looked over at Panther, sunlight glinted off her tears.

* * *

Panther and Gaitor had been sitting together talking for a long time, but although she wasn't close enough to hear what they were saying, Winter Rain knew Gaitor hadn't told his chief what was foremost on his mind. She understood that the words wouldn't come easily and maybe not tonight, but Gaitor couldn't remain silent much longer.

As a distant limpkin wailed into the growing night, she left the shelter Gaitor had built for them, keeping to the shadows because she didn't want to draw attention to herself.

Gaitor's wife.

She'd said the words over and over to herself since he'd given her marriage gifts, and still it seemed unreal. Whenever she looked at him, it was all she could do not to cry because he had ended her loneliness. She might always love Panther a little, but she'd learned to survive without her mother, and she would survive without Panther because a big, black, and gentle man loved her.

Calida was just leaving Turtle Follower's *chickee*. The woman glanced over at where Panther and Gaitor were seated and then headed toward the creek. Calida had knelt before the creek and was dipping her hands in the water when Winter Rain called out to her. Although it was nearly dark, Winter Rain realized she'd startled the other woman.

"I am sorry," she apologized. "You want to be alone?"

"No. No. it's all right." Calida held up her dripping hands. "I just wanted to clean myself. Caring for children is dirty work."

"The night does not bother you, does it? You often seek to be alone."

"I don't know if I seek it. I just know I don't try to avoid it." Calida inched off the rock she'd been squatting on, indicating Winter Rain could use it if she wanted. Instead, she continued to stand and watch as Calida stepped into the water. "What is it?" Calida asked softly.

"Our men are together. They speak and yet they do not."

"What do you mean? They're talking about Osceola."

"And Gaitor wants to hear what Panther has to say, but that is not all."

"Not all?"

Calida was waiting for her to say more. For a moment Winter Rain hated the other woman for knowing so much about her thoughts, but the emotion didn't last long because she wouldn't have followed her out here if she hadn't needed to talk. "I cannot speak for Gaitor. Perhaps I should say nothing."

"Perhaps."

A pain throbbed against Winter Rain's right temple. Trying to straighten her thoughts, she rubbed it. Calida seemed to have nothing to do except watch the water. Either that, or she was reluctant to leave the creek and return to where Panther might be waiting for her. "We cannot stay here," she blurted. "When the army comes, and they will come, Gaitor will no longer be free."

"You don't know that. The—"

"Do you think General Jesup will let him go to Oklahoma? Do you believe Reddin Croon will allow it to happen?"

Calida shook her head. It was too dark to see what was in her eyes, but Winter Rain could guess. After all, Calida's fate was the same as Gaitor's: Unless they were killed, they would again become slaves.

"That is why we have decided to leave here," Winter Rain said. The words came more easily than she'd thought they would. "Why we believe we have no choice."

"Leave? Where would you go?"

"Into Piahokee's belly."

Calida scrambled out of the creek and came to stand beside her. Despite the dark, Winter Rain was struck anew by how light-skinned Calida was. "Alone?"

"No. There are others. Only a few now but maybe more once they face the truth."

"The truth?" Calida asked.

"You know! The army's word cannot be trusted. They say one thing and then another. Always those things are for the army, never the Seminole. I think—" Winter Rain paused to give herself strength. "I think that if the army men see me with Gaitor, they will treat me as they do him."

"I've thought about that. I wish I could say different, but I can't." Calida held out her arm and slowly turned it first one way and then the other. "Our color isn't that different, Winter Rain. You were born into a Seminole clan, but that won't matter to the army."

Frightened and yet resigned, Winter Rain nodded. "They will look only at my Negro blood. They will make me a slave."

"Not just a slave." Calida gripped her arm with such strength that she winced. "I'm sorry. I didn't mean to hurt you. And I don't want to say what I'm going to, but you have to understand. Understand everything. You're young. Beautiful."

"Beautiful?"

"White men will like the way you look. They'll want your body. They'll use you. Force themselves on you."

"I would rather be dead."

"Yes. You would." After Calida released her, she didn't seem to know what to do with her hands. "I think it would be worse for you than it was for me because you were born free. I never knew what it meant to call my body my own, not until I came to live with the Egret clan, but you did. You'll fight the ropes they throw over you. You'll hate—you'll fight." Calida ran her fingers into her hair and clamped down so tightly that it must have hurt. "If you have children, they won't be yours."

"Not mine?"

"The man who owns you will do whatever he wants with them. Maybe take them from you."

"No!"

"Yes. Oh god—Winter Rain, I know what I'm talking about."

"This happened to you?"

Calida's hands dropped to her sides, and she seemed barely able to stand upright. "When will you leave?" she whispered.

Leave? They'd been talking about something else; Calida had been drowning in whatever that was. Not caring what she was saying, she told Calida that the time hadn't been set yet, but it wouldn't be much longer. Gaitor had decided to kill a couple of the white men's cattle so they'd have meat to take with them. Calida barely reacted to news that the whites would have even more reason to hate the Seminoles.

"Come with us," Winter Rain insisted. "Panther will go where you do."

"No. No, he won't."

"You believe that?" Winter Rain asked, although she already knew the answer.

"He can't leave his people. He'd never do that; he's a *tastanagee*."

Slowly, deliberately, Winter Rain pressed Calida's cold hand between her two warmer ones. "You are not a *tastanagee*, Calida. You are a slave."

"Not anymore! Not anymore."

"You will be again if they capture you."

"I would rather be dead."

Holding Calida's hand was like trying to still a frightened bird. "Then come with us. Alone, if that is how it must be."

"Alone?" Calida started to pull away but stopped as if still needing the human contact. "Alone," she whispered.

"Do you think I want to say this? Panther is my chief and a man of my heart, but he must do as he must; it is the way of a Seminole *tastanagee*. What is honor to him may kill you."

"It may kill him too."

"I know." Tears welled in Winter Rain's throat, but she willed them away. "So much of what is happening is beyond us. Although we breathe our ancestors' air, the old ways no longer serve. Sometimes—sometimes I think Breath Giver is no more."

"Winter Rain, no!"

"Do you think I want to say this, to fear— I cannot stay with you tonight. Gaitor will be looking for me. Listen to me. He and I do not dare stay in this place. I will not have my husband become a slave again! I would rather kill him myself than that. What will it be for you, Calida?"

What will it be for you? No matter how desperately she fought to rid her mind of Winter Rain's question, Calida couldn't. In truth, the other woman had forced her to face something she'd been hiding from for too long. In her heart of hearts, she believed Panther wouldn't run again. He was a *tastanagee*; he couldn't, wouldn't walk away from his clan, his people. These days few had the strength or will to go back to being fugitives. They felt safe back on holy land, or maybe the truth was, they'd decided to stay here until the army men said they could leave for the reservation. Panther knew how dangerous it was for her to remain by his side, but he hadn't spoken of that, and she guessed he was waiting for her to say what she must. If she left with Gaitor and Winter Rain, would it matter to him?

Of course it would.

Panther was already in the shelter he'd built by the time she reached it. Because night fires might alert army scouts to their where-abouts, none had been started. The moon had shrunk down to noth-ing and hadn't begun its journey back to life. The stars were out there, but it had rained late this afternoon, and the clouds lingered. The heavy air smelled of more rain. It was fitting; after all, a storm raged in her heart, didn't it? Thinking briefly that she no longer cared whether she ever saw another lantern or lamp, Calida ducked under the low-hanging roof and stepped toward Panther. He lay on his back on their mat bed. When he was silent like this, she knew he was thinking about the heavy burdens in his heart. She didn't want to add to them, but what choice did she have?

"What did Gaitor say?" she asked. In a minute she might be brave enough to join Panther, but not yet.

"He is leaving."

Hurting for both men, she couldn't stop herself from imagining how painful that conversation must have been. It couldn't be any eas-ier for brothers to separate than it had been for her to leave her mother. "When?"

"In two days, maybe three. Sit with me, Calida."

She did, dropping heavily beside him. She'd told herself she wasn't going to touch him until she'd said what she had to, but now that he was so close— The flesh over his ribs felt warmer than the air pressing around her, and she sensed a humming in her finger-tips she knew was his heart.

"Will you go with them?" he asked.

He wouldn't try to stop her; she already knew that. "I don't know," she said when it was much more complicated than that. She could have told him she'd rather die than be back in Reddin Croon's hands. She could have whispered that leaving him would kill her, but it wouldn't.

"What do you want from me, Calida? To beg you to stay? To tell you I will walk away from my chief and my people for you?"

"No. No." She didn't dare go on touching him, because if she did, the storm of love she felt for him would drown her and what she had to say would remain trapped inside her. "I know what you have to do. I'd never ask you to change who you are."

"And I would never try to change who you are."

What she was was a runaway pursued by a possessed master. "Go."

"Go?" she echoed.

"There will only be a few of you. You can move swiftly. Gaitor will provide you with meat. Before the army knows what has happened, you will be far from here."

You don't want me to stay? Please don't say that. "You—I don't know . . ."

"Even Reddin Croon cannot search all of Piahokee," he pointed out. "And if Osceola and the other chiefs and I are here, this is where the army will remain."

"What are you saying? That you'll sacrifice yourself for—for me?"

He didn't answer, and she lost herself in the silence. The storm was building, tightening the air until it had to explode. When the time came, maybe she'd explode with it. "I can't let you do that."

"Do not speak of this, Calida. My head is full of things I do not want. We have tonight; tonight is all I want."

Was he wise beyond her comprehension or afraid to look at the future? *Wise. Wise.* The answer drummed through her until her own head felt full to the bursting. "I wish it would rain," she moaned. "This waiting—" When lightning briefly scarred the night, she stared up at the energy and felt it arc through her. "Everything we do is determined by the world around us," she mused. "In the summer I feel more dead than alive because it's so hot. Even in winter, it seems as if the sun never lets go."

"Calida?"

"What?" she asked when she wanted him to remain silent.

"This time is for us. I need to know what is in your heart."

"My heart?"

"Don't," he warned and clamped his hand over her leg. "You are like a butterfly, Calida. You flit close to me. Sometimes you rest on my flesh and I feel great peace. Your life enters me and I tell myself you won't fly away again. But you have always kept a part of you separate from me. Why will you not trust your heart to me?"

His words were killing her, ripping her open when she needed— needed what? To curl into a tight and safe and lonely ball? She'd hurt so long, and now . . .

"No more silences, my wife. I have not given you marriage gifts because I cannot promise you the kind of home a warrior should give his woman, because I do not know if you would accept my offerings, but you sleep by my side and you have given me your body."

I know. Oh, how I know.

"Why does your heart remain apart?"

"Panther. Please—" She tried to slip away, but he sat up and gripped her around the waist. Before she could stop him, he pushed her down. She lay looking up at him, seeing lightning explode behind him, and when it died, she remembered his powerful silhouette. His hands pressed against her shoulders, and he brought his face so close that she felt his breath.

"If you leave with Gaitor, I will never know you."

"Never know? I—I'm your woman."

"It is not enough."

No. It wasn't. It was night. He couldn't look into her eyes and find the anguish, the pain she knew lay there. "I'm afraid of you."

"Have I ever hurt you?"

No. What he'd done was give her a reason and a place to live. More than that. "I'm afraid of what I feel for you. I never wanted— never wanted to feel vulnerable around a man."

"And you do with me? Why?"

"Because you're my life, and I don't want it that way." Horrified, she tried to take back the words, but it was too late. Besides, it was the truth.

"Your life?" he whispered. It started to rain. The fat, heavy drops plopped on the roof and ground and insulated them from the rest of what remained of the clan. "I am your life?"

"Yes," she whispered. She wanted to sit up and bury herself in his chest, but he still wouldn't let her move. Maybe he was afraid she would run if he didn't hold her captive. "I didn't want—I never wanted . . ."

"Calida?"

She had to tell him, now, with rain threatening to bury her words with its noise, before she left with Gaitor and Winter Rain. "I'm carrying your child."

He might have muttered something; she couldn't tell because the rain now sounded like thousands of feet pounding against the earth. "I didn't—" Her mind shattered, and she couldn't remember what she'd been going to say.

"My child?"

"Y-es."

His hands on her shoulders gentled. One trailed down her body to rest over her stomach. His fingers sought, gentle as a butterfly, to reach his baby. He leaned down and kissed her, a lover's kiss, a husband's kiss. "My child," he repeated. Despite the storm, she knew he was, for the moment, at peace with himself and touched in ways he'd never been before. "A son. I will have a son."

"Or a daughter."

"A daughter. She will look like you, have your eyes. You will teach her how to read, and she will be ready for a world I may never understand. I want . . ."

"What do you want?" she asked despite the terrible danger to her heart.

"To hold our child. To watch it at your breast."

She'd only missed one bleeding. Except for being more tired than usual and her breasts swelling slightly, there'd been no change, but she knew. Oh sweet Jesus, she knew. There was a child inside her. And it wasn't the first.

Turning her head from him, she fought her inner storm, but it was no use. Sobs tore at her; she was drowning in them, being killed by them.

"Calida? What is it? You are thinking that this war—"

"Not the war." She couldn't keep her voice even, could barely speak.

"You believe we will not be together when it is born?"

How hard it was for him to say that; she sensed his agony in every line and curve of him. "Not—that," she was forced to tell him, although that too added to her agony. "Not that."

She thought he'd demand more from her, but maybe he knew she'd said all she could. He pulled her into his arms and held her while she fought emotions she didn't understand. Or maybe the truth was, she understood all too well. She couldn't think about the past. She couldn't! If she did— "My—my mother said she had no control over her emotions when she was carrying me. I—I'm the same."

He nodded, and she prayed he would be satisfied with that explanation. He whispered something about her going to an old woman who knew whether babies were boys or girls before they were born. She tried to tell him that the old woman had been wrong twice since she'd come to the Egret clan, but she might start crying again if she spoke another word. She shouldn't have told him tonight. She should have waited until she was stronger. But would she ever be?

"I wish your mother was alive," Panther said.

"My—mother?"

"A woman with child needs the wisdom of another woman. Pilar could tell you many things."

What Pilar had done was tell her how to destroy two babies, not because either woman wanted that, but what life was there for an infant torn from its mother's breast and sold like cattle? Remembering that horrible, desperate time, Calida's sobs began again. Panther had called her a butterfly. That's what she was, a butterfly caught in a violent storm. Only, the storm was inside her, shattering her, killing her.

"Calida! What is it?"

"I'm not—I'm not worthy."

"Of having our child? No."

She shook her head to let him know he was wrong, but she couldn't speak. Her head pounded. Her throat felt raw. Her eyes burned and ached, and if Panther hadn't been holding her, she might have exploded into a thousand pieces. Even with him here, she lacked the strength to fight.

"Calida, Calida. Your heart is breaking. Why?"

Why? Tell him. Tell him, because if you don't tonight, you never will. "My babies."

"Babies? The others," he said softly. "The ones who came before. That is what you are saying?"

She nodded.

He stroked her hair, stroked and held and rocked her. "Tell me."

"You—know."

"Not enough. They are still inside you. They still live in your heart. I know that but no more."

They still live in your heart. Burrowing as tightly against him as possible, Calida tried to lose herself in Panther, but she couldn't because there was too much pain.

"Calida, listen to me. This is our child. It will know life. It will never be torn from your side; I promise you that."

He couldn't guarantee that; neither of them knew what the future would bring. But until she felt stronger, she would believe him. "I'm not worthy," she whimpered. "Not worthy of you."

"You are!"

"No. I—I destroyed . . ." She couldn't go on.

He'd stopped rocking her, but now he began again. She smelled the rain and even her closed lids weren't enough to keep away all of the lightning's impact. Thunder made the earth beneath her dance. She didn't know where she left off and where Panther and the storm began. Maybe everything had been thrown together.

"Calida, tell me. When you forced them from your body, did you cry for them?"

No. I didn't dare.

"Did you?"

She shook her head, hoping that would be enough for him, knowing it wouldn't.

"Why not?" he asked.

"I—" She could tell him she'd been terrified Croon would find out and that terror had overruled every other emotion, but she didn't want to lie to him tonight or ever again. "I couldn't."

"Why not?"

"I killed them. Tears wouldn't take away my sin."

"Sin? Is that how you see it, sin?"

"Yes!" Her throat burned; if only she could stop crying. "I—I did—"

"Calida, quiet! That was yesterday. We have today, tonight. Maybe only tonight. Listen to me. Mourn them. Say good-bye to the children you will never have. Let them know you loved them."

She was already doing that; didn't he know they were the source of her tears and heartache? "I—wanted to cry. I felt as if I'd been killed when . . . I was afraid that if one tear fell, I would never be able to stop."

"And so you buried what was in your heart, a mother's heart. Only, the love you felt for them didn't die, just as their memory didn't. And tonight that love, that loss has returned."

He was right.

"Cry," he encouraged. "Cry as long as you need. I am here. I understand."

"Pa-nther?"

"Hush. I'm here. Say good-bye to the past, my wife. Think of the future. Of the child you will one day hold. I understand."

He did. And that's what made her love him.

Dunlawton Plantation south of St. Augustine consisted of little more than a few blackened timbers. Although the Seminoles had set fire to it nearly two years ago, the stench still clung to the area. Reddin would never understand why General Hernandez had decided to bivouac here for the night—unless he hoped the sight would fill his troops with indignation. The way Reddin looked at it, the plantation was a painful reminder of everything that had gone wrong since this damnable war began.

Still, he had much more to think about than what the main house had once looked like. General Hernandez sat to his right. John Philip, head nearly dragging on the ground, knelt before them. The once militant slave's hands were tied behind him, and a burly private held the end of a rope snaked around John Philip's neck. Taking a long draw from his pipe, Reddin drew out the moment. Victory. How damnably good it felt!

"You're not holding back anything?" General Hernandez asked. His tone was so gentle that one would have thought he and the miserable slave had been talking about what they were going to have to eat. "You've shown us everything?"

John Philip lifted his head a few inches. "That's all, massa. I swears it is."

"Hm. I'll know in a couple of days whether you're holding out on us."

"A couple of days," Reddin interrupted. "Damn it, he's drawn the maps. Hell, I was with him this morning when he led us to where Coacoochee is staying."

"Coacoochee is only one chief. He isn't Osceola."

Or Panther. In his eagerness to bring the savages to their knees, Reddin had almost forgotten that. However, armed with the nigger's maps, it wouldn't be long before he was aiming a musket at Panther's miserable head, and this time he wouldn't miss. Content to simply listen, he smoked while the general went back over the details with John Philip. Yes, the nigger kept insisting, every clan had accompanied him when Osceola decided to return to their ancestral grounds. Although they were staying in different spots, runners could quickly take news from one clan to another.

John Philip didn't know where the Egret clan was staying; no matter how much he'd been "persuaded" to improve his memory, he continued to contend that Panther kept his location secret from all but a trusted few. What the hell did that matter? Once Reddin had his hands on one of those "trusted few," that would change.

25

Waves of helpless rage erupted through Panther. He wanted to whirl and plunge into the wilderness. Instead he stood and listened.

"They must have heard nothing," the exhausted runner said between deep breaths. "Otherwise, they would have defended themselves. Everyone was asleep. They woke to find their hiding place surrounded. Too late. It was too late."

"No one was killed?" Gaitor asked.

"None. The army men were most happy to discover they had captured King Philip. I heard them laugh. I understand enough of their words to know they made much fun of the chief's nakedness."

The past year had been especially hard on quiet, somber King Philip and his followers. Pursued relentlessly, the Seminoles had seldom had time to hunt. The last time Panther had seen him, he'd been shocked by how haggard, thin, and dirty the chief had looked. The runner, a youth not yet old enough to have had his baby name replaced with his warrior name, had managed to slip away unnoticed. If he hadn't, no one would yet know what had happened four nights ago, or afterward. When Gaitor asked how the army had so easily found the Yuchis clan the night after King Philip and his followers were captured, the youth explained that from his hiding place, he'd watched Tomoka John lead the army to the second camp.

"Was he forced?" Gaitor asked, his lips barely moving.

"No." The youth shook his head. "There were no ropes on him."

Wishing Tomoka John was here so he could plunge his knife into someone who could no longer call himself a Seminole, Panther asked if any of the Yuchis had been killed. The youth had seen an army man fall dead and was afraid several clan members had been wounded, but they had been surrounded by at least a hundred soldiers while they slept. By the time they'd awakened, it had been too late.

"I should have done something," the boy admitted. "Stopped the army somehow. Warned the Yuchis."

"They would have killed you if you'd tried. You said Osceola already knows?"

The boy nodded. After drinking deeply from the water-filled gourd Gaitor had given him, he explained that he'd hurried to Osceola as soon as he felt it was safe to travel. Osceola would decide what to do once he'd talked to the other *tastanagees*.

"He say whether he gonna fight?" Gaitor asked.

"He is sick. I looked at him and saw that, not the warrior he used to be."

Panther looked around for Calida but didn't see her. The thought of having to tell her this filled him with dread beyond what he felt for the captured Seminoles. He pointed at the closest *chickee* and told the boy to go there for something to eat. He could stay here until tomorrow before leaving for another clan.

"Two clans captured," he muttered. "They were taken without a fight. Have the Seminoles become wounded deer?"

Gaitor's chest expanded as he sucked in air. "Two," he repeated as if not yet believing. "Prisoners. What's gonna happen ta 'em?"

Panther couldn't concern himself with those whose weapons had been taken from them. The Egret clan was his responsibility; at the moment it felt as if it had always been his burden. Looking at them, he was forced to admit that although they weren't as beaten as King Philip's clan had been, neither were they the same strong and proud people they'd once been. There'd been too many moons of hiding.

"You know what's gonna happen, Panther. They's gonna be sent to that damn reservation."

The end. It's the end. Angry, he tried to shake himself free of the thought. He was going to be a father. He wanted his son or daughter to grow up knowing the same land he did. He wanted that child's mother—

There would be no reservation for Calida.

"We are like the others, wounded deer," Panther said. He felt the weight of the world on his shoulders.

"No! Never!"

"Saying it is not so does not change the truth." He hated the words, hated everything about the day. "A trapped deer then. That is what I am. Trapped."

"No." Gaitor stalked closer and planted his hand on his friend's shoulder. "The only way you's gonna be trapped is if you lets 'em take you. Come with Winter Rain 'en me 'en the others. Damnation, ya gots to come with us."

"I cannot."

Gaitor's eyes had flashed with exploding emotion. With Panther's words, the light went out of them. He let his hand drop back by his side. "I know," he whispered. "You's *tastanagee.* You's never gonna turn yur back on yur clan. Whatever happens to 'em, you's gonna be part o' it."

Whatever happens to them. The Egret clan had spent the summer hiding like rabbits. He could order them to do it again, only he couldn't because they were tired of running. Too many would hear what had happened to King Philip and the Yuchis and wait for the army to come for them.

Feeling exhausted, he stared at where he'd last seen Calida. She'd been different ever since the night she'd cried for the children she'd never have. He knew that despite their uncertain future, she was happy to be carrying their child, but it was more than that. It was as if her tears had freed her from the past.

He wished he felt the same.

"I makes you a promise, Panther," Gaitor said. "Long as we can, we'll stay here with you."

We. Calida was part of that. When Gaitor decided that his small group of followers had to flee, she'd leave with them. She had to know she had no choice. But he was a war chief.

"You mean it?" Reddin asked.

Looking disgusted with the question, General Jesup repeated his decision. The weeks since the capture of two clans had been ones of both triumph, because they now had King Philip's son Coacoochee as well as the old man, and keen disappointment because there'd been no wholesale surrender. Obviously, however, the loss of so many had finally gotten through to the savages. A number of chiefs had just sent word that they were willing to come in for a parley. What had elicited Reddin's outburst was that the general had just said he had no intention of letting any of the savages walk out of Fort Peyton.

"We've been waving a flag of truce for too long, and look what it's gotten us—nothing," General Jesup continued. "Every time Osceola decides he wants something from us, we put down our weapons and act like lapdogs. Well, the newspapers may have folks thinking he's some kind of great chief, but I'm tired of him believing he's in control. We've been made fools for the last time. This damnable war is ending, now."

The other officers muttered approval. They might say something different behind Jesup's back, but in public they supported their general's decision, glad that he was the one who would have to answer to the President and politicians. Reddin kept his own counsel. What happened to the rest of the savages didn't matter; the only one he cared about was Panther—Panther, who had cost him more money than he would think about today. Panther, damn it, had better be among those who accompanied Osceola. He'd give anything, anything to see the look on Panther's face when he realized he was trapped.

"How are you going to do it?" someone asked. "You're not going to shoot—"

"Not if there's any other way of handling things, I'm not," Jesup said. "There's one thing I'm going to say now, and I want everyone listening to me. Whatever happens, Osceola *will* come out of it alive.

I'm not going to have all those Indian lovers down my throat, understand?"

Fine, Reddin thought. Treat Osceola as if he was a goddamn king. Panther was another story. He deserved to have his head separated from his body.

But not before the savage had told him where to find Calida.

Osceola was sick but not beaten. Heartened by the large, glittering eyes and determined stare, Calida stood before the Seminole chief. Panther was a few feet away, his silence speaking to her, pleading with her to walk away from this meeting.

But she couldn't. Not yet at least.

"You have heard?" Osceola asked. "You understand that the army general has agreed to meet with us and that it will be a peaceful meeting, a time for all to talk about what they need and want?"

"Panther told me. I have to ask though. Do you really trust General Jesup?"

"I do not know this man. I have not sat down with him and looked into his heart, but once, years ago, a general placed me in chains." His mouth tightened. "Many whites said this was a terrible thing to do and he was forced to set me free. Later I killed him. The army will not make the same mistake twice."

Calida wasn't sure that was true, but she also knew the army and Seminoles couldn't continue as they were much longer. Both groups were tired, frustrated, eager to get on with their lives, even if that meant the Seminoles had to leave their homeland. She'd heard that Osceola had raged like a madman when he found himself in chains. Shamed, he had never forgiven Wiley Thompson and had been responsible for the Indian agent's death. Unfortunately, Osceola was no longer the same fighting man he'd once been. Panther had taken his place, at least in that respect.

"Has the time for the meeting been arranged?" she asked. Osceola hadn't said why he wanted to talk to her, but then he didn't need to. "Where will it take place?"

He told her that runners had brought word that a flag of truce had been erected over Fort Peyton. Most of the army's troops were at St. Augustine, far enough away that they didn't constitute a threat. "I have heard many things about what the army and its government want the Seminoles to do. It is time to hear those things from General Jesup himself."

"You know what they want," Panther insisted. "For all Negroes to be surrendered to them. They won't talk about what is to be done with us until then."

She should be horrified at the thought of being turned over to military men. Instead, Calida's thoughts fixed on something else Panther had said. *Done with us.* Were those the words of a beaten man? Looking at him, she knew that wasn't true. Still, could a single warrior go to war with the army?

It had to end! The Seminoles needed peace, a quiet place to live their lives and raise their children.

Their children. Why couldn't Panther put them first?

"I want you by my side when this meeting takes place," Osceola said.

Panther cursed. Calida simply waited.

"If I am presented with what the whites have written down, I want to know the truth."

"No," Panther insisted. "She isn't safe. You know that."

"Panther, please," Calida said.

Osceola's eyes flickered from one to the other, then settled on her. "There is more. Sometimes the army men use words that are foreign to me, to all of us. You have spoken their language since childhood."

"So has Gaitor."

Already tense, Calida became even more so when Panther said that. According to Winter Rain, Gaitor was still here because he was torn between loyalty for Panther and the great clan and the need to go where he would be safe. Last night Winter Rain had told her that Gaitor had decided to stay until he'd learned the results of the parley. Now Panther was saying he wanted Gaitor to interpret. "Not Gaitor," she insisted. "He can't read."

"She is not a warrior," Osceola interrupted. "The army has no reason to hate her as they do Gaitor."

Not giving Panther time to speak, she quickly asked Osceola when he wanted her. He and the others would be leaving for Fort

Peyton in the morning, he told her. "I will be there," she said.

"No!" Grabbing her arm, Panther pulled her around to him. "I should not have let you come here. You cannot. He—"

"I can't turn my back on my people, Panther. The Seminoles are my people, the Egret clan my family, you know that."

"You would risk your life? Our child's life?"

How dare he do this to her! Didn't he know how terrified she was of entering the fort, of maybe coming face-to-face with Reddin Croon? But Gaitor had stayed because he believed General Jesup's word that there would be no violence during the peace talks.

Peace.

How she hated war!

"Do you think I want to do this? But I don't want our child to be a child of war. Of hiding and running. It has to end. It has to!"

"End?"

"Yes. Please, Panther, tell me you understand."

His eyes darkened, reminding her of storm-filled clouds. "You carry life inside you, Calida, but you do not put that life before everything else. This I do not understand."

He didn't understand.

General Jesup wasn't here. From General Hernandez, Reddin had learned that Jesup was so nervous about the outcome of the so-called parley that he'd decided to wait in the wilderness around Fort Peyton along with the troops who'd been brought here to spring the trap. Hiding was a damn mistake on Jesup's part, the decision of a coward. The Seminoles and niggers still with them might be dull-witted, but they weren't stupid. If they didn't clap eyes on the head of the army, they would be suspicious, and rightly so.

Too nervous to eat, Reddin paced. From what scouts had told him, some seventy warriors as well as a handful of women and niggers were coming in with their leaders. They'd left their children behind.

To hell with the children.

Calida might—Calida might . . .

Wiping away the sweat that had beaded on his forehead, he ordered himself not to think about her, but it didn't work. As far as he knew, she was the only one in the whole stinking bunch who could read. Osceola would be a fool not to want her along. Panther, on the other hand—

His body went hot. According to John Philip, Calida was sleeping with Panther. Calida was his property, damn it! The savage would pay for what he'd done with his life, and nothing Jesup or Hernandez did or said would stop him.

The Seminoles were coming. News of their approach rippled through the fort. Reddin checked his pistol, yanked his stiff and dirty collar away from his neck too damn many times. His first impulse was to run to the gate to see if Panther and Calida were among them, but he forced himself to remain in the shadows because if they spotted him, they might not enter the trap.

The trap.

He had them! Finally.

With a nauseating show of ceremony, General Hernandez greeted Osceola, who was dressed in a colorful shirt, baggy pants, and ornately decorated moccasins with an equally colorful blanket thrown over one shoulder. Osceola immediately asked where General Jesup was. After a momentary hesitation, Hernandez explained that Jesup had the measles and didn't feel well enough to attend. However, Hernandez was authorized to speak for him. Hernandez was delighted to see Osceola and took that as a sign that the Seminoles were serious about finding a way to end the stalemate. Nodding at Coa Hadjo, who was another *tastanagee,* Hernandez asked why Micanopy, Jumper, and Cloud weren't with them. Straight-faced, Osceola said that those chiefs had the measles.

Tension knotted Reddin's belly. If the Seminoles smelled a trap—

They must not have, because at General Hernandez's suggestion the entire bunch filed inside and started toward the circle of logs set up in the middle of the fort. Osceola walked like an old man. Coa Hadjo looked disgustingly healthy. Reddin didn't care about Micanopy, Jumper, or Cloud. Where the hell was Panther?

Hernandez waited until the principals were seated and the rest of the savages bunched as close as they could get before asking that question.

"He comes in his own time," Osceola said. "I am ears for the

Seminoles. Tell me, what is the word from your President?"

Knowing Osceola's low opinion of the man the Seminoles referred to as Old Mad Jackson, Reddin doubted that Osceola would easily accept any words of peace from the President. His face didn't change expression as Hernandez explained that the President was eager for the costly war to come to an end and for the Seminoles to go to the reservation as they'd agreed long ago. Pulling out a rolled document, Hernandez explained that it contained the President's exact words. Costly, Reddin thought. Costly didn't explain the half of it. He'd all but brought ruin to his plantation and he still didn't have anything to show for it.

But soon—

Osceola lifted his arm in a semi-salute. At the signal, a brave who'd been standing by his chief's shoulder started toward the gate. "I do not understand talking leaves," Osceola explained. "I call on one who does."

Willing himself not to give away his excitement, Reddin drew even further into the shadows. It made hearing the conversation difficult, but he didn't dare let Calida see him until the trap had been sprung. For the first time since things got started, he thought about the big nigger who was said to be Panther's co-chief, but the man wasn't anywhere to be seen. Either he knew better than to show his black face or he was off somewhere in the wilderness with even more braves, waiting for the chance to attack.

Calida walked like a nervous deer. So graceful that it took his breath away, she stepped inside the fort and looked slowly, warily around. She wore a short dress that left her long legs exposed and moccasins that hugged her feet like a second skin. She was, he acknowledged, dressed for running. And she wasn't alone. Panther's features were carefully neutral. He carried a musket, and a knife was strapped to his waist. Arrogant as hell, he wore nothing except a loincloth, which accented his fit physical condition. What was it with the savage? The greater the hardship, the stronger he became? Like Calida, Panther assessed his surroundings. When his mouth tightened, Reddin guessed he was upset because he couldn't see into every nook and cranny. *You will soon enough, you savage. Only, by then it'll be too late.*

Neither Calida nor Panther sat, but that didn't seem to bother Osceola, and General Hernandez chose to ignore their breach of etiquette. After too damn much conversation in Seminole, Osceola indicated that Calida would translate the President's document for him. When Hernandez started to hand the paper to Calida, Panther grabbed it. He studied it so intently that it was all Reddin could do not to laugh. Finally, Panther slid his knife under the ribbon that held it in place and extended it toward Calida. The two exchanged long, studied looks.

Calida began reading, but her voice was so soft and low that Reddin couldn't hear what she was saying. Osceola, Coa Hadjo, and Panther all leaned forward, their eyes intent on her. The rest of the Seminoles stopped muttering among themselves. Only Panther occasionally glanced around. Once Osceola grunted approval of something Calida had said, but no one else spoke. Seconds pulsed by.

When Hernandez pulled on his starched collar, the gesture looked so natural that none of the Seminoles took note of it. The general didn't so much as take his eyes off Calida. Reddin, watching Panther, noticed that something had changed about him. If anything, he looked even more wary. Slipping a few inches away from Calida, Panther studied Hernandez so intently that after a few seconds, the general stirred restlessly.

Calida finished reading. Silent, she handed the document to Osceola. Panther started to say something, but he never got the chance. Suddenly, over a hundred well-armed soldiers rushed through the open fort gate. Reddin had only one thought: to disarm Panther. Taking advantage of the now-milling Indians, he hurried close. Panther was trying to reach Hernandez and protect Calida at the same time. Unfortunately, he couldn't do either because so many Indians crowded around him.

"You lie!" Panther bellowed. "White tongues know only lies!"

Osceola jumped to his feet, but someone jostled him and he started to fall. Grabbing the chief around the waist, Calida struggled to support him.

"Calida, run!"

Galvanized by Panther's command, Calida drew away from Osceola. Osceola bellowed something Reddin didn't understand. Calida whirled and began plowing her way through the bodies. Reddin could hardly believe his good fortune when she headed his way!

He was reaching for her when she looked up, and their eyes locked. Loving the horror mirrored in her stare, he took advantage of her shock by throwing himself at her. They went down in a tangle of arms and legs with him landing on top of her. The moment he wrapped his arm around her neck, she dug in with her nails. He slugged her once, twice, three times before she stopped struggling. Breathing raggedly, he hauled first himself and then her to their feet.

The Seminoles were already surrounded. Although the majority of them had been armed, only a handful had pointed their weapons, not that it mattered. Next to the well-armed soldiers, the Seminoles' rusty old muskets or primitive bows and arrows were no match.

Out of the corner of his eye, Reddin saw that Panther had managed to distance himself from the others. Musket pointed at Hernandez's belly, he waited.

"It won't do you any good, Panther," Reddin yelled. The fingers of his left hand were locked in Calida's hair. Careful to let Panther see what he was doing, he pulled out his pistol and pressed it against her forehead. Her arms sagged at her side, and he guessed it took what was left of her senses to keep her legs under her. "You shoot the general and I'll kill her."

"No!"

"You think I won't? Or maybe she doesn't matter that much to you."

"Panther . . ."

Panther. Yeah, he looked like one all right, tense and wary, trying to decide when and where to attack, only he'd been defeated even if he didn't yet know it. "Do you have any idea what would happen to you if you killed a general?" Reddin challenged. "They'd hang you. You don't stand a chance. Don't you see that? Maybe you won't live long enough to be hanged. Maybe you'll be so riddled by bullets in a few seconds that it'll all be over, and you'll never know what happened to her."

He had him. Damn it, he had him! Eyes glittering with hate and something Reddin took to be fear for Calida, the savage slowly lowered his weapon.

26

Alone. Alone with Reddin Croon.

Fighting both nausea and dizziness, Calida concentrated on placing one foot after another. She hated being dragged along by him but lacked the strength and clearheadedness necessary to fight. With every step that took her farther from the fort and Panther, she struggled against her weakness.

That and the sick memory of watching an army man throw ropes over Panther's wrists. He'd been a prisoner the first time she'd seen him. Would that be her last memory of the man she loved? If so, she wished Reddin had killed her instead of rendering her unconscious.

"You should have stayed out there," Reddin said. "Should have never come in. 'Course, if you hadn't, he probably would have stayed with you, and I wouldn't like that. Wouldn't like that at all."

She didn't care what Croon said or did to her. All she could think of was Panther's helpless rage—that and their baby's safety. At that thought, a fresh wave of nausea stole her strength. She fought it until it was under control, but the effort left her too weak to resist. Croon still had his pistol, although it was now tucked back in his belt. He also carried a knife.

"Do you know how long I've waited for this?" he asked almost conversationally. "To have you back again—your mama's dead, isn't she? Isn't she?" he insisted when Calida didn't immediately answer. He released her hair but quickly grabbed her upper arms and squeezed. Pain shot through her. She tasted blood from her split lip. "Look, you're not knocked out anymore. You can talk. Listen to me. You're still a little bit of a thing, a sweet piece, all right. You've gotten stronger though. I can feel your muscles." He roughly massaged her arms to accent his point. "I won't forget that." A frown touched his forehead. Still holding her so tightly that she was losing circulation in her arms, he cocked his head to one side. "Can't hear them anymore. That means no one's going to know what happens between the two of us, not that I give a damn."

She'd already guessed what he'd carried her out here for, why he'd waited for her to regain her senses, but hearing him say it sent a shudder through her. To her horror, that made him laugh. "You haven't forgotten me, have you? I didn't think so. We're going back, you and me. Back to the plantation. Nothing's changed. Nothing except that Isiah is as dead as his ugly daughter and everything he ever had is now mine."

Reddin had killed Liana's father; Calida had no doubt of that. She wished she understood what could make a man do something like that, what had made his pursuit of her so relentless, but it didn't matter.

Nothing did except protecting her baby. Hers and Panther's.

Reddin released her right arm but kept his fingers clamped over the left. For a heartbeat it didn't register that he'd drawn his knife and was holding it up for her to see. Then he touched it to her throat, and she froze.

"You think I'm going to kill you? Not too likely, not after what I've spent and done hunting you down." Turning the blade, he sawed at her neckline until it gave. He sliced some more until the fabric fell away, exposing the tops of her breasts. They'd become slightly swollen since the baby began its life inside her. Would he notice?

Resheathing the knife, he released her arm and ripped her dress off her. It fell in a heap on the ground. Shivering despite the heat, she forced herself to stare at him. Slave. She was a slave again. "Getting uppity, are you?" he asked. "You didn't used to look at me while I was bothering you." His big hand closed over a breast, and she gagged, wondered if she was going to pass out. When he captured her other breast, she took an involuntary step backward and ordered herself not to panic.

"Don't move. You know what's expected of you."

Expected. Oh yes, she knew. She could never forget.

He pushed her until he'd backed her against a tree. Then, smiling a little, he pulled off his belt and unfastened his pants. He didn't bother to remove any more of his clothes, only yanked down until he was exposed.

Panther. Panther!

But Panther was the army's prisoner.

Leaning toward her, Reddin braced himself by planting his hands on her shoulders. She turned her head to the side to escape his breath. Still, that did nothing to diminish his impact. Before she could react, he rammed his manhood against her. Legs clamped together, she denied him.

"Damn you, Calida!" He balled a fist and shook it under her nose. "You know better. I'm waiting. Damn it, I'm waiting."

He wanted her to lay herself open to him as he'd forced her to long ago. Unable to breathe, she stared at the ground.

"Now." He pressed his fist against the underside of her jaw. "Now, before I make you sorry."

Brain burning, she started to spread her legs. He rocked back, smiling. Watched. Instead of taking her, he ran his fingers over her breasts, his mouth slack. "You've changed, Calida. Gotten even riper. No wonder I couldn't get you out of my mind. I must have known—damn it, I've waited so damn long."

Changed. That was the only word she heard. *Changed.*

Willing herself to wait, she remained passive as he slowly, intimately explored her breasts. When he was done, he pressed his hands possessively over her hips and belly. She thought about her baby nestled safe and hidden inside her. When, if, Reddin learned about it, he would—

He would kill Panther's child.

Reddin's breathing came faster and more labored. He'd begun

moving in a jerky way that told her he wouldn't wait much longer. He no longer held her captive, but why should he? She was his slave. His willing, obedient, frightened slave.

Only, she'd changed.

His hands trailed lower. He pressed his thumbs against the inside of her thighs, opening her to him. He was coming closer. Bringing his manhood—

Screaming, she rammed her knee upward. Bone connected with soft, vulnerable flesh and she screamed again. Gurgling, he doubled over and dropped like a deer with an arrow through its heart. She screamed for a third time but not as loudly this time, not so insanely. For a moment she couldn't make herself move. This man, this huddled, hurting mass had once owned her. He'd captured Panther, had tried to take her again. But he'd failed!

Eyes never leaving him, she reached down for his belt. She pulled out the knife and gripped it, feeling its deadly strength. Her head still throbbed from her earlier beating, and she had to be careful not to move too quickly.

She had to kill him. Had to!

Breathing heavily, she backed up a few steps. He continued to jerk about, looking helpless, pitiful.

Her fingers were cramping. She needed to let up on her grip but didn't dare because if she did, she might lose her courage for what she had to do. What part of his body was the most vulnerable? His manhood was cradled in his hands, and she couldn't get to him there. His neck. Could she slice his throat? This man, this monster had so terrified her that she'd destroyed her babies to keep them away from him. Hers! Not his!

Using her foot, she pushed on Reddin's shoulder until he was on his back and looking up at her. His eyes bulged, and she read hatred so powerful it sickened her. Hatred and something else. His throat was nearly hidden beneath his graying beard.

Her babies! And now this one—hers and Panther's!

She'd just started to crouch when Reddin kicked out and up. His boots connected with her belly, doubling her over. She tried to breathe. Couldn't. Tried to regain her balance. Couldn't.

Panther!

* * *

The ropes around his wrists cut into his flesh, but Panther barely noticed. Fear for Calida made it impossible for him to keep track of the amount of time that had passed since Reddin Croon had left with her. What he did know was that Osceola had agreed to send out word for the rest of his clan to come into the fort. Since most of his warriors were already here, that meant the fort would soon be filled with women and children, all of them wondering what would happen next.

Panther knew. They'd be forced to leave the land of their ancestors and taken to some strange, faraway place, made to live a new way. The chiefs might be—what was the army word?—*exterminated.*

He couldn't think about that.

Calida was with Reddin Croon.

Feeling both hot and cold, he willed himself not to give in to rage and fear unlike any he'd ever known. His hands had been tied behind him and a length of rope held him to a stake. Occasionally someone looked at him, but for the most part he was left alone while the army men talked excitedly among themselves. Why shouldn't they feel triumph? They'd made a lie of a flag of truce and captured the greatest Seminole chief.

Seeking distraction from thoughts of what Calida might be enduring, Panther looked over at Osceola, who hadn't moved from his log. General Hernandez was sitting beside him, gesturing urgently as he tried to explain something, but Osceola said nothing in return. Was his chief beaten?

Did the rest of the Seminoles feel like their leader?

Acknowledging that over seventy braves had given up their weapons without a struggle made Panther want to bellow until his throat bled, but he didn't dare give in to despair. If he had more time, he would wait until dark and then convince one of the Seminoles to cut him free. But by then it might be too late for Calida.

And for their baby.

Feeling as if he was drowning, he forced himself to study his surroundings. There was so much confusion, such heavy lethargy. The Seminoles had no leader, or rather Osceola had resigned himself to the inevitable. He might be dying; if he was, his sickness had stripped all fight from him.

With a violent shake of his head, Panther dismissed his chief. He strained again, but he'd been tied too tightly, and there was no way he could free himself. If he hadn't allowed fear for Calida to rule him, he would be stepping into the void left by Osceola's surrender. He would be chief of a splintered people.

Either that or dead.

Was Calida dead?

"Panther?"

Instinct warned him not to acknowledge the low whisper. It was a woman's voice, but not Calida's, when that was the only one he wanted to hear. After a moment, he felt something hard and thin graze his wrists. His arms fell free, but mindful of the soldiers, he managed not to let them drop to his side.

"What—"

"Quiet," Winter Rain hissed. "They must not see me."

"Where is Gaitor?"

"Outside. Hiding. He wanted to come but he does not dare because too many would know who he is. No one looks at me."

After assuring himself that none of the army men was watching him, he glanced over his shoulder at Gaitor's wife. Winter Rain had padded her body with layers of clothing, rubbed dirt in her hair and pulled it down around her face. If it wasn't for the knife held in her long fingers, he might have taken her for a shuffling old woman.

Ignoring his aching arms, he asked how she'd learned what had happened and managed to get into the fort. She told him that Gaitor had intercepted the runner Osceola had dispatched. When they learned that the fort had been turned into a prison and Panther captured, she'd thrown on her disguise and taken Gaitor's knife. Gaitor had begged her not to risk her life, but she'd insisted that only she had a chance of freeing Panther. She'd waited until the guards went inside to see what was happening before slipping in herself. "They are so full of themselves," she whispered. "They think the Seminoles are beaten. Panther, are they?"

There was no time to answer her, to seek the truth. In a harsh whisper, he told her what had happened to Calida. Looking pale,

Winter Rain said she and Gaitor hadn't seen Calida or Reddin, but then there was more than one way to enter or leave the fort. Panther already knew that because he'd seen Reddin dragging Calida toward a small opening at the rear. "Give me the knife," he insisted.

She stared up at him, and for a moment he couldn't move. Winter Rain had risked her life coming in here. If there'd been no army or Calida he might have loved her. Finally, she held out the knife, and he took it. A sensation like hundreds of tiny, sharp teeth raced up his arm. He touched her cheek with his free hand and then, moving silently, buried himself in the middle of a large group of Seminoles. Several of them stared at him in recognition, but he didn't take the time to explain what he was doing free. As soon as he dared, he began slipping toward where he'd last seen Calida. Reddin had kept to the shadows earlier, but shadows didn't care whether the person they hid was army or Seminole.

Calida! He had to get to her! Nothing else mattered.

It took only one slash to cut the rope now holding the rear door in place. Without looking back, Panther slipped through the opening. The wilderness was no more than fifty feet away. Reaching it, he spotted a dim foot-trail leading away from the fort. Running, straining to hear, he put more and more distance between himself and where his people had been trapped. He prayed that Winter Rain would be able to leave as easily as she'd snuck in. He prayed Gaitor would be waiting for her and that they'd leave this place.

Head deep into Piahokee and find safety in its embrace.

Calida had been unconscious when Reddin carried her out of the fort. Much as he wanted her to be all right, he prayed she was still locked in nothing where Reddin couldn't reach her. If she wasn't—

If she wasn't, she'd fight Reddin with every bit of life in her body. The slave she'd once been no longer existed, would no longer claim her. She—death—

He'd stopped before he realized he'd heard a scream. A woman's scream. High and thin. Inhuman. Slipping forward a few more feet, he filtered out every other sound except for his heart's wild beating. The scream wasn't repeated; he might have only imagined it and he might have—

Not taking time to finish the thought, he began running again.

A turtle was just ahead of him. He leaped over it. He couldn't see far enough. If he wasn't careful, he might run right into Reddin. His mind filled with the echo of that scream and prevented him from thinking of anything else. Calida, sounding as she never had, as he'd never wanted her to.

Calida dying?

Despite fear so intense it nearly paralyzed him, Panther forced himself to stop his wild plunge. Leaving the trail, he slipped into the dense foliage and trusted instinct to take him to the woman he loved. Brush and branches reached out to stop him with every step. If he was a turtle, he could—a turtle was too slow. He was too slow.

Sweat ran down his chest and back, and his left foot stung from something he'd stepped on. Ignoring the discomfort, he ducked under a large, trailing branch. When he straightened, he saw that he was at the edge of a small clearing.

Calida, naked, stood in the middle of it. Calida! He willed his legs to move but they refused. Couldn't. What—

Reddin Croon lay at her feet, a knife protruding from his exposed belly. His pants were tangled around his hips, and he didn't move.

"Calida." He tried to repeat her name but couldn't. Alive! Breath Giver, alive!

Looking as if her arms and legs had turned into stiffened tree branches, she slowly turned toward him. Blood coated her lip. There were several red marks on her upper arms, and her chest heaved with each breath she took. He didn't remember reaching her. All that mattered was holding his arms out to her. She jerked toward him, one step, two. She wasn't crying. Her eyes, huge and black, seemed to look through but not at him.

"Calida," he whispered as he drew her away from Croon's body. "Calida," he repeated when what he wanted was to demand she tell him she was all right. Her arms felt all bone and muscle with no softness. No giving. Not sure how to reach her, he slid his fingers over her flesh and knew he'd never get enough of her. She started to jerk away, then blinked and her gaze settled on him.

"Panther?"

"I'm here, my wife." His throat constricted and he tried again. "You're safe."

"Safe," she whimpered. The word awakened something in her, and she sagged against him. Enveloping her, he pressed her body against his. His heart swelled so he wondered if it might break. *Calida. In his arms. Alive.*

They didn't reach where Gaitor and Winter Rain and a half dozen others were hiding until after dark. He'd had to lead Calida away from where she'd killed Croon because she'd forgotten how to place one foot after another. He'd put her dress back on and used vines to repair what he could of the damage Croon had done to it. He hadn't asked if Croon had had his way with her before she'd killed him; when she felt strong enough, she'd tell him. He'd covered their baby with his capable hands, protected it. She remembered that. And his shaking had matched hers.

Still holding Panther's hand because she couldn't get enough of him, Calida listened as Gaitor explained that two of Osceola's wives and their children had already joined him in the fort. Osceola's sister had gone too, as well as three warriors who'd stayed behind. The Negroes who'd been staying with Osceola's clan, Winter Rain's father included, had also turned themselves in.

"He will not live," Panther said somberly. "The army has taken the life from my chief."

"What's done is done, Panther," Gaitor muttered. "You cain't help him no more."

"I know."

How beautiful he was, Calida thought. How strong and wild. The months of trying to stay out of the army's grasp had taken none of that from him. Courage flowed around him, the courage of a man who has seen the only world he'd ever known end. "What you gonna do?" Gaitor asked. "I ain't stayin' here, you know that. I doesn't dare. Neither does Calida."

Hurting for Panther, she waited him out. He was a *tastanagee,* his clan's leader; she'd never want him to be anything else. But his clan no longer existed. He would be a father soon, and that had already changed him, would change him even more once he held his baby in his arms. If nothing else, she could give him that.

Breath Giver, thank you.

"It is a new world," Panther was saying. "Different. What I always believed, what I have always done, is like morning mist. Gone."

I'm sorry, Panther. So sorry.

"I do not want this! My ancestors, my father's ghost, those things will live within me forever."

My love, I can't give you back the past.

"The Seminoles are no longer a nation," he whispered. His eyes looked both old and ageless. "We are scattered. We will scatter even more while the army seeks those they did not capture today."

"I don' want it like that. You knows that," Gaitor said, his voice both harsh and laden with emotion. He was holding Winter Rain's hand.

"I know, my brother. I know because our hearts beat the same." Panther took a long, deep breath, then swept his gaze over their surroundings. It seemed to Calida that he was trying to drink in the wilderness and make it part of him. "I say this; I believe this. Our hearts will continue to beat only if we walk into Piahokee's belly and lose ourselves there."

"Panther . . ." Calida began but couldn't continue.

"I walk a new way," he whispered after a long silence. "Into a new tomorrow."

"You—you mean it?" she asked.

"I do what I must, my wife. What will protect our child. I pray to Breath Giver that my son or daughter grows up free. That is my marriage gift to you. Freedom for us and for our children."

Freedom.

Author's Note

Osceola and approximately eighty other Seminoles were captured on October 23, 1837. They spent several months imprisoned in St. Augustine before being transferred to Fort Moultrie at Charleston, South Carolina. Some say Osceola died from malaria on January 30, 1838. Others maintain he died from a broken heart.

What is known as the Second Seminole War finally ran itself out, neither won nor lost. Between 1835 and 1842, some four thousand Seminoles were relocated west of the Mississippi. However, approximately five hundred remained hidden deep in Piahokee, their presence ignored when the war was declared over on August 14, 1842. Those fugitives' descendants still live in southern Florida, part of and yet separate from today's world. Free.

It is this writer's dream that Panther and Calida's children formed the core of those survivors, and that they were joined by the children of Gaitor and Winter Rain.